# white ghosts

## will rhode

**POCKET BOOKS**

LONDON • NEW YORK • SYDNEY • TORONTO

First published in Great Britain by Simon & Schuster UK Ltd, 2004
This edition published by Pocket Books, 2005
An imprint of Simon & Schuster UK Ltd
A Viacom company

1 3 5 7 9 10 8 6 4 2

Simon & Schuster UK Ltd
Africa House
64–78 Kingsway
London WC2B 6AH

www.simonsays.co.uk

Simon & Schuster Australia
Sydney

A CIP catalogue record for this book is available
from the British Library

ISBN 0 7434 4030 7
EAN 9780743440301

Typeset in Stone Serif
by Palimpsest Book Production Limited,
Polmont, Stirlingshire
Printed and bound in Great Britain by
Cox & Wyman Ltd, Reading, Berkshire

# Acknowledgements

I would like to thank the following people for their kind support and love – not just with the writing of this book, but also during some difficult times. My family and most especially my brother Michael, my amazing mother-in-law Brenda, my very close friends Jonty Woodhouse and Shai Hill, my agent Andrew Nurnberg, my editor Suzanne Baboneau, and also Melissa Weatherill at Simon & Schuster. I would also like to thank my wife – everything started after I met you, Maria. Finally, to Neil and Dinah – we miss you and think of you always.

For my mum

Michael wanted the first picture to be of her face.

After all, it was her face that made her: the soft nose, almond eyes and olive skin. She had beautiful lips, even then, very kissable. Traces of baby hair ran forward over her forehead, unlike the rest of her hair, which she normally would have worn slicked back.

Not that he could see her hair. Somehow her face was cut off along the lines – the specific contours that make a face. Across the jaw line, up past the ears, along the hair-line. It was just a fluke, of course. The way the meat cleaver fell – no one could have intended to exact that degree of precision. It was just a fluke.

At the end of the beach Michael found a granite rock – flat and black and gently angled. He could see Repulse Bay curving.

The sun flashed against the water.

Michael handled her – it – delicately, like an eggshell mask, balancing the cracked ridges of bone on the tips of his fingers. He rested her gently on the rock, a small flap of skin catching on his index finger as he removed his hands. There wasn't any blood.

He took out his camera. Clickety, clickety, clack. A shadow caught a line just under her eye. Her face was so perfect for the task. Oval and open and forward and warm and now, it seemed, very removable. It was more than just photogenic – it *said* something. The Chinese Saving Face thing. Michael liked that, the pedestrian irony of it. It was all going to be in that first picture.

Below the granite rock, towards the sea, ran a flat patch of tide-swept sand. Untouched, it had a wonderful, delicate quality – crusty, the type he used to create miniature canyons with when he was a kid. Michael picked the rest of her limbs from out of the bloodied tarpaulin and placed them carefully. Stiff ridges of sand gripped the parts like teeth and kept them in the desired pose.

He stood back to get an overall sense.

It worked. The way he had arranged her. It was a little less inspired perhaps than a perfectly removed face, but it definitely worked. She looked as if she was sunbathing, partially buried in the beach. Michael was about to feel pleased when something caught in his throat.

Breathe . . .

Just breathe, he reminded himself.

. . . Breathe . . .

. . .

He wondered what the headlines might say.

SHARK ATTACK!

Or maybe:

BOAT TRAGEDY!

That might be more appropriate. Cleaved limbs were probably considerably less ragged than those gnawed by a shark. And he had to admit, her bits did seem very clean, very sheer, like sashimi.

As to how the accident might have happened, that would be anyone's guess. She was wild enough to have taken a late night swim, on her own, drunk, naked. It wouldn't matter. The important thing was that people accepted this as an explanation. By doing this, Michael was presenting an answer, an answer that would finally silence the questions.

People would accept this.

And if they didn't?

Michael felt prepared for the police. His fingerprints on the victim, the fact that he was the one to find her, the fact that he knew her . . . all of this could be easily explained.

After all, it wasn't as if he'd chanced upon her. Someone had anonymously tipped him off. A person might consider calling him before the police, especially if there was a pay-off involved. The *Hong Kong Herald* often paid for tips. Michael wouldn't even be expected to reveal the source.

The rest could be put down to panic. How else would he be expected to react? She *was* one of his closest friends. It wasn't his fault if, in a moment of shock, he touched her. He only wanted to help. And it was only when he knew, knew for sure, that she was dead that he took the pictures. He had to. It was his job. That was who he was. It was his way of saying goodbye.

There was some truth in all of that.

Michael paused. He looked at her, tilting his head to one side in contemplation. Then he picked up a foot and hurled it into the water. He watched it splash. Then he looked back at her and re-assessed.

Even though the sun had risen quite high now, the shadows were still sharp. She looked more and more cubist each time he checked, all dysfunctional and shifted and yet somehow forming a whole.

Funny how the mind fills in the gaps, he thought to himself.

# Chapter One

'Go on, sing Inky Pinky again.'

'No. It's boring.'

'It's not.'

'You're snot.'

'Ha, ha, very funny.'

Bunk beds creaked and whispered on top of each other, the odd giggle surfacing. They weren't in the same bunk bed. They were next to each other, in lower beds, at right angles. If they reached across the bars at the end, they could feel one another's head. They'd often wake each other up in the morning that way – tickle an ear, stick a finger up the nose, anything as long as it was gross. It was still better than the wake-up bell clanging two inches from your face.

'Go on, sing it,' Marland pleaded.

'I've got a much better song,' Clarke replied.

'I like Inky Pinky.'

'This one is much better,' Clarke assured.

Marland pondered how it possibly could be. Inky Pinky was brilliant.

'Why?' he eventually asked.

'It just is.' Another pause. 'I'll teach it to you if you like.'

'You will?' Marland couldn't believe his luck at this second chance. Clarke had given up trying to teach Marland all the words to Inky Pinky. It was just too long. The only bit he could ever remember was the chorus:

*Par*
*Inky Pinky*                    *-lez*          *vous-*              *-ous*
                                                          *-ooo*

'You'll have to come over here. I don't want anyone else to hear it,' Clarke whispered.

'OK,' Marland whispered back conspiratorially.

Marland had been in Clarke's bed before. He liked his *Star Wars* duvet cover. The first time, they'd snuggled in with a torch and counted all the C-3POs and R2-D2s they could find.

C-3PO was definitely a Bender, they'd concluded.

*Benny, benny, benny . . .*

That was the school chant for anyone who was gay. It didn't take much to be gay at school. All you had to do was stand out of line in the lunch queue. That made you a Bender, because the line wasn't straight any more.

Sometimes there'd be a fight.

*Woozie, woozie, woozie . . .*

Marland didn't get accused of being gay for sleeping in Clarke's bed, though. Maybe people just didn't know. After all, they only did it when everyone else was asleep. But Marland couldn't see how it remained a secret. There were nineteen of them in the dorm – someone, some night, must have heard. He certainly knew about Browne and Hurd, Jeffreys and Miller, even Miller and Oxenbury. They only climbed into each other's beds when it was late, too. Was he supposed to not know? Or did they just share the same secret?

Maybe sleeping together simply wasn't bent.

He crept across the two-metre chasm separating them. He could hear Davis snoring in the top bunk. Clarke opened up the duvet for him so he could climb in. They were both wearing their blue pyjamas. It was because it was Monday night. Laundry had just been done so they had the pick of the bunch. They loved blue. That was one of the things they discovered they had in common. That was how it all started: their friendship. They also had the same sense of humour. No one could make Marland laugh like Clarke could.

'Are you ready?' Clarke said.

'This'd better be good.'

'It is. My brother taught it to me.'

'Go on then.'

He whispered it to the tune of something patriotic.

*We bought two Belgian bunnies,*
*One was a Belgian buck,*
*We put them on the mantelpiece to see if they would . . .*
*Father went to the market to buy two dozen eggs,*
*Twenty-two in the basket,*
*And two between his legs!*
*Lucy in the garden hanging out the bits,*
*Along came a bumblebee and stung her on the . . .*
*Twice she called the doctor,*
*The doctor's name was Hunt,*
*He took the nurse's instruments and shoved them up her . . .*
*Country horses are the best,*
*They carry heavy loads,*
*What they don't carry on their backs they carry up their . . .*
*Holy Moses had a dog his name was Dirty Dick,*
*He tried to jump a ten-foot wall and landed on his . . .*
*Prickles grow on bushes,*

*Prickles grow on trees,*
*Prickles grow on ladies' legs*
*Halfway up their knees.*
*Pull down your knickers,*
*Show your fanny to your Granny,*
*Knees up Mother Brown,*
*Woo!*

He was panting heavily by the time he'd finished.

'Wow, that was brilliant. Sing it again,' Marland said.

'Gimme a minute.'

After he'd got his breath back, he did.

'I didn't understand the Holy Moses bit,' Marland said.

Clarke tutted impatiently at him. 'Holes,' he said, over emphatically. 'It stands for holes.'

'Holes?'

'Yeah. Horses have holes. They're gross.'

'Oh.' Marland said. He paused. 'What's Lucy hanging out?'

'The bits.'

'What's the bits?'

Clarke sighed heavily. 'Bits. You know bits. It's an expression for laundry.'

'Oh.' He paused again. 'Will you teach it to me then?'

'OK,' Clarke said enthusiastically, turning on his side so that their faces were close together. That was another thing Marland liked about Clarke. He was always enthusiastic. 'I'll teach you two lines tonight and then I'll teach you two more tomorrow, until you get it.'

'Brilliant.'

'But I'll only teach you two new lines once you've repeated to me what I've already taught you. That way, I'll know you're remembering it all.'

'OK,' Marland replied.

They rehearsed the first two lines.

'I've got it,' Marland said eventually.

'Yes. I think you have,' Clarke replied proudly.

They didn't say anything for a few minutes. Then Clarke went down under the duvet. He pulled down Marland's pyjamas and pulled on his willy. Then he put it in his mouth. Hot and nice. Marland pushed it in and out. It was hard. He shifted up an inch, adjusting his angle. He rested his head against the metal bars at the end of the bunk bed. They were cold.

He couldn't understand why it was nice but it was nice. Only eleven years old, Marland couldn't come yet. Clarke was making sucking noises. Then he stopped. Marland felt Clarke wiggling up against him. His head popped out of the top of the duvet.

'Do me now,' he said.

Marland went down. Clarke was already hard. His willy was very different to Marland's. For starters, it was bigger. Much bigger. His had hair all around it. He was a year older than Marland but, already, he seemed years away, years ahead. Marland certainly couldn't see how his willy was going to become like Clarke's in the next twelve months. It would take a lifetime for his to do that.

The dormitory door creaked open.

Marland froze under the duvet, next to Clarke's leg. He could hear footsteps. Shoes, not slippers. Heavy and clumping, like a man's. Oh no! It must be Fishface Haddock! The housemaster! Marland's heart started pounding. He didn't move. The footsteps moved with tortuous deliberation through the room. Torchlight swung on to Clarke's bed. It was bright even through the duvet.

Marland heard Fishface say: 'Clarke. Where is Marland?'

'Don't know, sir. Maybe he's gone to the toilet, sir.'

Clarke's voice sounded muffled.

'Fetch him.'

The light from the torch seemed to fill the duvet. Marland could see three C-3POs just in front of his nose.

'Do I have to, sir? I was sleeping, sir.'

'NOW CLARKE!'

The whole dorm shook. Everyone would be awake by now, Marland thought to himself. Once Clarke climbed out of bed, Fishface would see Marland and make him get out and then the whole dorm would see and then he'd be caught!

*Be-nny, be-nny, be-nny . . .*

Marland felt Clarke shuffle and shift beside him as he tried to climb out of bed while creating a mound of duvet around Marland. Was there any way Fishface wouldn't see? Marland saw a C-3PO settle on his nose as Clarke climbed out of the bed. Marland heard his slippers flap against the linoleum floor. Then the dorm door creaked as it opened and closed. Marland realized that Fishface must have turned his torch off, because it wasn't bright any more under the duvet. It was blue again. Marland listened to the sound of his own breathing. It was so loud. Then he heard Fishface take a footstep, then another, and then . . . Clarke's bed suddenly felt like it was capsizing and the metal springs sounded as if they were going to snap as Fishface sat down right next to him!

Marland felt his heart stop. He could smell Fishface – those cigarettes. Was there any way Fishface might miss him? How could he possibly not tell that he was there, right next to him, through the duvet? Fishface must know. He'd been caught. He was going to be expelled. What would his mummy say?

*Bear-neeeee . . .*

Marland wanted to die.

That was when he felt Fishface put a hand on his leg. First, he just stroked him through the duvet and then, slowly, the long fingers spidered their way through a fold and gently touched Marland's arm. Marland didn't move. Fishface's fingertips padded their way down and across his stomach. They felt damp and hard, even though Marland could tell that they were trying to be gentle.

Suddenly, the dormitory door swung open and Marland heard Clarke say breezily: 'Marland's not well, sir. He's gone up to Sani, sir.'

Fishface's hand snapped away from Marland and then he was up and off the bed and away, away, away. Marland felt like laughing with relief. But he didn't. He just breathed. It was very hot under the duvet.

'Right. Fine. Very good, Clarke. Thank you. Back to bed now, and no more messing about. I want everyone in here,' he paused, allowing the words to fall, 'to go straight to sleep.'

No one replied.

After the door had creaked open and then closed, Marland threw the duvet off the top of his head and felt Clarke climb in beside him.

'That was close,' Clarke said.

Marland panted. It was so hot. Eventually, Clarke reached over for Marland's hand and pushed it down, back down into the duvet. Marland snapped it away and quickly tried to clamber over Clarke and out of the bed.

'Where are you going?' Clarke hushed at him.

'To bed,' Marland said in a normal voice, knowing that all the other boys in the dorm could hear. He wanted them to hear. He wanted them to know. He wasn't a . . . he didn't want to be . . . he wasn't going to be one any more.

Besides, it was too late for whispers. They'd been caught.

'Stay,' Clarke whispered. 'Finish me.'

'Finish yourself,' Marland snapped. Then he paused before saying what he really wanted to say. 'Benny.'

Clarke quickly let go of Marland after he said that. Marland could tell he'd hurt his feelings. But he didn't care. Suddenly he was out of the duvet and into the refreshing cold of the dormitory expanse. He could finally breathe.

He hugged himself into the clean cool of his own bed. But then, quite suddenly and inexplicably, Marland felt very sad. Why was he being mean to Clarke? Clarke was his best friend. Marland didn't understand anything. He needed to tell Clarke what had happened. He turned and whispered, 'Clarke.' Nothing. 'Clarke, please. I need to talk to you.' Still nothing. 'Please, Clarke, I need to tell you something. It's important.'

But Clarke didn't reply.

# Chapter Two

Coming into Kai Tak was a total head-fuck.

The Chinese stewardess shook Michael out of several hours (or was it minutes?) of vertical un-sleep. He snapped his eyes open and glared at her as she reached across to adjust his seat. He felt like a killer robot suddenly switched on. Not that she took any notice. She tugged, politely irritable, at his starched headrest doily, forcing him to move forward and break his stone-cold stance. Suddenly humanized, Michael thought. Damn, he was handling this journey much better as the Terminator.

He looked out the window to see a thick swirl of murderous purple clouds and a disturbing number of toy-sized jets circling thousands of feet below. Instantly disconcerting. He had no idea why he'd insisted on a window seat. His legs were too long and, frankly, he was scared of flying. The last thing he needed was to see what was going on outside. Maybe he thought things were safer if he was keeping an eye on them. Just in case – you know – he ever needed to take control. Yeah right, nice one.

He glanced across the aisle. All the Chinese were sitting together. The cabin lights made everyone seem green. Or maybe that was just the reflection of the upholstery. He couldn't understand why he had a spare seat next to him, while everyone else was packed together like cattle. Maybe he just got lucky. Or maybe he was sectioned off on purpose. Quarantined.

He noticed the angle of the plane. Definitely going down.

He looked outside again. The tips of three Hong Kong humps were faintly visible now, the dragon's-back archipelago gently snaking. It seemed very dark outside for midday. The pilot told the cabin crew to take their seats for landing.

They hit an air pocket and plunged. Mouths gasped, hands grasped. Michael could almost picture the pilot pressing down on the lever, white knuckled, as the engines rumbled. He'd watched far too many disaster movies. He looked for some wood, a lucky charm of any sort to touch, even though he knew it was too late to take any superstitious precautions. You can't wish for luck once it's run out. That's the whole point. You have to refill along the way. Everyone knows that.

Ten minutes and two more turbulence tumbles later and they were careening through the skyscrapers, close enough to see people clearly through their windows – life-sized, not minia- turized like most things from a height. A spray of wetness whipped against the double Perspex window. Michael spotted an old lady wearing just a bra in one apartment as the plane righted itself off a steep left bank. She stared vacantly at him as they slid by, seemingly slowly. Long grey pubic hair standing out without shame, like a big fat arrow pointing down, the same direction the rest of her body was moving in.

Then the wings – not just the tips – the whole of the fucking wings shook as the plane pressed its way through another air vacuum. They banked again. Hard right, a little left, there was another skyscraper: fuck me, that was close, Michael mouthed, left a little more, BANG! Another three hundred feet or eight straight down, vertical drop, two tons bouncing on air. People were screaming and crying. Michael gulped his guts back into place. He was feeling scared now. Adrenaline. They were playing Pavarotti on the Tannoy. It did not mix well with the sound of Asian wails.

The runway suddenly bloomed into view below them. A girl with big hair, a plastic grin and an unlit cigarette looked caught in time on a bright-green billboard advertising menthol 555s. Michael watched the runway rush away below. He looked up. The girl was gone. Another billboard advertising ginseng flashed. The runway carried on rushing.

Shouldn't they be landing by now? he asked himself. How much runway could there be? And what was at the end? Oh yeah, water, Michael remembered, suddenly recalling newspaper pictures of a plane that had overrun its landing once.

Down, down, down, Michael muttered to himself soundlessly. But they just kept on flying, speeding a few feet above. It was as if the electrical storm had charged them, the runway and the plane – two alikes, now magnetically repelled. Michael could practically feel the force humming them apart.

And then, quite suddenly, something snapped and the wheels slammed down onto the tarmac. Three overhead cabins popped open and ejected contents. There was a bounce, a little wobble, another gasp from the gang, and then they were down in a wet spray of brakes and jet propulsion.

Michael tried not to join in when the passengers erupted into tearful applause.

# Chapter Three

They met at Leeds University, as part of the public school movement to the North. Leeds was cool. It was different. They were different. They didn't want to go to Bristol, Durham or Edinburgh. Those universities were full of public school twats. They weren't public school twats. They were public school cool.

And being public school cool meant broadening one's horizons. It was like an extension of the Gap Year only more daring. Instead of travelling to India, South America or Africa, it meant venturing north of the Watford Gap. Scary!

But they were brave. They were adventurous. They wanted to 'see how the other half lived'. It would be nice to make some Northern friends, for a change. Their parents simply couldn't understand it. Leeds? How ghastly! Which, of course, was part of the reason they went. They didn't want to be like their parents. They weren't snobs. They didn't care about the class system. They were going to change the world.

Either that, or they were too stupid to get a place anywhere else.

Of course, when they finally arrived and realized with full tower block horror just how grim the North was and, more importantly, how much the locals hated them, it slowly became an enormous relief to discover a thousand other rich kids thinking of themselves as unique.

At first, it was hard for the public school crew to comprehend just how venomously they were hated. Maybe they were in denial, desperate to still believe that they *had* made the right choice, that they could handle it, that they might yet, in time, transcend the class barriers.

But, gradually, the full reality sank in. There were the odd pointers. Like getting beaten up at Elland Road for supporting Leeds United. They eventually discovered that it was safer to support Leeds from the away end – at least then they got a police escort out of the grounds.

And then there were the housing estates. It took them a while to realize that they weren't actually living in Hyde Park and Headingley out of choice or because they were affordable (many of them hadn't come into their trust funds yet). They lived there because they had to. The locals had a way of cornering all the *Southern pooftas* off with the *Pakis* into ghettos so that they could collectively spit on them.

The North was so cold that the rich kids had little choice but to huddle together for comfort. They only felt secure in large groups. Surrounding themselves with the same accent made them feel as if they didn't have to disguise it.

It never occurred to them, or suddenly seemed quite secondary, that they had become just like all the other Sloanes at other Oxbridge-reject universities. It didn't matter if they hung out in large groups saying Ra-Ra-Radley too loudly in public places any more. They realized that individuality and cool came secondary to something far more fundamental: physical safety.

Which was really the beginning of how they all became such good friends.

# Chapter Four

The stiff immigration officer stamped Michael's passport: six months, work permitted, no questions asked. She handed it back to him with an expression that seemed to say: *It won't last.* Then it was through baggage pick-up, past customs, nothing noticeable. All airports are the same, Michael briefly considered.

The automatic doors to the greeting hall slid open and there was a rush of noise and then long rows of expectant faces slowly falling and shifting slightly to one side, moving Michael out of the way, out of their field of vision, eliminating him from their search. It felt mildly embarrassing, like someone should want him here, at least one person. But, of course, there wasn't anyone. Why would there be?

He had to call Sean.

Past McDonald's and then a Seven Eleven Michael found a telephone booth. It had a red sign doing something swishy and dynamic (the speed of telecommunication) and the reliable words *Hong Kong Telecom* on top. The call connected before Michael heard it even ring.

'Nobucorp. Sean's phone.' A south-of-South London accent came on the telephone line, full of the potential to shout. Michael never could understand what the exact name of Sean's company was, even less what he did for a living – something in the City. 'THREE SIXES . . . hello, Nobucorp.'

'Can I speak to Sean?'

'Lunch.'

'When will he be back?'

'THREE SIXES OVER THE SEVENTEENTH, EIGHTY-NINE AND A QUARTER, EIGHTY-EIGHT AND A HALF . . . hello, Nobucorp.'

'Sean . . . when will he back?'

'Dunno. Call back in an hour.'

'Can you tell me where he lives? I'm a friend. I'm at the airport.'

'Mid-Levels, I think. Tai-ping Shan. Try Mansion Flats, near Man Mo Temple. They all live there.'

Who's 'they', Michael wanted to ask. 'Do you know the flat number?'

'No.'

Michael put the phone down, picked up his bags and headed for a second pair of automatic doors, the exit. As soon as he stepped outside he could feel it, the wet heat. It was like walking into a shower with all your clothes on: instantly uncomfortable.

Michael found the taxi queue. It wasn't difficult. It was the painfully long line of people right in front of him. He shuffled himself into place. So fucking hot. And wet. Hot and wet. *Which is good if you're with a woman, but it ain't no good if you're in the jungle* . . . Michael knew that as soon as he'd thought of that he wouldn't get Robin Williams out of his head. *Goooooood Morrrrrning Vieeeeeetnaaaaam!*

People were already starting to collect behind him. The taxi queue wound its way through barriers, Hong Kong vaguely discernible in the distance. Michael couldn't get a good view yet because the taxi shelter obscured things. Still, it was there, definitely there, in the distance.

Impossibly humid. So humid, Michael couldn't think about anything else but the humidity. An unforeseen side effect, that. Michael was used to blaming the London grey for his general inertia but he had never anticipated Hong Kong might be so stifling. For some reason he'd thought the weather would be . . . exotic, inspirational. At least, that was how it had seemed in the travel brochure photos. He was finding it hard to breathe. It was too hot to move. Hot and wet.

*. . . which is good if you're . . .*

Oh, shut up!

The queue was taking for ever. There were plenty of cherry-red taxis but too many people waiting. It was the dispatch that was slow. He felt a trickle of sweat run from under his armpit down the side of his rib cage. He writhed in his T-shirt, coaxing the cotton into absorption. He sighed. A woman in front of him followed, and then a man behind did the same. The queue crept forward another single businessman.

Buses occasionally careened past. Taxis edged. Feet shuffled. Bags sighed as they were picked up, swung and then set down again. The queue almost stampeded forward, a whole family this time!

Finally, it was Michael's turn.

The taxi lurched and the boot clicked casually open. Michael swung his bags in and threw himself onto the back seat. The seats felt immediately cold, like sitting on ice. Ahhhhh! They swished as he slid across them. The air-con, which was blasting, smelt toilet-bowl fruity. There was a toy dog on the dashboard nodding its head. The taxi driver didn't turn round when Michael got in. Grey hair lined with black, like a barcode. The meter displayed red numbers.

'Err, Tai-ping Shan, please,' Michael tried.

The taxi driver yanked down the gear lever behind the wheel, American style, and pulled away without saying anything. That suited Michael fine. He preferred to travel in silence.

They passed the runway. There was a fence defending it from the road with barbed wire curling on top. It made the airport look like a concentration camp. Michael could see a jet turning off the end of the runway and then BOOM! a 747 hovered above them, seemingly uncertain that it should be there, hanging in the air like that, before adjusting its trim with purpose and quickly floating down. They passed a basketball court, teenagers in long shorts hopping. Next to that, a five-a-side football pitch, adults in full kit, socks held high with garters.

'British?' The taxi driver suddenly asked, his head still not moving.

'Yes,' Michael replied.

'Long flight.'

'Yes, very long.'

'First time in Hong Kong?'

Michael wasn't sure how to answer this. The driver might scalp him on some dodgy route. Maybe he'd end up in a shop selling fake Rolexes, or, worse, in some Triad-infested backwater without his trousers. Meat cleavers and scarred faces.

'No, third time.'

The taxi driver didn't answer. Could he tell that Michael was lying?

'Just visiting,' Michael added. It didn't sound right when he said it.

'What is your job?'

'I'm a . . .' Michael paused. What was he now – now that he'd left England? Was he still a politics student, hung up on his 2:2 and working on a Masters degree to hide the shame? Was he still a manager in a wine bar in West London? Or was he even a foreign-language teacher? Everyone seemed to have a TEFL these days.

Truth was, up until two weeks ago, Michael had been all of those things, lost and undefined. But now? Now things were different. He'd made a decision. He was on a course to a final destination, first stop: Hong Kong. He wasn't going to answer in the negative any more. That was all part of his new self-determination, a part of the New Michael that had bought a plane ticket and come to Hong Kong, inspired into action by his distressed best friend, Sean. His answer was going to reflect that now. Even if it wasn't true, at least, not yet.

'I'm a journalist,' he said.

'You've come for Handover?'

'Partly.'

'Which paper you work for?' The taxi driver asked.

Err, OK. Michael quickly realized that if he was going to be this new self he might have to think things through a little better, have a more rounded understanding of the person he was projecting himself to be.

'I'm freelance.'

The taxi driver didn't say anything. Michael didn't know if that was a good thing or not. Maybe it didn't matter. The important thing was he'd negotiated his first identity inter-rogation as the New Michael. He felt pleased with himself.

'I need a writer,' the taxi driver said after a while, as they approached a tollbooth leading down into a tunnel. Michael searched the wrinkling eyes in the rear-view mirror to see if he was being serious. 'I need someone to write company brochure,' the driver added.

'Yeah?' Michael said. 'What type of company do you run?'

'Property, import-export, many things. Interested?'

'I might not be good enough,' Michael hedged. After all, he may have been the New Michael but he didn't want to make out like he was Ernest Hemingway or anything. The only journalism he'd ever done was write an article on refugees in Croatia for the Leeds University weekly.

The taxi driver laughed. 'I don't need literature, my friend. I just need someone English. My English no good.'

*My English no good.* Somehow Michael knew that was a lie and, for some reason, it made him like him. The taxi driver paid the toll and then they were underground . . . or underwater, Michael couldn't tell.

Yellow neon lights pulsed to the beat of cat's eyes thumping against the tyres.

'I'll think about it,' Michael replied.

The thin eyes smiled at him in the mirror.

As they emerged from the tunnel Michael saw that they were suddenly in the city. He'd hoped that he might get a view first, a panorama or something. He'd been on the wrong side of the plane when they'd landed so he still had no idea what Hong Kong looked like as an overview. He felt he needed that as an introduction to the place.

He whirred the electric window down and craned his neck to see the skyscrapers. The warm air mixed quickly with the air-con chill and, for a few seconds, Michael thought he felt something close to a normal temperature. The sky was definitely clearing in places and Michael could see large patches of brilliant blue brushed now against the bruised clouds. The drama of the view was doubled up in the mirrored windows that seemed to cover every office building. It wasn't an overview but it definitely made an impression. The New Michael felt like He Had Arrived, which was exactly the sensation he had been hoping for. He immersed himself in it as he breathed in the ever-so-slightly toxic air. Hong Kong quickly felt like The Centre of the World. No. It was better than that. It was The Last Outpost at the Edge of the World. The Final Frontier. Michael could practically hear the rumble of the South China Sea cascading into the Universal abyss just beyond the horizon.

Well, OK, perhaps not.

But it was definitely an improvement over London, whose low-hanging skies only ever made the world seem half as high to Michael. Here in Hong Kong, at least, clouds or no clouds, heat or no heat, the sky really did feel like *The Limit*.

The taxi meandered its way through a tagliatelle junction (the highways seemed a little squatter here, a little fatter, to accommodate heavy traffic on little land, Michael assumed) and then ramped up the Garden Road on a direct course for Mid-Levels. As the road took them away from the city centre Michael noticed an architectural anomaly, a low-rise gleaming white building with a greedy driveway and flags: The Governor's Mansion, the driver told him.

And then, on a suddenly steep and sweeping downward slope, they arrived at Sean's towering apartment complex. The buildings seemed to lean back against the hill for support. Michael stepped out onto the pavement, hauled his bags out of the boot and walked round to the driver's window to pay. He was surprised at how young the taxi driver looked, considering the grey in his hair. With the exception of three laughter lines clawing across each cheekbone, he had smooth brown skin that looked like polished wood. Maybe it was the diet, or all that *Tai Chi*. The taxi driver wrote his name and telephone number on the back of a business card that wasn't his and gave it to Michael.

'In case you decide,' he said.

'Thanks,' Michael said, handing him the fare plus a tip. 'Keep the change.'

The taxi driver laughed. 'No tips in Hong Kong,' he said. 'First lesson.'

'Oh, right,' Michael said gratefully, before holding his hand out to take back the money.

The taxi driver laughed again and said, 'And this is second lesson,' before suddenly speeding down the mountain with a triple honk on the horn.

Now Michael hadn't expected that.

# Chapter Five

Sean was having a wank.

He'd recently discovered *Amateur Allstars* – an absolute classic, according to the boys at work. Sean was getting to the stage now where he could truly appreciate classic porn. He knew all the names of his favourite actors. He knew just who and what to look for in the seedy second-floor room in downtown Wanchai, the one with the blacked-out windows and the shelves that looked like they should be used for drying dishes, not stacking CDs.

He wasn't even embarrassed about it any more. Sean was now a porn connoisseur.

But this scene was getting the better of him, the one with Jennifer Ames, the Atlantis fantasist. He just couldn't get it out of his head. He'd already lost three nights sleep tossing and turning (quite literally), floating between various levels of consciousness on a circular tide, so nearly reaching an island of rest before being swept back out, despairingly, to sea. He had to get over her. He had to wank her out of his system. She was driving him mad. She was also making his dick very sore.

That was why he was back at the flat, wanking (his fourth for the day), when he should have been at work. The CD-ROM whirred as he clicked on the chapter screen. He put the head-phones on (the walls in these apartments were thin and they'd had complaints from the Chihuahua upstairs).

'Well, folks,' started Jerry Langer, one half of the Dirty Duo that had invented *Amateur Allstars* (all first-timers, no actresses, no fake studios, just real people having real sex, and real orgasms, supposedly, on camera). 'This is Jennifer Ames, from Atlantis. And she has a fantasy. Isn't that right, Jennifer?'

'Hmm-mm.'

Jennifer Ames.

Not a stunner by any means. Big peroxide blonde hair. Fat lips on an almost walnut-shaped jaw. Nice eyes, though. Blue, or maybe green. It was hard to tell on Alex's computer monitor. The resolution wasn't so good. Physique not imme-diately obvious as she sat on a cheap, leather sofa in her brown suede jacket with diamond sequins and a black cotton dress that probably reached her knees but now rode high on her thighs as she sat, legs crossed. She was obviously very nervous.

'What is it?'

'I want to be in a blue movie.'

The slightest of rural drawls. Perfect. So girl-next-door.

'Why?' Jerry asked.

'I think it would turn me on. I love being watched.'

'So it's not for money. You don't want us to pay you?'

'No.'

'And it doesn't worry you to think that people will see you having sex, that they will masturbate over you?'

'Not at all. I think sex is a beautiful thing.'

Good answer. Considering the circumstances.

'I see.' Jerry said slowly. 'Well, why don't you come here then?' He reached for Jennifer Ames's wrist and she smiled nervously again as he pulled her over, on to her knees, between his jean-covered thighs.

'*I'm a little scared,*' she mumbled.

'*You're doing just fine.*'

Jerry took her head in his hands and Jennifer Ames looked up at him and smiled slightly. Sean could see that her hands were trembling against his legs. Jerry pecked her, encouragingly, on the lips and then let her take the initiative. She pulled his shirt up over his chest and kissed his stomach.

Eventually, he said, '*Wanna suck me off?*'

'*OK.*'

Jerry stood up and pushed his trousers down. Jennifer Ames, still kneeling, looked with an open expression at his semi-erect penis, which was now just a few inches from her face. He gripped the base of it so that it stood slightly alert, horizontally hard, jutting towards her mouth.

'*You've got a lovely mouth,*' he said, probing a finger between her teeth to part them. Assertive. Controlling. Directing. After all, this was a porno. This was what she wanted. Jennifer Ames opened her mouth slightly, still a little unsure. Jerry pushed the head of his penis in, out, in, until, slowly, gradually, she forgot the camera. She moved and met, back and forth, back and forth.

After a while, Jerry took his trousers off completely and sat down.

'*You like to give head?*' he asked as he pushed her head into his groin.

Jennifer Ames didn't say anything. She licked his balls.

Her hair started to fall down over her face and obscure the action so Jerry considerately combed it back with his fingers.

'*That's it, baby, that's it.*'

Jennifer Ames had her eyes closed now, the odd moan

surfacing. She writhed her head across his genitals. Jerry stood up.

'*Turn around,*' he said, standing over her.

She shuffled round on the floor, turning her back towards the armchair, a little unsure of what he wanted her to do. Jerry guided her by pushing her head back onto the seat, her hair washing over the leather cushion. '*Stay there,*' he said.

He stood over her and stroked his penis across her mouth as she pouted and licked. Then he climbed up onto the seat of the armchair and squatted over her face. He dangled his balls – daring, coaxing, masturbating – before slowly lowering himself. She paused. And then she started to lick his anus.

She started moaning. Not just moaning in an *Uh, uh, uh* way but moaning in a writhing-on-the-carpet way. She pushed one hand between her crossing thighs and pulled her dress down over her right shoulder, exposing a handful of milky breast.

Nice! Jennifer Ames had nice tits.

She reached up and grabbed Jerry's white shirt and pulled him down, deeper down onto her face as she buried and rolled it between the cheeks of his arse. Her knuckles bled white with lust. She wiggled onto her side, twisting her fist between her thighs, reaching with her tongue deeper. Her dress rode up, exposing the darker shadows at the top of her hold-ups. Sean stared as she licked and rubbed and forgot herself.

'*You like to lick my ass?*' Jerry teased. '*Tell me how you like to do it on camera.*'

Jennifer Ames broke into giggles, turning her head to one side in a flush of embarrassment. '*I love to lick,*' more giggles, as she reached up with an index finger and lightly, playfully, touched his anus, '*your ass on camera.*' Full, honest, spontaneous laughter before Jerry lowered himself and she started to lick and wank and moan again.

Sean groaned as a mild shiver passed through his palm, down the head of penis, and buried itself somewhere deep into the recesses of his groin. Christ! Jennifer Ames was loving it.

She Was Loving It.

After a few minutes of rimming, Jerry climbed off, and Jennifer Ames – this was a nice touch – slid the shoulder strap of her dress back into place, re-covering her breast, almost for the sake of decency. How wonderfully coy, Sean thought to himself. This was what Sean wanted from porn. This was reality TV at its truest. He was sick of watching Japanese girls barking as some guy rammed them from behind. It was so obvious that they were hating every minute of it. Where was the turn-on in that?

'*Get on your hands and knees,* ' Jerry commanded.

Jennifer Ames had a medium big arse. Not the greatest of figures. Probably the right sized arse considering the tits, Sean weighed. It didn't matter. Big arse, little arse. Jennifer Ames was sexy as fuck, on the floor of some unknown room, on all fours in black sheer hold-ups, no knickers.

'*Let's see that ass. Spread those cheeks.*'

Jennifer Ames obeyed. Her face pressed into the carpet, she slid both hands round her arse, reaching tentatively with her fingertips to the centre, her hips shifting.

'*Nowwww . . .*' Jerry drooled as she tapped herself lightly, the moans mounting: '*SHOW ME!*'

Jennifer Ames didn't wait. She massaged her clitoris through a thick bush of hair (not shaven, and zoomed in on, loose lips and dangly bits flapping, like in so much tacky fake porn). Her moans stepped up a pitch as her hips barrelled and rolled, her fingers reaching into her mound. She was coming. The way her body shivered and shook in time with the grunts and cries. It was all too perfectly synchronized to be fake. She was coming.

Sean and Jerry masturbated.

When it was over, Jerry reached down and stroked her hair reassuringly.

'OK, Let's fuck.'

Turning, smiling, sweeping hair from her face, Jennifer Ames sighed and nodded.

'Let's fuck for EVUR-EEE-BOD-EE watching.'

Jerry knelt behind her. Sean stared at the computer monitor with a small crushing feeling as she wiggled her arse back – pleading, begging with her groin for him to enter her. Jerry slid himself in and she gasped. They started fucking. The camera watched, square in front of her face now, her body snaking back against Jerry's midriff. Jennifer reached between her thighs again. Then she flashed a look straight into the camera lens. As she rubbed and got fucked, she looked directly at Sean, into his eyes. He watched her.

Rubbing. Moaning. Rubbing. Bucking. Yelling. Rubbing. Bucking. Screaming.

Fuck me, Sean thought to himself, I don't know if I can do this much longer.

'Lie on your back,' Jerry said.

Jennifer Ames rolled over, legs parted.

'Jesus,' Jennifer Ames said, looking up at Jerry benignly. 'I'm so wet.'

Yes, baby, Sean mouthed. You love it.

Jennifer Ames threw her legs high in the air as Jerry entered her missionary style. A few more pumps. Jennifer Ames looked up and deeply into Jerry's face.

'God that feels so good. Please,' she begged. 'Please fuck me harder.'

But Sean could see that Jerry couldn't hold on much longer now. His pumps had slowed as Jennifer Ames continued to grind herself up and against him. Sean could see the red pressure circles on her knees from all the doggy action. Eventually, Jerry pulled out and walked round to kneel over her face.

Jennifer Ames continued to writhe around on the carpet, thighs and knees spread, driving her middle finger in and out of her cunt ready to bring herself to orgasm for a third time. Wanting to. Jerry squatted over her mouth and this time Jennifer Ames didn't need any coaxing. She craned her neck and licked his scrotum, then his arse again.

'That's it, baby,' Jerry said. 'Lick my ass! LICK IT!'

She thrashed and bucked underneath him, before Jerry eventually pulled back and ejaculated over her beaming face. Jennifer Ames smeared the come across her mouth as it spurted – just like a real professional. Sean waited. He didn't want to release yet. He wanted to see the scene through, right to the end. And then he'd rewind it. He was too bewitched to come now.

'Suck it,' Jerry said, as the spasms subsided. 'Take it in your mouth.'

Sean watched Jerry's posture collapse when his penis finally slid out of Jennifer Ames's mouth.

'Was I OK?' Jennifer Ames said, looking up at Jerry, come all over her face, grinning, half laughing.

'You were great, sweetheart. Fucking great,' Jerry sighed, resting his hand on his knees and slouching down onto the backs of his ankles.

'You were right, I completely forgot where I was,' Jennifer Ames said, full of naked honesty. 'I was just screwing. I was really screwing.'

*'You certainly were. Phewww!'* They laughed together as she wiped some of the come from her mouth. Then, leaning across her, his head in his forearm, resting against the arm of the sofa, Jerry sighed, *'Well, Jennifer, I definitely think you've got a future if you want one and, if you don't, well then, now you've got a past.'*

They both laughed heartily at that.

*'I really enjoyed myself,'* Jennifer Ames said privately to Jerry as he smiled down at her. *'Thank you,'* she said quietly before he kissed her.

Scene edit: a Greyhound bus driving off into an orange sunset.

*'Well, Ben, off she goes, back to Atlantis.'* Jerry said to his side-kick behind the camera, Ben Melody, the other half of the Dirty Duo. *'Jennifer Ames. A born natural.'*

It was easy to detect the wistful nostalgia in his voice. Perhaps one of the best fucks of his life and there she went, back to Atlantis, never to be seen again. Still, they'd captured her, hadn't they? Ever immortalized on camera – Jennifer Ames, the Atlantis fantasist: one of the few truly poetic moments in porn.

*'She was a really nice girl,'* Ben said simply before the screen faded out to black.

# Chapter Six

Michael looked up and scanned the concrete giants in front of him. How was he going to find Sean's flat among this vertical maze? he thought to himself. Then he spotted an England flag flapping from a window on the first floor. Leeds United was written in black marker through the horizontal bar of the cross.

That helped.

Michael heaved and huffed his way up skin-coloured stairs, bags on shoulder and in hand, and found what he thought must be the appropriate door. He couldn't see a bell and he noticed that the security gate was sitting on the latch, so he pulled it open and knocked on the front door. It swung slowly open.

'Hello,' Michael called out, peering through the gap. 'Anyone home?'

No answer.

'Hello,' he called out again, a little louder, this time poking his head through.

Definitely Sean's place.

The flat smelled of. . . rabbits. It was dark and dank. None of the lights were on and daylight was obscured by bars on the windows and the shadow of the neighbouring complex.

Three beer cans – two open, one lolling on its side – dominated a plank of plywood pretending to be a tabletop. An ashtray gave birth to a litter of fag butts. Ethnic sheets attempted to make a pair of sofas look more comforting and somehow managed to make them look much worse. A fantastically large television screen stood guard in the corner.

Michael walked in.

'Hi. Sean, it's me,' he announced to the sofas.

Still no answer.

Michael could see three doors, one to his left, open – an empty bedroom beyond it – another two at the end of the apartment. He couldn't decide what to do. He looked at his bags. He didn't fancy the prospect of lugging them all the way back out into the heat on the street only to hail another taxi to take him to some Destination Unknown. And there definitely didn't seem much point in waiting in the car park all afternoon for Sean to finally show up. He was already starting to sweat again. He stepped slowly through the flat, half hoping one of the fake floorboards might creak and announce his presence.

'Sean?'

He reached the two doors at the end of the living room. He could see through a 45-degree gap in the door to the right. Another empty room. The door to the left stood forbiddingly closed. For some reason Michael could sense a presence behind it. He had no idea why he thought Sean should be in there but it *was* the only room he couldn't see into, and the flat *did* look like Sean's place, sooooo . . .

'Sean?' he tried.

He knocked. No answer. He rapped. Still no answer.

Suddenly, a random panic gripped him. Maybe there'd been an accident. Maybe Sean was lying helpless beyond the two inches of dark-brown plywood standing in front of him. Maybe he'd gone ahead and actually done it. Suicide. Like Sean had said he would that time they'd talked on the telephone two weeks ago. He had sounded incredibly depressed, lost. That was part of the reason – the real reason – Michael had decided to come to Hong Kong in the first place. He wanted to help Sean. He was here to save him.

But was he too late? Had Michael underestimated the urgency? Could Sean actually go through with something like that? Michael had a vision of two shoes clanking together as they swung from a ceiling, a human metronome. Something was obviously wrong. Why had the front door been left open? Why was no one answering?

Michael suddenly felt that he had to *do* something.

He reached for the door handle, twisted it and threw himself into the room, opting to take the moment in like a freezing river dip, instead of a gentle immersion. Best to get the shock over in a short, sharp hit.

'JESUS!' Michael jumped as Sean suddenly yelled. It took his eyes a long second to adjust. The room was even darker than the one he'd just come from. There was a yellow sheet pinned to a window, pretending to be a curtain. Michael could see that Sean was sitting on a charcoal office chair, one which had wheels and swivelled. At first Michael was simply happy to see Sean, sitting in front of him, seemingly in fine physical health. Then there was a very strange moment as he tried to digest the entire scene: Sean, headphones on, trousers round his ankles, eyes wildly wide and hands frenetically fumbling.

A pot of Vaseline fell against a computer keyboard and on to the floor.

Sean turned to look up at Michael, one hand loosely cupping

his groin. His face froze and then an enormous twinkling grin quickly erupted across his face.

'OH, CHRIST, IT'S ONLY YOU!' he shouted. 'FUCKWIT!'

Michael stared at him. 'What *are* you doing?'

'WHAT?' Sean screamed, wild eyed still. Then, removing his headphones, 'What?' Michael could hear painful moans travelling loudly through the headphones. That was when he noticed the computer monitor, green flesh and black hair flashing.

'I said, what the fuck are you doing?' Michael repeated.

'What does it look like?' Sean panted, still beaming. 'Christ, you scared the shit out of me.'

Michael could only watch, incredulous, as Sean stood up unashamedly full frontal and still beaming boyishly. He bent down, pulled his trousers up quickly and jiggled himself into position. He zipped up his zipper as if to say, 'There. No harm done. What's next?'

'Christ! Are you wanking? Aren't you meant to be at work?' Michael said.

'Yeah, well,' Sean said a little guiltily. He looked at Michael gently.

Sean was very handsome. Even now, in this dark room, porn pumping beside them, Michael could appreciate it. His features were slender in a feminine, refined way. He had very high cheekbones, a long slim nose and a broad forehead that made him look noble. His blonding brown hair was layered, thin enough to control and long enough to look cool. Michael could see that it was shiny with product and was swept back carefully, Godfather-style. It was a bit of a joke, the hairstyle. A parody of Sean's 'ardness. After all, he was a broker now, the hippie days long gone. His green eyes beamed mischievously at Michael, the flash of a wicked twinkle within them.

Michael also noticed through Sean's open shirt that he'd kept his athletic figure: a God-given six pack on a pair of muscle-defined legs. Sean had always attributed his flat stomach to healthy bowel movements. Four a day, he recommended. Michael didn't know how on earth Sean managed that. Whenever Michael had attempted that kind of regularity he'd ended up with haemorrhoids.

'You're unbelievable,' Michael said.

'I thought maybe you were the dragon from upstairs or, worse, Alex. He's been bitching because we all use his computer to watch porn. The keyboard's gone sticky. And he's blaming me!' Sean said grinning.

Michael could only laugh.

'I can't believe you're here, Mikey. After all this time,' Sean said, reaching for him.

Michael recoiled, backing up against the wall and throwing his forearms up in self-defence. 'Can you wash your hands first?'

'Yeah, sorry, you're right,' Sean said, backing off – almost laughing. 'Tell you what, why don't you chill next door while I tidy up in here, OK?'

'Tidy up?'

'Yeah,' Sean said, a smirk in his smile now. 'I'll just be a minute. Promise.'

Michael sighed. 'Christ, Sean,' he said, shaking his head slightly, 'you're such a fucking pervert.'

'I know,' Sean beamed back. 'I'm sorry.' Then, as Michael started to leave, he added, 'Hey, Mikey.' Michael paused and they looked into each other for a moment. 'It's fucking good to see you, mate,' he said gently. 'Really fucking good.'

Michael turned and left without saying anything.

# Chapter Seven

Baxter stared across the field at Marland. Just stared. Right at him. There must have been twelve, maybe thirteen other boys on the line. But Baxter wasn't interested in them. He wanted Marland. This was a moment for Baxter. Marland could see it as he shrank under Baxter's glare. Baxter was going to get him. They were playing British Bulldog. Baxter was going to get him, and then he was going to kill him.

Marland didn't know why Baxter hated him so much. Maybe because it was Easter term. Easter terms were always the worst. Marland always returned to school with so many toys in January. Mummy always gave him lots of toys for Christmas.

Baxter never had any toys. All Baxter could boast about after Christmas was how many turkey necks he'd wrung. Baxter lived on a turkey farm, in the country. He had one brother, younger, also at the school. They killed turkeys together for the Christmas season.

But Marland tried to be friends with Baxter. Shared his tuck, shared his toys, sucked up to him, tried to buy him off. It only made Baxter despise him even more, though.

The only person who could help was Clarke. He was good at sport like Baxter, was in the same year as Baxter, one above Marland. If Clarke was around Baxter left Marland alone. Baxter usually did what Clarke said. Baxter respected Clarke. That was the only reason Marland was still alive. Because Clarke was usually around. Not today though.

Baxter had made Marland play British Bulldog. Maybe because he knew that Clarke wasn't around. Baxter was going to kill Marland.

'BURR-ITISH BULLDAWWWWG!' Came the war cry.

Three of them. Three bulldogs. There to tackle anyone and everyone they could. Twelve boys. All trying to get past, all trying to reach the end of the field. If they went down or out of touch, they became bulldogs too. Last man standing was the winner. A physical game, you might say.

Baxter was grinning. Squatting. Grinning. Ready. Waiting. Huge.

Marland started jogging, three steps, across the frost.

The other boys were running. Baxter was waiting. Marland could feel the thump of feet through the hard ground. Cold air formed itself against his breath. He had to run. He was getting left behind. Exposed. Baxter was waiting. He started running.

The sound of wind. The white lines of the rugby pitch bordering his vision. Baxter in the middle, waiting, grinning, like a huge ape. He slashed a finger against his throat as Marland started to approach. Close now, twenty, fifteen yards. Coming closer. Marland was running. Straight into Baxter's arms.

GO!

Marland sprinted. Wind rushed in his ears. But his legs weren't moving as fast as he wanted them to. The frost was slippery. It felt like Baxter was sucking the energy out of his thighs. Marland felt weak. Tired. Drained. He wanted to leave this school. He was tired of getting picked on. He wanted to make a new start. But he couldn't. Mummy wouldn't let him.

Baxter just waited.

Five yards, less. Marland dummied to the left, a slight feint, then darted right, hard angle, towards the touchline, fast, faster, pinching his toes through his slippery black shoes, gripping, scratching out the hard, cold ground.

Baxter flowed with him like a reflection, following his move to perfection. For a brief instant he loomed large and then BANG! He bundled on top of Marland in a collapse of thick clothing, heavy, hot bodily weight and then SLAM! Into the hard cold of the ground. Marland's neck jarred and his head banged in a way that made him taste metal from somewhere in the middle of his head right through to the back of his nose and then down his throat.

'Got you,' Baxter panted calmly into Marland's ear, while Marland played dead underneath, submissive, willing, scared.

Baxter fingered for Marland's wrist. Marland could feel him seeking out the place for pain.

'Bagsies, bagsies,' Marland tried, knowing that attempts at surrender were pointless. Baxter had him. Baxter wanted him and now he had him.

'I can't hear you,' Baxter whispered, full of anticipation.

'Bagsies,' Marland panted one more time, the cold melting underneath him. Wet. Then the pain shot through. A jerk. Hard. A twist. Round the wrist, the arm bending up and into his back, the top breaking, Marland could feel it. Fear. What was he doing to him? Something bad. Then another quick movement in the wrong direction. Marland felt his arm give, unnaturally. Scream. No tears. Not yet. The pain, a reactive, instinctive, fearful yelp. Marland could almost feel Baxter grinning behind him as he pushed and pulled.

'Bagsies?' Baxter asked.

Marland couldn't speak. Tears now.

'Bagsies?' Baxter repeated. And then another yank and that was the snap. In the wrist, which was strange because all the pain had been in the upper arm. Baxter must have done something that Marland's body couldn't understand. It was so unnatural. It couldn't relay the correct information. It was confused. Marland whimpered in response.

And then with a sudden, blind rush of feet, a reverberation through the hard ground, a whoosh of power that became a hard push and then a gasp as Baxter flew, flailing, off Marland into the air and across the frost . . . there was immediate freedom. Marland's arm fell limply into the general vicinity of where it should have been. He'd been released. He turned, holding himself. Through the distortion of tears, Marland thought he could make out a vaguely recognizable shape. Bearing over him, strong, standing. It was Clarke.

Clarke had arrived.

'Why can't you just leave him alone, Baxter?' Clarke said, panting. 'We could all hear him screaming, you bastard.'

Marland smarted. Bastard! Clarke had called Baxter a bastard. No one ever called Baxter a bastard. Bastard was the worst thing to call anyone in school. *Benny, moron, Joey Deacon* . . . anything but bastard. The unwritten rule was never insult the parents. Never the parents. That meant *bastard* and *son of a bitch* were strictly off-limits. *Are you saying my parents weren't married when I was born?* Through the pain, Marland was scared for Clarke then. He'd called Baxter a bastard. A bastard!

Baxter shifted against the frost, panting hot fury, and then he was quickly on his feet before charging, down, low, yelling.

'ARRRRRRRGGGGGGGHHHH!'

THUD!

The sound of their bodies was like two worlds colliding: dense and unrelenting. They crashed to the ground in a rustle of winter clothing and muted punching sounds. A crowd of boys was suddenly around them.

'WOO-ZIE! WOO-ZIE! WOO-ZIE!'

Boys, different sizes, different faces, some hammering the air with their fists to the rhythm of the chant, some smiling, others mouths dropping. Baxter and Clarke! This was the biggest fight in the history of the school. Two of the best sportsmen: fighting.

'WOO-ZIE!  WOO-ZIE! WOO-ZIE!'

Marland managed to climb to his feet and edge himself into the crowd, silent, aghast, holding his arm, tears now encrusted in the cold against his face. He shivered. He was scared for Clarke as Baxter mounted him and punched. Punch, punch, a fury. One after the other. Clarke had to win. He had to. Baxter was winning. Come on, Clarke. Get him. Get him. Get him. You've got to get him. Clarke had saved him. And now he was being beaten. Marland caught a flash of Clarke's face. His nose was bleeding. Clarke's nose was bleeding. Clarke, please. He had to get up. But he wasn't. He was getting beaten.

Then there was a sudden deep voice resonating and the crowd quickly parted as Fishface Haddock pushed and strode his way through, big, fat legs reaching, another teacher, Mr Gibson, following, long nose twitching, both booming: 'BREAK IT UP! BREAK IT UP!'

Gibo grabbed Baxter from behind by the arm and then quickly snaked it into a Nelson's grip, heaving him up and off, high above Clarke. Baxter still kicked, one blow connecting, as Gibo pulled him away. Clarke heaved himself up. Fishface Haddock immediately grabbed the top of his arm in half-hearted restraint before Clarke broke away and threw himself across the space to drive a fist straight into Baxter's throat. There was a gruesome sound of cartilage cracking, like soft shell. Baxter gurgled and collapsed slightly in Gibo's grip as Clarke prepared another blow, this time to come from the left, high and down and into his face, except, except, except . . .

Fishface Haddock lunged forward for Clarke from behind and right and low, reaching for his other motionless arm. Clarke's reaction was immediate. Unthinking. Furious. And hard. As Fishface swivelled him, the blow intended for Baxter simply pirouetted in the air and landed straight on Fishface Haddock's mouth. His dull lip split effortlessly along a seam, as though the blow was releasing some unseen pressure. The cut gaped cleanly. Purple blood exposed and showed briefly before pouring.

Time stopped. No one moved. Rough patches of red complexion in both of Fishface's cheeks turned grey. Gibo released Baxter, who held his neck and coughed and spat. Clarke breathed.

Eventually, Mr Gibson managed to move. He reached for Fishface Haddock. Held out a hand. Touched his shoulder.

'Are you all right, Frank?' Gibo said.

Fishface blinked, his tongue pushing against the cut. He looked at Clarke. Clarke looked back. Fishface Haddock nodded at Mr Gibson.

Gibo turned. 'Right, you two. Headmaster's office, now!'

No one moved.

'NOWWWW!' Gibo suddenly screamed at them, striding forward into the crowd, which immediately pulled back, frightened, reactive, timid. It parted. The four of them left. Marland watched them. He watched them walk across the fields, a teacher in between, towards the Headmaster's office. The crowd splintered into agitated hushes.

*Clarke punched Fishface, Clarke punched Fishface . . . He's going to get expelled, Clarke will be expelled . . .*

Marland wanted to run into all of them and say, 'No, no, no. Clarke didn't punch Fishface. Clarke saved Marland. He didn't punch Fishface. He didn't. He didn't. He didn't.' But he knew that Clarke had. He didn't move. He just stood there, holding his arm as the crowd evaporated. He watched the Four walking to the Headmaster's office. He didn't say anything, because he knew it was true. Clarke had tried to save Marland and had ended up punching Fishface. He had. And now there was nothing that could be done about it.

# Chapter Eight

Michael rifled through his luggage for his duty free Camels. He definitely needed a cigarette after that vision. Sean. He'd always been a filthy boy, but wanking on his lunch break? Wasn't that getting just a little too wretched? He wondered how much further Sean might have fallen since arriving in Hong Kong or, more likely, since he and Candy had split up.

Michael feared for Sean. Worse, Michael feared for himself. After all, he looked up to Sean – couldn't help it. Where would Michael be left if – when – Sean hit bottom? Michael understood that Sean could go low, much lower than Michael could ever imagine himself going. And yet Michael would follow him there and then, in the end, it would be Michael that would be left underneath, that one rung further down – deeper, darker, closer to hell.

Get out!

Get out now, Michael found himself suddenly thinking. While you still have a chance. Leave now and forget him. He's beyond you, out of reach, you can't help him, he'll only take you down, he'll destroy you. But that only lasted a second. Michael couldn't leave Sean. Of course he couldn't. He'd come here to help him. This was simply the nature of their relationship. They shared each other's fates, probably out of some primitive sense of British loyalty. They were *Best Mates* and everyone knew what that meant. Follow blindly first, have regrets later.

And besides, when he weighed up the actual events, Michael managed to convince himself that he was being melodramatic. It wasn't that bad. It wasn't as if he'd found Sean hanging from the ceiling, was it? He'd just caught him with his pants down. They'd all be laughing about it in the pub later. Michael told himself to relax.

Just then Charlie walked into the apartment. Michael's heart sank immediately. Michael hated Charlie. Or, to be more precise, he hated Charlie because Charlie hated him. Truth was, he didn't really know the guy.

'Oh, hi,' Charlie said unenthusiastically surprised, looking at him.

Charlie was medium height, not quite six feet, and slim. He had salt-and-pepper hair, a thin mouth and even thinner eyes. His nose was long and you could see sinews crossing his jaw whenever he clenched his teeth – which was quite a lot. He was dressed plainly in a blue shirt with the top button undone, a pair of grey school-like trousers and black brogues. He looked innocuous, the kind of person not worth noticing.

But that was just his camouflage.

Michael had always perceived Charlie to be shifty, untrustworthy, much more sly than his twenty-six years. The guy was so insidious Michael couldn't see how everyone else failed to notice. More to the point, Michael couldn't understand why Sean didn't see it. Or maybe he did, Michael mused.

Ultimately, Sean was a gentle soul – at least, that's what Michael liked to believe. But he also had a dark side, potentially . . . evil? Maybe that was why Sean liked Charlie. Maybe Sean liked Charlie *because* he was sly, deceptive, deviant. And maybe Michael only appealed to Sean's softer nature. Maybe Charlie and Michael hated each other because they both wanted Sean to themselves, like the devil and the angel sitting on each shoulder, vying for the man's ego. Maybe it was a simple matter of jealousy. Maybe too many maybes.

'Charlie! How are you? It's great to see you,' Michael gushed, jumping up from a squat, all smiles and handshakes. Michael felt acutely aware that he had the weaker social standing, being the new guy in town and everything.

'Where's Sean?' Charlie said, after nodding his own hello.

'In there,' Michael replied innocently, pointing at the bedroom door.

'Really?' Charlie said, surprised. 'He should be back at work.' He moved across the living room, full of purpose.

'I wouldn't go in there if I was you,' Michael warned. Charlie turned and flashed a 'Why not?' expression. Michael quickly used vulgar sign language to explain.

'What? Now?' Charlie said.

Michael nodded.

'Christ,' Charlie muttered. 'He's such a fucking pervert.'

'I know,' Michael agreed.

'Oi, Sean, you fucking pervert,' Charlie shouted through the bedroom door. 'Stop spanking the fucking monkey and get your arse back to work.' There was an uncomfortable silence as Charlie waited for a reply. Nothing. Michael didn't say anything. 'How long are you in town for?' Charlie eventually asked, turning back to face him.

'Dunno,' Michael replied, grateful that they were on to something else. 'I've got a six-month visa.'

Charlie nodded slightly. 'You're counting on a full stretch then?'

'Maybe.' For some reason, Michael felt he had to go on and

justify it. 'You know, I thought maybe I'd work here for a bit. London is shite.' He winced on his own Northern affectation, but he couldn't help it. Charlie was making him nervous. Michael was trying too hard and he knew it.

'That figures,' Charlie said, sneering at him.

'What figures?'

'That you'd turn out as filth.'

'Sorry?' Michael reacted with genuine surprise, almost with relief that the insults were finally out in the open between them. He had more than a few of his own to throw at Charlie given half the chance.

'Failed In London Try Hong Kong.'

It took Michael a couple of seconds to get it. 'Oh, right, yeah,' he said, trying to figure out why he was F.I.L.T.H. and Charlie wasn't. Weren't they all from London? Maybe that was what the bloke on the telephone at Nobucorp had meant when he'd said 'They'. Charlie smiled thinly at him before eventually sliding his way past the sofas into the kitchen. For some reason, Michael suddenly felt like he should just go home. He sat on one of the sofas and smoked.

Ten minutes later Sean limped out of his bedroom. Michael noticed his clothes. They weren't dissimilar to Charlie's but for some reason Sean looked more like an overgrown schoolboy in them than a devious malcontent in disguise. Michael wondered why Sean didn't pay more attention to his appearance. After all, this was Hong Kong – home of the tailor-made suit. And he had everything else: the looks, the charm, the humour, apparently the money. He could have been a real ladies' man with a little more effort – a French cuff and a sharp lapel, instead of the M&S look. Then again, what chance would Michael have if Sean actually made an effort? Maybe that was why he didn't say anything. He'd had enough of watching

Sean get all the attention over the course of the friendship. And now that he had arrived, in Hong Kong, making a fresh start, the New Michael was very much hoping to pull. It had been a while. A long while. That was another reason for leaving London.

Sean smiled at Michael before reaching for the packet of Camel Lights that Michael had unwisely left on the plywood plank and collapsing on to the opposite sofa.

'Help yourself,' Michael said sarcastically.

Sean put his feet up on the table as he lit his cigarette and then drew hard on it. He wasn't wearing any shoes.

'Feeling better?' Michael said.

'Much. Thanks.'

Michael just shook his head.

'So what's going on, Mikey?' Sean said, making Michael wince. That was the third time Sean had called him Mikey even though he knew Michael hated it. The Leeds Group had given him the nickname. Michael thought it sounded Sloaney. It sounded especially stark coming from a bloke. At school they'd only ever known each other by their surnames. Why were there all these soppy equivalents now? Maybe it was simply the female influence in their lives now. Michael was a someone-*ey*: just like a Katie, a Sophie, a Sluffy or a Muffy.

'How long are you staying?' Sean continued.

'Dunno. It depends.'

'On what?'

'You,' Michael said, knowing that he was being too direct, too quickly. *Always too serious, Mikey, always too heavy.*

Sean raised his eyebrows briefly.

'I wanted to see if you were all right,' Michael added, so there could be no confusion.

Sean didn't reply. He just looked at Michael and smoked.

Michael looked back at him. The smell of cigarettes was fermenting now with the smell of rabbits to form a cheesy aroma.

'Jesus, your feet stink,' Michael said, trying to back out of the *heavy* corner now. Insults had always been a good way to lighten a situation with Sean. It showed they were having 'fun'.

'I've gotta go to work,' Sean said quickly then, sitting up and feeling around blindly for his shoes under the plywood plank.

Michael was a little taken aback by Sean's abruptness. He hoped he hadn't gone in too strong just now. He knew that Sean needed coaxing, the soft touch, to come out of his shell. But the trip, and the previous couple of weeks preparation, had got the better of Michael. He was feeling anxious. Had been for a while. And who could blame him? The last time they'd spoken Sean had said that his girlfriend of five years had dumped him and he wanted to kill himself. The only thing that had seemed to matter after that was for Michael to get himself to Hong Kong as quickly as possible and make sure that his best friend was OK. But for some reason, they weren't clicking.

'Wait, Sean,' Michael said, a little beseechingly. Sean stopped to look at him. Michael tried to think of a meaningful adieu to see Sean through the afternoon but then realized there wasn't one. He *was* being overly dramatic. 'Which room should I sleep in?'

Sean's face fell slightly and then there was a small pause.

'Err, Mikey,' he said slowly, 'I wish you'd told me you were coming.'

Michael frowned. 'I did.'

'Not specifically.'

'Err, yes specifically. You said you had a spare room,' Michael said quickly, eyebrows positioned accusingly, loading up on the emotional ammo. He could sense when someone was about to drop a rejection bombshell.

'That was two weeks ago . . . and I was drunk. I forgot. Sorry.'

It was Michael's turn now to not say anything.

Sean cut to the chase. 'Charlie's already taken the spare room.' Michael felt the resentment quickly burn. Charlie? How could Charlie take preference over him? 'He just got here a week ago . . . from Korea,' Sean said. So that was why Charlie didn't constitute F.I.L.T.H., Michael quickly understood. He was glad he hadn't walked into that trap.

'Oh, right,' Michael said, trying very hard to take it like a man. It didn't matter that Michael felt Sean owed him more than this – *I've travelled six thousand miles just to help you . . . I haven't seen you in over three years and this is how you greet me . . . Surely I'm more important to you than Charlie?*

Only birds moaned like that.

Charlie stuck his head round the corner. Now that his name had come up he couldn't pretend he wasn't listening in on the conversation any more. 'Fancy a cup of tea, Sean?' There was a painful spring in his voice.

'No thanks, I'm just off,' Sean replied.

Michael wasn't surprised not to be offered one.

'Listen, mate,' Sean said, looking at Michael now. Michael could see that Sean knew he'd fucked up. He was maybe even feeling guilty about it. 'There's plenty of other places you can crash.' He paused in a way that said there was an easy remedy to this situation, that this wasn't a slight on Sean's part. He wasn't rejecting Michael. It was a simple oversight. He couldn't just turf Charlie out to make room for Michael. But he *was* sorry for the confusion and he'd do his best to fix it. 'Why don't you go stay with Candy?' he said eventually.

'Candy?' Michael replied, astonished.

'Why not?'

'Are you sure that's a good idea?'

'She'd love to see you,' Sean spun.

'I thought you'd broken up,' Michael said, a little too bitterly.

'No, no,' Sean replied quietly, almost with shame. 'We're back together now.'

Michael breathed through his nostrils. It *had* been a mistake to come here. He knew it.

'I see,' Michael said before quickly adding, 'That's good. That's really good.' He didn't want to come across badly. 'You must be . . . feeling much better then.'

Sean sort of smiled at him.

'Right,' Michael recovered. 'Do you mind if I use your phone?'

Sean stabbed out his cigarette and pointed at the Mickey Mouse statue collapsing on a beanbag, before moving carefully towards the front door.

'Her number's on the speed dial.'

# Chapter Nine

When Sean and Candy got it together it seemed, to them, like one of those things that *just happened*. But, to everyone else watching, nothing could have been further from the truth. To the boys, Candy was far too beautiful and elusive for sex with her to just *happen*. It was a question of superlative strategic skill and Sean was a lucky, lucky bastard. They all analysed privately how he'd done it.

And to the girls at university, who loved Sean unequivocally, Sean and Candy were destined for each other. They didn't *happen*. They were *meant* for each other. They gushed to hide their own jealousies, of course. Ahhhh, the romance! So beautiful. When would it happen to them? When would someone want them as much as Sean loved Candy? The more they burnt, the more they gushed.

But in spite of the fact that everyone perceived them to be the lucky ones, life wasn't plain sailing for Sean and Candy once they did get it together. Far from it. *Things* happened that made life immediately difficult.

For starters, there was Candy's course. She was studying Spanish, which meant she had to spend a year in Bilbao. That meant they had to decide, after just five months, whether the relationship was worth going long distance for. Of course, they decided that it was – things had been going far too well for them to just say '*see ya*', but neither of them had any inkling of just what a nightmare the long-distance relationship scene would turn out to be – least of all Sean.

For him, it was the beginning of the Blackness.

Sean had no idea how it all started, where it came from, the depression. At first, he put it down to simply missing Candy and he tried to adopt a certain stoicism. He talked to his friends about feeling unhappy, and, for the first couple of months, they sympathized. Mikey told him it was understandable for him to feel blue. He shouldn't feel too bad, however. She'd be back within a year, and then he'd have her. Candy! The Eurasian babe! What a lucky bastard!

Sean would smile when he said that but, really, he wasn't helping. Sean's sadness ran deeper than just missing Candy. He couldn't pinpoint it, but he could sense a deep-rooted self-loathing, black and all encompassing.

There were days, the occasional week even, when he didn't get out of bed. He'd lie there, watching the light turn, wallowing in the melancholy of the early evening, staying awake for the night so he could listen to the hum of the neon nightlights. Sometimes, maybe because he was playing with his sleeping patterns so much, he lost the ability to discern between the light of day and the light of the night. It all looked the same through his orange curtains.

Sean repeatedly tried to snap himself out of it. He wasn't the self-pitying type. He told himself that he had absolutely nothing to be depressed about. He was young, he had his health, he was popular, he liked Leeds (in general), and there was always the footie. Mikey tried to get him involved in a Sunday league.

But slowly, surely, as the winter months turned, Sean felt

his entire sense of self drain away, drawn towards this inner malevolence, as quickly and confusingly as water down an Australian plug hole. The Blackness was a malevolent force, capable of wiping out everything that was good in Sean. And it was growing.

When he did go out, he found that he wasn't happy, care-free, go-lucky Sean any more. He was frowning, serious, carrying-the-weight-of-the-world on his eyebrows Sean. He wasn't even athletic Sean. Winter had sucked the muscle out of him and now he was skinny. He started to think that he was losing his hair. He certainly wasn't one of the lads any more. He felt – and this was a first – shy.

He continued to shut himself off. He knew that he couldn't lean on his friends with the same old moan. He could see that Mikey was getting impatient. Candy had been away for several months. He should have been used to it by then, surely. He knew that they wouldn't understand. Why would they? He didn't even understand it. He started to use revision as the excuse to isolate himself, explain his long absences, squirrel away this new internal discovery, this new self-hating self – away from the gaze of the people he cared about, whose opinions mattered to him. He didn't want them – anyone – to see him this way. He also figured that the only sensible way to deal with this tide of emotion that Candy had seemingly unleashed within him was to channel it. The great wash was too much. He had to focus on work. After all, it was the year of Finals and Sean hadn't attended a single history lecture in his two years at Leeds.

He also concentrated on her.

When the darkness got bad, he used her, the mental image of Candy, to occupy his thoughts. She became a mental substitute for his issues. It wasn't the perfect solution. Sean knew that it wasn't Candy's physical presence he pined for, he understood that what he missed was companionship, someone he could talk to. But when he tried to write he found he simply couldn't express himself. And the telephone was even worse – what with all its long-distance pauses and crackling lines and lack of privacy (Sean could always hear people in her background).

He missed her too much afterwards, anyway. He didn't want to worry her.

So it was the thought of her that he concentrated on when he couldn't sleep (which had quickly become every night). Just the memory was enough. The way her hip angled its way into her stomach with such purpose as she lay on her side. The way her breasts breathed. Her smell when they were buried in each other under the duvet.

Then, one day, quite suddenly, with the summer and the sun and the longer days – she was back.

There was nothing disappointing in her return. Even though she'd become very large in his mind's eye, even though he had built her up into this person of God-like power (the only one who could save him, who he could talk to) she didn't fail to meet his expectations of her. She was just as sexy and desirable as she ever had been. There was the small, silent question of fidelity, but they didn't go there. The only thing that seemed important after she got back was whether they still wanted to be together, having both given up a year of their lives. And the answer was yes. Unequivocally, yes.

Sean stayed on in Leeds, after his 2:1. He took a job stacking shelves at the local supermarket, while Candy completed her course. They – or rather he – managed to put the darkness away, almost as soon as she returned. He found that her mere presence was enough to be happy about on a day-to-day basis.

It wasn't like he even had to conjure up the image of her in his mind. He could just open his eyes and she'd be there, next to him, in bed. He often watched her while she was sleeping and told himself he was happy, he was happy, he was happy . . .

In fact, after Candy got back, Sean found that the last thing he wanted to think about was his depression. He was busy now and she had exams. She needed his support. He didn't want to Sit On The Couch and drain her energies. He did things for her, like bring her tea, which helped him stop thinking, if only for a few minutes.

Slowly, he even managed to convince himself that he hadn't been depressed at all. He *had* just missed her. And now that she was back, the sadness was gone. But he knew, deep down he knew, that her return was only a temporary respite. The depression had never gone away. Not really. And after a while, with direct inevitability, the mental levee that he had erected to hold back the black tide broke again.

This time it happened after they left Leeds, while they were on a year off together. Their plan was to go to Turkey, India, Nepal, Burma, Thailand and Laos. It was going to be the best time of both their lives. This trip was going to *make* them, form the foundation for the good times and memories that they both hoped might ultimately materialize into something more permanent. Marriage? Maybe that's what they both wanted. Maybe they were both looking to unfairly tip the scales into the positive.

And then things went pear shaped. Sean wasn't exactly sure how it all started this time. It might have been the combination of malaria pills and Indian hashish. There were nightmares, of course, and some tearful midnight remembrances – it might have been the morning he noticed his long hair looking dangerously thin on top after a cold Himalayan river dip. Oh God, he *was* going bald, he'd thought to himself with horror.

In the end, though, it didn't matter how or why it had started. The only thing that seemed to count was that somewhere in North India, as the love of his life lay beside him, the Blackness overcame him, completely this time. It was relentless. Day in, day out, darkness. Pointless existence. Grim considerations.

Sean found himself staring at beautiful landscapes and feeling tears form. The more beautiful the world, the more depressed he felt. He'd look at Candy and feel his heart breaking. Beauty seemed suddenly so bleak to him. He'd always thought it had been the low Northern light that had got the best of him. But now he realized glorious landscapes were even worse.

It got especially bad in Thailand. He and Candy had found their very own private paradise, a small island in a nature reserve with seven simple huts built on stilts, which no one else lived in. Sean found he was unable to stop himself crying so he started taking walks by himself and making up excuses so she wouldn't see. He knew that his moods were becoming oppressive.

But one day she caught him. He was watching her swimming. She was a long way out. He watched the back of Candy's head, bobbing in the chrome, a beautiful black spot. Then her head turned. He could see her face, very clearly, even though it was a long way away. This was all he needed, a simple impression, in order to see the detail. He'd become good at that, while Candy had been away.

Eventually, Candy started stepping out of the water. Her long body dripped under a black string bikini, two bony bumps on her shoulders making her look skinnier than she actually was, almost skeletal. And the flatness of her stomach . . . was it starvation? No. She'd had a stomach bug but even after that, when he held her, she was full of soft places – small heavens of flesh on a lithe body that just seemed to go on and on and on. She was only slightly shorter than him.

She pulled through the length of her thin black hair and wrung the water out over her shoulders as she stepped through the shallows, the brightness beyond her, two more limestone islands bulging on the skyline – not swimmable, they'd already discussed it. Sean could see her feeling the wet sand through her toes. Soon she'd be on the hot, dry, grainy sand and then she'd have to skip. He'd only managed a minute or two out in the sun before having to move into the shade. It was midday. It'd get cloudy later and everything would turn grey, a bright grey, the same colour as the ocean. They'd probably make love and then go to the restaurant to eat fish. Candy would roll a joint. Sean might read something. It would get dark but they wouldn't go outside to look at the stars. They'd fall asleep. At least Candy would. And then Sean would watch her, listening to her breathing become a slow rhythm. They'd open their eyes together at dawn.

And then it happened. Candy looked up and saw him, sitting in the shadows between the palm trees, and Sean watched her face seize with panic. It was then that he knew that he was doing it again. And he hadn't even noticed. He'd simply slipped into it and now, as he felt it on his face, it was engulfing him and now she could see it and he felt terrible because he knew that he'd let her down.

'Sean!' Candy had cried out, running towards him, kicking up sand that stuck to the wetness on her calves, making amazing shapes. 'Sean, darling, please, don't . . .' She'd beseeched before finally collapsing in front of him, splayed on her knees. She pawed at his face and used the salty palms of her hands to smear the tears from his cheeks and kiss his eyes and hold him and try to rock with him and then hold his face in her hands and ask why/what happened/please tell me, over and over and over and over . . .

But Sean had no words. All he could do was sit there, terrified in his own despair. The tears surged from his eyes like blood from a deep wound. If only you could apply pressure. If only tears would clot. Who knew how long it went on for? Who knew how long it would last? Sean was lost in the vast Black and he was melting, slowly dissolving, becoming nothing, less than nothing, a shadow.

It was a dreadful discovery. It was as if there was finally no place to turn. He could find no sanctuary, no escape. Everywhere he turned it was dark. The only thing that was keeping him going was the beating of his heart, and he spent most of his life now willing it to stop.

Candy was great. She was brilliant at reassuring him. Sean learned to close his eyes and just listen to the sound of her voice. She told him things like she would always love him and that she understood, more than understood. She listened to his rambling analysis, why he might be feeling like he was (when he didn't know why) and then she'd suck his dick and look up at him and tell him how large he was – which made him laugh.

Eventually, as before, the depression eased without any real explanation and without any real sign. It wasn't cured and nothing was ever solved, but after a few weeks Sean simply found himself able to contain his emotion once again. The blackness subsided into a manageably soft grey. He stopped smoking dope, which helped enormously, and he tried not to talk, or even think, about his feelings too much. There were even moments when he felt happy.

After the second wave subsided, Sean made a resolution. He decided that it had been the thinking, the too-much-time that had been his undoing. He promised to get busy again, like he had been at Leeds. Travelling had unravelled him. He would not allow himself the time to think. He was always going to be good-time Sean from then on, carefree and funny and never-a-care-in-the-world. He wanted society to identify him as such. As long as the people round him always saw him as happy, he'd have a constant reminder to *be* just that. He wouldn't be able to forget himself again, or, at least, the Self that he wanted to be. He didn't want to get lost in that hole again. It was just too much.

And there was a big part of him that worried that if he had carried on much longer with his brooding Candy would have eventually just fucked off. There was certainly no denying the fact that by the time the year off was over the chemistry between them had changed. Candy loved Sean more and he loved her more, but it was no longer equal. Whichever way he twisted it, Sean knew that he depended on Candy now. He had let her into his head. He'd needed her help and she'd given it but, in doing so, there was no way his life could con-tinue without her. He could be Mister Happy-Go-Lucky, but only as long as she was there, available. She now commanded a seat, like a benevolent dictator without whom his normal psychology couldn't function. She held the crown to his mind.

Not that he didn't want her there, necessarily. There was no one else he could have trusted more to occupy that posi-tion. But, it *was* slightly irksome – the thought that his mental well-being depended on someone else. Sean needed Candy now. He couldn't go on without her. Sean knew that if, *when*, it ended (an unbearable thought in itself), he'd be fucked. It wasn't just about her, and how much he loved her any more. It was about the Blackness. It was about keeping that at bay. And he knew that he needed Candy in order to do that. If she left, it would be the Blackness that would fill the void. He knew it. He was now in a psychological relationship. He didn't want to be, but it was too late to do anything about it. He had let her in and there was no way now for her to leave.

Which was why, in the end, he let her convince him to go with her to Hong Kong. Looking at the precedent they had set themselves, it was destined for disaster. What worse idea could there have been than to follow a girl to *her* hometown, where *she* spoke the language, had *her* own job, *her* own family, *her* own friends and *her* own life?

But he didn't let himself think about any of that at the time. After all, it had been the thinking that had been his undoing, the thinking . . .

# Chapter Ten

Candy lived in Pokfulam, with her parents. Not affluent but nice, according to the guide book. Not quite in the same league as the Peak but a lot more comfortable than Mid-Levels, certainly less crowded. Somehow it felt like a small consolation. Michael didn't like the idea of staying somewhere out-of-town. He felt isolated enough as it was.

But, then again, he didn't have much choice.

He cheered up a little on the double-decker bus, which had the same smell as the taxi – a sort of fruity air-con, strawberry this time. Michael noticed English-style road signs everywhere with their green backings and white borders, which looked odd against the tropical jungle backdrop, yet mildly reassuring. Any familiarity was a comfort at this point, he supposed.

The stormy weather was still deciding on whether to clear and its ambivalence made the ocean views immediately impressive. Sun rays beamed between the clouds in random shafts, turning patches of water a deep jade. The bus wound its way slowly through the mountains and negotiated impossibly small roundabouts. It made a nice contrast to the city. It wasn't so much an I Have Arrived feeling as a traveller's feeling. It was more like an I'd Like To Stay A While type thing. It was nature. There were beaches.

The bus dropped him off at the end of Candy's road. Michael was relieved to get off. He was starting to shiver, the air-con had been so cold. He stamped his way down a steep hill with two bags on one shoulder to reach her house, a hundred metres or so, and was sweating by the time he found the front door. Hot, cold, hot, cold, hot. Hong Kong couldn't make up its mind what it wanted to be.

No one answered the bell and, after several bewildering minutes, Michael finally spotted a set of stairs leading down the side of the house. He walked down them to an iron gate before calling out.

'Hello, anyone home? Candy? It's me.'

A heavily coated Alsatian quickly bounded into sight. The dog thrust its snout through the iron bars and salivated at Michael's crotch.

'Hello, boy,' Michael said, nervously amiable, as a concerned-looking Filipino woman slowly appeared. 'Hi, I'm a friend of Candy's,' he announced, beaming. 'She's expecting me.'

'Candy no here.'

'Oh, right,' he paused. 'Errm, do you know when she'll be back?'

'Candy in Stanley.'

'Right, OK. Do you know when she'll be back?'

'Candy in Stanley.'

'Right.'

Any euphoria Michael had caught sight of on the bus journey now rapidly evaporated. He was getting fed up with his friends being flaky. He'd literally spoken to Candy on her mobile minutes before leaving Sean's place. She'd said she'd be at home waiting for him. In fact, she didn't stop going on and on about how excited she was that he was here. How *wicked* it was. And now: Candy in Stanley. Wherever that was.

He didn't bother to ask the Filipino lady if he could leave his bags with her or use the telephone. Somehow he knew exactly what she was going to say. And by the time he reached the top of the street to wait for the next bus to take him who knew where – he hoped there was a direct route to Stanley – Michael saw black thunderclouds reforming from over the mountaintops ascending in front of him. Within three minutes, hot thick drops were pelting the tarmac. The weather was about as reliable in Hong Kong as his friends, Michael thought to himself. He didn't bother standing under the bus shelter. For some reason, he found he wanted the rain.

# Chapter Eleven

Candy was drunk. Which was part of the reason she had her tongue halfway down this stranger's throat, she realized. The other part was because he was absolutely gorgeous. And besides, she reminded herself, it didn't matter any more if she kissed guys. She and Sean had agreed. Snogging other people was now 'OK'.

But when the stranger started to push her into a nearby alleyway and force his hands into her top, which was still soaked through from the thunderstorm, she soon realized what was happening.

'Stop, hang on, wait,' she gasped, falling back against a wall.

Mr Gorgeous pulled his head back and leant his crotch into hers, as if by accident.

'What?' he asked, quietly, gently, full of controlled passion. Candy looked into his steely blue eyes. She found that she was trying to remember his name. Not that it made any difference. She knew now that she definitely wanted to fuck him. He was so hot.

'Nothing,' she said, grabbing one side of his face and throwing herself back into him, hooking one leg over his and grinding.

'CANDY! CANDYYYYY!' She could hear Sasha calling. She

tried to block it out, lashing her tongue deeper into lover boy's throat in search of oblivion. 'MIKEY'S HERE!'

The name inspired – dare she admit it – fear . . . and guilt . . . and a range of other emotions she might normally have expected to associate with her father. Fuck. Mikey. She'd forgotten all about him. Admittedly, she was drunk when he'd called, but now she suddenly remembered her promise to meet up with him at her place. And she would have done, had old Blue Eyes not walked through the pub door. Damn, Mikey's here. He was the last thing she needed in her life at the moment.

She quickly pulled away. 'Gotta go, babe.' Blue Eyes mumbled something and firmed his grip on her hips before making another lunge for her lips. She looked at him. 'Get your fucking hands off me now or I scream.'

Blue Eyes suddenly looked incredibly stupid. Candy took the opportunity to break free and jog down the alleyway into the street before stopping. Then she turned and ran back, kissing him wetly one last time. She'd done it, she thought, with a self-satisfied sense of achievement – a harmless snog and nothing more. Poor Blue Eyes, she thought to herself. He didn't want to get messed up with a girl like her.

The new Candy Newman: *femme fatale*.

# Chapter Twelve

Sean was Candy's first. Sort of. She'd slept with a guy, once, way back, when she was on a French exchange programme in Canada, but it hadn't felt like she'd done it. For starters, neither of them had known what they were doing. She was only fourteen. It was during a weekend. Boys from the nearby school had sneaked into the grounds and shared cigarettes and vodka. Next thing Candy had known she was in a barn in a field, with this guy (she'd since blocked out his name – Jason or something) doing all the normal stuff. She'd said something silly about how a friend had already lost her virginity and that she was jealous. She hadn't meant it as a cue but he'd taken it that way. Then he'd found a red and green window-pane rug behind a log pile. She could still remember his face when he'd discovered it. The fortune!

She'd pulled her blue woollen stockings down to her ankles and then laid down, legs together, on the rug. She could feel the pinch of wood chips through it. There was a smell of sawdust. He'd climbed on top of her, instantly stabbing. She wasn't sure if he was doing it right. It didn't feel like he was doing it right. She remembered saying to him: 'This is worse than the dentist.' His face had an expression that seemed to agree. And then that man had seen them and they'd had to run for it.

All in all, the whole experience had been humiliating. She'd felt like a child playing an adult's game. And the fact that they'd been caught! That was awful. It hardly fitted in with the romantic notions she held about womanhood. She told herself that it hadn't happened. That he hadn't penetrated her. That she'd been given a second chance. She decided that she wouldn't sleep with anyone ever again for the sake of it. She wanted to wait until it was special.

And she waited a long time. Seven years, in fact. Her looks were part of the reason things took so long. Candy was beautiful. She knew it. Boys always looked at her, wanted her, badgered her. For the most part she liked that. After all, she liked boys. She knew that much. But she hated the way they pawed and begged and pressured and forced whenever they got a look in. Kissing to them was always an angle into fucking. None of them ever seemed able to let things build. They had one purpose in mind and they were all making a beeline for it – like she was something to be conquered. In the end she'd always have to say no. It made her cringe but it was the only way to make them stop. She found saying no embarrassing. She resented men for making her say it. She resented the pressure on her to please. She wanted to please. But she couldn't go *there* again. She'd promised herself. And they were always so determined. She had to learn, even though it didn't come naturally to her, to say no. And the very word: *no* – in and of itself – came to represent all the resentment she felt because she was having to say it, because they were the ones that were making her say it, making her feel like the bad guy, the one to disappoint. It put her off them. The word no. It made her immediately unforgiving. It was like a trigger. All those boys, committing sexual suicide in their blind lust, and they didn't even know it. Some took it well. Most took it badly. Candy earned a reputation for being a prick tease.

Eventually, slowly, she learnt to shut herself off entirely, turning off her emotions, never making eye contact, smothering the pheromones and trying her best to ward men off the scent right from the very beginning. It was the only way to avoid having to say that word, that no, again and again and again. Secretly, she feared, if she was forced to do that too many times, she'd start hating men altogether. And then what kind of life would she have?

Candy didn't fancy Sean at first. She didn't even think about it. Maybe she'd been shutting herself off from all that for so long by then, her feelers were out of touch. But, looking back on it, he certainly played his hand coolly. She had to give him that. He didn't make a single move. While all the other boys panted, he didn't even look at her. He was always charming, funny, friendly and kind. He treated her like a mate, which of course, was what she was. And he saw other girls. It wasn't like he couldn't get the attention. A lot of Candy's girlfriends said he was the best looking bloke at Leeds, he certainly had the best arse. But, still, Sean never looked at her. *Why not?* she one day wondered.

And that was when she started fancying him.

In the end, it just *happened*. What Candy had supposed she would determine, in fact simply occurred. Sean had just split up with another girlfriend, quite a long-term relationship by university standards (six weeks). And then, one afternoon, Candy had found him sitting in the front room of her house smoking a cigarette. She'd asked him if he was OK and he'd looked up at her sadly and said, 'Sure.'

And that was when she just knew, and he seemed to look at her like he *just knew,* and before she knew what she was doing she had put her fingers in his suddenly beautiful hair and he had stood up and their faces were opposite each other and then they'd started kissing and then she wanted him, seven years of wanting, suddenly concentrated on Sean, and she didn't even think about it as she scrambled out of her black leggings and pulled him down on to the swirling, seventies-carpeted floor of the living room and he pulled his trousers down and she took him in her hand and she put him inside of her and then she drowned in the pain and the release.

They made love for eight days. They didn't leave his room, except to make a sandwich or get a cup of tea. She often screamed. They even had complaints from the other housemates, but she didn't care, they didn't care. Sean said they were just jealous. She couldn't see exactly what she could do about it. She was in ecstasy. Sean made love to her in a way that was total. Or perhaps it was the other way round. She just threw herself into him, hoping she would melt like snow in a fire. She wanted to dissolve. And she did. Again and again and again. She couldn't stop. She wanted him all the time. She had a lot to give and she gave it all to Sean.

After a few months she had to go away. She knew it was coming. It had always been there. She had tried not to think about it. The only thing that had seemed to matter when Sean entered her life was to open the door as wide as possible and see how much was inside. All of it had to come out. And quickly. Because part of her realized, as they came together, that she had squandered her time abroad. She'd wasted the freedom of being alone, away from her parents' stern gaze. She understood, almost too late, that that had been her deal, her lot, as a half-caste. Adolescence, freedom, fun – abroad. And after that? Back to Hong Kong. Back home. As a good Chinese girl. It had never been expressed but an inner sense told her that that was the trade-off. Maybe it was a programme written in her blood.

That was why she entered the affair with Sean so completely, without reserve. She couldn't help but fall in love with him. In a way, he'd saved her. She'd almost missed out completely. She'd nearly thrown away all her liberation, her international half – all because of that one mistake, at the beginning.

But, with Sean, all would not be lost. She could realize herself before it was too late, even though, deep down – subconscious and unacknowledged – she knew it was doomed. Candy knew she would abandon Sean for the sake of her bigger Chinese-self. After all, she'd always be more Chinese than Western – at least, that was what Mother always said.

*Just look at yourself in the mirror.*

It was just the way things were.

For the first two weeks in Bilbao Candy found it hard to stop crying. Then, quite naturally, she discovered an inner resolve, a hardness, an ability to cope. Maybe it was because she was a woman. Or maybe it was because she was Chinese. Or maybe it was both. However much her love for Sean pulled, Candy knew that she simply had to get on with *It*. Her year in Spain was important. It was her university degree. Daddy had sacrificed a lot for this. She'd cry about Sean later, she told herself. When it was really over.

Candy knew that she was in Spain, learning the language, because one day she'd marry a Chinese, probably a Hong Kong Chinese (the languages – French, Spanish, Cantonese, Mandarin, English – would make her very eligible). At the end of the day, that was her path – marrying local wealth, becoming a *Tai-tai*, someone's Number One. *Tai-tais* were at the top of society in Hong Kong. She knew that her future husband would have other lovers – mistresses, not concubines like in the old days but they may just as well have been. She also knew that a Number Two would only ever get taken to the second best restaurant, bought the second best things, the occasional hand-me-down even. Candy had seen the difference between the *Tai-tais* and the second place whores at Hong Kong's society events. It was in the very dresses they wore. Who wanted to be somebody's second?

That might have seemed shallow to anyone on the outside, but it was the reality for a woman living in a male-dominated Chinese society. And besides, Candy often told herself, she wasn't just doing it for her. She wanted to marry for the sake of her family. As an only daughter (no sons – very painful) she had always been made to feel the inadequacy of Father's mediocre success on the Island, the fact that they lived in Pokfulam – not the Peak or Shek O. And the fact that he'd nearly impoverished himself giving her a private education. Marrying a wealthy Hong Kong businessman was the very least she could do. At least that was what Mother said.

And it wasn't as if Candy had a better solution, any viable alternatives. She certainly didn't know what she wanted to do with her life. She wasn't about to make large amounts of her own money. Even more than that, she knew that Sean was a no-hoper. There was no way a life with him could provide the wealth, both in real and cultural terms, that her marrying a rich Hong Kong Chinese would one day bring the family, which, in turn, would give her the parental approval she so desperately sought. Maybe that was all it was ever about.

When the year in Spain was finally over, Candy held Sean for weeks. He loved her. They loved and fucked. He helped her final year pass quickly. She got a First. And then she took Sean and they left. Travelling. That was the one thing

Candy wanted to do before going back to Hong Kong for good. See the world. Explore new places. Be free. In love. With Sean.

Which was why, when Sean started to get depressed, she found it hard, almost impossible to understand. After all, what was there to be depressed about? These were the good times. It simply didn't make sense. And he couldn't explain. At first, Candy did the only thing she could do. She managed it. She didn't try to solve things for him, she just muddled. After all, it was all so random. Where had it come from? It was bewildering. Presumably, one day, it had to go away. Until then, she'd just try to make him feel as good about himself as possible. There didn't seem anything else to do. It must be a phase, she told herself.

But then there were days when she found it hard, claustrophobic. Sometimes she wondered if she had ever loved Sean. Maybe all she'd ever wanted to do was fuck and, having made up her mind to do it, she'd chosen Sean and then mistaken it for love. Some days she couldn't even remember what it was about Sean that she loved so much, what characteristic. She tried to remember if she had missed Sean at all when she'd been in Spain. Maybe that was all he had ever been about to her: helping her lose her virginity, making up for seven years of lost adolescence, lost freedom.

That insight made her feel base and it made her realize that Sean's depression was killing them, all that was good about them. Turning the love into doubt. So she changed her strategy. She started to fight it. She fought his depression with all her emotion. Any inkling of love she felt in her body for Sean she doubled it, tripled it, in an enormous final push to make everything that they had meaningful and full – before it all ended, before she went home.

She loved Sean. She loved him harder than she had ever loved anything. The more depressed he got, the more committed she became. She determined to herself that this relationship, the one she had sacrificed her 'virginity' for, would be as special as all her childhood dreams. This would be true romance. She suddenly didn't care about the consequences. She didn't care about her future, her destiny to return to Hong Kong, to marry a Chinese. She wasn't going to let it down, their love. She wasn't going to give up on him. She was going to work for them, even if Sean was changing, even if she was confused, even if she was scared. She focused herself on that one single objective: Sean and her. She wouldn't let his depression destroy them. She wanted their love to keep. She wanted it as a memory possession. She wanted it preserved. She didn't want it to die. She wanted it to be something beautiful and cut tragically short by the Fates.

Maybe she was even more Chinese than she thought.

Part of her also knew she was trying to make it last because it was forbidden, because it couldn't be perpetuated, because – one day – it had to end. Sean didn't know that. He was missing that piece of the puzzle. He was naïvely assuming that they were going to go on. He took it for granted that they would continue. Maybe that was why he indulged his darkness – because he couldn't perceive the End. And, if she'd been using her brain, Sean's depression would have been the perfect angle out of the relationship. Nice and clean. She could have sent him back to England and she could have moved on to Hong Kong and eventually forgotten about him, and fulfilled her path. And she would have forgotten him. One day. Just like she had while she was in Bilbao.

But, for some reason, when it was all happening – the travelling and the loving, the drama and the depression – she found that there wasn't a single part of her that wanted to do that. She wanted it to last because she knew it couldn't, it mustn't. She wanted the love she couldn't have, even if some of it had to be manufactured. It wasn't sensible. In fact, it was more than stupid.

But then, when it came to love, who ever did the *right* thing, the *sensible* thing?

No one, that's who.

# Chapter Thirteen

Seeing Mikey again was disturbing. Candy always knew it would be. Mikey was Sean's best friend and there had always been a vague mutual mistrust between them. Of course, they had never said, or acted, it out loud. That would have been stupid. Too much depended on them pretending to be friends. The Leeds Group depended on it. Anything else would have amounted to insurrection. On the surface, everything had to remain rosy. That was part of the deal in the Group dynamic. At the very least, everyone had to appear to love each other. Taking ecstasy together had taught them that.

But Candy had always been aware of Mikey watching her. She knew that he was looking out for Sean, making sure she didn't break his heart. She also knew he was jealous. Mikey was one of the boys that had panted at her at Leeds. And there was that night she'd kissed him. What a mess that had been! Mikey was one of Candy's *no*-men. So things had been understandably terse at times. She liked Mikey, and she believed that he was capable of liking her. But somehow, a little unsurprisingly maybe, the fact that she was sleeping with his best friend got in the way of that. All Mikey seemed interested in when it came to being friends with Candy was watching out for the moment when she split up with Sean. And, sure enough, now that it had finally happened, five years down the line, he was here, right on cue, at the scene to assist. Jesus, it had only been two weeks. The only thing to be grateful for was that she and Sean had since agreed to get back together again . . . sort of.

But it wasn't this history that disturbed Candy when she saw Mikey waiting for her with his bags, soaked through and looking exhausted outside the pub, trying to smile as Sasha mouthed words at him. No. Candy was disturbed by something much more serious than that.

'Mikey,' she called out as she approached.

Mikey was tall, one of the few people from Leeds that could really stand over her. Candy was five foot ten and a half (and, yes, the half did count), so she figured Mikey to be at least six one, six two – taller than Sean, in any case. Like Sean he had brown hair, a little darker maybe, but his was much shorter. Was it receding? He had soft features – big dimples on a bulbous pair of cheeks, a flat nose that she immediately knew the Chinese would prefer, and a big red smile. She could see chest hair fighting its way out of the top of his T-shirt and the shadow of his beard looked very dark. He wore sideburns. He'd filled out from when she'd last seen him. His shoulders looked bigger and he stood well. As he hugged her in his long arms, Candy felt like she was being cradled. His body felt soft against hers. She should have remembered from their raving days – Mikey was one of the best huggers.

'It's so great to see you, Mikey. We've all missed you,' she said as he broke his hold and looked at her with grey, expressive eyes.

'Are you sure it's OK for me to stay with you, Candy?' Michael asked, half hating her for not being reliably at home. If he hadn't bumped into Sasha in the street (Stanley was thankfully small – a fishing village with just two streets and a string of bar/restaurants on the shore) he'd have been screwed.

'Of course it is,' Candy said, snaking an arm through his. 'We're going to have *soooo* much fun.'

'Shall we go get something to eat?' Sasha offered in a *I-think-you-need-it* type way to Candy. Sasha was herself very attractive. Petite with short black hair, spiked, and sharp cheek-bones. She wasn't ageing quite as well as Candy, however. She was thin in a drained way. No more of the youthful energy that they all remembered from Leeds. She looked hard to the touch now. 'Come on, guys, I'm *starrrrrving*.'

Just then Blue Eyes walked past. Candy had to hand it to him, because he didn't say anything, didn't even look their way. But Candy found it hard not to glance at him. She wondered if Mikey had noticed that they'd both emerged from the same alleyway. He must have figured. She felt him watching her. Oh well. There was nothing she could do about that, so she simply turned and smiled at him and said quietly, looking into his eyes, 'I've missed you.'

And, in a funny way, as she said the words, she found she had.

# Chapter Fourteen

Michael thought Candy was being weird. Maybe it was just that they hadn't seen each other in a long time. It was late. They were alone. Sasha had gone back to Mid-Levels soon after finishing her *dinner*, which had actually consisted of four Absolut and tonics gulped down in steady progression and synchronized perfectly with the inhalation of fifteen cigarettes.

Candy was finishing off making up Michael's bed. He was to stay in a room in the basement. It was the kids' den. There was a TV, video, some board games stacked in a corner, a small white desk under three white shelves laden with an adult's idea of children's books: *Treasure Island*, *The Happy Prince*, *Gulliver's Travels*.

'This is our guest room,' Candy explained as she shook a pillow into a green case. 'Sorry, I know it's not up to much.'

Michael had found it hard not to look at her all evening. Candy was even more beautiful than he'd remembered. It wasn't anything specific. It wasn't as if there was any one feature that stood out and made her beautiful, it was just . . . she was composed well. Normally, Candy wouldn't have been Michael's type. He went for the fair look and Candy was, well, Chinese. Her hair was very black, almost blue. Her skin was perfect, darker than Asian, more like Mediterranean. And it was flawless – she didn't have a blemish to scar her. Her cheek-bones weren't particularly high and if there was to be any crit-icism Michael might have said that her face was chubby, but it wasn't like he ever thought that. To him that just made her soft. And, besides, her cheeks went with her lips. Those lips – the perfect shape and colour – Michael could imagine himself kissing her for hours. He didn't like it when she wore lipstick – make-up couldn't do justice to that mouth. Maybe that was her outstanding feature.

But then there were her eyes. They seemed to bounce off her other features and stand out, even though, looking at them closely, they were little more than a simple light brown. The trick was that you were expecting black eyes, Chinese eyes. Candy had her father's eyes (were they in fact green?), and it was the special touch that balanced her identities, made her Eurasian and very stunning. Candy wasn't too much of any-thing. She had the Chinese look but it was tempered. Her eyes weren't shaped like a Chinese person's. They weren't shaped like a European's. They were like almonds and their lightness and shape leapt off the rest of her face to illuminate it.

And then there was her figure. Candy's was definitely a model's figure. She was tall even by European standards. Again, this wasn't Michael's taste – he thought models were really lanky and gangly and awkward – but even though Candy was slim, too slim maybe, there didn't look to be a hard place on her. When they'd hugged he could feel her breasts, which were small, pressing against him. And she had a good arse. It was a little bigger than she probably would have wanted it but to Michael it just made her more feminine. The point was, even though she was tall and slim, she wasn't all in a straight line. Candy could have stood next to a model and held her ground but she could never have been one. Her face wasn't frozen in pre-pubescence, her body wasn't a gawky, adolescent heap of bones. She was woman – with hips and breasts and lips and tenderness.

'Is this where Sean slept?' Michael asked, mainly because he couldn't think of anything else to say.

'Are you kidding?' Candy said. 'My parents would have gone mad.'

'Why?'

'Mikey, this is Asia. You don't sleep in the same house as your boyfriend when your parents are just down the corridor. That's inappropriate.'

'I didn't know you had such a traditional family,' Michael said.

'Well, now you do,' Candy said. There was a moment of silence as she rustled the pillow into place. 'Right,' she sighed eventually, throwing it onto the bed. 'You're all set.'

'Cheers, Candy, you're a star,' Michael said, settling down onto the floor and pulling out his cigarettes. Candy sat down beside him. He handed her one. 'So your parents won't think I'm your boyfriend now then?' he teased.

Candy snorted. 'They'd probably approve if you were.'

'Why?' Michael replied, surprised.

'Well, put it this way, they'd rather I was seeing anyone but Sean. They probably wouldn't even mind the public disgrace of us sleeping in the same house. Anything, as long as it wasn't Sean.'

'I didn't know your parents hated him that much.'

'A lot has happened since we last saw each other, Mikey.' Candy sighed as she blew out smoke.

'Yeah, it seems so.' He paused. 'Do you want to talk about it?' Michael asked, innocently enough, as he tapped his cigarette on the edge of an oyster-shell ashtray.

'What? About me and Sean, you mean?' She said, curling her eyebrows up at him. Michael noticed that there was a very fine line of sun-bleached hairs trimming the top of them.

'Yeah.'

'Not really,' Candy replied, rolling her eyes. Michael could see that she was still drunk. She didn't seem to be focusing properly. He also noticed that they were sitting very close together. He didn't say anything for a while.

'So this is your guest room then?' he tried weakly, glancing around.

'Yeah,' Candy smiled. 'This is where I come to behave very badly.'

Michael could feel her looking at him. He forced himself to look back at her. He suddenly felt nervous. They hadn't been this close since, since . . . He didn't dare to remember that dawn, all those years ago. He had spent so long forcing it out of his mind, desperate to forget and kill his longing. That one night when he had foolishly, foolishly believed he could make her his, only to watch her throw it back in his face. He promised himself he'd never give her that satisfaction ever again. He promised himself he'd never even consider her again. He wanted to be able to joke about it and not care. Things were much simpler that way. What was the point in pining for something that you could never have? Especially, and most painfully, when the two things you wanted most only wanted each other.

And not you.

# Chapter Fifteen

Candy knew she was flirting. There was a part of her that had wanted Mikey as soon as she'd seen him, all soaked through and so obviously pissed off that she'd blown him out. She'd tried to tell herself during dinner that it was the alcohol, or Blue Eyes, or the fact that she was this killer chick now, snogging innocent guys mercilessly and leaving them trailing in a wake of desire behind her.

Acting like the *femme fatale* was small consolation for the heartbreak Candy was going through with Sean, but it at least gave her some sense of control in her uncertain times, in her uncertain mind. Control. That's what Candy wanted these days. After years of being pushed around, told what to do, being unable to say *no* – her past, present and future all mapped out for her, Candy was finally taking charge of her own life. And to do so she was using the most powerful weapon in her arsenal. Sex appeal. She knew she had it. And it was time she used it. To her own advantage, for her own pleasure. After all, this might be her last chance.

But it was different with Mikey. It wasn't as if he was innocent. He knew who she was and there was no way she could have got away with treating him like Mr Gorgeous. No way. But when she saw him something just clicked inside her. She wasn't sure what. She'd never found him attractive before. There was that one night many years ago when she was high and he had got all upset because it was a mistake. She hadn't actually meant to go that far with him, she was just trying him on for size because he had been badgering her for so long about it.

Maybe it was just that he was the New Guy in town. Hong Kong always had a steady turnover of people. It was like a bus station or airport. One of the main buzzes that happened here was the arrival of someone new. It was part of the soul of the place. Fresh meat. Hot off the press. The New Guys. Like Blue Eyes.

'Probably not a good idea,' she said, before realizing too late that she was thinking out loud.

'What?' Mikey said, full of genuine interest.

'Staying up so late.' Candy quickly recovered. 'I've got to be at work by eight.'

'Oh, right,' Mikey said, leaning back.

The new distance spread between them like fresh air. Candy smiled and breathed in the moment with relief.

'Do you want me to wake you in the morning?' she said as they stretched themselves to their feet.

'No,' Mikey said, immediately turning and pulling his shirt over his head to get ready for bed. 'I'll probably be jet lagged.'

'Night then,' she said as he started to rummage aimlessly around in his bags.

'Night,' he said, without turning to face her.

She waited for a small second to see if he might kiss her goodnight. But she could tell he didn't want to look at her any more.

# Chapter Sixteen

It was raining. Hard. Marland peered through the blackness, across the rugby pitches. He could smell the earth. He felt naked in just his pyjamas. He was cold. Starting to shiver. That was probably fear.

'Come on, Marland,' Baxter said behind him. 'Now.'

'I don't want to,' Marland replied weakly, a little tearful.

The whole dormitory laughed and jeered.

Don't want to, don't want to, Mummy, Mummy, Mummy . . .

'Marland, you fucking bender, you have to,' Baxter said before punching Marland in the back. Marland's foot caught on the doorstop on the edge of the French windows and he tripped, catching his knee on the concrete step as he fell. It burned. Tears automatically flashed. Everyone was laughing. He could hear them. All of them were laughing at Marland. He was in the earth now. He hated the smell of it. The smell of wet grass and mud. There was mud on his face. It was raining hard. He heard the French doors locking. He turned and looked at all their faces – laughing silently into torches.

He had to.

The dare was to run to the end of the fields and back. It wasn't even a dare. Baxter just called all his orders dares. It was his way of making out that bullying could be a game. Not that Marland understood that. All he knew was that Baxter hated him. And he didn't know why.

There was only one Elm tree in the whole grounds. All the others had been cut down because of Dutch Elm disease five years earlier. The dare was to pick an Elm leaf and return. That way they knew you'd been to the bushes. The bushes where the Bummer Man hid.

That year, the year the Elms were cut down, one boy went missing. He was never found. The Bummer Man got him. The Bummer Man. He bummed that boy and then he cut him. Cut him up into pieces. That was the legend. Apparently there were police guards every night in the bushes for six months afterwards, waiting for the Bummer to come back.

Marland moved onto his good knee and then his feet. He was wet. And dirty. And shivering. He begged them to let him back in. But he knew they wouldn't. No one could save Marland now. Clarke had been suspended for a week. After the fight. Fishface Haddock had tried to get him expelled, but Gibo told the Headmaster that it had been an accident. Clarke explained all this to Marland before he left. Not that any of that made any difference now.

He cried. He couldn't move into the fields. He was too scared. He knew the Bummer was there. Waiting for him. He just knew. But they didn't open the doors. They didn't open the doors.

Eventually, he walked out into the rain. So cold. His slippers were wet. He could feel mud and pieces of grit filtering through the fabric, between his toes. He stepped into a mud puddle by mistake. His pyjama bottoms were wet now too. He cried. He thought he might not be able to move.

But he did. He kept going. Looking at the fields still

stretching out before him. The Elm tree clawed for him. The bushes shuffled together, barely able to contain their excitement.

He's coming, he's coming, he's coming . . .

Marland started to run. He didn't know why. Maybe he realized there was only one way to end this. He had to run. Get it over with. He ran. And ran. Then he slipped. Onto his grazed knee again. Ow. He yelled out. He couldn't help it. He scrambled with his nails back up onto his feet and then ran again. His little willy flapping helplessly, naked inside his wet pyjama bottoms. The wind rushed through the open fly. He was so naked in his little cotton pyjamas. Naked.

His throat started to burn. He coughed and then he thought he was going to be sick. But he held on and carried on running. Towards the bushes. Across the fields. Into the Elm. All he could hear was the sound of his own breathing, heavy and loud. And then something cut through it. A noise. A snap. He froze.

Marland turned. He stopped breathing. He looked. There was nothing. No light. The House was in darkness. The torches were out. It was hard to see. He was closer to the bushes now than the House. They wouldn't be able to see him from here. He was in the dark. Naked. Wet. In the dark. He wasn't breathing. He couldn't see anyone.

Breathe, he told himself. But he couldn't. He turned and looked back at the Elm. It called for him. He could hear it rustling now. Huge and hanging and leaning towards him. He started walking towards it, not breathing. Two steps. Three steps. Four, five, six, seven, eight, SNAP!

Marland froze. 'Who's there?' he called out, the air rushing from his lungs before he caught it and drew in deeply. 'Please, who's there?' Panting. 'Please.' Nothing. Just breathing.

Then he saw him. Standing in the dark. By the bushes, which rustled. He was large. Motionless. Black. Standing there. Waiting for him. Marland could see him. Near the Elm tree. Baxter had sent him. The Bummer Man was waiting. Waiting for Marland. Waiting to take him away. He wasn't moving. He was just watching Marland. Waiting for him. Marland couldn't move. His legs were starting to crumble. He was peeing now. Hot liquid in his legs. He started to sob. He wanted to turn round but he couldn't move. He wanted to run back to the House. But all he could do was look at the Bummer. The Bummer looked at him. Marland didn't want to die. He was sorry. Sorry, sorry, sorry. Then the Bummer started to come. Marland could see him walking. Walking towards him. From out of the bushes. He came for Marland. Marland watched him walking in the blackness.

He found his feet and turned.

The sound of breathing.

Heavy, thick and hot.

In the rain. Marland ran and ran and ran. He started screaming. The house started swelling. Larger and larger. Lights went suddenly on in the dorm and flooded the rugby pitch. Marland was running under the posts.

The sound of footsteps.

Squelch, squerch, squelch, squerch.

In the mud.

Slipping in his slippers.

He was close now. So close now.

Open the doors, open the doors, open the doors.

Marland was screaming.

But then, quite suddenly, it was too late.

The Bummer grabbed him. Marland kicked and punched. But it was too late. The Bummer had him. By the chest.

Naked, cold, in the dark. It was raining. Hard. The Bummer held him. Huge, manly hold. Wet through. His little willy. The wind rushing. The Bummer, the Bummer, the Bummer.

'You are in a lot of trouble, Marland,' Fishface Haddock said.

# Chapter Seventeen

Mangoes cut in slices sat in a bowl on the table. There were three glasses, filled with freshly-squeezed orange juice, rind lining the rims. Lilies stood in a crystal vase. They weren't open yet but Candy could see that they were white. Just as father had always insisted – white lilies, every day, always unopened. He'd fired six *amahs* that Candy could remember for not getting that right, as well as everything else on the breakfast table. He could be very particular about things like breakfast. *How could the day be good if one got off to the wrong start?*

Outside, the birds were screaming. It was a beautiful day or, at least, the beginnings of one. Hong Kong weather was only delightful in the early morning, like now, or during each month that framed either side of winter, just as the chill was turning. The sun was already high on the sliver of sea that Candy could still see from their kitchen window.

Candy threw her painkillers, her vitamins, her Chinese medicine and the Pill down her throat in one go and swallowed her orange juice.

'I see we have a guest,' Father said as he strode through the kitchen door, full of businesslike purpose. It made Candy jump slightly, though she couldn't tell if it was because of the sound of his voice or the fact that he'd almost caught her swallowing her contraceptive. Father believed she was still a virgin. Well . . . almost.

She turned and smiled sweetly at him. 'Good morning, Daddy.'

'Well, who is he?' he said stiffly as he presented his cheek.

Candy kissed him and adjusted his tie affectionately. She noticed the starched edge on the collar of his black and white striped shirt. It looked sharp enough to cut and it was buttoned tight, a size too small, pinching into the skin on his neck.

'Don't fuss,' he snapped at her, breaking away and reaching for his orange juice (momentarily pausing to check the layout of the table, first). 'You're worse than your mother.'

'Where *is* Mummy?' Candy asked.

'Resting,' he replied.

A vision of her mother lying in a dark room, on a cool bed, the sound of the ornamental waterfall tinkling in the distance flashed across Candy's mind. She wondered if they'd had another argument and that made her wonder if they'd ever loved each other. Maybe it was true, what Mummy had told her, about how Daddy's family had ostracized them, said they could never have a life in England, forced them to live in Hong Kong. All because she was Chinese. No wonder she hated *gweilos* so much. Maybe that was why they didn't get on any more. Because Daddy was white. It had always been white people that had made Mummy's life so hard. At least, that was what she kept saying.

'You still haven't answered my question,' Daddy said as he spooned out a slice of mango and bent down to slurp it into his mouth, being careful not to make a mess on his tie. 'Not a boyfriend I hope.'

'No, Daddy,' Candy replied, hiding her irritation. It was too early for a fight. 'He's just a friend . . . from Leeds.'

'Well, how long will he be staying?' Another slurp on a mango followed by a sip of mint tea.

'I don't know. Till he finds a place, I guess.'

'Heeyahh, what is this place? A traveller's lodge!' Daddy said in his Chinese accent. That was one of the things he'd picked up here, along with things like mint tea, a non-confrontational terseness and a heavy suspicion of outsiders. Sean said that Candy's father even looked Chinese he'd been here so long. Candy thought maybe things were actually the other way round. Daddy seemed to have a naturally Chinese disposition. That was probably why he was here, probably why he'd married a Chinese girl. 'I work hard to live here and all you do is fill it with your *gweilo* urchin friends who do nothing but leech and sponge.'

'Please, Daddy, it's only just past six. Can we talk about this later?'

'Like when? Like tonight, when you're off gallivanting around town and not coming home until two in the morning always drunk.'

Another mango slurp followed by a twisting, piercing stare. Candy took a deep breath and slid over the kitchen floor towards him. He looked at her as she approached. She shimmied her way into his lap, her face just inches away from his and smiling. There was a small patch on the edge of his cheek where stubble was growing.

'You missed a bit,' she said, stroking the black roots. Daddy sucked air in between his teeth and shook his head imperceptibly. She could smell his aftershave, the same aftershave he always wore, the smell that always made her smart whenever she smelt it on another man.

'He's not to come upstairs,' he said, his breath skipping across the nape of her neck.

'Thank you, Daddy,' she whispered.

'I don't want him in the house.'

'No, Daddy. Never.'

'Remember, men can't be trusted, especially *gweilos*.'

'Yes, Daddy.'

'They can destroy you.'

'Yes, Daddy.'

'Never allow them to destroy you.'

'No, Daddy.'

He squeezed.

'Always strike first.'

'Yes.'

The sound of two footsteps before the kitchen door made Candy jump up. Her father quickly repositioned himself against the table as the door eventually swung open. Then there was Mikey's face smiling and breezily announcing:

'Good morning!'

'You're up early,' Candy said, almost seamlessly she felt.

'Must be jet lag,' Mikey replied, hovering, still uncertain, waiting to be introduced.

'Couldn't you sleep?' Candy added, buying time for Daddy, who she could tell was flustered.

Mikey shrugged his shoulders as he walked over to Father without shame. 'Hello,' he said, presenting his hand. 'You must be Mr Newman. My name is Michael.' Candy cringed and didn't breathe, waiting to see what Daddy would do, half expecting him to explode.

But he didn't.

'Pleased to meet you, Michael,' Father said, taking Mikey's hand. 'Would you care for some breakfast?'

'Oh, yes please, that's very kind,' Mikey said, moving towards one of the chairs.

Father quickly grabbed the top of the chair, blocking Mikey's way. 'I'm sorry, but we weren't expecting you, so everything laid on the table is already spoken for,' he started. Candy watched her father tensing and having trouble holding it. 'We can easily arrange to have breakfast sent down to your room if you like.'

Mikey's face queried initially but Candy was already prepared. 'Come on, Mikey,' she said, quickly taking his hand. 'We'll have breakfast together, OK? Daddy's a slow starter.'

'Oh, right, sure, yup, sorry,' Mikey said, letting Candy lead him towards the door. Candy felt her father staring into her back as they left.

She resisted the urge to turn.

# Chapter Eighteen

Michael's initiation into Hong Kong life, or, to be more specific, colonial Hong Kong life, began the following Saturday. For the previous two days he had simply got his bearings and tried to spend as little money as possible. Before arriving he figured he might survive comfortably for four weeks on his work savings. Now, he calculated, he had just two weeks to start work before running out of cash completely. Everything was three times more expensive than he had expected.

In an effort to save, Michael found himself spending a lot of time getting lost in freezing, air-conditioned shopping malls that didn't have toilets. McDonald's was a haven and so was Asian Foodcourt. Other times he stared into the designer stores that sat smugly on the streets. In his impoverished condition he was disgusted by these overt displays of opulence. But, then again, the *Tai-tais* breezing into Prada were just too minxy to ignore. Asian babes!

Michael had arranged to meet Sean for lunch in a basement pub in Soho (*South-of-Ho*llywood Road), and for the last day or so he had been excited about it. He'd missed getting drunk with Sean on Saturday afternoons, as they had done so often together at Leeds.

The taxi pulled up outside the Down Under and Michael

climbed out onto yet another sloping street. With the exception of the city centre, which was almost flat, everywhere in Hong Kong made Michael feel as if he was falling.

A vertical sign with green Chinese characters hung from a building with brown-tinted mirror windows. For some reason the building reminded Michael of the seventies. In fact, a lot of the buildings in Hong Kong reminded Michael of the seventies. A period of affluence, he supposed. Like the nineties. The newer buildings were slightly easier to detect. They were much taller and gleamed silver techno.

He walked through the entrance to the bar. The sun didn't penetrate the narrow steel staircase that wound its way down a floor to the smoke-filled Australian pub below ground. He could see now why it was called the Down Under. It took Michael's eyes a long time to adjust. It was like Sean's flat, another dark musty hangout.

Michael spied Charlie in one corner, who waved half-heartedly at him to secure his attention. Michael tried to disguise his disappointment. He had been looking forward to having Sean all to himself, a real one-on-one. He wanted to get Sean to open up. Now he had Charlie to contend with as well.

'What are you drinking?' Michael asked as he approached the table.

'Boddies,' Charlie replied, tilting his quarter-filled pint to one side as if to consider and then confirm.

Michael turned to the bar. Anything was better than getting stuck in a conversation with Charlie alone – even buying him a drink. The barman demanded a hundred Hong Kong dollars (ten quid!) for two pints. Then Sean came up and punched Michael on the right shoulder blade.

'Mine's a Stella, Mikey.'

Michael groaned silently. He'd been hoping that he wouldn't have to buy a full round.

'Sure,' he said reluctantly. He couldn't afford to spend fifteen quid.

Michael watched Sean as the barman poured the pint, envying his filled-out frame and natural movement. Every limb seemed to flow with an innate sense of grace. He walked on the outer edges of his soles, high arches helping him to slide between the tables like he was dodging football tackles: neat and smooth and assured. Michael would have tripped up on a chair leg if he had ever tried to imitate that kind of effortlessness.

A few seconds later Charlie and Sean were pealing with laughter. Michael felt like they were laughing at him. He tried to look relaxed as he carried the pints, triangle-style, to the table. A jukebox played Oasis.

'What's so funny?' He dangled before setting the drinks down.

'I was just saying how my heart fucking fell out of my mouth after you barged in on me jipping the other day,' Sean said.

Michael snorted. 'Yeah, Jesus. That *was* frightening.'

'What have you got to complain about?' Sean replied, still smiling. 'It wasn't like you were the one caught with your trousers round your ankles.'

'Yeah, but I *was* the one that had to see you stark bollock naked after twelve hours on a plane.'

'You're just jealous 'cos I've got a nine-inch dick,' Sean said.

'If your dick is nine inches long then I'm Jennifer Ames,' Michael replied quickly.

'Jennifer Ames. MINE!' Sean said suddenly, throwing two flat palms in the air, knuckles out, like a trader in the pit. 'I fucking love that movie. Never manage to get past her, though.

Always shoot my load before I can see the rest. She's such a slut.' He paused. 'How come you know about Jennifer, anyway?' he asked, using her first name as if he knew her intimately.

'I watched it after you went back to work. Charlie and I couldn't believe the stack we found in your cupboard.'

'Yeah, mate,' Charlie said, looking at Sean. 'You are a filthy fucking boy.'

'Fucking class, that's what I say. I love porn. Except for those Japanese ones that go all blurry around the good bits. Fucking YOURS!' This time palms out-facing and thrust forward, away from himself.

'What is all this MINE! YOURS! bollocks?' Michael asked.

'MUH—EYE—NNN,' Sean exaggerated, palms in and slightly cupped.

'It's trader talk,' Charlie explained, looking at Michael. 'You know, mine, yours, done.'

'So you've sold out now have you? Fucking barrow boy,' Michael said, shaking his head with feigned disapproval at Sean.

'Better than being a fucking hippie cunt like you.'

'It wasn't so long ago that I remember you with your *Vibe Controller*, Sean.'

Even Charlie laughed genuinely at that one. During his raver days Sean had been known on more than one occasion to mount the stage and wave a gnarled stick that he'd found on a beach over the crowd, showering the acolytes with *good vibes man, good vibes*.

Sean smiled wryly at Michael – a mischievous look in his eyes. Michael could see that Sean enjoyed having the piss taken and that made Michael feel happy and relaxed. Sean was acting much more like himself. He certainly didn't seem upset. Far from suicidal. Hard to believe they'd actually had *that conversation* two weeks ago. It had sounded like his whole world was ending back then.

'Yeah, well, the only thing worse than the hippies are the fucking Chinese,' Sean restarted. 'You know some fuckhead taxi driver just tried to skank me on my way here. They are such a bunch of cunts.'

'Really?' Michael said innocently enough. Secretly he was a little shocked. He'd never considered Sean a racist. He figured he must be joking or, at the very least, he decided he should probably give him the benefit of the doubt. After all, Sean had only just started being nice. 'Why?'

'Because you can't trust them,' Sean replied.

'Is that right?'

'Yup. And they're rude,' Sean added.

'I see.'

'They only care about money,' Charlie added.

'What else?'

'What more do you need?' Sean said.

'Well,' Michael said, as if weighing up the evidence, 'had you ever considered that maybe it's because of our history here? The British haven't exactly treated the Chinese well. Had you ever considered that maybe they hate your guts?'

'Err, Mikey, you're stating the obvious, mate,' Sean replied.

'Well, there you are then,' Michael said, unable now to resist getting on the soapbox. He frequently found himself getting on his high horse about things like racism. He didn't care if Sean was being friendly. *It* just wasn't right! 'You shouldn't hate them. They're just people. Like you and me. Except the responsibility is on our shoulders to build bridges,' Michael rallied, like a politician. 'We have to learn the language. Communicate. Try to see where they're coming from.'

Sean shook his head. 'Good luck,' he said.

'Are you going to learn the language then, Mikey?' Charlie asked.

'I might,' Michael replied, knowing that he wouldn't. He told himself it wasn't his fault if he was terrible with languages. 'Anyway, Sean,' he restarted, changing the angle, 'if you hate the Chinese so much aren't you sort of living in the wrong place?'

'Probably,' Sean conceded.

'And what about Candy?'

'What about her?'

'Well, isn't she half Chinese?'

'She doesn't count.'

'Why not?'

'Because she's practically British. She's spent more time in England than here.'

Michael didn't reply. He looked at Charlie, who was finishing off his pint and not offering to get another round in. That figured, Michael thought to himself.

'You'll soon know what I'm talking about, Mikey,' Sean said. 'By the time you leave here, you'll hate the Chinese even more than I do.' A small pause. 'You know what they call us, don't you?'

'No.'

'*Gweilo.*' He pronounced it *gwhy-low*.

'What does that mean?'

'Foreign devil, white ghost – something like that.'

'Well, that just goes to prove my point, doesn't it?' Michael tried. They looked at him. 'It's a term for imperialists. Foreign devils. See what I mean? It's high time the British left Hong Kong.'

'You're so wrong,' Sean interrupted. '*Gweilo* is like the

Chinese equivalent for nigger, except it's for white people. They don't see us as imperialists. They see us as inferiors.'

'Well, we probably are,' Michael said, snorting.

'I can't believe we're going to have to put up with you for the next six months – all green and fucking loving the Chinese,' Sean said, shaking his head. 'Now give me some money to get the next round,' he added, stretching slightly before standing up.

Michael stared up at him, incredulous. 'But I got the last one,' he started weakly, ready to point his finger at Charlie.

'Christ, Mikey, I'm only joking,' Sean said, grinning again. 'Nice to see that you're still a tight-fisted bastard, though.' He paused then and looked down at Michael, real happiness quickly in his eyes. 'Mikeeeee!' he exclaimed, grabbing him by the neck and shaking him. 'It's good to see you again, mate. I've missed having someone around I can be mean to.'

Michael smiled up at him. It was nice to finally feel wanted.

# Chapter Nineteen

Michael's initiation was completed that night at a 'Fetish Fest'. *Everyone* was going to be there, Sean had explained, and Michael was surprised to find out that everyone really did mean everyone. After the pub they went back to the Mansion, which was the name Sean kept using for his flat. Michael couldn't figure out if he was being ironic (the place looked tiny to him) or if it was because he lived in Mansion Flats. Probably both, he told himself.

It was good to see so many old faces from Leeds knock on the front door. There was larger-than-life Emma and her ultimate nice guy boyfriend Ben. Then there was Fat Nick, who was skinny but had to be differentiated between two other Nicks in the gang: Little and Big (who both arrived later, Big Nick with his girlfriend Katz). Then there was Sophie and Clarissa, Alex and Jimmy, Jules and Ali (both the female and male versions). . . the list went on. They were all there, in Hong Kong.

Sasha and Candy were the last to arrive. They turned up arm-in-arm and giggling.

Michael was pleasantly taken aback by the flood. With the exception of Charlie, he was on good terms with almost everyone in the room. Until then, it had never occurred to him that his university gang had landed in Hong Kong. He could remember the odd departure from London among them, but he hadn't realized just how extensive the general migration had been in the three years since graduation.

But as they caught up on old times, he soon understood why they had all come here.

As Alex explained how his father, a director at Appleton Smythe, had helped Candy get her job at an art gallery and Sophie a job in the firm's debt markets division, he understood. As Emma, Ben, Fat Nick and Jimmy gushed over the lovely day they had just spent water-skiing off Emma's family yacht, he understood. And when Sasha detailed the history of her grandfather's arrival on the island and a company called MacFarlane Cheung, he knew what that meant.

Michael's friends were rich.

Not just middle-class rich. Not just public-school rich. Nor just we-have-a-house-in-the-country-and-a-flat-in-London rich. But rich rich. Offshore rich. Multinational empire rich. Opium War rich. These were the kind of people who never paid taxes, owned a Rolls Royce (but drove a Mercedes), flew in private jet planes and – most important of all – never, ever mentioned money.

Maybe that was why Michael hadn't seen it until now. He started to realize that among them, talking about money – more specifically how much they had – had always been a taboo. The deliberate way in which the subject had been avoided. Michael remembered the only time he'd ever seen ultimate nice guy Ben lose his temper was when Michael had attempted to look over his shoulder at a cash machine in Leeds. It was as if their wealth was the social equivalent of a hunchback or some other gruesome physical deformity. It was so extreme it simply couldn't – mustn't – be acknowledged.

They'd certainly never joked about it before and somehow, there'd always been an implicit understanding: don't take the piss.

Maybe they were embarrassed. Maybe they just wanted people to like them for who they were, rather than how much money they had. Michael could relate to that. That was the reason he gave himself for his own parsimony. He hated the idea that people might be using him.

Or maybe it was all part and parcel of their public-school-cool persona. They weren't proud of their wealth. If anything they were ashamed of it. Why should they be judged? It wasn't *their* fault their parents were so loaded. They didn't *ask* to be this wealthy.

Or maybe Michael was simply being over sensitive to the fact. Even though they'd all played the game at Leeds – the poor students – none of them had ever struggled. He'd known that. There'd always been money in the bank, even if they did talk about student loans sometimes. And he'd been the same. He was middle class enough to have enjoyed that much privilege.

But now, for the first time, there was a divide. Michael saw that the difference between himself and his friends was that they didn't have to struggle *after* university. By the time Michael left Leeds his funds had dried up. He'd carried on being the poor student after graduation because, well, he really was one.

But Michael's friends weren't playing the poor game any more. They were here, in Hong Kong, to claim their birthrights as more than just the middle class. They were the privileged expatriates, the imperials, the post-colonials. Life for Michael's friends now was clearly about living it large on unmentionable inheritances and high-paying nepotistic careers. And with Michael here, in their hometown, they weren't nearly as ashamed as they should have been to show him the true extent of their wealth. More likely they probably understood they could no longer hide it from him.

This realization made Michael feel jealous and more than a little inadequate. He liked his Leeds crew but he slightly resented the fact that they weren't all in the same boat any more – they couldn't even pretend to be. Being wealthy was one of those games you could only play if you were . . . well . . . wealthy. It wasn't a question of class or accent, it was simply a matter of being able to afford to do things, go to parties, have fun, buy drinks. You either could, or you couldn't.

How was Michael going to float? How was he going to go out and buy rounds like it didn't matter? He knew he wouldn't be able to get away with sponging for too long before earning himself some terrible label. Besides, his pride would never have let him do that. Michael forced himself to not think about it. Everyone seemed so super-pleased to see him, and they were going so out of their way to make him feel good and wanted – a part of the gang – that he didn't want to blame them. There would be plenty of time, Michael told himself, to appreciate the kind of friends he had.

*You'll have to come on the yacht with us next Saturday, Mikey* – Emma had gushed. *It's soooo great that you're here. I'm totally psyched.*

At the end of the day, who was he to argue with that?

Everyone was dressed appropriately for the party – tight PVC trousers and mini-skirts, handcuffs and feather dusters. Fat Nick even had a gimp mask. Michael, of course, had nothing to wear. He hadn't exactly packed for a fetish party so, after two hours of coaxing, he unwisely accepted Candy's offer to make him up as a girl.

And two hours after that Michael – drunk and stoned –

found himself walking blindly into the party, slathered in red lipstick and black eyeliner. After they arrived, Michael decided to separate himself from the gang for a moment to parade the scene. He'd never been to a fetish party before and he wanted to check it out for himself.

Everything was very dark. The party was in yet another basement. Michael wasn't surprised. Hong Kong only seemed to happen in the shadows. Black pillars held up the ceiling. A few people danced as hardcore techno raged. It didn't take Michael long to figure out that this wasn't a real fetish party, more like a gimmicky theme for a rave. He found two empty black-lit rooms and then the toilets before finally discovering a brightly lit room, covered wall to wall and tabletop to tabletop with mirrors.

An indiscernible number of people, but no more than fifteen, were tipping wraps of white powder into piles as two guys dressed in pin-stripe suits and wide-brimmed velvet hats crushed the mix with credit cards and lined up lines as long as snooker cues. Three very attractive petite Chinese girls, dressed in St Trinian's uniforms, sat on plastic orange chairs in one corner.

I really have arrived, Michael thought to himself as he licked an index finger, reached down to one of the five lines nearest to him and dabbed an end surreptitiously onto his tongue.

'Oi!' One of the pimps suddenly turned.

Michael had been spotted in the mirrors.

'What the fuck are you doing?' he said.

The pimp was disconcertingly large – both in height and width – with long, thin brown hair, tied back. His face was covered in thick stubble, almost a beard, that extended high up his face, almost to the edges of his eye sockets. He wore a clip-on silver earring on his left lobe, which must have been part of his costume. He didn't exactly look like the type to wear clip-on earrings.

Michael smiled at him and flashed the palms of his hands submissively. 'Sorry, no harm done.' I must be drunk, he told himself as he flushed with embarrassment.

'No harm done? What do you mean no harm done? That's my charlie, you fucking mincer.'

Michael caught sight of himself. The pimp had a point. Candy had done a real number on him. Michael couldn't help noticing the three Asian girls looking at him. In fact, the whole room seemed to be staring. The music seemed suddenly quiet.

'Listen, I've said I'm sorry, all right. Just simmer down, OK?'

'Oh, right, yeah, OK. Forgive me. Go ahead. Help yourself. Dig in. Make yourself at home,' he sneered. 'You shirt-lifting, perfume-poncing, back-passage-mongering, love-it-up-the-Gary slaaaaaag!'

There were sniffs of laughter. Michael looked at the pimp, who stared impassively back. He couldn't think of anything else that would salvage his dignity, so he reached across, swiped one of the white lines with his middle finger, licked it and presented an American fuck off signal squarely in his face.

It didn't take long for him to fly across the room and find himself pinned up against one of the walls. The pimp sneered in his face and demanded to know *just who he thought he was*. Michael noticed his cutting accomplice smiling uncomfortably behind him.

There was a lot more shouting and name calling and Michael was starting to wonder where it was all going when Sean suddenly slid into the room, one finger pointing triumphantly in the air, singing the chorus to 'White Lines (Don't Don't Do It)' by Grandmaster and Melle Mel.

Then he bent down and snorted what seemed to be a

forearm's length of coke. Michael watched the whole room stare as Sean stood up straight, eyes watering, and quickly did a shuffle – not unlike an Irish jig – to the words:

*Orang dang diggedy dang di-dang*
*Orang dang diggedy dang di-dang*
*Orang dang diggedy dang di-dang*
*Diggedy dang di-dang diggedy dang di-dang*

By now, the St Trinian's girls were grinning. Sean, always the funny guy, Michael thought to himself as the pimp turned to say in a whining voice: 'For fucksakes, Sean, that's my fucking coke, you bastard.'

'Oh, sorry, Lenny,' Sean said beaming. 'I didn't know.' Then looking directly over the pimp's shoulder at Michael he added, 'Have you had any of this yet, Mikey? It's blinding!'

Michael shook his head vaguely as Sean turned and looked directly at Lenny's friend, the other *pimp*, and said matter-of-factly: 'Who's this?'

'Err,' Lenny started. 'This is Bob, Sean. He just arrived, a month or so ago, right?'

'Bob?' Sean said, looking at him.

'Rob,' he replied softly.

'Agh,' Sean shrugged. 'That doesn't mean anything, mate. Bob, Rob, Robbie . . . Half the people I know here have three or four different nicknames. Just look at Lenny. He used to be Herman. And his real name is Andy . . . I think.'

Bob and Lenny – Herman, Andy, or whatever his real name was – looked at each other as if this were a moment of truth between them.

'Lenny?' Bob said to Sean. 'Why Lenny?'

'Because he's a fucking Lennnnnnieeeeee, isn't he? Just look at him.' Everyone was looking at Lenny now, boring into his Achilles heel. Michael marvelled at the way Sean had turned things round. Did Sean mean to be rescuing Michael this way? Did he see that Michael was in trouble? Or was he just taking the piss? Lenny started to shift under everyone's look and the moment started to feel a little too personal, maybe even hurtful. Sean backed off and said affectionately: 'Lenny! What a chap! Come on,' he encouraged, reaching into his pocket and pulling out three wraps. 'Let's rack 'em up!'

The tension quickly broke and the whole room seemed to turn towards the mirrors and proceed with the industry of getting mash up. Scraping from sachets, rolling up notes, crushing lumps, chopping with credit cards, dabbing, snorting, licking.

Michael didn't move. He still felt a little intimidated as Lenny continued to stand very close to him and started to joke about something loudly. But then, as Sean bent down to do a line, he looked across the room and passed Michael a note with a wink. Two mischievous dimples showed brightly.

# Chapter Twenty

Sean stood in a dark corner watching Candy dance with Bob, the cocaine numbing everything, even itself. He could tell that she wanted to sleep with Bob. Maybe she already had, he considered grimly.

Sean told himself to stay cool. Two weeks ago, Candy had accused him of being paranoid, jealous, possessive and over-bearing. He didn't want to give her any more excuses to leave him. He was hanging onto her by the tips of his fingers as it was. In fact, that was why he had agreed to the new terms. Candy had seemed so set on them.

*I only love you, silly. It's not as if a few harmless snogs will change that.*

Mikey came up and put an arm across his shoulder. 'Good party,' he said, sniffing.

Sean threw his arm around Mikey's waist and grinned. 'It's good to see you, mate,' he said, turning to face him. 'Really good.'

'I know,' Mikey said, a steady euphoria in his voice. They stood together and surveyed the dance floor. The cocaine was making Sean nostalgic for their friendship, even though Michael was standing right next to him. He felt like going over old times. Maybe it had something to do with the fact that he knew he was losing Candy.

'Some fit birds,' Michael said.

'Tell me about it,' Sean replied.

They continued to watch, and Sean could tell that Mikey was thinking exactly what everyone else was. It was hard not to notice Candy's mini-skirt riding high up her thigh as she straddled and ground herself against Bob's groin. Her suspenders were showing.

'Let's dance,' Mikey said, eventually.

'I'm mash up,' Sean replied.

'Exactly. Come on,' Michael said, pushing Sean forward and standing behind him, hips grooving, forming a makeshift dance zone of their own, so Sean couldn't retreat. It wasn't long before Sasha walked up and they were all dancing together, a unit of friendship, congregating around Sean, supporting him. At least, that was how it felt.

'Hey, Mikey,' Sean shouted through the darkness between them.

'Yeah?'

'I'm sorry about all the confusion over the room and everything.'

'What?'

'I said I'm really sorry about giving your room to Charlie. It was just a mix-up.'

'Yeah, yeah,' Mikey shouted back at him, in a way that was clear he still couldn't hear him.

Sean realized he was using and losing too many words so he moved to simply hug Mikey and say what was really between them, acknowledge *that conversation* (as Mikey kept calling it) that they'd had on the phone: 'It's fucking great to see you, Mikey. I've missed you. I'm glad you've come.'

Sean felt Mikey hug him back tightly and he was about to close his eyes and fall into the embrace when Candy strode up and beamed at him.

'Am I interrupting?' she said.

Sean and Mikey simultaneously relaxed their grip and let each other slip away and turn to face her. Candy quickly stepped across the thread that was still connecting the two men and put her lips against Sean's ear.

'I love you,' she whispered.

Sean looked across Candy's shoulder as they hugged and found Mikey's eyes. It looked like Mikey was smiling. But he couldn't be sure.

# Chapter Twenty-One

Sean pushed Candy's head down.

'Go on, lick, don't suck,' he said.

Candy licked his balls.

Sean pushed her head down harder and raised his buttocks off the mattress, coaxing her to go lower. 'Go on, baby, that's it, show everyone how good you lick arse.'

Candy mentally paused, but she didn't stop. Part of her hoped that maybe Sean was joking. It was four in the morning. They were still wired. Candy had agreed to leave the party early because Mr Gorgeous Blue Eyes, now AKA Rob, had come a little too far into her world for comfort. Sasha had warned her that Sean was watching. She was immediately defensive, of course, and claimed innocence.

But, later, when Sean begged her to leave and spend the night at his place she found herself instinctively agreeing, even though she didn't want to. Maybe it was because she found it so hard to say no, or maybe she was just covering her tracks in front of the Group. If she left with Sean then he clearly didn't mind her dancing *that way* with Rob, so why should they?

Sean shuffled and shifted, pushing her head down further, towards his arse. Candy resisted but didn't stop licking his balls. Eventually, Sean slid himself up the mattress. Candy couldn't figure out what he was doing. She was about to ask him what the matter was when he got on his feet and stood over her on the bed.

'Wank,' he ordered.

'I'm sorry?' Candy said, lying on her side, looking up at him. Sean cut a slightly ridiculous figure, still wearing his brown socks, his penis jutting out.

'Show me how you do it,' he said.

Candy shrugged her shoulders and slid her hand down to between her thighs.

'That's it, baby,' Sean coaxed as he started to stroke himself. 'Show me how you do it, show everyone how you do it.'

Candy could not figure out where Sean was coming from with all this. She found it vaguely annoying. For starters, it was off-putting. She wanted to have sex. Dancing with Rob had got her really worked up. And she was high. She especially liked to fuck when she was high. Why was Sean messing around? She wanted him to get on with it. She wanted him inside her.

'Yeah, that's it,' Sean said, as she rubbed herself half-heartedly. 'That's it. Show everyone.'

Candy wished he would shut up. Sean used the arch of his right foot to push her right shoulder down so that she rolled off her side and lay flat on her back against the mattress. She found that especially irritating. Candy had a natural aversion to feet. Maybe it was an Asian thing. She'd always thought them dirty.

'What are you doing, Sean?' she said, looking up at him across the profile of his hairless legs, his pointing penis, the slim panel of his stomach and the blur of his chin in the vertical distance.

'Just relax, baby,' he said. 'Just relax.'

Sean stood over her face. The mattress gave under his weight and her head nearly knocked against the sides of his feet. Then, without any warning, he started to squat. His arse loomed as he lowered. For a frightening instant, Candy thought he was going to sit on her face. Then she realized he *was* going to sit on her face! She froze.

'Go on, babe,' he said, his balls dangling against her chin, his arsehole just inches away from her mouth and nose. 'Lick me up.'

Candy couldn't move.

'Go on, do it,' Sean said. 'Show everyone how good you lick arse.'

Candy decided she had had enough. She put both hands on his left buttock and pushed Sean to one side of the bed as she rolled herself from under him, to the other side of the mattress, as far away from him as she could manage.

'What are you doing?' she snapped, as Sean collapsed beside her, a slightly shameful expression on his face.

'What?' he tried innocently.

'What are you fucking doing?'

'Nothing.'

'What do you mean *nothing*?' Candy said, pulling up a corner of a yellow sheet to cover her breasts.

'I just wanted to try it.'

'What? Sitting on my face? I don't think so.'

'Why not?' Sean said then, a little petulantly.

'Because it's fucking disgusting, that's why.'

'I lick your arse,' Sean replied matter-of-factly.

'That's different.'

'Why?'

'Because I don't ask you to do it. I only let you because I think you like it.'

'Oh fuck off, Candy. You know you love it when I do it. Don't lie.'

Candy paused. It was true. She did like it when he did it. But it wasn't the arse-licking that was bothering her anyway. It was the way Sean had gone about it. Like it was some pre-prepared script. It was as if he was using her to fulfil some other purpose. There didn't seem to be anything inspired about it. It wasn't passionate. It was mechanical, scripted.

'Have you got any cigarettes?' she asked.

Sean climbed out of the bed and slid onto the floor. He shuffled his way through the cheap plywood door that had only been painted white on one side, the other side showing splintering wood. It swung loosely open as Candy rested a forearm on her forehead and thought. Maybe she should be more considerate, she wondered. But then the idea of Sean's arse looming – ugh – it was enough to make her vomit. She wondered if she'd lick Rob's arse if he insisted. Probably. That was when it occurred to her. Maybe it wasn't Sean's arse that she found repellent. Maybe it was Sean.

Sean re-entered the room, kicking the door closed with the heel of his left foot before climbing onto the bed, sitting cross-legged, positioning the ashtray between them and lighting two cigarettes. He handed one to Candy. They smoked without saying anything.

Eventually, Candy said: 'What's with the big obsession all of a sudden?'

'It isn't an obsession.'

'Whatever.'

'I just wanted to try something different.'

'You could have warned me.'

'Look, I wanted to do it, you didn't and now we're not. So what? It's over. Forget it. It doesn't matter.'

'Yes it does.'

'Why?'

Why? Candy heard the echo. Why? Because I don't love you any more. That's why. If I did, I would have done it, she said to herself. She remembered those first few months when they were together. She would have done anything for Sean back then. He was such a wonderful lover. He showed her so much pleasure. And God how she had fancied him back then. She would have done anything. Now? She didn't want to do anything for Sean. Not any more, not for him. What had changed?

'There's something you're not telling me,' she said.

# Chapter Twenty-Two

Sean ground the cigarette into the ashtray so that the paper split and tobacco spilt out along the seam. Even after it was out, he carried on crushing the filter. He was furious with her. What a bitch, he thought to himself. This was the very least that she owed him. A tiny piece of rimming. That was all. Was it so much to ask?

After all the dancing she'd been doing with that Bob bloke, he deserved it. Right in front of him, in front of everyone! Part of him wanted to punch her. And she thought this was bad? This tiny fantasy. That was all he wanted. A little piece of Atlantis fire. Why wouldn't she play?

Sean looked at her.

'Do you still love me, Candy?' he asked.

'What? Yes. Of course I do.'

'You used to do anything for me.'

'I don't like being treated like a piece of meat. I don't like being ordered around. I need to be . . . you know . . . eased in. Just go slowly, OK?'

'So you'll do it?'

'What? Lick your arse?'

Sean nodded back at her and made himself look straight into her face. He knew what he was saying. He knew he was acting shamefully. Normally, he would have dropped it. But there was something about Candy that was bringing out the worst in him. The misogynist. Maybe it was too much porn. He was finding it hard to respect women any more. And the self-loathing. It was back. Small, like an acorn, but so poisonous. Sean could taste it. He no longer cared what Candy thought of him. She didn't love him. If she still loved him, she wouldn't be interested in other guys, guys like Bob. If she still loved him, she wouldn't have questioned it when he tried to sit on her face.

And knowing all that only made Sean even angrier. He hated her. He hated himself. She owed him. He was on the way out. Candy was dumping him. He knew it. She knew it. But he wasn't about to leave without a fight. Before she left him, she was going to give him this much. She had to. He was going to fucking well make her.

In the end he didn't have to. To his surprise (maybe it was the look he gave her that did it) Candy slowly nodded her head and reached for the ashtray. She stubbed her cigarette out and crawled out from under the sheet and across the bed to him on all fours.

'All right, you filthy boy,' she said, smiling slightly. 'Let me show you how I lick arse.'

# Chapter Twenty-Three

Michael was finding it hard to keep his eyes off Candy. She was lying on the deck of the yacht in a simple blood-red bikini. Her thin arms were crossed above her head, each hand gripping an elbow. She had three small moles that seemed to make a pattern along the trough of her stomach, the part that curved into her back. He could see, through the gap between her sun-glasses and her temple, that she had her eyes closed. Her feet were crossed. The line of her left leg angled steadily upward, on a gentle trajectory to the tips of her toes. Her toenails were painted red. Fresh red, like some Lolita tart playing grown-up with the make-up bag. They glinted in the sun.

'Don't you know it's rude to stare.'

The sound of Emma's voice made Michael jump. For a second he thought it might have been Sean, even though it was clearly female. His guilt could override anything, even the sound waves, it seemed. He was also worried that Candy might have heard. But she was at the front of the deck, upwind. She didn't even flinch. She seemed to be in her own world. Michael would have thought she was asleep if they hadn't only just set off from the Yacht Club.

'What?' he replied.

'You heard me,' Emma said as she negotiated the final two rungs on the ladder leading up to the deck – her brown, bobbed hair turning to chaos as she emerged into the wind. She grinned at Michael, two dimples showing, and handed him a can of beer as she sat down next to him on a white leather body-length cushion.

'Just admiring the view,' Michael smiled lightly, turning his head to the left. The Hong Kong skyline was dancing like a stock market graph along the shore as they cruised through the harbour, passing tugs and junks. To the right, Kowloon-side was lower rise and neon signed. The mainland looked grimier, more gritty than Hong Kong Island. It even had a slight yellow hue, the same colour as all the uncooked ducks Michael had seen sweating in restaurant windows.

Emma didn't say anything, but shifted beside him. She wasn't an attractive girl, but she wasn't unattractive either. Plain looking, perhaps. Her figure wasn't bad. Her legs looked smooth and tanned next to Michael's, but that wasn't saying much. His were translucent through the thick dark hair that spread across his calves. Michael didn't know why he was even thinking about it. He'd known Emma for so long now, she should have been sexless to him he supposed. Maybe it was just that it had been so long since they'd last seen each other. He was on the look-out for change. Or maybe he was just kidding himself. He'd known Candy for just as long and she wasn't sexless to him. Far from it.

'Cheers,' Michael said, offering his can. They clanked dully. 'Thanks for inviting me.'

'No worries,' Emma said. 'It looks like it's going to be a beautiful day.'

'Yup, another shitty day in paradise,' Michael said, feeling the newness in it. Pretty much everything Michael said and did still felt new and naïve. Even though he had been initi-ated, Michael still felt very much the tourist in town. After all, he had only arrived ten days ago. But there was also the sense that everything, more importantly everyone, was so established here. They all had jobs and lives and parties and yachts to go to. Michael felt at a loose end. He needed a job.

'So what do you think of Hong Kong? Do you like it?' she asked.

'Yeah,' Michael replied, his voice lilting upward with enthu-siasm. 'Yeah, I really like it.' Michael didn't know if this was true. He hadn't figured it out yet. All he did know was that he didn't like London so he had to like Hong Kong. And, besides, it would have felt rude saying anything else. After all, here they were, the Leeds crew, drinking beer on the deck of Emma's father's eighty-foot yacht in the blazing sun. What was there to not like? 'I'd like to stay,' he added.

'Well, no reason why you shouldn't.'

'Could do with a job.'

Michael had just spent the previous week CV-ing CNN, BBC, AP, AFP, SCMP, AWSJ, RTHK . . . and a lot of non-acronymed media enterprises too – only to attract zero interest. *It's because you can't speak Cantonese*, Candy's mum had offered as she'd swept through the living room in one of her more frantic moments to reach another part of the house. She let him use the phones while Candy's dad was at work. *How do you expect to get a job here without the language?*

Michael hadn't had an answer for that.

'Give it time, you'll get one,' Emma reassured.

'I don't know. A lot of newspapers aren't hiring unless you speak Cantonese,' he said without looking at her.

'Yeah, well, it's because of the Handover. Everything's changing.'

'Do you speak Cantonese?' Michael asked.

'A little. Well, not really. In fact, no.'

'You won't lose your job though, will you?' Michael said, trying to sound understanding but realizing, as Emma turned to raise her eyebrows and look at him through the tops of her eyes, that he was just being new again.

'Hmmm, I don't think so, somehow,' Emma said, clearly mistaking Michael's naïvety for sarcasm. 'Daddy does own the company I work for.' She meant it ironically: Emma the little princess, working for Daddy. At least she was self-aware, Michael thought.

He smiled back at her. 'Maybe he'll give me a job,' he said, half joking.

'I thought you wanted to be a journalist,' Emma replied.

'Yeah, I do.'

'Well, I'm not sure if Daddy knows anyone in journalism. I'll check for you.'

Michael might have despised the nepotism if he wasn't feeling quite so desperate. And, besides, he told himself, Hong Kong seemed like just the place to oil its mechanics on contacts. He bit his lip and suddenly felt very excited at the vague prospect that Emma's father might actually get him a job at a newspaper. A whole fantasy life suddenly revealed itself before him. Michael in Hong Kong: weekend trips on Emma's yacht, a tan, cocaine and all-night drinking sessions, fifteen per cent taxes, sexy *Tai-tais* and tailor-made suits. He'd live it large here and crack a secret Triad smuggling ring before eventually joining the *New York Times* as a world-famous Far East correspondent. It was all going to begin here. It was all going to begin now. Michael's New Life.

'If you're sure it's not too much trouble,' he smiled, showing all his teeth.

# Chapter Twenty-Four

Sean was water-skiing. Mono, baby . . . mono. He looked good and he knew it. Flat stomach, long baggy swimming trunks flapping casually round his knees, his hair flowing just how he liked it – slicked back: no sign of baldness today. He could hear Candy, Emma, Mikey, Fat Nick and Charlie all hollering and whooping from the deck of the yacht. The Chinese captain circled around them one more time so that he could cut the wake and attempt to spray them, just like Onatopalot or whatever the Russian girl in that James Bond movie was called.

He was on good form. There were days when his humour just fell into place. Everything he did and said seemed funny. And, for some reason, he was on fire today. Even Candy couldn't keep her hands off him. He'd very nearly convinced her to give him a blow job in the toilet after lunch. If it hadn't been for Mikey stumbling in on them, she would have, too. But he didn't mind. She'd promised to give him one on the way back.

As the yacht loomed, Sean veered out of the violent tumble of the wake and crossed into the flat calm of the bay. The water was like glass. The ski cut cleanly through the blue, barely disturbing it, no white horses, just the odd bubble. Sean could see the sandy bottom metres below. His shoulders were burning but he didn't care.

The speedboat turned giving him the angle he needed so he leant hard and fast, back in towards the wake, all of them jeering and waving and telling him to fuck off just a metre or two away as he sped past. He felt the spray start to kick from out of the back of the ski then, as he passed, he could hear the water splashing against the deck of the boat and all of them hurling abuse at him. He looked back to see Mikey, soaked! And Fat Nick waving a wanker sign at him. He beamed to himself.

He waved at the driver to circle back towards the yacht and eventually, arms shaking with exhaustion, he coolly landed, releasing the rope and sinking down into the water, arms stretched crucifix style. The life-jacket buoyed up over his shoulders and above his ears as he submerged. He took the opportunity to dunk his head back and make sure his hair matted down in straight lines, as he removed his ski.

Then, quite suddenly, there were war cries. He saw Fat Nick – big brown hair flying, ribs showing and knee-length Hawaiian swimming trunks almost falling off his hips as he leapt from the oak railing of the yacht, Mikey and Charlie just a split second behind. Even Emma and Candy joined in. They were dive bombing him. One of the boys, he couldn't see which, grabbed his arms from round the back. Mikey swam up, grinning: 'You're fucked,' he said, laughing.

Sean broke an arm free and managed to get a palm flat on Mikey's head before pushing it under the water. He was vaguely worried that the rough and tumble might reveal his lack of hair. Mikey grabbed his wrist and came up spluttering and laughing. Sean was pinned again. That's when he noticed that the girls were under the water. They were pulling his trunks down. Oh shit!

For a moment he struggled. He kicked, but after he connected with Emma's arm he realized it would be safer to simply let them de-bag him. After all, he didn't want anyone to get hurt. And, besides, he was too drunk to care. Candy finally emerged, victorious, spit and seawater spilling out from her mouth as she laughed. Emma's head appeared next to Candy's.

'Got 'em boys, got 'em,' they laughed before backstroking their way to the yacht.

'Serves you right,' Fat Nick said, treading water beside Mikey. Charlie and Mikey were laughing on either side of him.

'Bastards,' Sean said.

Once the girls were clear, the boys let him go and started swimming back to the yacht. Eventually, everyone was on the deck taunting him as he floated in his life-jacket.

'All right, guys, joke's over. Toss 'em back,' he tried. Mikey seemed to be especially enjoying the moment, taking charge of hiding the trunks.

There was nothing Sean could do so, after a few deep breaths, he plucked up the courage to get back on board the boat, trunks or no trunks. He climbed his way slowly up the ladder. He could hear them on the deck. Once he was high enough, the back of the boat still shielding him, he could see them, reclining on seats, finding fresh beers, waiting for the matinée performance.

'OK, guys, this is your last chance,' Sean said, looking at Mikey. 'Don't say I didn't warn you.'

More jeering and cheering.

Sean climbed up the ladder and emerged, full frontal (with the exception of the life-jacket) in front of them. Candy cheered. Mikey and Charlie shook their heads and grinned. Fat Nick's mouth actually dropped and Emma said: 'Fucking hell, Sean, you've got a huge dick.'

They all laughed.

Sean put his hands on his waist and said: 'Right, Mikey, you're next,' and lunged for his groin.

'No fucking way,' Mikey said before leaping off the side of the boat and belly flopping into the ocean.

Sean turned to Candy, who screamed and kicked as he picked her up, slung her over his shoulder and then jumped with her in his arms back into the sea. Fat Nick and Charlie grabbed Emma and threw her, on the count of three, her bikini top coming loose in the process, over the side railing. Fat Nick and Charlie dive-bombed. Sean could hear the music now, The Fugees, blaring from the boat sound system.

Sean sang along, turning to Mikey and grinning. He grabbed Candy and emphasized each word double-entendre style. 'You love it when I strum your pain don't you, babe,' he said, grinning at her.

'I love it,' she said, mounting him and kissing him deeply. She tasted of salt. Sean heard Emma ask one of the crew members to throw a bottle of champagne into the water to open. Candy reached down and fingered him.

'Who's my big boy then?' she said, laughing.

He laughed back as he noticed Mikey swimming over to join the others, who were now guzzling.

'Oi, save some for us,' he called over to them. Charlie flashed him a fuck-off sign. Sean smiled. This had to be one of the better days of his life, he thought to himself before making a conscious effort to bank it into his memory.

# Chapter Twenty-Five

Candy couldn't think of a way to break the news to Sean. She'd been making an effort all day – being sure to puff him up, furnish him with self-esteem, wrap him in a layer of protection to soften the blow. Trouble was, she'd done such a good job of it she now found herself facing an impossible reversal. It had been a wonderful day – just like old times. But she had to. Actually, it was more complicated than that. She wanted to. Didn't she?

Father had arranged it but, of course, they all knew that Mother was the one that had set it up: a date with Stephen Ching, eldest son of the property magnate Sun Ching – one of the richest men in Hong Kong. Ching – Candy smiled as she repeated the name silently to herself as they sat on the front of the deck, watching the sun starting to set. The name said it all really. *Ching*!

Candy was determined not to feel guilty about it. After all, hadn't she always known that she was going to marry a Chinese man, a rich Chinese man? Hadn't it always been there? Something she had inherited. Something genetic. Programmed. Drummed in. Understood.

So why the guilt? Why the big conundrum?

Hong Kong.

That was the problem.

Candy had never anticipated that so many of her English friends would find their way to Hong Kong. Even the ones that came from here. For some reason, she had naïvely assumed that they would stay on in England. Just like she would have done, given the choice. She'd assumed that they saw Hong Kong simply as the place they started life, spent their first years, a kitsch childhood memory. It wasn't home. At least, she hadn't thought that they might see it that way.

Even now, she didn't believe they were here because they saw Hong Kong as a place to live, work, love and die. They were here because of the Handover. It was an historical time. Something not to be missed. They were here because they had nowhere else to go. Nothing else to do. Couldn't get jobs in England, so they'd come back. Easy to get a job in Hong Kong.

And it wasn't just her Hong Kong friends that had returned. They'd brought everyone else with them. The rest of the gang, the rest of the Leeds Group. Boyfriends and cousins. All here, together. One big happy English family in Hong Kong having fun. It really was wonderfully colonial. And it meant that Candy was trapped. Between it all. Between two cultures. Her Eurasian dilemma perpetuated. She'd wanted to migrate seamlessly into her Chinese destiny. And she'd thought that once her education was complete, and once she'd returned to the Island, it would all happen. So strange for her parents to create that conundrum for her, she often thought: send her abroad only to insist she eventually use that education to settle at home. They'd explained that an international education was simply That Much Better, but even so, it seemed a very odd logic.

And now it meant she was finding it impossible to fulfil her destiny, the path they wanted her to take. How could she do it while her Leeds friends were around? She loved them too much to reject them outright, to their faces, while they all lived just around the corner from her, kept on telephoning. What was she meant to do? Not return their calls? Refuse to see them? Impossible. They were like a second family to her.

And yet that was what she needed to do to create the simplicity, muster the single-mindedness of purpose it would take to become Chinese. The Hong Kong Chinese themselves would never accept her while she socialized with the English. As long as she behaved like that she'd never belong. She knew that. Indeed, how could her parents not have foreseen that? Maybe they'd made the same mistake she had: assumed the English would stay in England.

Candy understood that the only real way to leave her friends, and her Western-ness, behind was to go somewhere else, do something else, be someone else. Just like she had during her year in Spain. She'd been able to forget them then. Time would have healed the wound, the cut from her past – if only they hadn't been around.

But they were. Just like Sean was still around. And now the Handover was just three and a half months away. And Candy was in the same place she'd started. English boyfriend. English friends. It had to end. They had to end. The colonial world of being English in Hong Kong was too small for her to survive in. It would eventually kill her, the real her, the eventual her. Indeed, it had already started. She was even losing her Cantonese! How could that happen while she was living in Hong Kong? No wonder her parents were freaking out.

So now the time had eventually come. After three years, Candy had to start making changes. She was going to make the impossible prospect possible. She wasn't going to feel guilty about it. It had been understandable for her to fall into the position she was in. But now it finally had to end. She had to dump Sean and she had to start to not return calls. Her friends weren't leaving and there could be no seamless transition. That was just the way things were. She wasn't going to feel guilty about it. Not any more. She'd been feeling guilty about everything for too long. She didn't want to hurt anybody. She didn't want to hurt Sean. But this was her destiny. Candy was going to marry a rich Chinese businessman. End of story.

A haze was settling, turning the island view opaque, like some Oriental watercolour painting. The water rushed forward in white, like it was trying to run away from the boat as it ploughed. Candy looked at her feet as they dangled over the side of the boat. She was glad to see that the sun and sea hadn't damaged her nails. She'd had them done especially. Sean rubbed her forearm before passing her the joint. She smiled at him as he looked into her eyes softly.

'What are you thinking?' Sean said quietly, turning to face her, his face still resting on his forearm as they leant against the chrome railings of the boat. The wind was rushing. The temperature was turning. Candy was thinking about what to wear for her date. She knew Stephen was planning something special.

'Nothing,' Candy replied before flicking the last of the spliff into the ocean.

'Wicked day,' Sean said, seeking confirmation.

'Yeah,' Candy replied. 'It's good to have Mikey in town.' She felt herself building up to the task this way, directing Sean's thoughts and energies onto his best friend. It was the sensible thing to do: hand Sean over from her grip into the arms of Mikey. She didn't want Sean any more. Mikey had been waiting for this. And now he was going to get Sean back. Candy was giving Sean to Mikey.

'Yeah,' Sean replied, half laughing.

'What did you say?' Mikey shouted across the deck at them. He was leaning with Fat Nick against the other railings, the starboard side. Emma and Charlie were somewhere inside. 'I can hear you talking about me.'

'We were just talking about how phenomenally dull you are,' Sean said.

'Fuck off,' Mikey replied.

They all smiled.

'What's the plan then?' Fat Nick asked.

'For tonight?' Sean said.

'Yeah,' Fat Nick said.

'Dunno. Lan Kwai Fong?' Sean tried.

Fat Nick groaned.

'Well, have you got any better suggestions?' Sean said.

Fat Nick shook his head.

'What do you want to do, Candy?' Sean asked, turning to face her, their legs and elbows touching.

Candy breathed in. This was it.

'I can't come out tonight,' she managed without flinching.

'Why not?' Sean asked, innocently enough, still not picking up on the imminent rejection – the fifth one in two months.

'I've got to go out with this guy,' Candy said, shaking her head as if it was a drag. 'My parents arranged it weeks ago apparently.' She added a small, impatient, can-you-believe-them sigh for effect. Sean's face suddenly creased into a heart-melting expression of hurt. He looked like a begging dog.

'Why didn't you tell me?' he said quietly, almost catching on the *me*, almost not making it through the question with dignity.

'I only just found out myself,' Candy replied, slightly indignant. 'This morning. I was going to tell you but . . . we were having such a good time. I'm sorry, Sean,' she said, touching his arm. 'I didn't think it was a big deal.'

Sean looked at her. 'Don't go,' he said, eventually.

Candy could feel Fat Nick and Mikey shifting uncomfortably behind them. She hated the idea of them listening. But there was no way to avoid it. She felt ashamed. Ashamed of Sean's pleading. Ashamed of herself. For rejecting Sean this way. It was like she was rejecting them all.

'I can't do that,' she said a little impatiently.

'Why not?' he asked.

'Because I can't,' she said, before pulling her knees quickly up to her chest and gripping the top railing so she could haul herself up.

'Please, Candy,' Sean said, holding her forearm as she stood. She looked down at him. 'Don't go. Stay with me.'

'I can't,' she replied, realizing it was for the third time. She looked down at him, straight into his weak eyes. She wanted him to see the way she despised him in this moment, despised him for being so public with their problems. Why couldn't he just let her go? It was the only way to give him the message. 'I'm cold,' she said, as if that covered everything. Then she turned and padded her way towards the cabin to get her sweater.

# Chapter Twenty-Six

Sean was putting a brave face on it. After all, it *was* Saturday night. Lan Kwai Fong – which was a strip of bars of the kind you might expect to find in a peak season Costa del Sol – was heaving. Indeed, the only difference between Lan Kwai Fong and the Costa del Sol was that Lan Kwai Fong was packed *all* the time. It didn't have a season. Its season was simply night time. Monday through Sunday, three hundred and sixty-five days a year, for everyone who worked too hard and played too hard in the Oriental Metropolis. Maybe because Hong Kong was a temporary place, a kind of holiday camp, something akin to university – but for working adults. Every night in Hong Kong was a good night to get wasted. Or it could have just been a symptom of the claustrophobia of the place: the only real solution was alcoholic annihilation.

Open-fronted bars with names like Perestroika and 49-ers screamed the Top Ten at one another. People spilled out onto the street like overflowing beer. There was the sound of drunken chat-up lines being yelled in the air and the vague aroma of Tequila slammer sick mixing with pizza and fast Thai food.

Sean, Mikey and Fat Nick were in Le Bistro, the open-air terraced bar set slightly away and above the rest of the pink, sloping streets. Like everywhere else it was stuffed. People lined the steep steps waiting to 'get in' and the dark, dripping, slime-slipped narrow alleyway (which squealed with rats), the only other entrance to the bar, was blocked off. Everyone was sweating. Somehow, the night seemed much stickier than the day had. Or maybe that was just the crowd.

Most of the Leeds crew had managed to meet up – Ben, Big Nick, Katz, Little Nick (who seemed to be chatting up Sophie – bit weird considering she used to go out with Ali, Nick's best mate), Jimmy, Alex, Jules, Sluffy, Muffy and Bee-bee. There was also some of the extended gang, friends of the Leeds hard-core that had come into the social fold since arriving in Hong Kong. There was Lenny, Roo, Fi Fi, Munkie, Loo-loo, La-la, Jarv, Spunk . . . lots of people anonymous in their nicknames and various abbreviations.

Sean noticed Rob, Bob, whatever he was called, standing in a corner talking animatedly with Muffy and Roo. Sean didn't like the way they seemed to laugh at whatever it was he said, particularly Muffy. She was meant to be a good friend of Sean's, part of the original posse. Hadn't she seen the way Candy had danced with Bob at the fetish party? Whose side was she on anyway? The social side, it seemed, the having-a-good-time side. Typical, Sean thought to himself. *But he's a really nice guy*, he could hear the girls cooing.

Yeah, fuck off. Really good looking you mean.

Sean told himself to ignore it. He had his own audience to deal with. At least fifteen people (among them six girls, two quite fit) were yelling and laughing around him. He was taking bets on a game he'd invented in a fit of drunken charisma: Spot the Cockroach. It was brilliant in its simplicity. Three red plastic cups, which they'd all been drinking Sea Breezes from, were used to hide one cockroach – or *'cacker-roach'*, as Sean was calling them, Al Pacino style. Sean had always fancied himself as a bit of a Scarface. He had the hairstyle for it. Which reminded him to sweep his hand through it one more time. He had to be careful. Couldn't let a revealing strand fall forward while he was bending over to shuffle the cups. After all, there were birds present.

'Place your bets, ladies and gentlemen, place your bets,' Sean said, swaggering slightly. 'Remember, if your ante's not down, you're not playing.' He pronounced down 'dan', like the cockney bouncer in that rave tune.

Mikey, his trusty sidekick, was in charge of taking money and grinning. Fat Nick was in charge of ushering the cockroaches, enormous silver-black armour-plated monsters that were the length of fingers (not including the antennae). Charlie had slipped off somewhere earlier with Emma, clearly up to the no-good they had started on the way back from the boat trip. For his part, Sean found himself wondering where his allegiances lay: with boyfriend-Ben or flatmate-Charlie. Best not to get involved, he had decided. Maybe Sean was more like every other member of the gang than he liked to think.

Candy. How could she do another blind date to him? Sean couldn't believe it. He blamed her parents. They'd always hated Sean. And they were doing a good job of splitting them up. There wasn't much Sean could do about it. He knew that if he had forbidden Candy from going, she'd have accused him of being 'paranoid', 'overprotective', and then she would have gone anyway. There was no choice. He had to let her go.

*If you love something: let it go,*
*If it comes back, it's yours,*
*If not, it never was. . .*

Sean had seen that on a poster in a Chinese hairdresser's, depicting a large waterfall and a deer that looked like it had been painted on for target practice. He hadn't found it very reassuring.

One of the girls (not a fit one) screamed as a wayward cockroach feeler brushed against her naked ankle. She was wearing tablecloth shorts and espadrilles. Nick ushered the victim into the circle of cups and covered it. Three dead cockroaches, smashed and splattered, dark yellow innards oozing around them, randomly filled the circle. Sean had tried to minimize the killing but what could he do? One of the boys watching (who Sean could tell was trying to slice off a piece of female attention from the three Game Masters) had stamped on a cockroach after he had lost his bet – much to the amusement of the male crowd. Now anyone who lost was doing it, unless the cockroach scurried away first. Sean didn't suppose that it mattered. There were plenty of victims to choose from.

'OK, the bookie is closed, bookie closed,' Sean shouted.

A final flurry of hands, some clapping and other casino-type catcalling. *'Come on baby, come to Papa. . .'*

Sean bent down. 'Now, ladies and gentlemen, watch closely . . .' He shuffled the cups, dummied, pulled the left cup back, in the middle, no, back to the left, slip, slide, shimmy. A slight divot in the concrete caught on the edge of the cup and an antenna was suddenly revealed. Huge roars from the crowd. Sean kept shuffling the cups but it was no use. The antenna was showing, there was no point hiding it. Everyone was clapping. This time they'd lose everything!

He stood up and everyone was thrusting bills at Mikey, who looked at Sean beseechingly.

'CHRIST, NICK, DID YOU HAVE TO CHOOSE SUCH A LARGE FUCKER?' Sean shouted above the din.

*IT'S IN THE MIDDLE, IT'S IN THE MIDDLE . . .* Everyone was screeching. *HUNDRED DOLLARS, IT'S IN THE MIDDLE!!*

'FUCK OFF, IT'S NOT MY FAULT,' Nick shouted back.

'YEAH, SEAN, WHAT WERE YOU DOING?' Mikey joined in. 'WHY DID YOU HAVE TO DO IT SO FAST?'

*MEER-DUL! MEER-DUL! MEER-DUL!* Everyone was chanting now. Money flying.

'OK, people, OK,' Sean said, arms raised, palms pleading. No one listened.

*HUNDRED DOLLARS ON THE MIDDLE! MINE!*

'OK, order!' Sean tried.

More chaos.

'ORRRRDEEERRRRR!' he screamed.

Finally, a hush descended. Some of the Leeds gang were turning now to see what was happening. Somehow, things had got just a little out of hand. Well, at least bets were confined to those that had placed antes, Sean said to himself. If everyone started muscling in at this late stage, they'd be screwed.

'OK, now listen, because I have something very important to say,' he started. The crowd eyed him suspiciously. 'We *will* be taking your bets,' Sean said, pre-empting the general scepticism. 'But I feel that I have to remind everyone here of the risks of this game.' The crowd groaned. 'Seriously, people,' Sean said, glancing at a nervous Nick and a very concerned-looking Mikey, 'I feel obliged to warn you that *all* bets are final. Is that understood?'

'GET ON WITH IT!' one of the males jeered.

'YEAH! I want a hundred Hong Kong on the middle,' said another.

Sean looked at Mikey, who looked back at him. 'OK, Mikey, are you ready?' he asked.

'What are you doing? It's off,' Mikey exclaimed. 'How can you take bets? It was a dud round.'

*MEER-DUL! MEER-DUL! MEER-DUL!*

The chant had started up again. Sean looked at Mikey. 'Trust me,' he said.

'Trust you?' Mikey replied. 'We'll lose all our money! Don't you understand?'

'Trust me,' Sean said again.

Mikey shook his head. 'You're crazy.'

Sean grinned at him. *Yes, I am a little crazy*, he thought to himself. *Because I'm a betting man, a broker, with nothing to lose.* Everything that meant anything to him was out on a blind date. Sean discovered that he didn't care any more if he was going down.

*Goiinnngg Daaahhhnn!*

'Ladies and gentleman, the bookie's is now open,' he suddenly restarted. 'Please, if you will, puhhHHH-LACCE YOUR BETS!'

Mikey scrambled to catch all the money. Fifteen hands flying at him, all bets on the middle cup. Within a minute he'd collected eighteen hundred Hong Kong dollars. Two hundred quid if you counted the ante. They were looking at a possible loss of four hundred quid, two to one odds for the winner: those were the rules.

'All right, all right,' Sean said when the hands eventually stopped thrusting. 'All bets are in, all bets.'

A hushed tension settled over the crowd and spread throughout the bar. Mikey shifted nervously next to Fat Nick, who was glancing over the railings behind them to see how far the fall would be if they had to jump. Sean was smiling a little insanely.

'This will be the last bet of the evening and everyone here, I wish to restate, is aware of the risks. Am I right?'

*GET ON WITH IT!*

'Right,' Sean said slowly. 'Middle cup, please, Mikey.'

Mikey looked at him. 'You do it.'

Sean looked at him, slightly exasperated, that *Trust me* expression sewn into his broad brow.

Mikey sighed and bent down to remove the middle cup, the one with the antenna still pointing out shamefully. He gripped the top of the cup in the ends of his fingers and snapped it up quickly.

Empty.

The crowd was stunned. People in the rest of the bar started muttering, wanting to know what had happened.

*Empty.*

*But how?*

'Ladies and gentlemen,' Sean said slowly, 'I'm afraid that this brings our evening to an end . . .' Sean turned and looked at Mikey and Nick, signalling with his eyes to start moving through the crowd.

*Must have been an antenna from a previous game.*

*No . . . It would have been from one of the dead cockroaches on the floor.*

*Yeah, it must have caught on the cup.*

*Which idiot started stamping on cockroaches?*

*Yeah? Who came up with that brilliant idea?*

*It was him!*

*No, it wasn't it was him!*

*Fuck off . . .*

By the time the crowd had figured out who they wanted to blame, Sean, Mikey and Nick had squeezed their way, hearts racing, down the stairs and were melting into the chaos of Lan Kwai Fong proper.

Eventually, when he was sure that the crowd had completely consumed them, Sean reached into his pocket, grabbed the cockroach that had spent the last three minutes pinching his thighs with writhing legs and gnawing mandibles, and slipped it down the back of Mikey's shirt. It took him a second or so to react.

'Uh, uh, ug, help, errr, fuck, shit.' Mikey writhed in his shirt. Twisting and reaching round the back. 'Christ, fuck, help me, what is it, WHAT IS IT?'

Sean couldn't contain himself as Mikey eventually ripped his shirt off, the cockroach tumbling to the ground and scurrying off only to get crushed into yellow smithereens fifteen pairs of feet later. Nick was laughing, too.

'You fucking bastard, Sean,' Mikey said, grabbing his collar. 'I'll kill you.'

Tears were streaming down Sean's face. He started waving two cupped palms in towards himself, *muh-eyne*-style, as Mikey threatened him.

'Fucking two thousand dollars, mate,' Sean cried, grabbing Mikey's face. 'TWO FUCKING THOUSAND!'

The realization slowly eased into Mikey's expression. They were rich. Rich! And Sean had done it. The crazy fucker had duped them all. Nick, Sean and Mikey ran whooping through the crowd, arm-in-arm, and they didn't stop until they were well clear of the Lan Kwai Fong madness, eventually stopping on Pedder Street, near a corner busy with HSBC ATM machines.

'Right,' Sean said eventually, panting. 'There's only one thing for it, lads. We're off to the wank shop.'

# Chapter Twenty-Seven

Candy was having a miserable time. Stephen Ching may have been loaded – so far they'd taken his father's private hovercraft to Macao, drunk bellinis and were currently dining at the five star Pousada de Sao Tiago (no less) – but, Jesus, he was boring. He wasn't even *that* good looking. Far less impressive than when she had eyed him from afar at the social events or in the society pages of the *Hong Kong Herald*.

'Penny for your thoughts,' Stephen said, looking at her. He was so smooth, what with his perfectly groomed, perfectly black hair and his manicure. He was even wearing a tuxedo. But his lips looked colourless and it was hard to see his eyes. The shadow of his forehead, which seemed to overhang slightly, hid them. Candy didn't find these unusually closed features attractive at all. She liked typically Chinese faces: open. Ironically, that's why she liked Sean's face so much. Even though he had cheeky eyes, his face was open. You couldn't prise Stephen Ching's features open with a crowbar.

'Just how beautiful it is here,' Candy replied, smiling flatly. A breeze billowed the silk curtains separating their table from the private balcony. Candy could see the crimson walls of the seventeenth-century Fortaleza de Sao Tiago, just beyond the garden below. It was a surprisingly cool night. She was wearing a pink shawl over her black dress, an elegant and slightly risqué number, a semi-transparent outfit, cut on the bias. Mother had picked it out.

*Try not to let your father down now. You know how much tonight means to him, how hard he's worked for this. And we all know that he's doing this for you, that this is for the best, don't we? You look absolutely stunning. I love you, darling, you know that. And I know that you'll make Stephen happy, that you can make all of us happy . . . if you try. You will try now, won't you? It's for the best, definitely for the best . . . I'm almost completely certain of it.*

'It is, isn't it?' Stephen said before going on to explain the historical significance of the place. He didn't say anything she didn't already know. He sounded like someone reciting the text from one of the tourist brochures you could find in the hotel reception. Candy drifted off.

She couldn't stop thinking about Sean. And what a bitch she was being to him. And how she hadn't *really* wanted to come on this date. Mother had made her do it. OK, so when she'd said the name *Stephen Ching*, yes, she'd been impressed. But now that she was on the date she understood that she didn't want to be on it. Why were her parents trying to split her and Sean up? More to the point, why was she allowing her parents to split them up? Was it because Sean wasn't Chinese, was it because Candy wanted to be a *Tai-tai*, because she wanted to be rich? Well, yes, obviously it was that.

But then, if that were the case, why was she messing around with Rob? If all she was ever about was marrying a rich Chinese businessman like Stephen, why was she snogging Mr Gorgeous Blue Eyes? Was she deliberately trying to hurt Sean? Why would she do that? She loved Sean. Didn't she? She'd only suggested that they open up their relationship, see/snog other people so she could negotiate her way into her Chinese destiny, go on these blind dates arranged by her parents, get on with her future. So why was she using that now as an excuse to have an affair with . . . another Westerner?

Because she fancied him, that's why. Christ, she fancied Rob. How had her desire for Sean died?

It hadn't just been the fact that Sean wasn't Chinese, couldn't speak the language, had found it so hard to get a job, had depended on her for so long for . . . everything – food, directions, friends – when they first arrived in Hong Kong that had first made her have second thoughts about him. It hadn't just been those things, though they had got her thinking. The moment Candy had started to have second thoughts about Sean was when he'd taken his job at that bank, brokerage, or whatever it was. It turned him into such a . . . what was the right word? . . . Lad? No. Worse. Yob.

Almost as soon as he'd gathered a small measure of independence from her, and started to *live* in Hong Kong, Sean suddenly seemed always too busy, or too tired, but, most often, too drunk for her. She hadn't liked that. She hadn't liked that at all. He was suddenly shallow. Hong Kong had got to him. And very quickly, too. He was susceptible. So fresh. So open to the infection. Everything was immediately money. Which, of course, was something Candy could appreciate.

But maybe it was the speed of it. The fastness of the cash. Sean became wide. He lost all his class. Which definitely didn't fit with her socialite persona at all. How was Candy the Art Dealer meant to discover new Chinese talent and sell paintings to the island's rich, with Sean the Banker Wanker on her arm? OK, so she wasn't actually selling paintings yet (just filing for a gallery on Wyndham Street) but that was hardly the point. She'd preferred Sean when he'd been depressed – the stifling Sean, the dependent Sean. The weak one, the gentle one, the innocent. Hong Kong had corrupted him.

Maybe it was simply the claustrophobia of the place that brought out the worst in people. And maybe that was why Candy had eventually given in to her parents' insistent suggestions that she go out on all these dates they had arranged. Not so much because she was determined to start her life but simply because Sean had changed and she'd fallen out of love with him.

Even so, her parents had certainly known how to dangle temptation, known how to woo her away from Sean's grip. The Chinese had style, Mother had reassured her. They were more comfortable with their wealth. Candy knew that her Mother pined for the right marriage for Candy because she regretted her own, even if she was too stubborn to admit it. She had believed in Daddy when they'd met, believed he'd make it just like he'd said he would, just like everyone else was making it back in those days, Hong Kong's halcyon days.

*Love! What good did that ever do anyone?*

Those words had stayed with Candy all the way through her relationship with Sean. And she watched her mother, watched what she had become. All Mother wanted now was to be able to hold her head up high – in front of her family, in front of her friends, in front of everyone that had succeeded. And if that meant sacrificing her only daughter to the cause, well then, so be it. Or maybe Mother simply understood that going against the grain was a mistake. Just look at where it had gotten her – in a crappy three bedroom house in Pokfulam.

Mother was probably right. She wasn't sacrificing Candy. She was rescuing her. From love, from Sean. After all, Candy could already see it. She didn't want what Sean was becoming. If only all those guys he worked with weren't so, so . . . common.

Now Rob. He had style. Even more than Stephen.

His voice filtered tonelessly back into her consciousness.

'The Fortaleza da Barra was one of the fortresses built in the seventeenth century by the Portuguese to defend Macao against hostile European nations and local pirates. One hundred years later a chapel was built within its walls and dedicated to Saint James, the patron saint of the Portuguese garrison. Today, much of the fortress and the Chapel have been preserved as part of the Pousada de Sao Tiago, which is where we're eating now.'

He smiled at her, very pleased with himself. Candy smiled back at him.

'More wine?' he said, reaching for the bottle. Normally there would have been three waiters on hand to pre-empt any such effort on the part of Stephen Ching, but he had dismissed them at the beginning of the meal. He wished to have privacy.

'No thank you,' Candy said.

Stephen ignored her and filled her glass anyway. She looked about the room in silent protest. It was very gaudy looking, reds and golds and clashing greens, but there was a certain Catholic charm to the place, a kind of innocent decadence, as if bawdy colours and clashing fabrics were all part of a 'good life'.

And then she saw that Stephen had moved and was now standing beside her, his crotch meeting her face. He was looking down at her. He reached and held her hand, which was resting, gently arched, on the starched white tablecloth. In his other hand he held a black velvet-lined case with a silver clasp. It was open. The multi-coloured flash of diamonds zig-zagged across Candy's face. A necklace. A dazzling diamond necklace the length and weight of all Macao! Candy's mouth fell involuntarily open and went dry. She couldn't say anything for a moment.

Stephen took the opportunity to free her hand and place the case on the table. He pulled the necklace out and held it in front of her. It looked like the Big Dipper on a clear night. It was practically the same size.

'Oh, Stephen, I can't,' she finally managed.

But by then he was already sealing it round her, like some silent agreement. *And with this necklace I own you.*

It was utterly inappropriate. And ostentatious. And absurd. How could Candy accept this from Stephen Ching? She'd only met him properly two hours ago, and now he was giving her this? The stones felt wonderfully cold against her skin. She could still see them shining, even though they were under her chin. They radiated colour. She reached up to touch them. They felt like . . .

And that was when Stephen bent down to kiss her. Candy saw him approaching, and she was frozen. It was just like old times. The enormous pressure to please. The feeling that she *had* to kiss him, even though she didn't want to, even though she didn't fancy him. But it could make him *so* happy. He seemed to want it so much. Just like all the other boys who begged. And what was a kiss to Candy? A kiss was nothing. It was important to make him happy.

But what if he wanted to fuck? What if she had to say *no*? The word dangled in front of her, that single word that she knew would trigger her resentment, her disgust, instantly put her off him, kill any chance that they might have together. Candy told herself that she mustn't let her father down. After all, what was she protecting now? Her virginity was long gone.

That ghost had been happily exorcized. A kiss was nothing. A fuck was nothing. If Candy was going to be a *Tai-tai* she'd have to get used to the idea of sleeping with someone that she didn't love. She knew that. She told herself that she could learn to fancy him.

Stephen's colourless lips hovered, but not with uncertainty. He just needed to negotiate the best angle. He was coming in. And then, like something cruising in to dock, he landed his lips simply on hers. So what did Candy do? What did Candy do? She kissed him back. Of course she did.

Oh well, she thought to herself, as Stephen slipped his hand into her loosely bound hair. At least I'm not doing it because of the diamonds.

Well, not entirely . . .

# Chapter Twenty-Eight

Michael was slightly horrified to discover that he'd have to remove all his clothes, Roman Bath style, before the massage, so he spent several minutes in the Happy Endings changing room slapping the head of his penis against his inner thigh in the hope of generating a not-too-obvious semi-erection.

'Hurry up, Mikey,' Nick hollered through the wooden-shuttered door.

'Coming.'

Michael watched Nick's flip-flopped feet through the knee-high gap at the bottom of the door as he walked away. He cursed the booze. *Come on*, he mouthed. Eventually, there were stirrings. Michael held the two erotic images that seemed to work best in his mind, and finally exited.

He may as well not have bothered. As soon as he was out of the changing room and into the jacuzzi/shower area, he realized that he'd never be able to hold his effort. Fat Chinese men wobbled across blue-slatted plastic mats. There were thin Chinese men, too, of course, naked and skinny and pigeon chested, ribs showing, but all Michael could see was the cig-arette-filter flesh and the black pubic triangles showing like vaginas.

He spotted Nick and Sean bubbling in an Olympic-length jacuzzi to his left. Thankfully, they still hadn't seen him, so he walked around and behind them to a set of ladder steps leading into the pool, slipping inconspicuously into the water and allowing the bubbles to smear the reality.

'Fuck, it's hot,' he said once he was comfortable.

Sean smiled vaguely at Michael and then turned back to Fat Nick and said, 'So what happened after that?'

'Well, I just told her I couldn't come unless she took her top off,' Fat Nick replied.

'And did she?'

'Yup.'

'Result,' Sean said. 'And then she let you come on her tits?'

Nick nodded back.

'Good work, fella.'

'What are you two talking about?' Michael asked.

'The Game,' Sean replied.

'What game?' Michael asked.

'The game we all play whenever we come down here,' Sean continued. 'To see how far we can get with the girls.'

'Aren't they all hookers?' Michael replied, unimpressed.

'Oh no,' Nick and Sean said together. 'This is just a massage parlour.'

'But I thought we were here for sex,' Michael said.

'They only give hand jobs here, Mikey,' Sean explained. 'At least, those are the rules. That's how the whole idea of the Game started. To see if . . . you know, if they'd go any further.'

'How do you get them to do that?' Michael asked.

'Ah, well. Now you're asking,' Sean said.

'Well, how far will they go?'

'I got a blow job once,' Sean said, smiling proudly.

'Fuck off you did,' Nick said.

'I did,' Sean replied calmly.

'I don't believe that,' Nick said.

'You can believe whatever you like,' Sean said beaming. 'I'm telling you, I came in her face like a milk float hitting a brick wall.'

They all laughed.

'The best I've ever got is a fishy finger,' Nick said.

'How many times have you played this game?' Michael asked.

'Many,' Sean said, emphasizing the 'M' as if it was an innuendo of some kind.

'Sounds expensive,' Michael said.

'That's the best thing about it,' Sean said. 'It's all on the company Amex card. I bring clients here. It's great for business. A few thousand dollars in here can bring in millions for the company.'

'Christ,' Mikey said.

'Yeah, well, don't knock it, mate,' Sean said. 'Happy Endings is the best wank shop in town. Any one else might have taken you to Wanchai or some other shit-hole. If you'd hadn't noticed, everyone else here is Chinese. Always a good sign, going local. Happy Endings in North Point. It's Hong Kong's best-kept secret.'

'Come on, come on,' Nick said impatiently, standing up. 'Let's go. I'm getting a blow job before I leave here tonight.'

'OK,' Sean agreed, grinning at Michael before moving to pull himself out of the water.

Michael hovered, waiting until their backs were turned before heaving himself out behind them. Nick and Sean led him from the bathing area into an adjacent room filled with towels and bathrobes. A petite Chinese girl with acne handed

Michael a fluffy white robe with thick collars and two extra towels. Sean and Nick both placed one towel round their neck and folded the other over their forearm. They moved into the next room.

There were four long rows of brown leather seats: two rows against the walls and two more, back to back, running down the centre of the room. Television screens flashed horseracing and betting odds in each corner. Chinese men filled most of the seats, many with their feet resting on footstools. There was a bar in the far-left corner of the room. The boys found three seats together, silver ashtrays on broad airline-like dividers between them. A Chinese girl immediately approached them and offered individual cigarettes from an open box.

'Marlboro, Marlboro Light, Benson's, Silk Cut, 555s?' she asked.

They all helped themselves before she presented a large seventies-style lighter with a fist-sized gas cylinder coated in bone enamel. They leaned forward to reach the flame as she passed it before them. Another Chinese girl arrived, this time with three clipboards in her hand. She handed one to each of them. Blue biros were clipped into the silver grip at the top. A piece of paper with a list of a numbers, a hundred or so in two columns, small black boxes typed in next to them, stood emptily on the page.

'Seventy-three, every time,' Sean said, his cigarette bouncing on his lips as he spoke, his eyes squinting to keep the squirming smoke out.

'Is she the one that gave you the blow job?' Nick said.

'Mind your own business.'

'Well, I'm going for forty then,' Nick said.

'You bloody well are not,' Sean replied. 'I found forty.'

'They're not yours, you know, Sean.'

Sean grunted with disapproval.

'How am I meant to know who to choose?' Michael eventually said.

'Don't worry, Mikey, it doesn't make much difference,' Sean said, turning to face him and pulling on the last of his cigarette with a reassuring wince. 'Trust me. I've tried most of them.'

'I'll go for ten then,' Michael said.

'A fine choice,' Sean replied.

Nick ordered each of them Scotch and Michael put his feet up and watched horses covered in coats slowly circling before a race on the TV screen. He smoked another cigarette. A man in a tuxedo occasionally called out numbers from the corner of the room and men stood up from their seats and disappeared behind a red leather door with gold studs.

Michael found himself getting increasingly excited. He loved the idea that he was in this room, just relaxing, in a bathrobe, smoking a cigarette, on the pretext of waiting for a massage, knowing that he was really here for a hand job. He was thrilled by the idea of finally crossing the sexual barrier implicit in a massage. And all with a simple slip of the palm. All that oil, all that nakedness, skin-to-skin touching, slipping, sliding, easy to just go below and ahhhhh . . .

'Ten,' came the call from the black-suited man at the end of the room. 'Forty.'

'Right, lads,' Sean said, as Nick and Michael got up. 'See you outside.'

Michael smiled a little nervously at him.

They passed through the mysterious door and into the gloom. There was the occasional sight of women slipping between rooms. Michael thought he could discern male grunts and cries of pleasure and the sound of lubrication, but that could just have been his imagination.

Nick peeled off as he was led by the man towards a door and then entered it without saying goodbye. Michael's room was three doors down. He walked in. It was empty except for a massage table, body length and plastic and with a face hole cut out of one end. Three white towels were stacked on the other end, away from the face hole. The faint sound of Chinese classical music clinked and chinked from unseen speakers. Michael took his robe off and hung it on a hook on the back of the door, before lying face down on the massage table.

He waited.

And waited.

And waited.

Finally, the door swung open. Michael lifted his head to steel a glance. He wanted to see if she was a babe. Even in the dim light Michael could see that she wasn't. She was short and dumpy and she wore a starched white outfit not unlike a nurse's uniform. He told himself she wasn't bad looking.

'Hello,' he said deeply, trying to sound seductive.

'Hello,' she replied, moving immediately round and beside him.

'What's your name?' he said.

'Doris.'

Doris? Michael felt disappointed. It was hardly Suzie Wong.

'My name's Michael,' he said, somehow knowing in advance that she wouldn't have asked.

She dripped oil onto his back. 'Nice to meet you, Michael,' she said.

'Nice to meet you, too,' he tried one last time before she started to press her fingertips into his back. The massage was half-hearted and unpleasant. Michael tried to tell himself to relax as Doris stabbed and jabbed, but he found that the only thing he could think about was the moment when she would finally ask him to turn over and he could get down to the Game. He considered the tactics he might use.

After ten or so minutes of strangely indifferent body rubbing, Doris finally said the magic words and Michael quickly twirled himself over onto his back. Somehow Doris seemed a little more attractive as he looked up at her now, greased up and oiled in the dimness.

She rubbed his chest three times and said: 'You like special massage?'

'Yes,' Michael replied quickly.

The very faintest of smiles appeared in the corners of her mouth. And then things went quickly. Doris slipped her hand under the towel and started to pump, hard and fast. There seemed to be a lot of oil and it was hard to feel anything. Michael concentrated on building his erection. He realized that he was a little nervous. He thought about telling her to slow down. He considered reaching across and grabbing her left breast. What about if she took her top off?

Then he felt something very strange – an alien insertion – deep and pressing.

Next thing Michael knew, sperm was ejaculating loosely onto his belly. It felt horrible, functional, not unlike taking a piss. It certainly wasn't an orgasm.

'What the fuck?' he managed.

The smile that Michael had thought he detected in the corners of Doris's mouth now shone in all its glory down at him.

Doris said: 'It's OK. Don't worry.'

She removed her finger from his anus.

'No,' Michael tried, slowly understanding the violation. 'No.'

'You want cigarette?' Doris said, moving away from the table and wiping her left hand with a towel that was folded in half in her pocket.

What would he tell the boys? Nothing like this had ever happened to him before.

'No,' Michael said. 'I want . . .' He looked down at his penis, pathetic and sticky with sperm. 'I want another one.'

Doris sniggered as she lit herself a cigarette. 'You want another one? You pay again.'

'But that's not fair,' Michael tried.

'That is special massage,' Doris said, as if it explained things.

'Fuck,' Michael said, collapsing back onto the massage table, his forearm on his forehead. Doris inserted the cigarette she had lit between his lips and lit herself another one.

'Lie down, smoke, relax,' she said.

'Fuck,' was all Michael could say.

'You want me to go?' she asked.

'No,' Michael replied quickly. He knew he had to kill time before going back out into the wash area. God only knew how long the other two would take and he didn't fancy the prospect of pruning in the jacuzzi. 'No,' he said. 'Stay.'

Doris sat down on the massage table as Michael shifted to one side to accommodate her. They smoked.

Michael said: 'Why do you do this?'

He knew it was a stupid question before he'd even said it but he had to glean something from the moment. Some intrusion into her private thinking, at the very least. If she wasn't going to wank for him then she could at least give him an idea of the *real* Doris. That would be something neither Nick nor Sean would ever know.

Doris looked at Michael with a mixture of derision and defence. 'For the money,' she said.

'Do you enjoy it?'

Doris snorted with laughter, smoke catching in her nostrils.

'Do you have a boyfriend?' Michael asked.

'Why you want to know?'

'Just do,' he said, shrugging slightly.

'Yes,' she said.

'And he doesn't mind that you do this?'

Doris looked at him and took a final draw on her cigarette. 'I go now,' she said quickly, sliding off the massage table and standing up.

'No, wait, I'm sorry,' Michael tried.

But he was too late. Doris had stamped out her cigarette into an ashtray and was brushing indiscernible flakes of ash, dirt, or whatever it was that she could see, off the front of her starched white dress with a slightly disgusted expression on her face. Then, as quickly as he had come, she was gone.

'Bye,' Michael mouthed as the door clicked closed behind her. He slowly elevated himself and sat upright on the massage table. He felt acutely aware of his nakedness, his self-imposed exposure. There was no generating a semi now. He'd just come and his penis felt as shrivelled and pathetic as it ever could. He regretted being here.

# Chapter Twenty-Nine

'**B**end over, Marland.'

Fishface's voice was deep and resonating. Marland could almost feel it vibrating in his chest. He needed to pee again. His pyjamas were still wet from the rain and the mud and the grass and the first time he'd wet himself out in the fields. He was shaking.

'But, sir, Baxter made me do it, sir, I'm sorry, sir, it was Baxter, it was . . .'

Fishface Haddock turned his back to Marland then and moved towards a cupboard in the corner of the study. The smell of old furniture and cigarettes. Books lined the walls. A bible. A lot of Maths and Chemistry texts.

'Bend over, Marland.'

There was something in his voice the second time he said it that made Marland realize: there was no point in protesting. It was resolve. No. Worse than that. It was a statement of fact, more than a command. *Bend over, Marland.* Like something that was simply fated to occur. Marland would bend over just as surely as the sun would rise the next day. There was no point in arguing. There was no point in getting het up about it. It was simply a matter of power – all-supreme and complete. Like God's will.

Marland put his hands on the back of the brown sofa and bent over.

He wondered, feared, what Mummy might say. He couldn't believe that he was about to get slippered. He felt so ashamed. All he ever wanted was to be a good boy. All he ever wanted was for Mummy to love him. And now he'd gone and let her down. He'd been naughty and now he was getting the slipper for it. He didn't feel outrage. He didn't feel anger. He just felt guilty. And ashamed. And scared.

He looked down at his feet and felt tears re-forming.

Rumour had it that anyone Fishface Haddock slippered couldn't sit down for a week afterwards – it was that bad. Everyone in the House knew that Fishface Haddock wasn't meant to slipper the boys, everyone knew that it wasn't allowed any more. It had been in all the newspapers – how to get rid of caning.

But for some reason, no one ever said anything. Maybe because a slipper didn't seem as bad as caning. Maybe because slippering didn't count, wasn't included in the definition of corporal punishment. Maybe because no one dared cross Fishface. Not while he was in charge. Not in his House. This was his world. He made this place. And he made the rules. That was probably the real reason. Fishface was in charge. No one questioned that.

Except for Clarke.

And he wasn't here. Where was he? Marland sniffed. Where was Clarke when he most needed him? Everything would have been different if Clarke hadn't punched Fishface, if he hadn't got into a Woozie with Baxter, if Marland had refused to play Bulldog. Why had he agreed to play Bulldog? Why was he trying to impress Baxter? Why did he do whatever Baxter told him to do? Why was he trying to be friends with him?

Marland only ever wanted people to like him. Maybe that's why they teased him. They could smell the weakness.

He could feel Fishface's presence behind him now. So large and fat and all encompassing. He was close, almost touching, the warmth of his body meeting Marland's.

'Pull down your trousers,' Fishface said quietly.

The tears started to rush then. Natural and flowing and pure: a reflex action. The naked dread. The humiliation. The fear. Marland couldn't speak. The tears just fell and he watched them fall. Towards his feet. He couldn't move.

'Pull down your trousers, boy,' Fishface said even more quietly, almost compassionately.

Marland sobbed. He heard himself say 'sorry' and 'can't' and 'sorry' again, but the words came out all in a jumble and he wasn't sure what he was saying. He felt like he was saying that he was sorry for being alive, that he couldn't go on, all he knew was that he was sorry, so sorry to be here, bending over and about to get the slipper from Fishface Haddock.

Poor Mummy. She'd be so ashamed. Would Fishface tell her? Of course he would. Even though corporal punishment wasn't allowed any more. Even though parents didn't want this. Why? Because Fishface was in charge. Everyone knew that. Especially Mummy. She wouldn't question it. Fishface was doing the right thing. He was punishing Marland for being bad. Marland was bad.

Marland felt Fishface hook a finger into the elastic holding up his pyjamas and shimmy them down gently, slowly, over his buttocks and down, down to his knees. He could feel his legs shaking, his thighs knocking together. Marland felt his nakedness. Standing, pink, against the warmth of the room. Naked.

Silence.

A heating pipe cracked. Fishface breathed. Marland blubbed silently, his lower lip flapping. Naked.

And then a whoosh as the slipper flew and then flapped, slapped and BURRRRNNNNN!

Marland gasped on the pain and the tears suddenly froze, suspended at the edge of his eyelids as his face snapped alive with astonishment before another, discernible rush in the air, *shooosh*, slap, whack, wallop and BURRRRNNNNN!

Now the pain filtered through and into his thinking. Marland could feel it between the assaults.

*Whoooshh*, *Wallop*, BURN! *Whoooshh*, *Wallop*, BURN! *Whoooshh*, *Wallop*, BURN! *Whoooshh*, *Wallop*, BURRRNNNNNNNNIIINNNNGGGG!

How many times? Marland couldn't count. He felt faint. And sick. The room was rushing round him. His legs weren't his any more. Nothing was his any more, his body had left him, and, in its place only pain. No fear. Just all-encompassing redness. Before his eyes everything a blood red.

He watched as his penis spurted urine onto the carpet. And then his knees gave and he was collapsing and Fishface was suddenly on him, one arm round his waist, holding him up, his other hand free, probing, massaging, rubbing, reaching. He molested Marland's genitals. Then there were gaps, lost consciousness. Marland couldn't tell if these were the moments Fishface felt the numb bits, the buttocks, the burnings, or if he was simply passing out, leaving the place. There was rubbing. Marland remembered that. In the blackness, there was rubbing against him. Against his buttocks. And then he knew. Knew for sure.

Fishface Haddock was the Bummer Man!

The Bummer wasn't in the bushes. He wasn't *Out There*. He was *In Here*. He was on him. The Bummer Man was Fishface.

Fishface Haddock was bumming him. Humping him in the numb parts. Groping, panting, on him, hating and breathing and the smell of cigarettes.

The Bummer Man.

It made Marland scream.

But that didn't stop anything.

It went on. On and on and on. For ever. The room elongated to suck in all Time, like a Black Hole, everything drawn towards an enormous gravitational vortex under the sheer mass of it all. Fishface's weight on top of him. Bearing down and suffocating and so much hatred.

Marland was going to die. The Bummer Man had him. Fishface had him. Just like the other boy. The one that had disappeared. The one the police hadn't found. They had searched the bushes but they hadn't found anything. Because they had been looking *outside*, when they should have been looking *inside*.

Marland understood everything now. Too late.

He was going to die. He knew that now.

Something caught in Marland's throat. A piece of lint or cloth, something ticklish. In the throat, at the back, blocking it. Then there was a hand, old and hard, over his mouth, stopping the screaming, stopping the breathing. There wasn't any breathing. Marland wasn't breathing. Everything was blocked.

And then, quite suddenly, he stopped.

Fishface's voice: 'Go to your bed now, Marland.'

Carpet. Brown and all round. Marland blinked. Then he breathed. He pulled himself upright and reached down for his pyjamas. Still wet. From before. Marland remembered now. There was a before. Now, he was in the After. He got up and walked to the door. It wasn't locked.

# Chapter Thirty

In the end, it was Sean that came through with the break Michael needed on the job front. Turned out he was friends with an editor at the *Hong Kong Herald*. Sean spoke to him whenever he lost a deal or a trade – or whatever it was that he did with his day (besides wanking) – to a competitor firm. There was nothing that pissed the financial world off more than the publication of a private deal, Sean had explained. His boss at Nobucorp openly encouraged the practice. It figured that Sean would have an angle on a parasitic profession like journalism, Michael had thought. Only he could charm his way around a relationship where he should have been the Used, not the User. Still, he could hardly criticize. Sean was now making the most of the relationship to sort him out.

The plan was for the three of them – Sean, the editor and Michael – to meet at the FCC (Foreign Correspondents Club), at the top of Ice House Street, near Central. It was a brilliantly fresh day, the air unusually clean and smarting on the skin, even though it was still hot.

Michael walked slowly up a paved, broad-stepped pedestrian alleyway, nearly at the FCC already, even though the meeting wasn't for another hour. He didn't like the idea of being early, but then it wasn't as if he had anywhere else to be and he was bored of designer store gawking.

As he reached the top of the hill, lightly sweating, Michael spied two white women begging on the corner. They immediately fixed his attention. For starters, Michael was surprised to see anyone – let alone two white women – living on a street in Hong Kong. He'd already noticed, and wondered about, the island's distinct lack of a homelessness problem. The only other beggars – all three of them – Michael had spotted thus far had been Asian of some sort, usually bald Buddhist monks with black robes and large brass bowls, chanting.

Maybe Hong Kong simply wasn't the sort of place to have a beggar problem, he had speculated. It was far too affluent for that. Or, perhaps even more likely, the government shipped all the homeless back to China – no need to soil the reflective gleam of all those mirrored corporate buildings with that kind of muck. Or, more generously, maybe Hong Kong had the world's only working social services system.

Michael didn't know the answer. Either way, it made the vision of these two white women, huddled together and muttering, utterly fascinating. And, as he stared, the vision became only more beguiling. For not only were they beggars, not only were they women, not only were they white – they were also identical twins.

Both had wiry black hair that met their shoulders with a crazy logic and their faces were filled with youthfully ageing features, Scandinavian, Michael felt, each the mirror image of the other. They were even dressed the same. They wore long, ankle-length red skirts, scratched with filth, and white blouses turning brown with wear. As Michael stared they flashed him a cursory, cursing glance that made his heart jump, and then they quickly huddled back into each other, furiously muttering and twitching.

Michael suddenly found himself interested to know who they were, how they got here, where they came from and what had happened to them. Were they relics of the colonial empire – suddenly destitute and helpless in a fast-moving modern world? Were they mad? Yes, as he turned back to watch them twitch and tut, it was clear that they were mad. But how could two people go simultaneously mad, or destitute for that matter? Was it a twin thing?

They were the first real anomaly Michael had seen in Hong Kong, a quirky crevice through which to gain an insight into the place. Michael realized that, for the first time in his life, he had A Story. He decided that he'd bring up the idea at his meeting with Sean's contact. It was bound to make a good impression.

# Chapter Thirty-One

Sean sat at his desk listening to everyone screaming. He looked at the pulsing green numbers on his screen. Then up at the Boards. Ralph was running around chaotically, trying to keep up as everyone shouted prices at him. In a moment of panic he'd used the black marker for the Yen when it should have been red. Now he was frantically trying to rub out his mistake with the edge of his hand – *You fucking twat, Ralph . . . Ralph, you cunt if you don't sort it . . . Ralph, you're a fucking spastic mongoloid . . .* He only succeeded in making more of a mess, the black ink smearing into the Dollar column.

Christ, what a fuck up! And Ralph thought he had problems, Sean muttered to himself, trying not to feel too sorry for him. It was a lousy job doing the Boards – the starting point for everyone, the lowest of the low. Sean remembered the abuse he used to get when he first started: *Oi! Posh cunt!* Still, it wasn't as bad as the place Sean was in now. The Baht ticked down another point against the dollar. No. No, no, no . . . Sean was fucked. He couldn't hold on much longer. It didn't make any sense. He couldn't understand why the market was moving against him. He'd get the sack for this. Christ! They'd probably send him to prison. Just like Nick Leeson.

Strictly speaking, Sean wasn't meant to take positions. The

whole idea of being a broker was to match up trades. One bank called up, offering a price. All Sean had to do was shout the price down the Box, relaying it to every one of Nobucorp's clients, to anyone interested in making a bid. Sean put the two together and then there was a trade, a tidy little tenth of a percentage point as commission for the company.

Nought point nought one per cent of ten million, fifty million, sometimes, rarely, a hundred million dollars . . . you do the maths. And it was happening every second in the Nobucorp office. Nought point nought one per cent here, nought point nought one per cent there. It was a good business, an easy business, no risk, just profits, like taking sweets from a kid.

Except things never worked out that way, not in practice. Competition was fierce. There were too many brokers all fighting for the same scraps that the banks threw under the table. So when a big offer came through – like the one Sean had just taken: five hundred million – you didn't fuck around. You didn't wait to find a bid. You just said it, without thinking, just knowing: MINE!

Sean had been sitting on this swap now for more than fifteen seconds and still no buyer. The bank must have known the baht was going to move. What a wanker – it was bloody Olly as well, one of Sean's best clients. The number of times he'd taken that prick to Happy Endings. And now he was screwing Sean. Totally fucking him. It was getting worse, too. As soon as Sean had shouted the offer down the Box everyone on the floor had stopped. Nobucorp didn't have a big trading room and Sean had been so excited he'd screamed it. The Thai currency swaps market wasn't exactly liquid. You didn't get deals this size every day. It would be probably be the deal of the year . . . if he could sell it.

The only good thing was, no one was listening now. They'd

all turned off when they'd heard the silence that had greeted Sean's cries, assuming that no one would take a five yard trade, that it was a dud offer, going nowhere, freezing the market like a deer caught in headlights.

They didn't know that Sean had accepted it already. And if he could, Sean would have denied it, turning the tables on his so-called friend Olly. But all conversations were recorded . . . you know, to prevent any misunderstandings.

Sean was fucked. He looked at the screen. NO! NO!!! The baht fell another three basis points. Just like that. 3.4, 3.3, 3.2, . . . Christ stop! Going down. The numbers just went down. Down, down, down . . .

*GOIINNNNNGGGGGGG DAAAAAAHHHHHNNNNN* . . .

Sean was going down. He was long five yards. The whole market had heard his offer and now they were working against him, like vultures, desperate to screw the competitor that held this position, knowing that there was a weak spot in the market, knowing there wasn't the liquidity to take it, smelling a kill. *It is not enough that I should win, everyone else must lose* . . . Where had Sean heard that?

Sean tried to breathe. He was sweating heavily now. His head was hurting, all the numbers swelling in the space between his brain and his skull, expanding, pumping, pressing in on him. He had to offload. How? His head thumped. Think! Come on, Sean, think! Should he tell Weasel? No. It'd be over if he did that.

Oh, God, please, please . . . Just turn. Please just turn. Sean stared at the numbers. They stopped flashing for a second. Please, please, please, he begged the market. If it moved another point Sean would be sitting on a loss of . . . all he could see were the noughts. There'd be no way to hide it. He'd have to tell Weasel then, and it would go into dispute. Without a counter-party Nobucorp would have to claim default. But still, they'd have to pay something, a lot, just to keep the client happy, even though it was the fucking client that had pulled a fast one. Sean would be asked to clear his desk by the end of the week.

He was fucked.

'Hey, Sean, where's the baht?' Ralph yelled at him.

Sean stared at the screen in a daze. Please. Please.

'Sean!'

Sean could feel people looking at him. He didn't dare look up. He knew that Wanker Wong was watching. Wong was waiting for the moment when Sean would fuck up. The only Chinese man on the whole floor and the Boss. He'd never liked Sean, and Sean had never liked him. The silent telephone receiver that Sean was still holding to his ear burnt.

'SEAN!' Ralph shouted at him. 'WHAT ABOUT THE BAHT?'

Sean didn't know why he snapped. He just did. He picked up the nearest thing he could find – a paperweight, solid metal – and just hurled it, watching it fly on a perfect trajectory to Ralph's forehead, straight between the eyes. Ralph managed to duck just in time and then there was a loud crack as it hit the white Board. Sean stood, staring, in shock, terrified of what he'd just done as the whole room burst into hysterics and Ralph's stunned face slowly re-emerged from behind a desk.

By now everyone was throwing things – albeit less dangerous items: *Ralphie . . . Spazmo . . . take this . . . fucking moron . . .* – lavishing credit on Sean for a joke that he hadn't meant.

Ralph tried to smile casually as the abuse flew. Sean tried to contain his breathing. He'd have to tell Weasel now. Then Weasel would have to tell Wong. It was over. Sean was fucked. A whole minute had gone by and still it wasn't moving. The baht ticked like a bomb. Weasel couldn't help him this time. Five yards! Sean was dead.

And then, it just happened.

'THREE AND A HALF!' Sean screamed, theoretically at Ralph but really to the whole floor, fuck, to the whole market. He pulled the Box closer. Could it? Would it? Hold on now. Don't let anyone know. The market forgets, remember, the market forgets. Who was doing this? The government? It didn't make any sense.

He watched: 3.6, 3.7.

Come on, Sean mouthed to himself. Come on, baby, come to papa. It kept moving. He could see Ralph furiously scribbling as Sean shouted out the numbers to him. The whole office had gone quiet again, watching him, wondering what all the panic in his voice was for. Telephones hung limply in wrists and loosely on shoulders. Even the topless swimsuit calendar models and the spread-eagled porno stars looked on as the market turned in Sean's favour.

And then it reached the offer price, even better, it passed it. Sean waited, his heart thumping in his ears. Higher, higher, go higher. He knew he was being greedy but he couldn't help it. He was in the money, IN THE MONEY. Come on, come on, go . . . let's see what you've got now, three, four, four-and-a-half points . . . He waited one second longer. The number hung on the screen as if dangling on a string. And then he just did it.

'FIVE YARDS, THREE YEARS, TWO YEARS FORWARD, FOUR AND THREE AND A HALF!'

The Box seemed to jump off the desk as everyone of Nobucorp's clients – all of them wined, dined and wanked-off compliments of the house – screamed: 'MIIIINNNNNE!'

Sean's phones flashed violently at him. One by one he took

their calls. It was over. He was safe. Fuck. He was a lot more than safe. He couldn't even think of the profit he'd made. It was undoubtedly the biggest trade of the year.

He did the right thing, the fair thing, sharing the spoils with as many of his clients as he could. Fifty million here, fifty million there. Everyone wanted a piece, and Sean gave it to them. Multiplying Nobucorp's commission several times in the process as well, of course.

When it was finally over and the trading floor resumed a more muted and admiring sense of business, Olly called him up.

'Well done, mate,' he said. 'I knew you could do it.'

'Fuck you, cunt,' Sean replied simply and hung up.

He beamed to himself. I love this job, he realized. You couldn't get further from the Darkness than this. Nothing like losing a million dollars to focus the mind, take you away from things too deep, away from the things that hurt. Sean became aware that he hadn't even thought about Candy in over an hour.

'Fucking hell, Sean,' Weasel turned and said between them. 'How long were you sitting on that trade?'

Sean shrugged his shoulders at him. 'Dunno. Seemed like for ever.'

'It was for ever, Sean,' Weasel said, looking more concerned than Sean had ever seen him. 'You can't do that, mate. You must never do that.'

'Fuck that, Weasel,' Sean replied. 'I just made Nobucorp a million fucking dollars on one trade. So put that in your pipe and smoke it.'

'Yeah,' Weasel said, suddenly beaming. 'You did. You fucking killed it. Let's go to the bogs and celebrate with a quick know-what-I-mean. . .' Weasel touched the side of one nostril.

'Yeah,' Sean replied. He could feel himself flying inside.

Then he heard Wanker Wong: 'Sean. In my office, now.'

'But I was just off to . . .' Sean tried.

'NOW!' Wong screamed.

'Shit,' Weasel said quietly. 'I think you're nicked, son. I think you're nicked.'

# Chapter Thirty-Two

As he approached, his stomach bunching with nerves, Michael realized he had already started writing the scene in his mind. He was acutely observational all of a sudden.

He noticed, for example, that the Witches' youthfully ageing features were actually the workings of make-up, eked out efficiently across the necessary parts. Lipstick lined the lips, not filled them, lending a full appearance only at first glance. Eyeliner sketched the edge of their eyelids, to much the same effect. Rouge was brushed lightly, one sweep no doubt, just to faintly hide the lines and fill their cheeks. All very efficient. All very eked out. All very poor.

They stared at him as he neared, muttering muted, twitches self-consciously held. Did that mean that they knew they were mad? He wanted to smile at them but he was too scared. The Witches. He wondered if they could cast a curse without saying anything, just by looking at him. Every inch of him wanted to flee. But he knew he couldn't, he knew he mustn't. This was it. His one chance. His big break.

Sean's friend at the *Hong Kong Herald*, David, had been well impressed by the pitch. Said he thought it might make a good feature for the *Sunday Magazine*. Said he'd often wondered himself about the only two white women beggars in Hong Kong.

And he loved the Witches angle. He couldn't have agreed more. They scared the shit out of him as well. Wouldn't go near them if he was paid, so he promised Michael one Hong Kong dollar per word, no more than two thousand words. Said he'd see about a permanent position at the paper – though it was hard these days, what with the Handover and having to speak Cantonese or Mandarin and it better being Chinese these days and all that.

Michael placed the two baguettes carefully down on the pavement between himself and the Witches, the sun burning through the shirt on his back, the sweat, trickling, as always, down his inner thighs. They stared at him, holding hands. Michael tried to think of something to say but there was nothing there. Instinctively, hating himself for doing it, he started to step back, away, all of a sudden scared that they might start screaming at him. *WHAT?!!! YOU THINK WE NEED THE CHARITY!! DO WE LOOK LIKE BEGGARS?*

After all, who was to say that his charity wasn't offensive? Especially since it wasn't charity. There was an ulterior motive at work. This wasn't altruism. Did that make it bad?

Three steps back and then, together, they spoke.

'Thank you,' they said.

For some reason it reassured Michael to know they were English. He slowly eased out of the humble hunch he'd found himself in as he'd crouched to place the sandwiches on the ground and stood up to look at them, relief dripping back into his system. Might they be normal? Might they be communicable?

He smiled.

'Thanks a lot,' they said again together, smiling back and leaning forward for the food. Michael watched them place the sandwiches in a communal bag that sat between their bodies and then look back at him.

'I . . .' Michael started and then felt the freeze reset. He forced himself to continue with the sentence, not sure what was about to come out of his mouth, all his rehearsed one-liners and self-introductions long since evaporated. 'I'm a writer.'

They stared back at him, eyes slightly narrowing.

'I'm a writer and I'd like to interview you for a piece in the *Hong Kong Herald Magazine*,' he blurted.

This time their eyes really narrowed. There was a long pause. There was the sound of exhaust as a bus passed down Ice House Street. Someone was singing opera in the rainforest canopy that sat in the space between the streets above, higher up on the Peak. It was morning still.

Then one of them, the one on the left (it was impossible to describe her any other way, they looked so identical) said: 'One thousand Hong Kong dollars, one hour.'

Well, at least there could be no confusion about it, was Michael's first thought. He was so relieved that there was an agreement, that the first hurdle on his path to journalistic success had been overcome, that he heard himself immediately replying, 'All right,' before understanding, too late, that he was being ripped off.

A thousand Hong Kong dollars! That was half the money he'd be getting for the story, assuming he only needed an hour to interview them adequately. Oh well, maybe they deserved it, he told himself. After all, they needed the money more than him. Maybe that was another reason he'd agreed so readily: a latent sense of guilt. After all, he was only doing this as an angle into a job. He *was* using them.

'Good,' the Right Witch said, and suddenly they were on their feet and saying together, dividing the sentence between themselves. 'Money in advance,' Right Witch said. 'Pay now,' Left Witch added.

Michael looked at them and felt his own eyes squinting a little. Was it necessary to be so caustic about it? He did feel like he was getting ripped off now, realizing that, somehow, whatever happened, they would get the better of this arrangement. Maybe they'd done this before, fleeced some other journalist. Did he really have an original piece? He told himself that he was too naive and they were too street for the negotiation to be any other way. He couldn't bear the idea that he didn't have a scoop and he promised himself that he wouldn't check.

'Half now,' he said, pleased that his bargaining mind was finally kicking into gear. 'Half after.'

'NO!' They both screeched at him and Michael jumped. 'ALL NOW OR NO INTERVIEW.' The words were mixed between them and he couldn't tell who had said which, but that didn't matter. He got the message. Seemed that they were Witches after all.

'All right,' he said, knowing they were in the more powerful position. He handed them the cash. Good job he'd been to the bank that day. 'But I want to record the conversation.'

They shrugged their shoulders at him and sat back down, preparing. It was a meaningless victory, less than Pyrrhic. Michael took out the tape recorder, an old school Sanyo that he'd borrowed from Candy's Mum and pressed Record and Play.

'OK, well, why don't we start with your names, shall we?' He said, almost jovially, like he was introducing the three of them to the technology: *Hello, Mr Recorder, we are . . .*

'Linda,' said Left Witch.

'Ruth,' said Right Witch.

'And your surname?' Michael said carefully.

'Next question,' they both said together.

Michael looked back at them and wondered what he'd get for his thousand Hong Kong. He knew he should have insisted on the half-now, half-after arrangement. Too late for that now.

'Errrm, OK. So . . . how long have you lived in Hong Kong?'

They both sighed at him. 'Seventeen years,' Linda said.

'Really?' Michael said, feigning fascination. He was using every trick he knew to draw them out. 'That's amazing.'

'Why?' Ruth said.

Michael was thrown. 'Err, I dunno. Guess you must have seen a lot of changes around here, that's all.'

They didn't reply.

'OK,' Michael restarted. 'Maybe you wouldn't mind me asking why you're homeless.'

Four eyes flashed. 'We're not homeless,' Ruth said with disgust.

'Oh?' Michael said, pleased he was finally getting something, however tiny, to go on.

'Christ,' Linda suddenly spouted venomously. 'You're so fucking stupid.'

Michael looked blankly back at her. 'I'm sorry.'

'Think we'd be homeless? You're so stupid,' Ruth added in confirmation.

She said stupid like *stoopid*, like a New Yorker or something. Michael tried another tack.

'Where are you from?'

They sneered before saying, together, 'England. Where do you think?'

'Yes, I figured that much. Where in England?'

'Oh,' Ruth said, almost as if she realized that, this time, she was the one being *stoopid*. 'Devon.'

They're all mad in Devon, in-breeds, Michael couldn't help automatically thinking to himself.

'Why did you come here, to Hong Kong?'

'My husband brought us here,' Linda replied.

Now we're getting somewhere, Michael thought, very pleased with himself. 'You're married?'

'No,' Linda replied.

'Divorced?'

'Widowed,' Linda said.

'Oh, I'm so sorry,' Michael replied obligatorily. He'd never felt comfortable extending apologies to the bereaved. Why should he be sorry? 'How did your husband die?'

'We killed him,' Ruth replied.

Michael felt his heart jump. He looked at them. They looked back at him, their eyes set like spirit-levels. They weren't joking.

'There was an accident?' Michael tried, knowing it was coming out wrong, that he sounded patronizing.

'No,' Linda said. 'We murdered him.'

'What?'

'Yes,' Ruth replied.

'How?'

'I shot him,' Linda said.

'And I cut him up,' Ruth added.

'And then we threw him in the harbour,' they said together.

'But why?'

'Because he cheated on me,' Linda said.

Michael didn't say anything. He didn't need to. Their story, *The Story*, had begun. As they talked, in sections, sometimes together, Michael began the writing. He knew that the article would have to start with the murder scene. It was the most dramatic piece of tension. He tried to direct his questions to the details of the murder. How precisely it happened, what the weather was like, how the scene was set, what the exact chronology of events was.

They weren't completely forthcoming but Michael didn't think that mattered. The notion of a joint murder, two twins conspiring, would hold the reader's attention, he knew that. It was enough of a frame into which he could fill the story of two lives: The Witches. How they went to prison, why they were released, into society, without any avenue by which to reintegrate, outcast and insane and now on the fringes of the street. There'd even be space for social commentary, an insight into Hong Kong expatriate life and what the story of these two women meant in the world. It was that good a peg. He'd have to check the facts, of course. But he didn't think they were lying. Why would they?

*You're so stoopid, so stoopid.*

The phrase kept cropping up, again and again and again, as he fired question after question, partly in disbelief at the fantastical nature of their lives and the way they had fallen from grace and from the affluent expatriate lives they had lived on the Peak. Love, betrayal and hate. Caught up in the claustrophobia of a hot, humid, colonial Hong Kong. Losing one's head in the heat. Or, in this case, two heads. The joint madness.

It was such a good story. All he needed now was a few pictures.

# Chapter Thirty-Three

The fish swam like zombies. Crammed in a tank, waiting for the slaughter. They mainly floated on their sides, eyes glazed over with a dull but partly reflective blue-grey film. They only shuddered to some semblance of life when they were chosen.

Maybe they knew, Sean thought to himself. Maybe they knew that they were here to be eaten and that their only hope was to look as unappetizing as possible, so that they'd never be selected. Not very likely. They probably were just as sick as they looked in their algae-infested, over-heated toilet water. That had been a scandal not long ago. The *Hong Kong Herald* had reported that the fish in these restaurants lived off the same water as the cisterns. The authorities had threatened to close them down. But they didn't.

Sean could hear the five lobsters that Candy's father had chosen screaming in the kitchen as they were dunked, alive of course, into pots of boiling water. After all, why dunk them dead? The meat had to be tender, Candy's father had grinned sickly at the waiter. Supposedly the screaming was just the sea-water trapped in their shells, steaming.

If truth be told, Sean hated this restaurant. The same fish restaurant Candy's parents always took her and her *friends* to, whenever celebration deserved it. And today it was Sean's twenty-seventh birthday. Candy's dad was treating them. Treating Sean and them all: Mikey, Sasha, Charlie, Ben, Big Nick, Katz, Jimmy, Jules, Sluffy, Muffy, Bee-bee, Lenny, Roo, Loo-loo, La-la . . . *How kind of you, Mr Newman,* Sean had said to him on the junk trip from the main island to Lamma.

But Mr Newman wasn't being kind. That much was abundantly obvious the moment he had turned his back on Sean in disgust as he had attempted to thank him. Mr Newman hated Sean. Sean knew it, Mr Newman knew it, everyone knew it. So why was he treating everyone to dinner? Simple. It was a matter of face. The oh-so Chinese Mr Newman treated his daughter and her friends to his wealth and beneficence (albeit his limited wealth and beneficence) whenever occasion merited it. Even though he wasn't Chinese, even if he was just an anally retentive Britisher gone native. That was simply the way in Hong Kong. Even so, he was damned if he had to be *nice* to the boy as well.

'Excuse me, Muriel, would you like some more wine?' Sean offered Candy's mum. He noticed that her long hair was going grey. Sean knew that half of Mr Newman's hatred for him came from her. He knew that she believed that he wasn't good enough for her daughter. And, although, unlike her husband, she was always overtly nice to him, Sean understood that she was an enemy.

'Oh, yes, Sean,' she said, momentarily turning to face him. Mrs Newman was talking to the female half of the table, seconding them for some society event. *It's going to be THE party of the year!!* she had shrilled. 'Thank you.'

Sean poured. 'Mr Newman?' he said gently, turning to his left.

Mr Newman didn't say anything. Unlike his wife he didn't

have a conversation to hold onto as a distraction or an excuse to not acknowledge Sean. He'd barely spoken to anyone all dinner. Sean could see that he despised them all. Why did his daughter have to have so many *gweilo* friends? Didn't she know she had to associate with the Chinese? How was she going to get on in Hong Kong without intermingling, without assimilating?

Without intermarrying, more like.

Sean could tell that Mr Newman wished he'd had sons instead of an only daughter. They'd tried for more but apparently there'd been complications with Candy's birth. Mrs Newman never conceived again. A son could forge a career. No daughter could make money, not real money. It simply wasn't feasible. Especially now that the Handover was just around the corner. Marriage, love – what a pair of wild cards to stake a future on, his daughter's future, *his* future.

'Mr Newman?' Sean tried again, quietly.

But the man, who had parted light brown hair, almost-boyish features and flat green eyes, just continued to look impassively out – beyond the open-air concrete terrace of the restaurant, past the low-lit jetties bobbing on the black water and across to Hong Kong Island itself, which sat on the horizon like a firework display frozen in time, an instant of light.

Eventually, Sean put the bottle down between them and less than three seconds later Mr Newman was picking it up and pouring himself a glass. Even Mikey, who hadn't believed Sean when he'd tried to explain just how much Mr Newman hated him, noticed the slight. Mikey twisted his eyebrows in sympathy at Sean. Sean could only smile and shrug his shoulders imperceptibly in reply. Sean also noticed Candy staring at her father, her eyes burning. For a terrible moment, he thought she was going to explode. He'd rarely seen her look so furious.

But Mr Newman acted like he didn't notice, or didn't care. Candy eventually flashed a glance at her mother, who also ignored her daughter, and eventually settled her eyes on Sean. 'I'm sorry,' she mouthed at him.

Sean shook his head at her slightly. He was glad that she hadn't forced a showdown. It wouldn't have helped. Best to be non-confrontational. The Asian way, and all that – even though there wasn't a single Chinese person except the Newmans at the table. Besides, it was his birthday. No point in making a scene.

But Sean couldn't help feeling depressed. He felt very trapped, like one of the fish in the fish tank. Hong Kong felt so painfully small to him now. This restaurant. They'd all been here a hundred times. And the energies: they were all just the same currents without an outlet. With nowhere to go they just kept circling, intensifying – like Mr Newman's hatred for him.

In the beginning, he'd tried to make Mr Newman like him. He'd explored every angle. Humour, flattery, charm, even gifts. The previous summer, knowing how much Mr Newman loved to gamble, Sean had managed to secure a private box through Nobucorp for the Happy Valley races. He'd invited the Newmans to a champagne breakfast before the day's excitement began. Only Candy and her Mum had shown – two hours late. Mr Newman had been called away on urgent business. On a Saturday. Yeah, right.

It didn't take long for Sean to figure out that the harder he tried to make Mr Newman like him, the more Mr Newman would hate him. There was nothing he could do about it. It was only ever going to get worse. Sean knew it. There was no point in fighting it any longer. The only reason he cared was because he knew that Mr Newman's hatred would ultimately trickle down onto and into the one person he did care about. Candy.

Even if she was being nice to him now, Sean knew that Candy would eventually go off him again. Why? Because her parents hated him. Because Sean wasn't Chinese. Because it was simply happening. Who knew why people fall out of love? It just happens sometimes, doesn't it?

Sean suddenly understood that the only way to break the cycle was to leave. But he knew he wouldn't. Sean would stay on in Hong Kong, with its misplaced sense of importance, and suffer the slights, bear all the hatreds. Why? Because he lived here now. He had a life. He had friends. He had a good job. Possibly

He was going to find out the following Monday if they were going to fire him. Wong had done an excellent job of screwing Sean. It was only because of Weasel that Sean hadn't been fired on the spot. He'd calculated just how much Sean had made the firm and chosen a suitable moment to call Head Office to tell them. Obviously they were impressed. Still, Sean had sat on a position and been caught doing it. That sort of thing couldn't go unpunished. Everyone knew that. He was under *review* now.

Part of him hoped they did fire him. Then he'd *have* to leave. He was suffocating here. They all were. Just like the fish in the fish tank. Crammed in on top of each other, not enough water between them to breathe. The air was strangling them, strangling all of them – slowly, surely. If Sean did get the sack on Monday, he'd come to. He knew it.

But it would only be brief, the living, the moving. And while it would be a relief to be removed from the warm, stifling, deadening water of Hong Kong like that, ultimately he'd be revitalized because he'd be fighting to stay alive in the cold killing air of the outside. He'd shake and flip and feel the final moment within him. Leaving would be futile. Because while Hong Kong was suffocating, it was the place he'd found himself caught in. It was the only thing sustaining him.

If he was ever to leave Hong Kong without Candy, there'd be only one eventuality. The Blackness. It was inevitable. It was hovering, looming, lurking in places, waiting. And if it was to finally settle, it would kill. He knew that. He couldn't leave Hong Kong. The Blackness was the world outside the tank, it was the world beyond Hong Kong. It was the customer waiting at the table, choosing its next victim to eat. It was God. And it wasn't benevolent. It wouldn't choose Sean from the fish tank only to set him free into the cool, open expanse of the ocean, his rightful place, his home. No. Because Sean had been caught in its net long ago. And placed in the tank. With everyone else here. Waiting. Waiting for the moment when the Blackness built up an appetite and decided to eat and pointed its finger and chose Sean. And Sean knew, the day that moment arrived, there would be killing and screaming. And it wouldn't just be water steaming.

# Chapter Thirty-Four

Munkie and Puffy were sharing birthdays. They'd organized two junks and everyone was on them now, getting wasted. Girls interlocked legs as they lounged on the upper deck, the sun making their skin shine. All of them wearing dark wraparound glasses and floral bikinis. The boys all shouted and competed to deliver booze, drugs, funny limelight jokes so that everyone would look at them or crowd them or make them look like they belonged.

No one really belonged.

Michael was having a hard time of it. Couldn't seem to penetrate the moment, get on top of his self-confidence. Maybe it was the spliff. He was feeling paranoid. He couldn't decide whether he was on the 'right' junk or the 'wrong' junk. They were parked next to each other in Sheung Wan Bay. He could have swum to the other one. Sean was on the other one. So was Candy. He could see that Sean had his arm round Candy's waist. Three people were all laughing as he greeted some lanky-looking bloke. 'Willage McWillables!'

Names. Michael couldn't remember anyone's name. Maybe that was the dope's fault. Short-term memory loss. But it didn't make sense. Michael should have known a lot of these names. They weren't short term. He knew 'that' person from Leeds, and 'that' one, too. Those three girls he remembered had gone to Edinburgh, but Jesus, he didn't know what they were called. Why couldn't he think? At least everyone could be 'darling' 'babe' 'mate'. That was one thing to be grateful for. The assumption of intimacy. Even with those he'd just met.

*Mikeeee, baby, how are you, darling? This is Jojo and Cob. They know Big Nick and Top Red really well. Just got here . . .* Hand shakes, mutual beams. Then their names – instantly gone. Just like that. Could have taken the opportunity to ask again and then made some mental log: *Jojo sounds like Mojo – I've got my Mojo working, Cob equals corn on the cob – right, got it, thank you very much, I'll remember you now and won't be so embarrassed about forgetting your name that I won't be able to talk to you later.*

But things moving fast, too fast. Got to be socially sharp at these parties. Focused, working, thinking, remembering, not getting sidelined, left out of the action, perceived as dull. Never pull that way. And wasn't that the objective? To get lucky? No one would snog the stoned Joey in the corner who looked too afraid to talk to anyone. Had to work, work hard, not forget and still get mash up, still look like you could partieeeee . . .

Could Michael leave? Could he just accept that he'd got too drunk too quickly – he might be sick later, that would be embarrassing – and leave and try again at another party and make sure the next time he remembered everyone's name and didn't fuck up and embarrass himself in front of a lot of people like he had just now.

'Hey, Benny boy, pass us the skins,' he'd said, but only because he'd wanted to look like he had something to say and something to do because he'd been standing in the corner all by himself for more than twenty minutes and he couldn't spend the whole afternoon that way looking like a twat. He didn't know anyone on this boat – no one he could trust.

The Olympic-looking man hadn't answered.

'Benny, Benji, Big bastard – give us the skins for fuck sakes.'

That had got his attention. The broad shoulders had turned round and held up the rizlas, sneering across the lower deck of the junk where there was Pimms and champagne and lots of beer, some wine and crisps and lots of people everywhere – they could all hear.

'Mikey, sort your fucking life out you cock, my name isn't Ben.'

'I know, just give us the skins.' Michael had recovered, he'd thought, quite well.

Everyone listening in now. Especially the girls, one of them, Tatty, could have been a model; Mikey quite fancied her, she had a tiny arse and her breasts were swelling under the fabric of her bikini so you could almost see the edge of a pink nipple aureole.

'What's my name?'

'Ha ha, very funny. Hand them over and stop being a nonce.'

'You don't know, do you?'

Michael's heart had started to race then, his face flushing with embarrassment, why couldn't he remember, he'd known this guy for three weeks at least and seen him around repeatedly but it didn't make any difference because he couldn't remember for the life of him and he was going to look like a fuckwit now *fur-shur*.

Maybe it wouldn't have mattered if people didn't like this guy so much. Girls fancied him. No one would like Michael, fancy him, if he couldn't even remember this guy's name – Michael wasn't one of *them*. He wasn't really invited. He'd just come. There wasn't any such thing as Not Fucking Invited. Everyone was always invited. He didn't know Munkie but he'd met Puffy.

Who cared anyway?

Michael hadn't said anything. He'd just grinned inanely, looking, feeling, being a twat.

'It's Marco, you prick,' the guy had said, hurling the packet of skins, which flew through the air and twirled in a light-weight paper way making it hard to catch. It had eventually ended up bouncing off Michael's forearm and onto the floor, so to add to the humiliation he'd had to bend down and pick it up like there was some sort of physical submission as well as a social one, and as he stood back up he saw that all the girls were talking to each other and giggling (probably at Michael), and then the guy had said something snide and that was when Michael knew they really were laughing at him and he was about to come out with some funny retort but real-ized as the words took shape in his brain that he'd forgotten whathisname's name again.

Shit.

Could he get off? Had to get off. He couldn't get off. He was trapped. Six more hours to go at least, they hadn't even had lunch and then there was the whole afternoon planned, the drinking would go on until late night, someone had brought acid, Jesus, that would make things scary. Michael wanted to leave. He was desperate. Had to get off this boat, sneak away, no one would miss him, it would have been so much easier.

He was finding it hard to breathe.

# Chapter Thirty-Five

It was fancy dress. Barbecue on the roof, a makeshift bar in the flat. Loud music. One girl no one had ever seen before had shown up. She was a dark little minx, dressed in a Brazilian carnival outfit, tight little tits on a sharp waist, dark bobbed hair and a wicked, filthy grin. No one knew where she'd come from but the boys weren't asking. A welcome addition to the usual conveyor belt, as far as they were concerned. It was the girls that were talking. Michael watched them all sneering and twitching and judging and sizing up and looking not very impressed in the slightest.

Not everyone was invited but they came anyway.

Who was she?

Maybe it had been the way she'd gone straight up to Alex and started flirting outrageously right from the very beginning. Where did she get the gall? Didn't she know that Alex had been going out with Sophie for three years now? Sophie wasn't at the party, so all the girls had to defend her honour – right? What the hell was Alex thinking?

No one could stop looking when they started grinding together in one corner, too drunk by then to really care who was watching. It was the rum punch. There was cocaine going round.

The girls huddled closer together in one corner and watched, forming their strategic attack. Michael could hear their shrieks of outrage desperately trying to disguise themselves as whispers. Gossip, sneer, bitch, kill. They managed to make a whole half of the apartment feel arctic.

Someone, it might have been Little Nick, eventually went up to Alex to warn him while the hard body left for the toilet.

'Mate, you all right?'

'Course.'

'Just wanted to check. People are talking.'

'Let them.'

'Cool man. That's cool. Just wanted you to know. Sophie might not be too happy.'

'That's my business.'

Little Nick had just nodded. Who was he to stand in the way of this guy's good time? Meanwhile the girls stood in the corner and came up with curses.

Hubble, bubble, toil and trouble.

Michael could see all their teeth moving.

When the little minx eventually returned, Michael watched Alex walk past the girls, who were all bitching, and take the girl by the hand and walk with her down the long narrow corridor and into one of the bedrooms, closing the door.

They didn't come out again.

The girls in the gang opened up the forum. Not feeling the need to just gossip among themselves, they spread the word as Alex and the minx fucked each other senseless down the hall. The barbecue had gone out, some people leaving now, no one had really eaten, there'd been too much cocaine.

*Poor Sophie. Poor, poor Sophie.*

*Men are shits.*

*Who does that little bitch think she is?*

*Do you know her?*

*Who invited her?*

*Poor Sophie. It's just too awful.*

*What will happen when she finds out?*

*Someone will have to tell her.*

*She'd never forgive us if we kept it from her and she found out.*

*Poor, poor Sophie.*

The party went on. As if *they* could have a good time too. Only difference was, they wouldn't have to *pay*, like Alex would be made to pay. He'd regret it in the end. The gang of girls would make sure of that. He'd wish he hadn't betrayed his girlfriend in front of all her mates, he'd wish he'd stayed with them and had a good time at the party and just had fun, fun, fun. They were all watching. No one could do just what they wanted, you know.

Who the hell did he think he was?

Michael occasionally looked down the corridor and wondered what manner of heaven was occurring behind the closed, locked door.

Samba!

# Chapter Thirty-Six

Lan Kwai Fong. Pint. Five gulps and then gone. Hard day at work. Top buttons undone, Windsor knots loosened as part of the uniform for the casual corporation career. No one would actually stay in these jobs. No one would actually keep this money. They only made enough to spend, they didn't have enough to invest, to make a life. Life was all about disposable income and the disposing of it. Designer suits and expensive jewellery.

Another pint. Get them in. Drink it fast. Gulp, gulp, gulp. Bitter always the easiest to swallow. One girl, Michael couldn't remember her name, laughing too loudly. Their eyes met. She wasn't attractive.

Someone told a story and then they went to the next bar, piece of pizza on the way, couldn't be bothered to sit down at one of those crappy plastic tables waiting for fast Thai/Indonesian medley food that only took five minutes to cook and one minute to eat, a lot of it going down the front of your shirt. Lots of laughing now, bring your pint, don't be stupid, Michael's shoulder brushed the girl's. What was her name? Who was he with? He couldn't remember, even as he looked at them.

Tequila slammers at the next bar, the first ones lurching,

the next four tasting sweet and even like they might be fun. Michael swayed to the toilet, a tiny room the size of a cistern with piss all over the seat and no loo paper. The girl he didn't fancy squeezed her way past him as he stumbled out.

Let's go to B-52's in Wanchai someone said, so they all piled into taxis, which were easy to hail because the drivers always picked up *gweilos* at this time of night they were so easy to rip off when they were pissed. They circled Lan Kwai Fong like sharks. The girl and Michael sat next to each other in one cab, their legs touching. She was wearing grey trousers to hide her fat legs.

They couldn't get into B-52's because it was Ladies' Night and there were only two women between eight of them so they went to Slap Harry's, which also had a Ladies' Night on, but when they walked in it was full of men and only three or four girls, probably whores, ten guys all dancing round each of them, a couple of really ugly women sitting all by themselves at the bar, one guy climbed up on a stool. He started singing 'Three Lions', the Euro '96 anthem.

On the dance floor, Michael kissed the girl and started squeezing one of her tits crudely. It was too late to ask her name.

American servicemen in Village People uniforms and Popeye hats were very large in white but someone had said something stupid and some sort of violence had ensued and then someone fell, smacking the girl in the back and so she'd fallen forward into Michael and as they'd landed in the wet filth of the dance floor, mud all over them now, she'd said maybe they should leave and Michael thought that maybe he'd be able to fuck her if he concentrated.

It was pissing down but they managed to get a cab.

Not thinking, Michael realized. He had not been thinking

when he'd agreed to go to her place because now there was no way out. He couldn't remember her name and he was trapped because he'd just tried to fuck her and it hadn't worked because the condom had killed what little sensation he could feel and she was trying to cosy up to him now and her affection was making his skin crawl.

She told him about how she'd been waiting for this. He closed his eyes and pretended to be asleep until the room started spinning so fast he had to get up but he didn't make it in time and he ended up tearing the toilet seat off as he puked violently into the bowl where he could see crap streaking the bottom. He fell asleep.

# Chapter Thirty-Seven

Michael was watching *Jaws*. The government-run Oyster channel planned on showing 1, 2 and 3 – one for each day of the week remaining – because an eighty-one-year-old lady had just been attacked by a shark that had somehow managed to get through the protection net at Repulse Bay. The pictures of her half-eaten body dragged up the beach by onlookers had been on the front page of all the Chinese-language newspapers. The English-language newspapers, like the *Hong Kong Herald*, had carried the pictures on page three – you know, for the sake of decency.

Michael was considering a 'review' for the following morning edition along the lines of: *With terror TV like this, you'd be better off in the water*, then a pedantic ramble about the small-minded mentality of Hong Kong government officials and the absolute, Armageddon-like interpretation of every misfortune – outbreaks were epidemics, the stock market was either booming or busting, and all sharks, of course, were Jaws – before smoothly segueing into the evil madness that was US foreign policy.

Indeed, turning the TV review pages into his own personal diatribe against the world and all its flaws was Michael's small rebellion against the paper that had refused him a meaningful position, even after his Witches piece – which had been such a success the paper was syndicating it out to newspapers throughout Asia. And without paying him extra! It was *theirs* to sell, they had said. And all Michael had got out of it was a measly thousand Hong Kong dollars, minus the money he'd spent developing the photos. Michael had made more money playing Spot the Cockroach with Sean.

Oh, but he'd also earnt himself a *job*, if you could call doing the TV reviews a job. It was hardly the launch into international journalism he'd been hoping for. But that was the other thing the paper had told him. They couldn't give out news desk positions to people who couldn't speak Cantonese. Not any more. Not with the Handover approaching.

Still, he was learning to quite enjoy his position, especially now that his column had attracted the attention of a small cult of colonial followers and a tiny measure of fame on the island. He was *funny*, they'd told him. Not that the editors at the *Hong Kong Herald* noticed the attention. After all, who on earth read the TV reviews? Certainly no one respectable.

Outside it was raining. Hard. The clouds were hovering darkly just beyond the barred windows of the thirty-fifth floor cigarette box-sized apartment off Hollywood Road. This was where Michael was living now, with Jamie and Roo – two relatively new additions to the gang (Michael had no idea what or where the connection was – the public school network probably).

Jamie and Roo were the type of people who spent so much time with one another, they'd even started to look like each other. They were often mistaken for brothers. They both had dirty blond hair that somehow parted in exactly the same way even though neither of them ever brushed it. Their eyes, despite being different colours, looked similar because early laughter lines marked their faces in exactly the same way. Maybe because they listened to all the same jokes. And their mouths wore the exact same expression: a kind of smirk that hinted at an innuendo that was never spoken, an in-joke that gave Michael the impression they were communicating telepathically.

But even though he couldn't help feeling like a spare wheel at their place (shouldn't he and Sean be together?) Michael kept telling himself he finally had a proper place to live now. The important thing was that he get going with His Life in Hong Kong, he had felt far too much like The Unwanted Guest at Candy's house. Even so, he found his accommodation depressing. The place was a pit, much worse than any of the student houses in Leeds, mainly because the heat and humidity made any leftover mess fester. And there was lots of leftover mess. The kitchen sink was filled with Ragu-coated pans balancing on strands of pasta (that remained from a cooking adventure three months earlier), the fridge was constantly empty (with the exception of a single cockroach no one had ever had the energy to remove) and the bathroom was so small Michael had to shower with one foot on the edge of the loo.

Michael had long since concluded that Roo and Jamie's flat was even more disgusting than Sean's place – if that was possible. And it was definitely much smaller. Only now did Michael realize that Sean wasn't being ironic when he referred to his place as the Mansion. After all, his flat had three bedrooms and it was that much bigger than most other flats Michael had seen in Hong Kong. Plus Sean paid for a cleaner once a month. Roo and Jamie spent all their spare funds on nosebag.

Christ, Michael wished Sean hadn't given the spare room to Charlie.

Michael looked again at the sachet lying open on the coffee table between him and the TV. It was there from the previous night. Roo and Jamie did coke most nights, often in front of the TV. On the weekends they did Es. Sometimes Michael joined in, most of the time he didn't. He simply didn't have their stamina. So many members of the gang, especially the peripheral people, seemed able to take unlimited amounts of drugs and still operate. Paranoid, delusional, neurotic – they were all of those things, but they still had jobs, they still got up in the morning. Roo worked at the retailer Beijing Bang and Jamie was in TV.

The sound from *Jaws* filtered back in as Quinn broke into his sea shanty about 'A fair Spanish lady.'

Michael felt a little sick. Then, out of sheer boredom, he reached across, hating himself, and aimlessly started to rack up two thick lines. The phone warbled. Michael snapped it off its cradle, grateful for the interruption (God must have been watching, he thought to himself).

'Hello,' he said with proud sobriety.

No answer. Michael could hear breathing down the end of the line.

'Hello,' he said again. 'Who is this?'

Michael thought he could discern a faint sniff. Then: 'Can we meet?'

It was Sean.

'Errr . . .. yeah, sure mate. What's going on?'

More silence.

'Meet me in Murray's. You know where it is?'

'Yeah, think so.'

Another sniff.

'Sean? Are you all right?'

'She ended it.'

'What? Again?' But as he said the words, Michael knew that the line was already dead.

# Chapter Thirty-Eight

Michael decided to take the Escalators down to Murray's in Central. He couldn't get a cab because it was pissing down. The rain bounced off the tarmac and travelled up his trouser leg as he ran down the street, skipping and shimmying his way under shop awnings. By the time he'd covered the hundred or so metres to the sheltered walkway that went from the top of Mid-Levels all the way down the hill into Central, the bottoms of his trousers were soaked through.

He leapt onto the slow-moving steps, shook his shoulders off like a dog and caught his breath. He was sweating. The rain was very loud under the Perspex shelter. Buildings that staggered their way down the hill seemed to be travelling upwards on their own separate conveyor belt as Michael travelled almost imperceptibly down into town.

The Escalators. They had seemed so amazing to Michael when he'd first used them. They were Hong Kong's equivalent of the commute, at least for all the twenty- and thirty-something *gweilos* with their respectable incomes and corporate titles that far exceeded their actual work experience. As he descended, Michael considered how, in some ways, the Escalators felt synonymous with the occupational leapfrog Hong Kong offered young white Western people living in Mid-

Levels. In the Snakes and Ladders game of Life, the Escalators were a moving ladder that took Mid-Levellers quickly and effortlessly to wherever they needed to go:

*Want to be in TV?* You can be a producer.

*Want to be a banker?* We'll put you in charge of trading.

In these pre-Handover days, young *gweilos* (Michael being perhaps the only possible exception) were enjoying the privilege of immediate promotion, even those that weren't rich or 'from here'.

The only catch? They had to live in Hong Kong, which, like the Escalators, hadn't seemed a bad prospect at all at first (in fact, it had seemed positively groovy: an exotic archipelago on the doorstep of Asia? Ace! A ten-minute assisted-walk commute into work? Bonus!).

Until you were actually doing it.

Like a lot of its mirrored buildings, Michael had quickly come to realize that Hong Kong was all sheen and no substance. The place was about one thing and one thing only: money. It was shallow, it was empty, and, worst of all, it was boring. The music scene was barren. No bands ever came to Hong Kong to play. New York, London, Tokyo, Paris, Berlin, Beijing even . . . all of these places were must-gos. No worldwide tour billing was complete without these cities. Hong Kong? Yeah, thanks, we'll skip that one. The same was true for art. How often would a collection of Picasso's work or anybody else's for that matter end up in Montreal or Sydney or Amsterdam? Hong Kong didn't even have a museum to put the paintings in, for Christ sakes!

Michael had argued extensively with Candy about this. She said that there was plenty of art in Hong Kong. All one had to do was go to the galleries. She didn't seem to get Michael's hang-up on museums – or rather, the distinct lack of them.

She said Hong Kong discovered art in the mainland, liberated it, even, from the authoritarianism of a Communist government. Michael said that that was nothing more than trading, just like everything else Hong Kong did. At the end of the day, it all came down to money.

Maybe it wasn't Hong Kong that was the problem. Maybe it was Michael. Maybe it was Michael's friends. Maybe it was the tiny expatriate world he'd fallen into here. Here he was on the doorstep of the world's most populous nation and, so far, the only people he'd met were white. He told himself that it wasn't Hong Kong's fault. If he spoke Cantonese he could integrate, make Chinese friends, listen to Canto pop, watch martial arts movies, appreciate the fruits of this barren rock. But deep down he didn't believe that. Michael understood that Hong Kong had nothing to offer him. Even if he did learn Cantonese and made Chinese friends, he knew that he'd always be their token *gweilo* friend. Hatreds ran too deep here for him to overcome them. It was just like Leeds. The *gweilos* hated the Chinese because the Chinese hated them. The only option was to huddle together and sneer at the other side. It was the only way to be safe, to be strong.

Even so, the tiny colonial society Michael had fallen into only ever felt as if it was getting smaller with each passing day. The warmth and general friendliness Michael had experienced during his initiation to the city now sat on top of him. It felt as if his entire social life was spoken for. Every party he went to was pre-arranged by some member of the gang and everyone (with a capital E) was always there. There was no such thing as Not Fucking Invited in Hong Kong. Part of sticking together involved taking part – whether you liked it or not. There wasn't space in this small, isolated society for individualism, for standing apart, for non-comformity. The most important thing was that they stick together.

After just two months on the island, Michael was losing. He was becoming just like the rest of them, just like Sean and Charlie had said he would. The signs were all there. The skyscrapers no longer impressed him, he just felt hemmed in by them. The Chinese irritated him enormously now. Hong Kong seemed incredibly crowded, it took ages to get anywhere. The oppressively humid weather depressed him. No. Worse. It offended him. It was so invasively wet. And just as all the good things about the Escalators had seemed to represent all the good things about Hong Kong, they, too, now represented the bad.

Michael often found himself furious with the heat. *Why couldn't they put fans in these fucking escalator shelters?* He found he could hate the Chinese with an irrational passion. *Why can't they get it through their thick heads to stand on the right so that I can pass?* He'd also find himself spitting at them, with no small measure of irony on his part. The Chinese clearly didn't consider spitting repulsive, so surely they wouldn't mind if Michael gobbed on them, right? He usually only victimized the old hags frying tofu in woks of fat who sat beside the Escalators and sold it as food to Chinese commuters. He found the intentional stench of *Chou Tofu* offensive, not unlike urine burning, so he figured they deserved it most. He also figured (correctly) that the old biddies wouldn't do anything. What could they do? Chase him? Throw a wok of fat at him? They couldn't afford to waste it. The peasants.

Thus, like the entire island itself, something as benign and enviable as an Escalator commute into work, standing in the air, the light and an orderly line, not crushed like cattle into an underground train or a bus, had quickly become a loathsome experience. Michael couldn't see how anyone could bear it in Hong Kong. He wasn't going to last six months. More to the point, Michael couldn't see how anyone could bear themselves after six months in Hong Kong. He wasn't like this. He wasn't a racist. This wasn't him. He didn't want to be a small-minded expatriate that knew nothing about the Chinese except how to hate them and have them hate him. It wasn't so much that he hated Hong Kong, it was more that he hated the person the place was turning him into.

He could leave now, he supposed, but where would he go? Back to London? It was too much like an admission of failure. More importantly there was Sean. Michael's allegiance to him meant more than his own failure to happily exist here. The only thing that mattered was that Michael be near Sean.

He started trotting down the Escalators, two steps at a time, in a hurry now to rescue his best friend (especially since the opportunity had finally presented itself) from suicide, from Candy, from his job, from Hong Kong, and from the big black hole that had somehow become his life.

After all, he owed Sean that much.

# Chapter Thirty-Nine

'Hello?'
Marland stared into the darkness and let the silence hang, breathing, so that she'd know he was still there.

'Hello? Who is this?'

The telephone booth was very hot under the stairs that ran up and round the main hallway of Holland House. Marland had cringed as the phone had clickety clacketied its way through the numbers, echoing all around. Making so much noise. He'd have to whisper. It was nearly three in the morning.

'Hello,' he whispered.

'Who is this?' The woman's voice came back.

Marland looked round, his eyes well adjusted to the darkness now. He could see the graffiti on the corkboard and the plywood walls. Blue biro and red felt tip pen.

*Ipswich FC*
*Mr Crewe*
*went to the loo*
*with Benny Lemanu*
*the big fat poo*
*Oxenbury is a Bender*
*Beware the Bummer Man!!*

'Can I speak to Clarke please?'

'Who is this?'

'Please, it's very important.' Marland was holding the door to the telephone booth shut tight. Sometimes it swung open by itself. The latch was broken from boys barging in. They often did that when someone was taking too long. They were only allowed to make telephone calls after Prep and that meant there was only an hour for everyone to have a go before bedtime. And that was if you were a senior. Juniors had to go bed straight after homework, no telephone calls at all. And they were the ones that needed to make the calls the most. Marland was a junior. Baxter was a senior. So was Clarke. But he wasn't here.

'This is Marland, Mrs Clarke.'

'Michael?'

'Yes, Mrs Clarke.'

'Do you know what time it is?'

'Can I speak to Sean . . . please?'

'It's three o'clock in the morning.'

'I know, I'm sorry.'

'Can you call again tomorrow?'

'No.'

Silence. Marland waited. He hated himself for doing this. He felt very nervous. If he was caught then Fishface Haddock would take him into his study again. The Bummer Man. Marland couldn't stop his leg from shaking.

'Wait a minute,' Mrs Clarke said, not unkindly.

The phone started beeping so Marland rushed to grab a ten pence piece from the pile he had been collecting by selling his tuck. He thrust it in the slot. The coin crashed and banged its way through the mechanics of the big box phone. The receiver felt hot against Marland's ear. He waited.

Eventually Clarke came on the line.

'Hello?' he said, groggy, tired, not there.

Marland didn't say anything, couldn't say anything.

'Hello?' Clarke said again, and then quickly, 'There's no one there, Mum.'

'Fishface Haddock is the Bummer Man,' Marland managed to blurt out.

'Michael?' It was the first time in ages that Clarke had called Marland Michael, that anyone from school had referred to him by his Christian name. It made Marland happy. 'Is that you?'

'Fishface is the Bummer Man, Sean. He's the Bummer!' Tears started to rush then and Marland had to pinch his leg through his cotton pyjamas (his blue ones, his favourite ones, their favourite) and grip his knee to stop. Mustn't cry, must not cry.

'What?'

'Please, Sean, you have to help me. Last night Baxter sent me out to the Elms and then Fishface caught me and then he took me into his study and he slippered me and then . . .'

BLEEP! BLEEP! BLEEP! . . .

Marland snapped another ten pence piece off the top of the phone and pushed it into the slot, his hands shaking, glancing into the cold night shadows hovering in the hallway just beyond the crack in the door. The coin slammed and it crashed and it echoed all round. Soon he'd be caught.

'Sean? Sean? Are you there? Did you hear me? Fishface is the Bummer Man!'

'It's OK, Michael, it's OK. I'm here. Just hang on a minute.' There was a small pause and then the sound of Clarke's voice, more distant. 'Michael's homesick, Mum. His Nan died.'

There was the sound of Mrs Clarke's voice and then a 'Yes' from Sean and then the words, '. . . turn the lights off when you're finished.'

'Okay, Mum. Thanks.' A pause and the sound of a door closing. 'Baxter!' Clarke suddenly hissed into the phone. 'Baxter sent you out to the Elms!'

'Yes.'

'I'll kill him!'

'And then Fishface caught me and he slippered me and then he, he . . .'

'Fishface! That bastard! Are you all right?'

'I don't know,' Marland said.

'Don't worry, Michael. I'll get them. I swear to you, I'll get them.'

'How?' Marland sniffed, already feeling better.

'I dunno. I'll think of something.'

'I don't want you to get into more trouble, Sean,' Marland said. 'I don't want you to get expelled. Please don't get expelled.'

'I won't. This time I'll wait. I'll get them when they're not looking. They won't even know it was me.'

'Really?' Marland said, not believing his own ears.

'Yeah.'

'And you're not going to get expelled?'

'No.'

'What are you going to do? Can I help?'

'I'm not sure yet. I have to think.'

'You could get Baxter in a rugby match. Kick him or something,' Marland suggested. 'Really hard, in the head.'

'Yeah, maybe. Or we could get him out of school, away from the teachers, when he's going home or something, so we won't get caught,' Clarke said, running with the fantasy. 'I've got my brother's knife . . .'

BLEEP! BLEEP! BLEEP! . . .

Marland grabbed another ten pence piece and slotted it. Crash, bang, ching, clink, click . . .

'Sean?'

'I'm here,' he said calmly.

'Why don't we just run away?' Marland said then, realizing as he did so that he was thinking out loud, that the thought had never occurred to him before but now that he was speaking to Clarke it all made sense. 'Let's just forget Baxter. I just want to get away.'

'No,' Clarke snapped and then, more softly, 'No. I'll be back soon. Next week. Then I'll take care of everything. You'll never have to worry about Baxter or Fishface again. OK?'

Marland felt relief rush over him. He knew that Clarke would be able to help.

'Promise?'

'Promise.'

'Hurry, Clarke.'

'I will, Marland. Just hang on. I'm going to take care of everything.'

BLEEP! BLEEP! BLEEP! . . .

Marland squeezed another ten pence piece that he already had in his hand into the phone.

'Sean? Sean? Sean?' Marland said, but the line was dead. Marland didn't dare call again. It didn't matter. Clarke would be coming back soon. He'd know what to do. He'd take care of everything. Just like he said. He'd get them. All Marland had to do was hang on. Just hang on and wait. He collected the last of his ten pence pieces and held them tight in his hand, gently replacing the receiver. Then he crept out of the telephone booth, the door creaking, and tip-toed back to the dorm, back to his bed. Everyone was asleep.

# Chapter Forty

Murray's was a black bar. Charcoal black – the kind of black that carried an air of professional sophistication. Offices and suits and computer keyboards – that kind of black. Enormous tinted windows filtered out the light beyond them and turned the whole world grey, which was exactly what it was since it was still pissing down, but Michael figured (correctly) that the tint might have had much the same effect on a clear blue sky. He also got the feeling that no one walking past would be able to see him, sitting in a red leather seated booth by the window drinking a beer. For some reason, that made him feel secure: obscured and concealed. Maybe that's why Sean liked it here, he thought to himself: another dark den for him to hide in.

What was Sean hiding from?

Michael was about to get up and call Sean (he was fifteen minutes late) when he spotted him walking quickly into the bar. He paused underneath a television screen hanging from the ceiling showing American baseball, yellow and red lights from a pin-ball machine beside him thudding dully against his dark suit. He scanned the bar and quickly fixed his eyes on Michael and then flashed a smile that looked customarily pleased, but which also seemed to hide depths of despair – or that might just have been Michael's projection. He walked over, sweeping a hand through his hair, and slid himself into the booth beside Michael.

'What are you drinking?' Sean asked.

'Lager.'

Sean sniffed. A coke sniff? A weepy sniff? A snort of approval because lager was Sean's kind of drink? Michael couldn't tell. Sean waved his arm at no one in particular and twisted his head like an owl, hoping to catch the attention of a waitress.

'How's work?' Michael began, knowing that he had to tread carefully with Sean, resist the temptation to dive straight in.

'OK,' Sean said. 'Thailand is starting to go to shit. I reckon the peg will break.'

'Really?' Michael replied, not knowing what he was talking about.

Sean didn't say anything.

'How was your review?' Michael restarted.

'Fine. They've offered me a job in Japan – good money – but it's just to break me and Wanker Wong up. Politics, you know.' Michael looked at him, nodding slightly, interested to know if Sean would consider taking the offer. That was when Sean said: 'Candy dumped me.'

Michael paused for a moment, trying to think of the best thing to say. All he could come up with was: 'When?'

'About an hour ago.'

'Why?'

'Dunno.'

'Oh come on, course you know.'

'No. I don't know,' Sean said, slightly exasperated.

'Well what did she say?'

'She said that there was no point in us seeing each other any more and that it would be better if we were just friends.'

'Wow. After five years, she gave you that shit?'

'Yup.'

'Shit, Sean, I'm sorry, mate. You don't deserve that.'

Sean didn't say anything for a while. He just looked past Michael, through the dim windows, into the pissing rain. Then he said: 'Do you know something?' It wasn't a question. It was an accusation. Do *you* know something?

'What do you mean?'

'I mean, do you know something I don't?'

'Like what?' Michael said, immediately feeling the pinch of playing dumb. Did Michael know something? Well, yes, he knew some things. He knew that he had fancied Candy from the moment he'd laid eyes on her. He knew that maybe he even loved her, but that his friendship with Sean had long since eliminated her from his list of attainable desires and that, nevertheless, he knew that he wanted her now, still, more than ever. Michael also knew that Sean's problems with Candy had indirectly rekindled some of the home fires that had been smouldering and burning in his soul like some private, living hell and that maybe that was even why he'd come to Hong Kong in the first place. Not for Sean. Not for his career. But for Candy.

'Like if she's having an affair.'

'An affair? With who?'

'What about that Bob bloke?'

'Bob? Naaaah.'

'I mean I know she's snogged him,' Sean said softening. 'I don't mind about that. We did come to an agreement.'

'What sort of an agreement?'

'We said it was all right to snog other people.'

'Really?' Michael replied, his interest piqued. 'Why did you do that?'

'She said she wanted to have some harmless fun, and I think I probably wanted to as well.'

'Well then, you're a fucking idiot, aren't you?' Michael piled in with overblown morality. Truth was, he was a little pissed off now to discover that Candy had been let off her leash like that. There was something about Candy being Sean's that had been bearable for Michael. He could effectively pigeon-hole her that way, place her in a box. Candy equalled his best mate's girlfriend, therefore she was off-limits. And it had taken him ages to master his jealousy of the fact that Candy was with Sean and not with him. Her being a free entity, however, effectively put him back at square one. Now he'd have to watch her go off with someone else, prefer someone else to him, effectively reject him all over again.

Sean stared angrily at Michael, as if he could read these thoughts, and Michael shifted uncomfortably under his stare. He'd rarely seen Sean angry before, with him in any case. He was usually so gentle with Michael, always more interested in cracking jokes at his expense and having a good time. If he was upset about something, Sean usually just shut his mouth and kept himself to himself. He rarely showed emotion. He didn't like confrontation. Usually.

'You always fancied her, didn't you?' Sean said. Again it wasn't a question, it was an accusation.

Michael felt his face flush. He didn't say anything. He felt embarrassed, caught out, exposed for the Judas that he was. Then he felt suddenly angry. Angry because Sean was angry with him. Angry because he'd been there first, he'd seen Candy first and yet *he* was the one playing second fiddle. Angry because he'd been biting his tongue for five long years, for Sean's benefit, for Sean and Candy's benefit, and yet he was expected to not want Candy any more, to believe the lie that they were just friends. Angry because Sean was right. Angry because he did still fancy Candy. Angry with Candy. Because she didn't fancy him.

A waitress came over to their table. She was wearing a white T-shirt cut off at the midriff. Her hair was dyed blond with black roots showing, and she wore a belly button ring. She smiled at Sean.

'Who's your friend?' she asked in a hoarse voice.

Sean looked at Michael and suddenly smiled, his charmer's smile, one that made his eyes shine. 'That's Mikey. Mikey, this is Karen. She's the babe of this bar, so be nice. I know that will be hard for you, but, well . . . try.'

'Hello, Mikey,' Karen said, flashing Michael an uneven smile. 'Nice to meet you.' She held out her hand. Michael took it.

'Nice to meet you too, Karen,' Michael replied, smiling.

'Well, what are you boys having?'

Michael wanted to say 'you', but congratulated himself three seconds later on holding his tongue because he knew he would have come across like a complete twat if he had. He told himself he was rusty. It had been years since he'd ever chatted anyone up – if, indeed, he'd ever chatted anyone up. All of Michael's girlfriends had typically been women that had simply migrated from being friends to girlfriends. Michael felt acutely uncomfortable when it was clear that sex might be on the cards, so he'd gone for girls he already knew and made all his moves like they weren't moves and acted like nothing was actually happening until, of course, it happened. The fact was, Michael was too petrified by the opposite sex or, more seriously, the threat of rejection, to ever officially and explicitly chat a girl up.

'I'll have a Stella please, Karen,' Sean said.

Karen looked at Michael in a way that made his heart rush.

'Yeah, sure, thanks. I'll have another,' Michael said.

Karen turned and both of the boys watched her oversized arse move underneath a pair of tight black jeans.

'Worth a shag,' Sean said.

'Definitely,' Michael said, pleased that they were off the contentious Candy issue.

'As if you'd stand a chance,' Sean said.

'I think it was pretty clear who she preferred, mate.'

'Yeah, you're probably right,' Sean said in a suddenly sub-dued tone.

Michael melted. Why was he putting down a friend, his best friend, after he'd been dumped by his girlfriend of five years? Michael hated himself sometimes. 'Hey, listen, man,' he said, stretching his arm across Sean's shoulder. 'It's going to be OK. You'll figure things out with Candy,' he added, finding that he genuinely hoped that Sean would. And not just for selfless reasons.

Sean sighed. 'I hope so.'

'I know so,' Michael encouraged. 'Look, Sean. Don't ever forget it. Candy loves you. There were thousands of people she could have gone out with but she chose you. Why? Because you're a beautiful, lovely, fun and funny guy. She'd be an idiot to let you go and I know she'll come to her senses. And when she does, the first thing you should do is get down on your knees and ask her to marry you. Because I never saw a couple more meant for each other than you two. I know that this is a hiccup, but you'll both get through this. Trust me.'

Sean looked at Michael and smiled gently. 'Thanks, Mikey. You're a mate.'

# Chapter Forty-One

The party was out on D'Aguilar Peak, home of Hong Kong's most exclusive and reclusive. Tommy was both of those things. First son of the *Taipan*. No need to clarify which company, which *Taipan*. Enough to simply say it like it was capitalized. The *Taipan*. Like God is He instead of he.

After all, that was what Tommy was: the son of God, the richest, most powerful man in all Hong Kong. Not that he acted like it. Tommy was painfully shy. He spoke very softly. And he stuttered. Candy felt that Tommy was one of those people too intelligent for their own good. She could see it in his eyes. The way he thought too much. And the fears he held onto – he was sensitive, too sensitive, as if he could feel all the suffering in this world. It made Candy want to hold him.

Everyone was stunned to eventually receive an invitation to a party at his house. It was supposedly to celebrate his return to the island, even though he'd been back three months already.

Candy waited for Tommy to finish his sentence.

'I might . . . I'm going to stay. I've set up a studio upstairs.' (Tommy was a musician.) 'I . . .'

He'd grown into a good-looking man from the child she'd known (they'd all grown up together, the Eurasians, the Hong

Kong internationals) in an unusual, inverse way, she thought to herself. His features had matured but somehow they'd done so youthfully. His face looked smooth, the Chinese in him keeping him hairless. Even so, wispy sideburns extended down from his very black hair, which he wore long and tied back in a ponytail. He had high cheekbones, a slight angling of the deep-brown eyes, and light, puffy lips. He almost looked effeminate but not. Just young, in an eternal way. Candy imagined he'd never have wrinkles, his tanned skin looked so firm it shone. Maybe it was simply because he was a few years younger than her, she told herself.

'I like the acoustics how are you,' he said in one breath like it was all one sentence, like he'd suddenly become aware that he was talking about himself and his studio and that he should probably be polite and ask Candy how she was and so the thought just fell in without a full stop to separate it.

Candy still waited a couple of seconds before answering, knowing that there might yet be something else he wanted to say, and then she said, 'I'm great, Tommy. It's so lovely to see you back. Everyone has . . .'

She was about to continue but Tommy started talking. 'Mu . . . mu . . . my D . . . Dad says I can use the room upstairs for a studio it has good acoustics.'

'Can I see it?' Candy picked up seamlessly.

'Sure,' Tommy replied normally.

This rare moment of clarity made Candy feel good. Then she spied Rob at the end of the room and she felt even better. He was *sooo* good looking. Blue eyes sparkling like diamonds. Sun-bleached hair. She was happily stunned to discover him at Tommy's party. He was the last person she had expected to meet. She hadn't seen him since the Fetish Fest thing. She had even thought that maybe he'd left town, and she'd tried not to feel sad about it since she was trying hard to give her and Sean another go. But that was then.

# Chapter Forty-Two

When it became clear that Bob was walking across the room to speak to him, Michael tried to think of something clever to say – like fuck off. After all, this was the guy Candy was supposedly leaving Sean for, or so Sean thought. And Michael had to admit, he didn't like the way Candy and Bob had spent the entire evening gawking at each other.

But as he got close, close enough for Michael to see him clearly (the only time he'd ever seen him before had been at the Fetish Fest party and it had been pretty dark then) Michael thought he recognized him and that threw him slightly. There was something in his expression that was very familiar, but that could have just been the public school thing, the same way Jamie and Roo had come to look like each other over the years. He had very blue eyes and the kind of hair that Michael envied – it didn't seem to need any attention. He wore it long. And he was tall, nearly as tall as Michael but not quite. He held his head high as he approached and looked directly into Michael's eyes, and then that look – it *was* recognizable.

By the time Bob actually started talking, Michael found that he was trying too hard to place his face to come up with a quick insult.

'How's it going?' he said simply, still looking into Michael's eyes.

'Cool,' Michael managed to reply, without giving anything away. He could instantly see what Candy found attractive about him. The man possessed the same sort of casual charm as Sean. And he was definitely good looking. He was dressed in a sharp black shirt and black jeans.

'I liked your Witches article,' Bob said, taking a drag on the spliff he was holding before passing it to Michael.

'Yeah?' Michael said, instantly hating himself for falling for the flattery. But the fact was Bob was the first person to directly compliment Michael on his inaugural piece. It felt good to have someone, anyone, a stranger no less, appreciate his work. Sean hadn't once mentioned it and if it hadn't been for him Michael would never have even written it. 'Thanks,' Michael added trying not to let his eagerness show.

'I thought the way you tied in the idea of joint murder was a clever idea,' he said. 'I'd never heard of anything like that before. Do you think they, the Witches I mean, do you think they did it together?'

'I don't see why not,' Michael started, knowing that he was letting himself be wooed and that he was betraying Sean this way. But he couldn't help it. There was something about the bloke. Sean had completely left Michael's mind. Michael was about to say something else but he decided to suck on the reefer instead.

'I like to write,' Bob continued, casually gulping on a clear alcoholic drink like it was water.

'Really?' Michael said, happy that they weren't talking about him any more. 'What sort of stuff?'

'Crap usually,' he smiled warmly.

'Join the club.'

'I think you're talented. I read your column every day.'

'Tell that to my boss.'

Bob smiled quietly and then took another swig on his drink.

'So . . . what do *you* do?' Michael restarted.

'Not much,' he breathed. 'Hung out with Tommy mainly.'

Michael listened as Bob explained how he and Tommy were best friends, and how Tommy was the reason he'd come to Hong Kong in the first place. The *Taipan* had arranged a high-paying job for him as a trader in the city. Accommodation and food: all free.

'What a result,' Michael said.

'I know. But let's face it, Hong Kong is pretty shit isn't it?'

He was the first person to have said it and Michael couldn't help liking him more for it. It simply confirmed to him that they shared a bond, thought the same way. One can't look for that in everyone, Michael thought to himself, practically glowing now. It's either there or it's not. And with Bob it was definitely there. It was only as Bob excused himself to go and talk to Candy that Michael remembered Sean again. But by then it was too late. He found that, even if he was duty bound to do so, he simply couldn't hate Bob now.

Bob seemed like a really nice guy.

# Chapter Forty-Three

Rob caught Candy's glance and grinned at her, so, with a slight nod of her head, Candy indicated that he should join her and Tommy just as Tommy was getting up to make his way to the stairs. Rob walked across the room towards her.

'Oh, hi, Rob,' Tommy said with relaxed surprise.

'Where are you two going?' Rob said, looking at Candy.

'To see Tommy's studio,' Candy replied, smiling up at him.

'Good, I've got a spliff.'

Tommy headed up a curving cream staircase with the two of them in tow, almost touching. Outside, Latin music was blaring and the sound of the swimming pool splashing echoed off the jungle-covered mountain shielding the estate. From a window Candy could see Alex and Jimmy, both bare-chested and soaked through, chasing Jules around the diving board. She was screaming as they threatened to throw her in. Candy could see sparse lights from Shek O below, and beyond that a silver sea winked in the full moon. Candy had forgotten how beautiful it was here.

Two hours later and they were finally alone. It had been hard to get rid of Tommy. Candy couldn't tell if it was because he didn't realize that they wanted to be left alone or if he was jealous. Despite his lack of communication skills, Tommy seemed to find it easy to perceive the sexual tension between Rob and Candy (it might have had something to do with the way she had sat on his lap). Candy got the impression that Tommy was willing *her* to leave. She wondered if Tommy might be in love with Rob. She wouldn't have blamed him if he was. Even she was starting to think she might be a little in love with the oh-so gorgeous Rob.

Candy thanked God for the eightieth time that Sean wasn't here, even though there was no reason why he should have been. After all, Tommy didn't even know that Sean existed. Candy had got Michael to escort her to the party instead. He'd said he didn't mind. He had something to talk to her about in any case, he'd said. Three guesses what that would be about. Candy was dreading a lecture from Mikey even though she knew it was coming. For some unforeseen reason Mikey was turning into an intermediary between her and Sean. That was the last thing Candy had intended or needed. She'd managed to spend most of the evening avoiding him, even though she could feel him looking at her sometimes. At one point she'd felt a shiver pass down her spine – like someone had just walked over her grave – and she'd turned to see Mikey staring into her, like a stalker or something. It was freaky.

She was glad that she and Rob were finally alone.

# Chapter Forty-Four

Michael couldn't sleep. He hadn't managed to get a room as the party had gradually died. The sofa and the bean-bags in the living room were full. All that was left was a Mastermind chair in the billiard room. He'd tried sleeping on it but after a few minutes it had made his neck ache.

And his nose hurt. Too much coke. He was drunk – nearing head-spinny. He was finding it hard to swallow. All those cig-arettes. Ugh. The thought of them made him feel wretched. He decided to get a glass of water to wash the brown taste out of the back of his throat – hopefully ease the queasy feeling too.

By and large the party had been worth the self-abuse. Tommy had laid everything on. There were decks: good tunes. And then there was the swimming pool. Some of the girls had got their tits out. That had been fun. And Michael found that he'd genuinely enjoyed the company. Making friends with Bob and Tommy made him feel like he'd finally met new people and that he hadn't just hung out with the people he knew from Leeds. All in all, the party had been a refreshing change.

He found the kitchen lights and flicked them on. They hummed a little. Then something caught in his throat and a sudden, violent nausea rushed over him. There were three blind seconds as he stumbled towards the kitchen sink and then he was vomiting. His stomach quickly back flipped and tears instantly rushed out of his eyes. Another heave and Michael found himself praying for it to end. He murmured 'Please,' and then there was another furious gut convulsion. Nothing came out this time. He stared into the basin. The sharp smell of sick biting.

Breathe, he told himself. Breaaaathhhhhhhe.

Another retch began and Michael closed his eyes tight to ride the wave as it swelled from below. He wanted to breathe but he knew he couldn't. Any minute now and he'd be under water, drowning in his own regurgitation. He felt his head throb and he winced harder to fight back the ache. Complete blackness. Purple blackness, behind his eyes. Inside himself now. Inside his body, as it revolted, inside his mind as he fought it. And then, and then, and then . . .

The image flashed. It was sudden. It was an instant. But it slowed within itself. As it began, it elongated, like something curled up and then unravelling. Unravelling and revealing – somewhere in a space between Michael's eyes and his brain. An internal vision, a subconscious insight. Michael saw . . .

A pair of hands. Oversized. Reaching. Beyond them stretched cardigan-covered arms. Green wool. The smell of cigarettes and old furniture. Big shoulders. So fat and lumbering. This entire entity, so physically overbearing, so all-encompassing. Michael felt powerless and surrounded. His arms felt weak. The body beyond him was growing, enveloping, as he himself shrank. Then, quite seamlessly, the big body was holding him down, smothering him. Michael could feel the weight. On top of him. Writhing. Michael struggled.

So he *had* struggled. Michael hadn't understood that before.

But he was too heavy, he was too heavy. And then his face.

Just the edge at first. Blond hair, combed back. So close. The smell, an old smell. Then a cheekbone and an eye. Blue. Quite an amazing colour. And then the lips detracted from the beauty. They were thin and malicious. A nose.

And then it was suddenly there. His face. His face. Inches away. His face.

The Bummer Man.

'HUUNNNHHHHH!' Michael yelled. The sound was primordial, instinctive, somewhere from below, somewhere from within, like a scream. It flew out with the final stomach heave and the last of his vomit, like an evil expunged.

The moment evaporated as suddenly as a squall.

He breathed.

Michael rested his head on his forearms, which were leaning on the edge of the kitchen counter. He stared at the floor. Terracotta tiles. And then he felt two tears, already in his eyes from the violence of the vomiting, re-form themselves into drops of sadness. Complete despair. He watched them swell on their new shape and then finally, under their own weight, fall to the ground. They seemed to drop for a long time before smashing. The two tiny puddles of darkness looked like small flowers against the kitchen floor.

Michael sniffed and took another breath. In and out. He stood and wiped his eyes. He let the tap run and wash the sick down. Then he washed his face. Two more breaths. He cupped his hand and caught water. He slurped in the relief slowly, so slowly. He felt tender. Timid. He wanted to hold himself and rock.

Eventually he stood upright and turned. He saw that there was a door at the end of the kitchen. He hadn't noticed it before. Maybe it was a bedroom, he thought to himself with relief. He deserved that, he thought. He felt tired. So tired now.

He walked through the kitchen and slowly twisted the handle. He watched fluorescent light from the kitchen flood into the darkness, revealing nothing. Just a bookcase and some carpet. He opened the door wider and then he saw a body, lying, on some cushions, on the floor, in a sleeping bag, like a caterpillar in a cocoon. The body quickly turned to meet the light and there was a darkly covered naked chest and a face with a hand shielding the eyes.

'What the . . .' the man said, and Michael realized it was Bob. Michael opened his mouth to apologize but in that instant there was more movement from behind his nakedness, shielded in the darkness, inside the cocoon. Another face emerged. Squinting, not understanding.

It was Candy.

# Chapter Forty-Five

The Hundred Handshake Club was on the fifth and sixth floors of the old Bank of China building, accessible only by a private elevator. It was colonial old school – the British had bought the building after the Bank moved – and it was traditionally not immediately accepting of Chinese members, though there was now a long list of Chinese on its books, filtered in slowly over the years. Maybe even the English had finally smarted at the obscenity of not allowing Chinese to enter the old Bank of China building. That kind of imperialism was a little too in-your-face for Hong Kong, a little too obvious. The British understood, even if not immediately, that they couldn't refuse admission to the Chinese in their own land. After all, they were only in Hong Kong on lease, by invitation. It wasn't like India used to be.

Inside the club there was a marble lobby with marble stairs running between the two levels. Downstairs a restaurant served dim-sum. There was also a bar. Upstairs there was a library and on Sundays there were debating competitions when young F.I.L.T.H. would hang over the railings that protected the books and shout and leer and pretend they went to Oxford. Men also went to the library to smoke cigars in large leather armchairs.

And, finally, there was the roof garden, which looked out directly onto the new Bank of China building, towering above a hundred storeys taller. That was as it should be, Candy thought to herself whenever she came here. The new Bank of China – a mighty, gleaming, vaulting symbol of power – overshadowing the old-school British club in the tiny building where the Chinese used to work. So fitting that the British should be forced, whenever they found themselves starting to relax in their old smoking club, to see just what China had grown into over the years and, worse, to feel, in the juxtaposition of the two buildings, just how far Britain, and its empire, had fallen. Not dead yet, just shrunken and shrivelled and having to look up, craning their necks, at the sight of Today.

Maybe that's why Candy brought Mikey here. To show him this.

But probably not. She'd brought him to the roof garden because she knew they wouldn't be seen here. And they had to talk. After all, he was the only person who knew, knew for sure, about her and Rob. Everyone had their suspicions, but no one had actually seen her do anything bad, really bad.

No one, except Mikey.

And so far he hadn't said anything. Candy had called Sean the day after the party to feel him out. She could tell: he still didn't know. That had been a big relief. Mainly because Candy genuinely didn't want to hurt Sean. Even if she was falling out of love with him, she still felt loyal. She still wanted him to be happy. She didn't see why her confusion should upset him. He didn't deserve that.

But there were selfish reasons, too. Candy was especially worried that her affair with Rob might shame her. For starters it would bring things with Stephen to a very abrupt end. And she was meant to be going out to dinner at his house later in the week. And if her parents were to ever find out. Going out with one *gweilo* had been bad enough, but two. Part of her honestly believed they'd kill her if they discovered the truth. The loss of face would be terrible.

It had made Candy angry when she had thought that. About her lot as a woman, worse, as a half-caste woman. The fact that one minor transgression, one small affair could ruin her so easily. In England she'd been known as a prick tease. And now, in Hong Kong, she risked earning the reputation of a slut. Just because. It was enough to make her rebel. Maybe that was partly what her affair with Rob was about: a rebellion.

But in the grey, overcast light of the day after, Candy realized that it simply wasn't worth it, fighting the way things were. She'd understood that for a long time. There was still no reason why she couldn't do what she wanted to do, why she couldn't still sleep with Rob. She just had to make sure no one found out. Rob was amazing but he wasn't worth losing everything over – Sean, Stephen, her parents, her face, her future.

She had to make sure Mikey kept his mouth shut.

He was leaning against the rooftop railing as she brought him a vodka tonic. She smiled as she approached. Her dress, long and slim and light – knowing that she was beautiful and using it. He smiled back at her. Spot-lit clouds swam between the skyscrapers. It would rain later.

'Cheers,' he said as she passed him the glass, the ice cold through it, the white napkins underneath already wet with condensation.

'Cheers,' she said, standing beside him.

'You know, when I first got here,' Mikey said looking up at the new Bank of China building, which seared like a gleaming silver knife under the lights, 'Sean managed to convince me that the lightning rods on top of the Bank of China were actually posts for golf nets, you know, so all the executives could hit a few in their lunch break.'

Candy grinned. 'And you believed him?'

'You know me, Candy. I'll believe anything.'

Candy snorted. It was true. Mikey was probably the most gullible person she knew. After all, wasn't that part of the reason she'd decided she could talk to him, convince him to keep quiet, bring him onto her side? There was a pause, which Candy allowed to hang like the start of a new paragraph. She looked at Mikey meaningfully.

'How *is* Sean?' she started slowly, as if now was as good a time as any to discuss him, seeing as Mikey had brought him up and everything.

Mikey shrugged. 'He's OK. Could be better.'

Candy nodded slightly and bit her back teeth. 'So he, er, he doesn't know.'

She'd meant it as a question but somehow her inner sense, her inner understanding that Sean was none the wiser, twisted the words into a statement.

'No,' Mikey confirmed.

Candy didn't say anything, letting silence do the work.

Eventually Mikey said: 'It's OK, Candy, I won't say anything. If that's what you're worried about.'

Candy nodded, knowing that Mikey would say that, that he'd feel uncomfortable enough to offer it, that he probably wouldn't have agreed to even meet her in the first place if he wasn't prepared to at least claim that he could keep the secret. But that wasn't good enough. Mikey might very well say that he wasn't going to say anything. But what would happen when he got drunk, or angry with her, or anything? It wasn't a binding enough arrangement. It would be too easy for him to let the information slip. No. A promise wasn't good enough. She needed much more from Mikey than just that. She needed a commitment.

'Thanks,' she said.

'No reason why he should suffer any more than he is,' Mikey said.

'No,' Candy agreed.

There was the sound of a plane in the distance.

'Do you love him?' Mikey said eventually. 'Bob, I mean . . . Do you love him?'

Candy didn't say anything. Mikey had asked her that question once before, just after she and Sean had got together, all those years ago. *Do you love him?* It was a trick question. Before, she'd given the wrong answer, in the hope that it was the best answer, the easiest answer. And what a mistake that had been. She had told Mikey that she didn't love Sean. She'd said it because she hadn't wanted to hurt Mikey any more than she had done already. She'd said it because she thought the alternative would only make things worse.

But it was after she had told Mikey that she didn't love Sean that he turned. That was when Mikey started hating her. Really hating her. He was clever and deceptive and he never showed anyone else his evil, but when they were alone, or if ever their eyes accidentally met, Mikey would pour out hatred, hurl the stuff out of his stare and from his body and every discernible crevice. There was no way she couldn't feel it. It was violent and hot and horrible.

It was only by avoiding him altogether that the naked hostility eventually eased. Mikey needed time and space to overcome his jealousy, the jealousy that was so much more intensified by the notion that she was with Sean in the beginning simply because she fancied him, and for no other reason. It was sex that fucked Mikey up. Like so many other men, it was the thought that Candy might want to have sex, pure and simple, in its own right, that drove him crazy. It took her years to understand, but eventually Candy realized that men, ALL men, couldn't bear to perceive a woman in any other way than as a creature that pined for love and security and only tolerated sex for these two higher emotional objectives. Yes, women might enjoy it. But only when they were in love. There was no way a woman could ever be allowed to just fuck. That was how men thought, that was how Mikey thought.

'I don't know,' she said. 'Maybe.'

She felt Mikey tense beside her as he turned. She could feel the lecture coming. 'Well, don't you think you should figure that out before you go destroying Sean's life.'

Candy made herself look back at Mikey, into his grey eyes. 'Probably,' she said.

Mikey looked back at her. She could see that she'd taken the wind out of his sails with that answer. She could tell that he'd been expecting her to resist, fight, argue, even break. But Candy wasn't going to break. She'd been through too much shit already to cry over something like this. After all, from a certain perspective, her whole life might very well depend on this moment. She had to be strong. She had to remember why she was here, justifying herself to her enemy. She was here for one reason, and one reason only. To make sure Mikey kept his mouth shut. And she knew just how to do it. All she had to do was wait for the right moment, the right opportunity. She watched Mikey breathing.

'You know, Candy . . .' Mikey started.

'What?' Candy encouraged.

Mikey looked back at her and then, after a small pause, shook his head slightly and said: 'Nothing.'

Candy looked back at him. It was OK. She knew what he wanted to say, what he was about to say: *I love you*. It was so obvious. He didn't need to spell it out. Mikey was committed, she knew that now. He'd never tell Sean about her and Rob. Not while he was still in love with her, not while he thought he was still in with a chance.

She smiled warmly at him.

# Chapter Forty-Six

Sean and Michael were watching *Scarface*. Michael had rented the video because Channel HK had pencilled it in for the following week's line-up. It would be the only thing worth watching so Michael thought that some research might be required. They were in Sean's flat. All the lights were off. Outside a typhoon lashed at the windows. The offices were closed. Sean had the day off. He was lying on one of the sofas, using an ethnic sheet to cover himself. He was only wearing boxer shorts. Michael could see his hand moving like some sea creature around his genitals.

'Stop scratching your nuts.'

'Fuck off.'

The volume was up high. The sound of the machine gun made the speakers on the TV rattle. They'd had complaints from the woman upstairs during the chainsaw scene. But Sean said he didn't care. Sean leaned over to the plywood plank and pulled the broken mirror towards him, separating four new lines from the pile that they'd already crushed off the rock.

'I thought we agreed that we'd only do lines when they did.' Michael said.

'And whenever they say *yeyo*,' Sean replied, before snorting a line, his eyes creasing with revulsion, the pain in the bridge of his nose almost tangible.

'They say *yeyo* about fifty times in this movie.'

'I know. It's such a wicked word. *Yeyyyyyy – yo!* Got to do a line to that!' Sean said, before snorting another line in the other nostril, still horizontal on the sofa, gagging afterwards.

Michael shook his head. 'We're going to be mashed,' he said, taking the mirror from Sean's outstretched hand.

'That is the intention, yes,' Sean replied.

Michael did both lines in his left nostril, the right one still blocked from the previous night. 'This coke is cut with toilet cleaner,' he said, pinching the bridge of his nose. It felt like his brain was burning. 'Where did you get it?'

'Sasha sorted it out.'

'Who from?'

'Dunno. Some dodgy geezer she's shagging.'

Michael realized for the first time that he'd never had to go and actually score for himself. Just as he'd fallen into his tailor-made social life, Michael had contented himself with everyone else's cut supply. Maybe that was why the quality was always so bad. He was a bottom-feeder fish happy to live off the crap floating in the ocean – less than the end of the food chain.

'Who?' he asked.

'Does it matter?'

'Well, it does if it's cut.'

'What are you going to do? Return it?'

'No. I'm just thinking that maybe we should find someone with better quality coke.'

'It's all the same shit, Mikey. The Triads cut it and then the dodgy *gweilo* go-between probably does as well. It's not really a question of choice, unless you want to go and deal with the Triads yourself. Now shut up and watch the movie.'

Michael considered this and realized that Sean was probably right. Hong Kong was crap in so many ways, why should the quality of the coke be any different?

'Why aren't the others here?' Michael continued, knowing Sean had invited some of the gang. 'I thought they were joining us.'

'They got trapped by the typhoon,' Sean replied.

A sheet of solid rain smacked loudly against the window, making Michael jump slightly. He looked out from the darkness of the flat and into the grey night that was the day.

'Are those windows going to hold?' he asked nervously.

Sean didn't reply.

Another lash, crack and shoooossshhhh, as the rain smashed and then relented against the glass before streaking down in broken droplets. The air-conditioning hummed. Michael was finding it hard to concentrate. His heart felt funny, ahead of itself, skipping on the beat. He told himself he was being paranoid. He reached for the packet of Marlboro Lights and lit himself a cigarette. The tobacco tasted good, mixing with the chemical taste in his nose and forming into something solid, almost like real food. They hadn't eaten for nearly two days. They were on a bender, a typhoon celebration. It was the only decent thing about this island, Sean had said. Some typhoons lasted three days. Three whole days to do nothing except stay inside, watch TV, drink beer and get totally mash up.

Outside, poor Chinese people were dying in mudslides.

Michael felt his heart flipping again. He was starting to feel seriously crap. Part of him wondered why he was doing this to himself. But not for long. Feeling good or having fun wasn't the point. The point was making sure Sean was OK, that he was happy. This was what he wanted to do, so Michael was doing it with him. It was about brotherhood, sticking by your mates. Needless to say, Michael had been shocked by the amount of shit Sean could take. He just seemed able to keep going and going and going. Michael's body was operating on less than reserves. He knew he'd have the flu afterwards.

The sound of thunder and the wind humming.

Michael had been lost in the scene where Scarface's mother throws him out of the house, so he couldn't tell how long Sean had been sobbing for. Slowly though, the wet sounds filtered into his consciousness. As if from a dream he turned, feeling the weight of his eyes in their sockets, and was shocked to see Sean sitting upright, his whole body shaking, tears streaming down his face, relentless, like the rain on the windows outside.

'Sean?' Michael said, quickly coming to, awake now, not zombiefied. 'Sean, mate?' Very concerned, slightly scared. 'Whassup? What's wrong?'

Michael jumped to the sofa where Sean was sitting and put his arm around him, their naked torsos touching. Sean's body felt soft next to Michael's thick chest hair. It was uncomfortably male. But Sean was too lost in emotion to notice. He was weeping mercilessly. Michael felt his ribs shaking.

'Sean, mate, talk to me. Is it Candy? Tell me. I want to help. Cummon, buddy. What's wrong?'

'They're all such bitches,' came the words through the stream.

'Who, Sean? Who are bitches?' Michael said, rubbing a shoulder blade, wanting to hug him but fearing it.

'All of them.' Michael didn't say anything. It would be better to just let Sean speak. Let him get it out. He had to let it out, get the pain out of his system. 'Women. All of them. Fucking whores. CANDY!'

As he shouted the word, Sean smashed a fist into the

plywood plank table and put his hand straight through it, the wood instantly splintering into his knuckles. The violence of the movement momentarily threw Michael back and away, and this new freedom, combined with the cocaine numbness and illusion of power, sent Sean off into a spiral. Before Michael could do anything, Sean was up and away and kicking everything in sight, flinging the rest of the table (and all the narcotics) into the wall, turning and finding a door and putting three fists into it:

BAM! BAM! BAM!

Rapid-fire succession. Then he turned and threw his head into a wall before twisting and finding a glass suddenly in his grip and hurling it at the window. It bounced back and sang on the floor as it landed, incredibly not broken, the glass from the window also intact. This show of resistance, from the most unlikely of substances, stunned Sean for a second and gave Michael – who was now standing – the chance to throw his arms around Sean from behind and hold him.

'Easy, man, easy.'

Sean didn't struggle. He could easily overpower Michael. They both knew it. But it was over. The spasm had subsided. Sean let Michael hold him. He wanted to be held. Sean stared at the glass, which was still spinning on the floor, and laughed through bittersweet tears.

'I hate them,' Sean said grimly.

Michael could see that Sean had cut his hand quite badly.

'Shoosh, it's OK, mate. It's going to be OK.'

'Why?' Sean said, seemingly random.

'Come on,' Michael said, pushing Sean gently from behind. 'Let's go to the kitchen. Your hand, it's cut.'

Sean looked down and the blood, which was pouring now and forming a black puddle on the fake wood floor, confused him. Michael felt a chill pass through Sean, his body clammy with sweat. Michael was worried about the amount of coke they'd done and whether Sean's hand would need stitches and if they'd have to go to hospital. One step at a time, he told himself. Nice and easy. Important to stay calm now.

'Come on,' he said again, releasing his hug and taking Sean's good (well, less damaged) hand and leading him gently towards the kitchen. He looked at Sean's face and noticed that he'd cut his forehead as well. Michael tried not to show his fear. The coke was surging through his system now, mixing with the adrenaline and making him shake slightly. He told himself to stay calm. Just stay calm. Breathe.

They padded into the kitchen and Michael twisted the cold water tap on, guiding Sean's hand into the blast. Blood surged into the basin, the odd wood shard coming loose and falling. Sean didn't react to the pain. He just stared, his face grey, a small line of blood seeping from his hairline. He looked out of the window that was above the sink. Outside, the rain was pouring in straight lines, large lakes forming in the car park below.

Michael tried to inspect the damage.

'Why?' Sean said again.

Michael removed his hand from the water and looked into the cut. It was bad, very deep, some white showing, which must have been bone. Michael felt a lump jog in his chest and he had to stifle a cocaine lurch. For a second he thought he was going to be sick. Eventually he found a dishcloth and managed to wrap it around Sean's fist, pressing tight.

'Sean, mate, you've cut your hand quite badly,' Michael said. 'You have to squeeze it tight to stop the blood.'

But Sean wasn't listening. He was just staring out of the window, into the rain, his lower jaw jarring and gnashing on the Charlie. So Michael held his hand, applying the pressure for him, trying not to look at the blood, which he could already feel dripping through the cloth. Christ! Sean's hand *would* need stitches. Damn it.

'Why do they treat us like that?'

Michael looked at Sean, trying to see now if the cut on his head was bad. 'Who, Sean?' Michael asked more as a distraction than anything else, not listening, just trying to deal with the not inconsiderable medical emergency that was suddenly on his plate. 'Why do who treat us like what?'

'Like Scarface's mother. Women.' Sean said, his back teeth grating.

'What are you talking about?' Michael replied.

Suddenly Sean turned and levelled a large look into Michael's eyes. 'You know what I'm talking about,' he said.

Michael looked back at him, still holding his hand, aware that from the outside it would look like they were naked, only their bare torsos showing, their lower halves shielded by the sink and the wall and . . .

'It's their fault, you know that, don't you?' Sean said.

Michael didn't say anything. He was finding it hard to let Sean carry on this way. Something inside himself knew where Sean was going with this. And it scared him. It scared him a lot. He blinked.

'Your mother,' Sean said. 'It was her that made you go. She was the one that made you stay even though you told her you hated it. Remember? It was her fault. Just like my mother. If she hadn't made me go back, things might have been . . . different. You know that, don't you?'

Michael was shivering now, the air-conditioning freezing all of a sudden. The fear in his throat. It was tight. The room was shrinking around Sean's face and making him all-consuming.

All Michael could see was Sean. Sean, in front of him, looking at him, seeing through everything and knowing.

'They're all the same,' Sean's mouth moved. 'All of them. Scarface's mother. Your mother. My mother. Candy. Women make us . . . it might never have happened.'

'Don't,' Michael said. 'Don't go there, Sean. It's best left. We said that. We always said that. Remember? Don't go there.'

Sean's eyes narrowed and he looked at Michael the way he used to look at him in school, when he knew what was what, when he called a spade a spade, when he understood what needed to be done.

'I never fucking left,' he said.

# Chapter Forty-Seven

It was a charity walkathon. Cancer. Leukaemia. Something like that. It was just a way to make the boarders run some energy off during the weekend. Weekends were always the worst. Especially for bullying. There was never anything to do. There was sometimes a movie in the afternoon. An extended bedtime, for some late-night TV. A couple of other activities arranged.

But apart from that, the only thing for the boys to do on weekends was lounge around, eat tuck, play ping-pong, read comics, get bored, masturbate. Everyone envied the boys that went home for the weekend. The ones that were left behind had to suffer the sheer extreme boredom of no one caring.

Except for that weekend. That weekend, everyone cared. The teachers cared, the boys cared. It was all for charity. It was a ten-mile hike across the Downs. Long, rolling inlands. There were woods. Sometimes fog. Like on that day, that Saturday. It was wet. They were wearing anoraks. Old school style. The ones with the fake-fur-lined hoods that looked like periscopes when they were zipped up all the way, just two eyes visible within a waterproof tunnel.

Who was there?

Marland. Baxter. Clarke. Miller. Oxenbury. Jeffreys. Browne.

Thirty others from three other houses, among them some lower schoolboys. Only seven, eight years old. Tiny little creatures. Only just more than babies. Ripped from the tit and sent straight to hell. Skinny wrists and slightly distended bellies because the muscles hadn't fully developed yet. Little legs. They'd only be doing the first half of the walk. They'd have to run most of the way just to keep up. They were the babies of the school. They still got sneered at, though, and called names and teased. At night, when the lights were out and the terror had finally abated, and it was just them under the duvet, and they were alone, they cried. They sobbed the way a baby can cry. Completely. They cried for their Mamas and their Dadas, so full of feeling and not hardened or reptilian-skinned or forgetful of what it was to actually feel – like the men that they would eventually become.

Indeed, this nightmare was why they would eventually become those men, isolated from and trapped by their own emotions, ignorant and afraid and unable to cry. Because it would ultimately become too difficult to feel, too difficult to cry like this, too difficult to keep on missing Mama and Dada and wishing they were here to help, to take them away from this hell. Because Mama and Dada would never come. They would never come because they didn't care. Mama and Dada didn't love them. That was the truth for every single one of the boys. Their mamas and their dadas didn't love them. Or if they did, it wasn't as much as Mama and Dada loved themselves, or their tea parties, or their businesses, or their lovers, or their social status, or their tax rebates, or their anything-that-had-something-to-do-with-them. Children were just another feature of their existence. Something that had to be 'taken care of', neatly compartmentalized in an arrangement of some sort. Just like everything else they lived and had. This bill gets paid then, this vase should be slightly over to the left, that boy will be at school for eight weeks now and I won't even have to think about what to cook him for dinner.

Eventually, the boys, the babies – they'd learn that there was no point wishing they weren't at St Luke's. Because they were there. Seemingly for ever. Six more years, in any case. And to a seven-year-old, six years was for ever. Nearly a whole lifetime.

Who else was there?

Three teachers supervising. Fishface Haddock, Gibo and Mr Harris – the vicar, a good man. One of the few, the only one who didn't punish or shout or discipline or terrorize. Mr Harris was a good man. He often offered comfort to those boys who were in despair. But he couldn't be there all the time, he couldn't deal with all the misery. There was simply too much. Mr Harris had taken the little boys back. Mr Harris wasn't there in the end. Nor was Gibo. He'd twisted his foot and gone back with Harris.

It was getting dark early. They were in the woods. Twenty, maybe more of them. Some still had the energy to run, play tag. The leaves were sodden, some edged with frost. Mostly they just walked. No energy for bullying now. Everyone exhausted. Even Fishface. He was at the back. Not much talking now. The boys didn't know where they were, or when they would get back. They had to finish the walk. It was only four thirty. But it was getting dark. It was getting dark very early. Maybe it was the fog. Maybe it was the woods. Maybe it was the wet.

It was winter.

Marland looked down at his feet kicking the leaves. Shushing and shovelling and shaking off condensation. His

will rhode

Green Flash were wet through. He could feel blisters. He had his hands in his pockets. Clarke was in front of him. They were slightly away from Baxter, who was walking with Jeffreys and Miller.

Very tired now. Everyone was very tired now. They'd have tea when they got back. Sausages and baked beans steaming and the sound of cutlery echoing because there wouldn't be the din of boys clamouring and laughing and shouting because they'd be too tired to talk. Even more, there wouldn't be enough of them to make a din. There would only be thirty of them in a canteen that housed three hundred. They were the minority, the ones that got left behind.

It was the sound of the road that sent up the final call.

'IT'S CHESSINGTON ROAD!' someone shouted.

'ONLY A MILE LEFT!'

'LAST ONE BACK IS A BENNY!'

Suddenly the sound of trees darting and dancing and the wind between them weaving as the steam from the leaves and the crystals of frost shook because they were all running now. Running in a final burst of energy, the main road an inspiration, the first landmark in a long line of landmarks they actually recognized.

'NO ONE CROSSES THE ROAD UNTIL I GET THERE!' Fishface Haddock's deep voice boomed, carrying across the high-pitched cries and settling.

No one would disobey.

The woods were a monotony, a claustrophobic, dark continuum without a break, without a respite in the view. Just trees and leaves and the sound of wood and birds reverberating. So when Marland finally saw the road it was a relief. It was something else. His legs ached. But Clarke had pulled him. They were running together now.

'You're too slow,' Clarke said as they panted together, running through the woods. 'I'm going to beat you.'

Marland grimaced happily. He was looking at Clarke's face, moving and yet staying still because they were in the same space, running at the same speed. Clarke was back from his suspension and he was with Marland now. Marland wouldn't be bullied this weekend. Not with Clarke. Not after the walk.

BUMPF!

And suddenly he was gone. Marland kept running, laughing, almost crying because Clarke – the best sportsman in school, ha! – had tripped and was now tumbling in on himself in a pile of leaves. His grinning face emerged from the dirt just as Marland shouted back: 'JOEEEEEYYYY DEEAAAACCOONNNNNNNN!' And then Marland turned forward to run in earnest, taking the lead and sealing the advantage.

The sound of cars speeding through the wet was its own sound, not like anything. Headlights streamed, the fog seizing some of the yellow light in ghostly snatches.

Marland slowed to a jog.

A body of boys was collecting by the side of the road. There was an HGV. Two, in fact. Long and large and parked one in front of the other. Everyone assembled, panting from the final run. Some pretended they were smoking while they waited, the air forming off their breath, small twigs in the sides of their mouths.

Marland joined them. He stood next to Jeffreys. Fishface Haddock arrived.

'Is everyone assembled?' he said to himself as he counted. Then: 'Where's Clarke, where's Baxter?'

*don'tknowsir*, came the communal mumble mixed with the shuffling of feet against the tarmac.

They waited.

Cars – whhhhhHHWWHHHHHHOOOWWWWWEEEINN-ggggggggggggggg. Shossssssssshhhhhhhhhhhhhhhhhhhh – as the drizzle resettled. Almost to a certain time, a certain beat. Humming and passing and speeding, the wet fizzing as it reshaped itself in the fog and the darkness.

They waited. Next to the trucks. How long? It was hard to say.

*coldsir . . .*

*canwecrosssir? . . .*

*weknowthewaybackfromheresir . . .*

*oooocomeonsir . . .*

'Curses,' Fishface Haddock said under his breath.

Marland could see what he was thinking. Marland was thinking the same. Or worse. Would it be now? His heart was thumping.

Fishface Haddock suddenly sighed. Marland could almost feel his thoughts. He wouldn't want the humiliation of catching those two fighting again only to take another punch in the face. And Clarke probably would punch Fishface in the face again now that he knew he was the Bummer Man. All he needed was an excuse to make it look like an accident. Another fight with Baxter would be ideal.

Yes.

Marland could feel what Fishface was thinking. He could see that he was nervous. Suddenly a situation. Those two boys again. And it was just him this time to control them. It was getting dark.

'Right,' Fishface suddenly started. 'We'll cross the road now,' he said, looking behind himself one more time. 'Wait until I say.'

'But what about Clarke, sir?' Marland said, looking up at

Fishface, strangely hardened to him, unafraid of him now that Clarke was back. Now that they had agreed.

Fishface looked at him, almost sensing Marland's impertinence, his bravery. A small sneer. 'You wait here for him,' he half barked. Then he looked left, two cars clearly coming. He looked right just as one was passing and then was gone.

They waited for the cars from the left to pass. The first car came.

WhhhhhHHWWHHHHHHOOOWWWWWEEEINNgggg-gggshossssssssshhhhhhhhhhhhhhhh.

A small gap and then the second.

whhhhhHHWWHHHHHHOOOWWWWWEEEINNgggg-gggshossssssssshhhhhhhhhhhhhhhh.

Fishface: 'NOW EVERYBODY!'

They all surged into the road, the kids not looking, already knowing it was clear, just running and Fishface with them.

And then . . .

SCREEEEEEEEECCCHHHHHHHHHHHHHHHHHHHHHHHH
. . .

In that pause, that eternal second that hung, everyone froze. After the tyres started scratching in the wet for grip and made that noise, that awful, terrible, slow-motion noise that echoed and couldn't control itself, no one could move. And then they all saw, before they even heard the thud, the sight that was travelling faster than sound.

A body flying. Quickly upside down. One foot strangely moulded over the top of the windscreen, the first feature of its form to twist and contort to meet the shape of the vehicle. Below, a pair of legs collapsed into the windscreen that quickly shattered into them, and then the rest of the body, its torso and head dancing horribly on the bonnet like a rag doll being violently shaken.

THUD!

The body, which was wearing an anorak, slipped a little as the car slowed. The car entered a small spin before eventually leaning into the oncoming lane and then collapsing against the grass verge on the opposite side of the road.

It was quiet then. Marland didn't move. He watched smoke from the car mix with the fog in the beam of the yellow headlights, which were still working. He saw the man's head, the driver, against the steering wheel. He couldn't hear the sudden footsteps, the sound of movement against the tarmac, the cries, Fishface Haddock shouting at the rest of the boys to get out of the road. Marland blinked and watched. He wasn't breathing. He watched them all, all the boys, running to the car. Another set of headlights suddenly approached and Fishface waved at them. The other car slowed down. It was wet. Getting dark very early. Cold. The body on the bonnet didn't move. It had come out from behind the trucks. Out from the blind spot. Three boys were staring through the back windscreen as Fishface screamed at them to get back. There was glass. The body didn't move. Marland still wasn't breathing. He just stood, waiting, like he'd been told, for Clarke.

And that was when he saw him. From the corner of his eye. Coming out of the darkness. Drifting, as if without feet, from out of the fog, floating towards Marland. He was coming out from behind the length of the HGV, the same place the other anorak-ed body had come from, the same place the person had run into the road from.

Clarke was moving. Slowly. And he was looking at Marland.

Gently. Warmly. Knowingly. Like God, after He has exacted some terrible truth, all because only He knows, only He can understand this law that has compelled Him.

He was smiling at Marland.

And so Marland smiled at Him.

# Chapter Forty-Eight

Sean and Michael were on their way to a bar to meet some of the gang when they decided – or rather, Sean suggested it and Michael agreed. The conversation, in the back of a taxi as it wound its way over the mountainous Peak road, went something along the lines of:

Michael: 'Christ, I hope I get lucky this weekend.'

'I know, what's wrong with you?' Sean replied. 'You haven't had a shag since you got here.'

Michael was silent. He didn't want Sean to know about the other night, his 'mistake'.

'You never were very good with women,' Sean added, gently pressing his bandaged hand. Somehow, the butterfly stitches Michael had made were still holding. 'Oh well, mate, you know what they say: You only find an oasis in the desert.'

'At this point I'd probably settle for a camel.'

Sean snorted with amusement. 'Why don't we go to Macao?' he said.

'Aren't we meant to be meeting the others?'

'Yeah . . .' He hovered. 'Or we could go to Macao and fuck whores.'

Michael felt suddenly excited. He'd always wanted to sleep with a prostitute. At least once, you know, for the experience. 'Can we . . . I mean, do you really think?'

'Why not?'

'I can't afford it.'

'Don't be stupid, I'll pay.'

'Really?'

'Yes,' Sean urged, slightly impatient.

'Let's go,' Michael replied.

Sean grinned and quickly leant towards the taxi driver. 'Shun Tak ferry terminal *m'goi*.' Then he turned and faced Michael. 'Some bird's going to get a pounding tonight!'

Michael shifted in his seat with boyish anticipation. He found he was unable to stifle a laugh of excitement. Some bird was definitely going to get a pounding tonight! It was hard to stay cool once he knew – absolutely knew (it was only a question of cash) – that he'd be fucking someone for the first time in months. Sean beamed back at him with the same sense of adventure, the same sense of enthusiasm.

It was practically like old times.

# Chapter Forty-Nine

'**W**hat are you doing?' Stephen said.

Candy cradled the telephone between her head and shoulder, using an open drawer in the desk to push her feet against so she could rock in her chair, her tight grey pin-stripe mini-skirt sliding up against her thighs. Sweat stood against her skin as if it had been sprayed on. The gallery was stuffy. The air-conditioning system had broken down. She'd closed the gallery until the repairman arrived. He was down in the basement now, fixing things.

'Nothing,' she replied in Cantonese.

'Let's go eat.'

'I can't.'

'I thought you said you weren't doing anything.'

'I'm working.'

'It's Saturday. No one works on Saturday.'

'Everyone works on Saturday,' Candy said, smiling without knowing why.

'Take the afternoon off.'

Candy looked round. The gallery was dark while the electricity was off. An abstract painting in the corner looked like it was shouting at her. She wiped her temple and looked at the sheen of sweat on her fingertips. Suddenly it did all seem a little unreasonable, her being here.

'All right,' she said quickly, without thinking.

They met down at the harbour an hour later. It was crowded. The sun was standing perpendicular in the sky and Hong Kong was momentarily a world without shadows, all things dark consumed by their form. Hired junks milled in the water, their broad bows rolling confidently in the chaotic wash like pimps on a violent street, waiting for their corporate *gweilo* tricks as they gathered on the pier.

Stephen was waiting for Candy as she stepped out of the taxi. He was dressed in cricket whites and he dazzled in the extraordinary brightness. There was a terrible smell in the air, which seemed to emanate from the pavement. It was worse than disgusting, an amalgam of revolting odours, rotting fish mixed with raw sewage and old milk. Candy almost gagged as Stephen greeted her, but his aftershave smothered the stench, so she pressed her nose into his neck when he held her.

Stephen's cigarette boat, a monster of inappropriate power, rumbled lustily on its own private mooring. People looked on enviously as they prepared to leave. Maybe they thought that this couple were famous in some way. Stephen would be driving. They were alone. No security today. He jumped down onto the boat and turned to take Candy's hand. She leaped down with a squeal and almost dropped her bag. This might be fun, she thought to herself, feeling the sun on her head.

# Chapter Fifty

Michael found that Macao had the one big thing that Hong Kong lacked: a sense of identity in the culture clash. It hadn't completely sold its soul like the whore that Hong Kong was. It wasn't all about money. It was also about living. There were houses, not just tower blocks of flats, and many of them were brightly painted: red or purple or green – some display of the individuals that lived within. There were narrow cobbled streets that shone and smelled fresh in the shade because the butcher or the jeweller or the coffee-house owner that plied their trade on them had washed away the filth with buckets of water. This wasn't exactly the conscience of a multinational corporate franchise chain.

And people had time. Fat old ladies with hairy chins and billowing coloured dresses chatted on doorsteps. There were men and boys on bicycles. The shopping arcade was an open-air square with stone benches and water fountains and the sound of laughter. There was a sense of community permeating the place. People seemed to actually *come from* Macao. They weren't just passing through it on their way to somewhere else, somewhere better. And while the Macanese themselves could still be boiled down into being basically Portuguese or Chinese, they were varying shades of each within it. As a whole – as a crowd of people to observe – they generally merged to become one. They were a single local identity. There was assimilation, not alienation.

Michael breathed in the place. He felt happy. The sun was shining. The rooftop on the Mini Moke that they'd hired at the ferry terminal was down. Actually, it didn't even have a roof, it was that much of a holiday hire car. And in many ways that was what Macao felt like – a holiday from Hong Kong.

Sometimes he closed his eyes.

# Chapter Fifty-One

Next thing she knew, Candy was drunk. It might have been the heat, which had been steadily concentrating itself in her black hair on the boat journey and which was now filling her head and swimming. She'd only had two glasses of wine. They were sitting at a small outdoor table in a quaint restaurant in an even quainter fishing village on one of the outlying islands. There was no umbrella. Maybe that was the problem. Stephen filled her glass.

'Nice wine,' she said.

Candy found that she was having a good time, even vaguely romantic. Not too much *gweilo* influence here, not too much confusion. Just a simple fishing village, seemingly untouched. The metropolis was invisible, round the corner of a sheltered bay and across two peninsulas, the day blinding the bright lights, the open space obliterating the density of buildings and people. Sampans waddled on a gentle swell like fat babies – smaller, more innocent versions of their junkie parents pimp-rolling in Hong Kong harbour.

Stephen smiled at her, his face cracking as he slid the bottle back into the bucket, the ice crashing.

'I grew up here,' he said.

Candy looked back at him, interested.

'Well, I mean, we used to come here on the weekends. The family.'

'I don't think I've ever been here before,' Candy replied. 'It reminds me of Lamma, in the old days, before they built the power station.'

'Hmmm,' Stephen replied, wincing through the brightness at her. Candy noticed that he wasn't sweating. 'Would you like to see my secret beach?' he said eventually.

'Sure.'

Stephen didn't pay the restaurant owner but shouted at him as they got up to leave in a dialect Candy couldn't understand. The pier jumped under their feet as they walked across it, the water licking the posts. The day felt windless and hot. The sun was burning. Candy almost fell when she got back into the boat, even though it was steady on the water. She *was* a little drunk. Stephen caught her. She felt his hand on her breast as he reached out but she didn't say anything. He helped her, a little patronizingly, into a seat at the back of the boat, but Candy didn't mind. It was too hot to care. When they started to drive, Candy's hair flew back. She liked the way it pulled on her scalp.

# Chapter Fifty-Two

After their brief tour of Macao, Sean and Mikey settled in at the five star, fifty-storey Landau Hotel, which had a pool appropriately shaped like a crab (for more than one reason, Sean felt), a massage parlour in the basement and its own casino/restaurant. The rooms were entirely windowed, huge panes of glass that started at the floor and ended at the ceiling, facing out to sea. From their room (which had two single beds and which they'd taken because it was on a thirty percent discount) they could see three of Macao's low-lying bridges skipping the surface of the ocean between its penin- sulas. They had a beer from the mini bar and then they did two lines of coke. Eventually Sean suggested they go to Ola's.

They drove at sixty miles an hour, but it only felt like they were doing ten because the Mini Moke was so toy-like. The sun was just starting to set and the temperature was turning. Mikey put on a sweater even though it wasn't cold. It was the longest period of time that either of them could remember that they hadn't actually sweated. Sean wore a baseball cap so that his hair wouldn't flail in the wind as they drove. He was worried about his bald patch showing.

'Christ, it's nice to get out of Hong Kong,' Mikey said at one point.

'I know,' Sean replied with real relief in his voice.

They travelled the rest of the way in silence, got lost and eventually found the restaurant as darkness fell. The tables were all taken so they ate at the bar. Grilled fish, spicy chicken, a bowl full of chilli clams, eaten with fingers and washed down with vino verde. Sean flirted with the waitress and she responded.

'I almost feel normal,' Sean said in the break before dessert.

Mikey smiled at him kindly and for some reason his expression made Sean feel instantly and acutely guilty. He realized that this was the first moment since Mikey's arrival that they'd really been alone together. He'd been so wrapped up in Candy and in his own tiny Hong Kong world these past months he'd barely understood that his best friend had come all the way over from England just to see him.

He heard himself saying: 'Hey, Mikey, it's really, you know . . .' The words caught in his throat. He wanted to say that he was grateful, or that he loved him, or something kind, but somehow it seemed suddenly easier to crack a joke. He started smiling enthusiastically at Mikey, hoping that maybe he'd say the words for him. 'You know,' was all he could manage second time round.

Mikey snorted. 'Yeah, Sean, it's good to spend time with you too, mate.'

Thank God! Sean thought to himself with relief. That was exactly what he had wanted to say. He sipped on his wine and grinned. 'It's been ages, hasn't it?'

'Not since university,' Mikey agreed.

'I'm glad, you know . . . that you're here.' Sean was surprised at himself. 'Mikey . . .'

'Please don't call me that,' Mikey said unexpectedly, casting a sideways glance.

'What?'

'You know I hate it,' he said, turning to look back at Sean.

'No I didn't,' Sean replied innocently enough.

'It makes me sound like such a . . .'

'Twat?'

'Sloane.'

Sean laughed.

'I think I preferred it when you called me Marland,' Mikey continued.

Sean didn't say anything. He liked indulging Mikey in his little tirades.

'I just don't see why everyone's name has to be abbreviated.'

'We only use it because we love you, Mikey,' Sean said, stirring him a little.

'But people who don't even know me call me Mikey.'

'Like who?'

'Roo and Jamie and Fi Fi and Munkie and all that lot.'

'They know you.'

'Barely, I only met them a couple of months ago.'

'Well, they probably don't know what else to call you. Everyone calls you Mikey, just like you use their nicknames.'

'That's exactly my point. I don't know their real names. If I did, maybe I'd use them.'

'Why don't you ask them then?'

'Oh, I dunno,' Mikey sighed heavily. 'It's not really the names that bother me, it's just . . . the whole expatriate gang scene. I find it pretty weird. I don't think I've had a proper conversation with anyone since I got here. It's always about what party to go to next, see you down at Lan Kwai Fong . . . all of that. It's a nightmare.'

Sean looked at him. Always too heavy, Mikey, always too heavy.

'Doesn't it drive you mad?' Mikey finished.

'I've never really thought about it before.'

'Oh, come on, Sean. I know that you find all this,' Mikey glanced across the restaurant as if he were casting his eyes across their lives in Hong Kong, 'to be a load of superficial bullshit. Doesn't it get you down? Having to make out like everything is love and happiness and a great time and just-like-university-was and how we don't have a care in the world and no one ever argues and everyone is just bestest bestest friends. It's stifling having to be friends with people you don't know, not even knowing if you really like them. I'm not saying I don't like them, I'm just saying I don't really see why I'm friends with them. All I know is, I arrived in Hong Kong and I suddenly had this whole social scene. I haven't made any of my own friends here. All my friends are people you or someone else we knew at Leeds has introduced me to. I'm friends with all these people and I don't even know their names. It seems so bloody false.'

Sean paused and breathed. Mikey had exposed the one key flaw in his attitude to life since coming to Hong Kong, since his decision to put his depression away. It *was* false. Sean had been living a lie in Hong Kong. Nothing but a lie. With a sudden dead weight in his stomach, he realized that perhaps this was how he'd lost Candy. By being something, someone he wasn't. She knew that he wasn't Mr Good Time All The Time. But he'd hidden this weakness from her, put on a mask. And the only thing it had achieved was confusion. Candy didn't know who Sean was any more so she'd fallen out of love with him. She'd lost sight of the man she loved. God, even he'd lost sight of the man he was. Wasn't that what the trading, the wide-boy persona, the porn and the prostitutes were all about – his pretending that everything was just about having a laugh?

'I . . .' Sean started, looking down at his plate. 'I guess.'

'So you agree?'

Sean shrugged his shoulders. Then, for some reason, maybe it was because they weren't in Hong Kong, because they were away from it all, he decided to explain. 'This is the best way for me,' Sean started conclusively, looking at Mikey now, determined. 'If I was going to really share . . . God, how do I put this?' he said, looking up at a lamp above him momentarily. 'If I was going to really share my thoughts with everyone else I don't think they'd want to know me any more.'

'What do you mean?'

'No one's interested in Heavy, Mikey. Half the point is to not think. Thinking fucks you. Everyone just wants to have fun, especially here, where no one is looking and they can do whatever they like.'

'What? Like shag whores?'

'Yeah, exactly, like shag whores. And get pissed and be stupid and just . . . God, you don't need me to tell you. You've seen it. Everyone just wants to enjoy themselves and that suits me 'cos I don't think I want to get real with people. I don't *want* to know their real names. I don't want them to know my last name. I don't want them to know about my problems with Candy, about how depressed I get, about how I'm going bald, how much I hate it here, about how much I hate myself. Who wants to know about all the shit that's inside my head?'

Sean heard the last sentence come out too violently. There was a long pause.

'I do,' Mikey said eventually.

Sean looked back at him and sighed heavily through his nose.

'Yeah, I know you do,' Sean replied quietly.

'So you're still getting depressed then?' Mikey asked.

'Hasn't exactly been a great year.'

'Do you still . . .' Mikey stopped.

'See,' Sean laughed. 'Even you can't say it any more. Hong Kong's getting to you, mate.'

Sean watched Mikey looking at him strangely.

'I'm not going to top myself in the immediate future, if that's what you want to know,' Sean stated.

'Good,' Mikey said.

They didn't say anything for a while.

'Are you really going bald?' Mikey eventually restarted.

Sean took his baseball cap off and tipped his head down to reveal the horror. He was stunned when he heard Mikey laugh.

'I know, it's terrible, isn't it?' Sean said, assuming the worst.

'God, if you think that's going bald, Sean . . .' He paused. 'Your hair is fine, Sean.'

'Really?'

'Yeah. I don't know why you'd think otherwise,' Mikey said. 'Come on, Sean, what is all this about? You've never struck me as particularly vain. You know you're a good-looking guy. Why are you so worried all of a sudden about your hair?'

'I dunno. A hairdresser mentioned it once.'

'Jesus, sometimes I really worry about you. You're so down on yourself all the time. Even though everyone loves you and thinks you're great and all the girls fancy you, all you can think about is how you're going bald and about how much of a loser you are and about how you're going to cope with life after Candy. You've got to give yourself a break, man. You've got to know that you're all right, that you're going to be all right.'

'You think so?' Sean said, looking at Mikey, loving him for being so kind.

'Yeah, of course. Look, Sean, maybe you just can't see it

because you're going through a rough patch, but you must know most guys would give their right arm to be you. *I* would give my right arm to be you. You want to see balding. Taking a fucking a look at my forehead. That's recession mate.'

'You're not bald, Mikey.'

'Oh, please.'

'Well, OK. Maybe your forehead *is* a little pronounced.'

'Piss off.'

Sean laughed and heard himself say, 'Mikey, Mikey, Mikey. I really have missed you. You're the only one who even vaguely understands, you're the only one I can really trust. If you weren't here . . . well, let, just say I'm going to carry on calling you Mikey,' he said, holding up his glass. 'I feel that we're close enough for me to deserve that right?'

'All right, Scanic. If you insist.'

They clinked.

'I do.'

There was a meaningful pause as they drank.

'Why don't you just leave?' Mikey said eventually.

'I should, shouldn't I?' Sean replied.

'You've been here long enough,' Mikey said. 'You've got your foot in the door of a career. Maybe you should take that transfer to Japan your company offered.'

'Yeah,' Sean nodded.

Mikey looked at Sean, both of them knowing he wasn't going anywhere.

'It's not going to help you, Sean,' Mikey said. 'Being in the same city as Candy, seeing her around all the time. It won't help you get over her, get yourself back together again. This place is destroying you.'

'Nothing will help me get over her,' Sean replied.

'Time will,' Michael said quietly.

Sean started crying then. The tears just formed and fell and when he felt Mikey's hand on his arm he had to swallow hard three times to control himself. He wanted to sob for all mankind, just once, just for a few minutes. Life seemed suddenly so sad. But he knew if he started he wouldn't be able to stop. He managed to pull back from the abyss . . . just.

After what seemed like a very long time, Mikey finally looked at him said: 'Shall we go fuck some whores then, or what?'

Sean managed a smile.

will rhode

# Chapter Fifty-Three

Before Candy knew what was happening (maybe she'd nodded off) the boat was suddenly lurching and banking and Stephen was quickly on the bow, reaching with a hook for a buoy in the sea. The white of the boat glared violently and for a brief instant the sun flashed against the water, swallowing Stephen. Candy squinted and cupped her eyes and he slowly reappeared – at first just a sketch without substance but then his form slowly filling, like a white ghost incarnating. Beyond him Candy saw land, another bay, the gentle green curving round them. The sight of it was easier on the eyes.

'This is it,' Stephen announced, stripping off his shirt. 'We have to swim from here.'

'I didn't bring my swimsuit,' Candy replied.

'There's a bikini down below,' Stephen said.

Candy raised her eyebrows but didn't say anything. She was secretly impressed with his style. Just as Daddy had said. Much more than Sean, perhaps even more than lover-boy Rob. For some reason, Candy found that she didn't want to think about the *others* at the moment. She was enjoying herself.

Down below, the cabin smelt of sun tan lotion. And freshly cleaned wood. Candy had to bow her head as she dressed, the ceiling was low. She let her skirt slip onto the floor as she changed her top. She didn't know why she did things that way. Backwards. Normally she would have changed her knickers first before taking off her skirt. Maybe it was the alcohol or the cramped conditions. Strip and then dress, instead of matching the moments with the corresponding bits.

And that's when she felt him. An inner sense screamed and she glanced up. Stephen was staring at her through a cabin window. Not lecherous or sick or scary – just impassive. Like she was an object, another feature of the boat, a part to consider. She didn't know what to do. The alcohol almost made her feel like it didn't matter – his looking at her.

But then she remembered herself and she rushed to cover her nakedness. An arm went across her chest and then she crouched to the floor, near her skirt – like an animal looking for cover – shimmying it pathetically back up around her calves. She looked up again and he was still staring at her, his face unreadable. She tried to hold his eyes. She thought about saying something. 'Fuck off' came to mind. And then, quite suddenly, he was gone.

She heard him diving into the water.

'It's nothing, it doesn't matter,' Candy said out loud to herself, shaking her head slightly. She breathed heavily to quell the nerves that were still bouncing. Then she finished changing into the bikini, which fitted her perfectly, and stepped outside. The surface of the boat was rough and warm on the soles of her feet. Stephen had started swimming and was nearly halfway to the beach already.

Candy dived in, the water pressing into her ears as she went down. It turned cold quickly so she arched her back and kicked. It was warmer nearer the surface. She started to swim.

When she reached the beach, feeling a little less drunk and a little more wary, Stephen was dressed in a burgundy dressing gown and was waiting for her with towels. She emerged, stumbling slightly on some pebbles that bordered the shore (why was she so unsure footed today?) and wringing the water from her hair in an effort to seem casual and hide the body language that said she felt very naked in front of him. *He had seen her naked.* She told herself again that it didn't matter.

'Well, you're certainly full of surprises,' she said to him, taking a towel and grinning as water dripped off her.

Stephen pointed towards a path that ran up the hill from one end of the beach. At the top, obscured by harsh bracken and trees, there was a house, concrete and white with a terrace and large sliding windows.

'I'm impressed,' Candy said.

She found herself looking at the shape of their footprints in the sand as they walked. For some reason, she wanted to see how his looked next to hers. But he walked too slowly for her to really see.

At the steps leading to the house he made her walk in front of him. Candy tried to tread lightly and not think about the fact that his face was just behind her arse.

It was cold inside the house – a shaded, concrete cold as opposed to an air-conditioned cold. The air felt different, refreshing. There was a dark corridor. It led to a living room, which was tiled and empty, with the exception of a white sofa and a long, low wooden table. Artwork hung on two walls.

'Is this where you used to come as kids?' Candy said, thinking to herself that it wasn't very homely, more like a bachelor pad. At least it was clean.

Stephen looked at her and Candy found herself able to look back. She knew what he was thinking, so she stepped towards him and took his hand in hers, their fingers entwining. She angled her face and then moved to kiss him, drawing him closer. She closed her eyes and let her lips open slightly and then she heard him say:

'No kissing.'

With the same kind of ruthless simplicity and cold logic that filled the house, Candy felt Stephen move her against the wall and prop himself against her. She looked at him and wondered if she was stupid. A house, in the middle of nowhere, on an island she didn't know, a secret beach, no one knowing where she was. Yes, she laughed. She was stupid, incredibly stupid.

'What's so funny?' Stephen said, holding her against the wall.

Candy could feel the alcohol. 'Nothing,' she said, as she moved to kiss him again, thinking that he must have been joking.

Stephen turned his head away. Candy stopped and looked at him, a frown emerging. She tried again, this time more determined. She wanted to kiss him. And again he pulled his head back.

'I told you. No kissing,' he said.

That was when he grabbed her bikini knickers and yanked them down. Candy froze. Stephen's hand went down and twisted like a crowbar between her thighs, spreading them as far as they would go with the elastic from the bikini caught round her knees. Before she knew what was happening he was inside her. He didn't look at her when he fucked her. He just stared across her shoulder and into the cold white of the wall. Her body jarred against the concrete. She watched him as he pumped. She tried to slow him down. She tried to ride with him. She kissed his neck. He tolerated that. She moved to take his face in her hands. But he pushed her back and held her against the wall until, eventually, after what seemed like a very long time, he grunted into her.

# Chapter Fifty-Four

The whorehouse was on the fourth floor of a five-storey complex that also contained a casino, a strip club, a singles bar and a restaurant. Each activity took up an entire floor and the buttons in the lift were labelled accordingly. Michael could tell that Sean knew where he was going as he pressed the Members Only button.

The lift doors opened and they were immediately in a white-tiled reception with a small podium-like desk and a thin micro-phone on a bendy length of metal flex. There was a Chinese woman with red lipstick. Behind her and to her left there was a long red velvet curtain. The woman smiled at them as they approached. Then, in one swift series of formalities, she said her greetings, took Sean's credit card, pressed a button and suddenly the curtain parted. As it swished, Michael noticed that there were three heavy-set bouncers standing against the walls.

Some of the women, all of whom were dressed in either bikinis or colourfully transparent negligés, looked up from behind the Perspex. A few of them smiled, a couple looked bored. Three of them were knitting. They sat on a set of stag-gered steps, slightly spaced apart, mostly with their legs crossed. They all wore numbers, golden, rounded numbers on thick white plastic pendants, threaded through an element of their clothing – more like a part of the costume than a painful signature branded onto the flesh, Michael found himself observing.

Indeed, it didn't look or feel like human slavery to Michael and he wasn't put off. In many ways he preferred this arrangement to the blind selection process at Happy Endings. He wanted to know what he was getting for his money this time. Of that much he was certain. One or two of the prostitutes – who all looked Thai – were stunning.

'Take your pick, Mikey.'

'Erm, twenty-eight.'

'I'm taking fourteen.'

The Chinese receptionist relayed their choices down the microphone and their two numbers efficiently stood and walked, both in platform heels, to an invisible white door that suddenly clicked open from an invisible white wall. Sean and Michael were led down a corridor and there they were met by the prostitutes and led silently into separate rooms.

Michael was a little drunk and the coke that he and Sean had done on the dashboard of the Mini Moke was mellowing as he followed the girl, who for some reason was starting to feel like his girlfriend, into the room. He giggled behind her and she turned and took his hand and guided him onto a bed-like massage table in one corner. She poured bubble bath into a jacuzzi in the opposite corner of the room and turned on the taps. The sound of water crashed. Michael noticed that there was also a sink, a school-like chair, some coat hangers on a hook and, just like Happy Endings, stacks of white towels and bathrobes piled in places. If they were trying to make the place feel clean, it worked.

'You'll have to forgive me, I'm a little drunk,' Michael said gently before hoisting himself up on to the table-cum-bed. 'And I've never done this before.'

The girl smiled at him and kneeled down to undo his shoes. 'That's OK,' she replied. One shoe slipped off easily. Michael was glad that he'd changed his socks. For some reason he found that he didn't want to make a bad impression. The moment was even starting to feel like it could be vaguely romantic. He decided that he wasn't going to do anything, he'd let her control things. After all, there was no Game to be played here. Everything – E.V.E.R.Y.T.H.I.N.G. – was available. The other shoe fell to the ground.

'What's your name?' Michael said as she stood between his knees and started to wrestle with his belt buckle.

'Mai,' she replied.

'You're from Thailand?'

She nodded back at him and Michael noticed that she was nervous too. It reassured him.

'Here, I'll do that,' he said, taking her hand away from the belt that she couldn't undo.

Mai turned around and started to undress by the chair. Michael watched her. She was wearing a complicated purple negligé that criss-crossed at the back and looped its way through the waistline of her knickers. In order to undo it she had to twist and turn and reveal. Michael saw the edge of one breast, the glimpse of a nipple, her stomach folding in two seams, the long, dark run of an inner thigh. It was as if the clothing had been designed to reveal her, the suggestion of nakedness as she undressed more exposing than a full-frontal display.

Michael started to get an erection. Mai had one of the best bodies he'd ever seen, perhaps the best that he'd ever seen in the flesh. Smooth, coffee-coloured skin and a gravity-defying orb for an arse. Michael pulled his boxer shorts down in the same movement with his trousers. She undid a clip in her hair. There was a brief, black tumble before she reached round and redid the same style using the same clip, just more tightly this time. When she lifted her arms above her head to adjust her hair Michael saw a breast in all its totality. It was larger than her frame would have suggested.

Michael resisted the urge to grab her from behind. He'd promised himself that she was the whore and that she would have to do everything to him. That was what he wanted for his (well, Sean's) money. And, besides, he wanted to make her feel comfortable. He wanted her to make love to him, he didn't want to fuck her – like all the other men? What other men, he suddenly wondered. How many other men? Tonight? Last night? Where was he in the list?

'How old are you?' Michael asked.

'Twenty-five,' Mai answered, still with her back to him.

Twenty-five. Seemed old for a prostitute. Maybe she'd been with a lot of men. Hundreds of fat, sweaty, greasy, toothless men that slobbered on her and ejaculated and then paid. Was Michael another one of these men? Was he just like all the other bastards that soiled this thread of beauty? He suddenly thought, did he want to do this?

She turned to face him. He looked at her and she looked directly back. Her face was made up but it still looked girlish and innocent. Maybe she'd been made up to look girlish and innocent. Either way, she didn't look like she was an 'old hand'. There was nothing about her that exuded the notion that hundreds of fat, ugly, sweaty, toothless, balding men had spent the evening writhing on top of her. All Michael could see when she turned, naked and perfectly shaped, was that he wanted her.

She walked towards him and helped him unbutton his shirt.

'Kiss me,' Michael said, looking up at her.

Mai smiled sweetly and kissed him on the cheek.

'Kiss me,' he said again, lustily.

She smiled again and said, 'No kissing.'

Michael didn't realize that they were both stealing lines from *Pretty Woman*.

'Why do you do this?' he said, true to his naïve form.

She raised her eyebrows. 'For money,' she replied gently.

'Do you have a boyfriend?'

'Yes.'

'And he doesn't mind that you do this?'

Unlike Doris, Mai didn't roll her eyes or sneer at Michael's interrogation.

'He not know.'

'He doesn't know?'

'No. He in Thailand. I save money so he come here and we live.'

Michael very nearly did back out when she said that. Mai was a person. A beautiful woman with a boyfriend and dreams. How could Michael use her like this? How could he contribute to the plague of human slavery and entrapment and abuse and, and, and . . .

But then Mai leant down to his ear and touched his penis and said: 'I want to have bath with you, Big Boy.'

# Chapter Fifty-Five

Sound was the first thing to come back. For a moment, everything had gone quiet, deadly silent, an instant of deafness. But it was only for a moment. Nothing more than a temporary block, a fleeting absence from this world, and then he was back, straight into the deep shit of it.

'Hey! Hey!' Mai's voice swelled into his consciousness. She was snapping at him from the bath, two, three fingers clawing. 'Hey! You OK? You OK?'

'What?' Michael asked, still dazed.

'You OK? You OK? AIDS? No AIDS!'

'OK? Am I OK?' Michael said, hearing the words. Time seemed to stretch and then snap, just like the condom that was now only a tightly coiled rubber ring strangling the base of his cock. 'Are you asking me if I've got AIDS?'

'You OK?' Mai said, more quietly this time.

'Errr, yeah! I'm fucking OK. What about you?' He wanted to accuse her of being the whore, the more likely risk in the equation. But he didn't. 'Are *you* OK?'

'Yes. I OK.'

'How do you know?'

'We test. Every week.'

Michael didn't exactly find this reassuring. He reached down and ripped the remains of the condom from his prick, already retrospectively going over the whole disaster in his mind. How could this happen to him? Then again, wasn't it typical? Michael – the man that had never shagged a whore in his life and the first time he did it the condom split. It was more than just typical. It was . . .

ARRRRRRRRRRRRRRRRRGH!

The dark prospect of HIV soon overshadowed his fury at himself.

Fuck.

Michael.

Mikey, Mikey, Mikey, Mikey . . . he muttered his nickname to himself, like some embryonic mantra, hoping that if he could just start with the basics – *Who was he?* – then he could rationalize things, get a grip on them, see the bright side, reassure himself in some way.

But then he looked down at his penis and he had to sigh heavily through another wave of nausea. There was no escaping it. Michael had just had unprotected sex with a Thai whore in Macao. This had to be considered one of life's more high-risk activities, right? Oriental Roulette – he could practically hear the wheel spinning – *clickety, clickety, clickety, click* . . . How long it would take for the ball to fall, or, more appropriately, for the bullet to find the chamber?

Fuck.

# Chapter Fifty-Six

When Sean saw Mikey finally step out into the reception area, there was none of the bravado he'd been anticipating – the calls of muh-eyne! Just a quiet smile and a lift in the eyebrows that suggested they leave. He was a little disappointed – not least because he'd been loving the way Mikey had been acting like one of the lads lately. He'd picked up the trader talk in no time (there was no end to the amusement of saying Mine, Yours and Done repeatedly at one another). And now he was shagging whores as well! Could this be the same Mikey? It may have been base and shallow and unreal and a lie and all of that stuff they'd been talking about earlier, but it was also fun. Like doing something naughty together when they were boys. Shagging whores was one of those things you could only do with your mates – it brought you closer. At least, it made shagging whores feel a lot less lonely.

'All right, stud?' he said, as Mikey came close. 'You took your time.'

Mikey shrugged his shoulders. 'Yeah, well, she fucking loved it.'

'Class!' Sean grinned back at him.

They stepped into the lift just as their two girls – re-dressed now in lingerie – stepped out into reception to wave them goodbye. Sean and Mikey cooed back at them as they squealed their farewells, like little schoolgirls.

Sean stabbed the button for the strip club. They travelled in silence. When the doors opened a wave of cheap techno music barrelled into the lift and curled back in on itself, crashing on top of them. There was the glare of flashing disco lights and strobes against a pitch-black relief. Three Chinese men wearing pastel-coloured suits bloomed into view, wanting to use the lift. Sean blindly led the way out. Mikey followed him.

The strip club was tiered. Tables closer to the stage were more expensive for drinks. Leggy Canadian women (there was a link between Hong Kong and Canada that Sean didn't fully under-stand yet – it had something to do with passports and money) were doing acrobatic things against metal poles. There was also a row of seats round the stage itself – but you had to slip tips into the strippers' tits there and Sean wasn't about to pay for anything with cash. He planned to expense this trip. He chose a booth in the middle of the club. It wasn't the best of views but it was slightly quieter and more private than everywhere else, and he was dying to find out how Mikey had got on.

Before they'd even sat down, a tall Chinese woman wearing a black leotard over black tights approached them and demanded they order drinks. Sean got them each a beer. He pulled out his cigarettes and lit one, leaning back into the purple velvet-covered booth, sweeping a hand through his hair. It was still wet from the jacuzzi.

'You're being very quiet,' Sean said, squinting as smoke squirmed into his eyes.

Mikey smiled faintly at him and reached for a cigarette.

'So come on then,' Sean started as the waitress arrived with their beers. 'What was she like? I tell you, mate, she was fine. I wasn't sure at first but when she came out to say goodbye – Lord!'

Mikey took a swig on his beer and then pinched the bridge of his nose with his free hand. There was a heavy sigh before he said, very dramatically: 'My condom split.'

Sean didn't say anything. He couldn't see the significance.

'I think I've got AIDS,' Mikey continued.

Sean looked at him for a moment to see if he was joking. But he could tell, Mikey was being deadly serious. Sean couldn't help himself from laughing.

'What the fuck is so funny about that?' Mikey said, glaring at him. 'I've got AIDS and all you can do is laugh.'

Sean shook his head. Only Mikey could be so melodramatic.

'Mikey, there's no way you've got AIDS,' he managed between his sniggers.

'How would you know?'

"Cos . . . well.'

Sean suddenly realized that he didn't know. He'd never really thought about it before. Well, maybe at first, way back, when Charlie first took him out whoring, but he'd never dwelt on it. There didn't seem much point. Everything had its risks. If all you ever thought about were the risks, there wouldn't be much fun in life. Besides, he knew loads of blokes that had shagged whores without protection and they seemed to be all right.

'Mikey,' Sean restarted, 'you'd have to be pretty fucking unlucky to get HIV on your first time with a whore.'

'Well, I am unlucky, aren't I? I'm a fucking klutz.'

'Condoms split on me all the time,' Sean said.

'Really?' Mikey seized.

'Yeah,' Sean said encouragingly. 'I really don't see what you're so worried about.'

'Fuck,' Mikey sighed, taking another drag on his cigarette. 'I knew I should have used my own. I told her I had my own. Maybe she didn't understand. She used hers – some crap fucking Chinese brand. God, I wish the condom hadn't split.'

'Listen, Mikey,' Sean said, genuinely wanting to reassure him now. 'Think about it. How long do you reckon you were inside her after the condom split?'

'I don't know. Couple of minutes.'

'Well, there you go then. There's no way you can get AIDS from two minutes of shagging. I mean, do you know how difficult it is for a guy to get AIDS from a woman? Your dick has to be all sliced up and shit. Is your dick sliced up?'

'No.'

'See?'

'Well, she *was* pretty upset when I came inside her. She seemed more worried that *I* had AIDS,' Mikey said, managing a vague smile now.

'Exactly,' Sean pressed, not letting Mikey indulge himself any further. 'She doesn't even have it. I'm telling you, mate, you've got absolutely nothing to worry about.'

'Sure?' Mikey said.

'Sure I'm sure.' Sean answered. 'Now come on, let's have another beer, sit back and enjoy the show, yeah? Everything is going to be fine, I promise.'

Mikey seemed to relax a little. After a few moments of relative quiet (the music had mellowed into something operatic for the sake of a new routine that involved a three-way lesbian act) Mikey managed: 'I have to admit, it was the best sex I've had in a long time.'

'I know,' Sean said, grinning. 'They're wicked, aren't they?'

'Yeah.'

'They love it.'

'Well, she certainly did.'

'They all fucking love it,' Sean said, beaming.

Mikey finally managed a smile.

# Chapter Fifty-Seven

An hour or so later and Michael still couldn't shake the feeling that he had AIDS. They were still in the strip club, neither of them saying much.

By now, the place was pretty much empty. Michael had tried to act like he was having a good time – he didn't want Sean to see him dwelling on his misfortune. But when Sean finally suggested that they leave (sensing Michael's lack of enthusiasm for naked women, no doubt) Michael found himself nearly begging that they stay, because the only place he didn't want to be, more than here, was bed. He knew that he'd never sleep. He was still coked up and he had the Fear bad. If only the condom hadn't split, he kept thinking to himself. If only, if only, if only . . .

In the end, though, he didn't protest, because he also had a spectacular headache.

'So what's next?' Michael said, trying to sound jovial as they reached the lift, the strobe lights echoing behind them.

'Dunno,' Sean said. 'Beer back at the hotel room?'

Michael groaned silently to himself. 'Cool,' he said quietly.

The drive passed without memory.

When they got back to the hotel, Michael suggested they do another line.

Sean looked at him like he was ill or something. 'I'm good,' Sean said, pulling beers out of the mini bar. 'You do one if you want.'

Michael didn't say anything but watched Sean as he collapsed back onto one of the beds and stretched. What was he going to do? He didn't dare bring up his worry again – he knew what Sean would say – but, at the same time, he had to think of a way to keep Sean awake. He didn't want to be alone. Not in the dark. Part of him believed he'd never sleep again. Michael was terrified. He wanted someone to hold him. Mummy. Anyone really. Just some tenderness. He felt so alone. He was very close to crying. He looked up when he heard Sean's beer thud against the carpeted floor.

Sean was asleep.

# Chapter Fifty-Eight

The sky was a sea of darkness, without the sun to light the way.

Under it, Sean was lost and adrift, floating in a vast, black ocean: a single human head and a pair of arms surrounded by seeming infinity. His legs and body dangled below the surface like bait. Not naked but feeling so because they were identifiable – a something drifting on the surface of a nothing, an unfathomable expanse of emptiness stretching below.

A shark might eat him at any moment, he thought to himself. Then it occurred to him that that moment itself would be another minuscule something in the midst of another infinite nothing: an instant in Time.

Enormous plains of water sighed around him, lifting him up and then slowly allowing him to fall. The black sea horizon melted into the sky so there was no longer a point of separation between the two. The only difference between *here*: this cold, liquid here, and *there*: that cold, ether *there* was the stars. Billions of them, smearing infinity like a stain.

There was no moon. The sky was a sea of darkness.

Sean stared up and carried on breathing. He was still alive. How long had he been lost? It was hard to say. Six, maybe seven hours. He hadn't thought it would take this long, that he'd have this much time to think.

He watched the darknesses merging more. Now the black sea seemed to rise up and meet the night. He could still feel the water supporting him, like a level, a point of resistance, a reference in the expanse. But the already all-encompassing Black was becoming bigger as it found itself and collected.

Being all alone in the dark like this . . .

Sean looked up at the sky again and suddenly noticed that the stars had disappeared and that the darknesses merging had actually been him descending.

As expected, his body panicked and his arms thrashed when he realized with even more horror that the surface, the point of resistance, was gone now. It was no longer below him, it was no longer supporting him. It was above and now it was pressing him down. He was under the water . . . deep below the surface. In the final death throes he kicked and swam and his lungs tried to perceive which way was UP but the stars were gone so it was hard to tell.

The sky was a sea of darkness.

He was down, deep below the surface of a dark sea. He may have even smiled before breathing in a sharp lungful of water, but he wasn't sure. Sean didn't see his life flash before his eyes.

Mikey's voice brushed somewhere, the outer reaches of his consciousness. Sean was suddenly aware that he was floating in the middle of his own universe, this was *his* Blackness, and now there was something beyond him. He wished the sound away. He didn't want Mikey. He didn't want life. This was what he wanted: the comfort of non-existence.

Sean knew he'd never have the guts to commit suicide. It was too violent. But given a choice, say by God, between Life and Nothing, a simple case of pressing a button ON/OFF, Sean knew which he'd go for.

But then he felt himself, as if drawn on a hook, travelling with increasing velocity away from the centre of the void and towards the edge, towards the imperceptible glare. Before he could hold himself back, Sean had reached a sickening light speed and then – quickly – he'd broken through, and the black universe shattered as Sean opened his eyes.

# Chapter Fifty-Nine

'What?' Sean said, blinking into the bedside light. 'What's wrong?'

'Can't sleep,' Mikey said, embarrassed, ashamed, sitting on the edge of Sean's bed, next to him.

'Why not?'

'I'm scared, Sean,' Mikey quivered.

Sean rubbed his eyes. What time was it? It was impossible to tell. Did it matter? He could taste cocaine and nicotine at the back of his throat, in the space where his nose drained into his mouth. He sniffed.

'Why?'

'I don't want to die.'

Sean sighed. 'You're not going to die, Mikey.'

Silence. Mikey breathed. Sean was naked under the sheets. How had he got there? It didn't matter. He could feel Mikey through them. They were touching. Mikey was in his boxer shorts.

'I . . .' Mikey said after a while. 'I'm sorry, Sean.'

Sean didn't say anything.

'I'm sorry I told on you.'

Sean blinked. It was weird how deep the understanding ran between them, the idea that they could communicate on two levels like this and always know what the other was talking about. Even though they were in Macao, even though it was the middle of the night, even though they were much older now, one of them only had to say a few words and they could carry the other right back – back to St Luke's, back to 1983.

'Why did you, then?' Sean said. He'd never asked before, partly because Mikey had always seemed too vulnerable, too weak to justify his betrayal, and partly because the opportunity to ask had never arisen till now. But Sean had always wanted to ask, even though he knew the answer. He still wanted to hear Mikey say it.

'I don't know,' Mikey said, his head bowed, his shoulders slouched. He looked like a beaten man. Easy to confuse him for someone else, this wasn't the Mikey that Sean knew. This was Marland. 'They . . . you know, I don't know. I was scared. I thought we'd been caught.'

'Caught doing what?'

Mikey looked at Sean then, their eyes meeting dead on. 'We killed him, didn't we?'

It wasn't a question, it was a confirmation. *We killed him, didn't we . . . that's what we got caught doing*. Sean looked back into Mikey's eyes. He wasn't angry, even now. He could see that Mikey still genuinely believed that Sean had pushed Baxter. Shit! There had even been times when Sean thought he might have – Mikey had seemed so convinced, especially back then, back at school. Maybe Mikey knew something, saw something, that Sean hadn't, that Sean had since blocked out, a case of selective amnesia.

But that wasn't the truth.

The truth was Baxter's death had been an accident. Nothing more. Sean remembered the day like yesterday. The way Baxter had seen everyone crossing but not the cars coming, because the trucks were in the way. He'd simply sprinted out from the woods and into the road. And then . . . it was just an accident.

So why did Mikey think it was something more?

Sean had his theories. Mikey had suffered more than anyone at St Luke's, mainly because he took it so bad, which only attracted more grief. And twelve-year-old boys. They could be particularly vicious. Sean had read about it once but he couldn't remember where. The mix of childlike imagination combined with the onset of sexuality . . . it established perversions. Sean didn't know about that, he wasn't much of a one for amateur psychology. But he remembered the evil.

And what happened to Mikey *was* evil, pure and simple. It was twisted and it twisted Mikey's mind – turned a simple road accident into a murder. Maybe Mikey had wanted Baxter to be dead so badly that, when it actually happened, he believed that he must have been in some way responsible, that it must have been his fault. Maybe it simply wasn't enough for Mikey that Baxter die. Maybe he had to be murdered, in Mikey's mind, for justice to be served. Maybe Mikey wanted to be blamed, credited even, with Baxter's death, but knowing that he could never have done it himself, being so weak and vulnerable and impotent, he'd projected the deed onto Sean.

After all, Mikey had always idolized Sean, thought of him as some kind of Superman. Just because Sean had stood up for him once or twice at school. It had been hard to live up to this expectation of him. Christ it had been hard. Sean wasn't a hero. He was a fucking loser. His girlfriend had dumped him. He did a meaningless job. He fucked whores. He wanked on lunch break. He was going bald. Couldn't Mikey see how pathetic and loathsome Sean was? Why did he look up to him? Why did he love him? Sean found it hard to handle the disappointment he saw in Mikey's eyes whenever he failed – which was a lot these days. A part of him even resented it. He didn't want to be Mikey's hero. He didn't want to be anyone's hero. Sean hated himself. Why couldn't Mikey despise him as he should?

'It was an accident, Mikey,' Sean said. 'It was just an accident.'

Mikey nodded, recognizing the words. 'I'm still sorry I told on you,' Mikey said.

'It's OK,' Sean snorted. 'It's not like I got into trouble or anything.'

'Only because the school didn't want the scandal,' Mikey said. 'Had to be one of biggest cover-ups of all time.'

'Yeah,' Sean grinned. 'Tishgate.'

They didn't say anything for a while. Sean looked at Mikey. He looked tired. Very tired. But still young, like a little boy. Sean gulped. Poor Mikey. He'd always be just a little boy. Even though he was a man now, he'd always be the weakling. The experience had made its mark on him at too early a stage. He was damaged now – irreparably so. There was never any changing that. Fear and insecurity had been sewn into his very being. Sean felt painfully for him then. They were very close. Everything was quiet. It was dark inside the room. They were alone. They were together. No one was watching.

'Come on,' Sean said, very gently, very quietly, almost imperceptibly as he shifted to turn out the light and make room in the bed. 'Get in.'

# Chapter Sixty

The hallway outside Mr Bride's office was tiled white, with shapes of green ivy set in the centre of squares. The door to the building, which was an elegant red-brick house with turrets and alcoves and a dark wooden staircase, had stained glass in it. The late sun shone low and through the door as Marland waited, casting cold shapes of coloured light on the ochre-painted walls.

Marland sat on a wooden bench, his head humming with nerves.

He'd only been to see the Headmaster once before, and not because he was in trouble. He'd come to collect a prize for a project he'd written about Crete after Mummy had taken him there on holiday one summer. He'd only worked so hard on the project because Mummy had told him a story about how she and Daddy had lived in Crete once, when they were young, before the divorce. He'd probably been conceived there, she'd said. After Marland had got the prize, they'd sent him up a year and given him a boarding scholarship. And that was how everything, the hell, had begun. It was only later, years later, that Mum told him he'd actually made a mistake. It hadn't been Crete. She and Daddy had lived in Corfu.

A large wooden door to the right of Marland suddenly swung

open. It was the Bursar's office, and out of it strode the Bursar. A huge balding man with kind, light eyes. He was dressed in corduroys. The Bursar looked at Marland, who looked back up at him as if he was expecting to be struck at any moment.

'Don't worry, boy,' the Bursar said gently. 'Everything is going to be fine.'

Marland just looked at him.

The Bursar smiled and then strode three steps across the tiled hall and into the Headmaster's office across the way. Marland gulped when he saw the Bursar rap on the door briefly and he heard the Headmaster's deep voice resonate, 'Come.' Even the Bursar had to ask permission to see the Headmaster. Mr Bride was that powerful – even more powerful than Fishface Haddock.

A cold through-draft rushed from a gap at the bottom of the front door when the Bursar entered Mr Bride's office, travelling across the tiles and up the bottoms of Marland's trouser legs. The silhouette of a birch tree danced outside and then a cloud passed and the hallway went quickly dark.

After a while the Bursar stepped out of the Headmaster's office.

'Mr Bride would like to see you now, Michael,' he said.

Marland found it hard to find his feet. His legs were already shaking. He watched himself stand and move, the sound of his school shoes rapping against the floor. He could feel the rough fabric of his trousers against his legs, the collar of his shirt rubbing into his neck. Basic good sense told him to stop going forward, but he couldn't help himself. He was drawn towards that door by an authority that had been instilled into him. There was no point resisting. When the Headmaster asked to see you, you went.

When he did eventually step into Mr Bride's office it was

like walking into another world. The carpet was a strange lime green and there was a big desk with two uninviting stiff wooden chairs in front of it. Light caught in net curtains that dressed a large bay window, making them seem very white. The room smelt clean. Not clean-like-the-rest-of-the-school clean, which stank of bleach. It smelt clean in a normal way, almost like home. It momentarily transported Marland into the outside world, the world beyond the bushes. And yet not quite. The culture shock wasn't total. The freshness still intermingled with the wood and the books and carried a vague trace of desks and education. This was presumably the image that the Headmaster wanted to present to the outside world, the image that camouflaged the vicious hell that spread among the fields beyond it. This was the smell of a sane place, a normal school, not St Luke's.

He must bring a lot of prospective parents here, Marland thought to himself.

Mr Bride was sitting in a large dark leather chair behind his large desk. He wasn't a big man and the large furniture only made him seem smaller. He had parted black hair that was wiry and full, and which was going gently grey at the edges. His face wasn't unkind but it looked a little stupid or, at the very least, easily led.

Next to him, in another chair, sat Mrs Gibson – a woman who had grown large on her one pregnancy and exponentially travelled from that point to become a huge, fat, wobbling whale. She had red hair that was curled. A hateful demeanour was hidden in sky-blue eyes. Her son was a day boy, a real *Benny* if ever there was one. Everyone knew about her ambitions for Mr Gibson and how desperately she wanted him to become a House Master, maybe even see him take over from Mr Bride one day.

They didn't invite him to sit so Marland stayed standing, lost in the middle of the room.

It was Mrs Gibson that started. 'Do you know who I've just been on the telephone with, Marland?' she said, her chin bubbling.

It felt especially harsh for some reason to hear a woman, a mother, address him by his last name.

'No,' Marland whispered.

'What?'

'No, Mrs Gibson,' Marland repeated, his head bowed slightly.

'I've just been on the phone with Jeremy's parents,' she said.

Marland could feel Mr Bride staring into him, his fingers crossed against his chest as he leant back.

'As you can imagine they're very upset.'

Marland didn't say anything. There was a pause as they looked at him.

'They want to know exactly what happened last Saturday.'

It was Monday today.

'Can *you* tell us what happened?' Mr Bride said.

'It was an accident,' Marland replied. He'd learnt how to recite the words from Sean on the Sunday. They'd gone over it. Over and over again. *It was an accident.*

'Yes, we know that,' Mrs Gibson said, to Marland's surprise. 'What happened? How did it happen?'

'Baxter didn't see the car coming.'

'Why not?' Mrs Gibson said.

'Because he was behind the trucks.'

So far so good. He was saying exactly what Clarke had told him.

'And where were you?' Mr Bride said.

'I was standing with the other boys, in front of the truc

'But you didn't cross the road?' Mr Bride said.

'No,' Marland replied.

'No, SIR!' Mrs Gibson exclaimed.

'No, sir,' Marland repeated.

'And why didn't you cross the road, Marland?' Mrs Gibson said.

'Fish . . . I mean Mr Haddock told me to wait.'

'Why?' she asked.

'He told me to wait for Baxter.'

'For Jeremy?' Clearly, in this world, you only got your first name back once you were dead. 'Why? Where was Jeremy?'

'I don't know. In the woods . . . I think.'

'Alone?' Mr Bride said.

Marland gulped. He didn't know how to answer this. He hadn't expected there to be so many questions. Clarke had said that it wouldn't take long. Why were they asking so many questions? Marland felt his bladder twitching. He was finding it hard to breathe. The room felt stuffy with radiator heat.

'Marland?' Mrs Gibson said.

'Yes?'

'Mr Bride wants to know if Jeremy was alone in the woods.'

'Err, no, I mean . . . I don't know.'

'Yes or no, boy!' Mrs Gibson said.

'No,' Marland replied quickly.

'Who else was with him then?' Mr Bride said.

'I don't know, sir,' Marland said.

Mr Bride stared at him. 'What do you mean you don't know?'

The carpet was starting to swim. Marland could feel his throat. His collar felt tight. It was now very hot in the room. Why were they asking so many questions? What did they want? Marland was having to try very hard to breathe.

'I . . . I'm sorry, sir?'

'I said, what do you mean you don't know?' Mr Bride asked

impatiently. 'If Baxter wasn't alone in the woods, who was he with?'

Marland was finding it hard to focus now. What did they know? Did they know about the *plan*? Was he in trouble? Marland couldn't face it if he was in trouble again. Would Fishface slipper him? Would they tell his mummy? Why were they asking so many questions? The room was boiling hot. Marland needed to pee. He could feel it. He looked out of the window. He could remember playing outside this office once, on his first day at the school, all those years ago. He wished he was outside now.

'MARLAND!' Mrs Gibson suddenly yelled.

Hot urine suddenly splashed down the inner thigh of Marland's left leg. He tried to hold on but the harder he tried the more it flowed.

'LOOK AT MR BRIDE WHEN HE'S TALKING TO YOU.'

Marland felt the tears forming. He simply couldn't face them. He was so scared. They'd been caught. He knew it, he knew it, he knew it. He knew that they'd get caught. They should never have done it. Baxter was dead.

'Now you listen to me, young man,' Mrs Gibson started, quietly this time, full of controlled fury. 'I think you should know. You could be in a lot – A LOT – of trouble, if you don't answer Mr Bride's question. Do you understand?'

Marland was sobbing now, his breathing shallow. Fishface was going to slipper him again. They'd been caught. And now Fishface was going to bum him. They were going to send him back to Fishface. The whole room was swimming now. Marland felt like he was falling.

'I SAID DO YOU UNDERSTAND?!'

'It wasn't me,' Marland whimpered. After that, the rest came out quickly. 'I didn't do it. It wasn't me. I didn't mean it.

Baxter . . . Jeremy . . . he, we . . . Baxter used to pick on me. He used to . . .' The words caught in his throat. 'It was Clarke. He said it would be OK. He said he'd take care of everything. He tried to help me. I'm sorry, I'm sorry. I didn't think he'd die. We only wanted to hurt him. That's why Clarke pushed him. We wanted to get Fishface into trouble.'

All Marland could hear after that was his own sobbing, wretched and raw and soaked in piss. His knees felt like they would crumble at any minute. He wanted to collapse into the lime-green carpet, which was still spinning. He wanted to die. He wanted it all to end. Anything to not be here, in this room. They knew. They'd always known. What were they going to do to him now?

It felt like he was crying for a long time before they said anything.

'Clarke?' Mr Bride started eventually. 'Are you saying that Sean Clarke *pushed* Jeremy Baxter into the road? Good heavens, boy, why on earth would he do that?'

Marland could hear the frown in his voice, even though his tears blurred everything, even though he couldn't see, couldn't breathe. Marland's heart was pounding still.

'We wanted to get him,' Marland sniffed. 'We wanted to get him. Baxter was . . . Baxter was a bastard!'

They gasped when he said it.

Marland could hear Mrs Gibson shifting in her chair. It screamed in agony when she did so. There was another long silence. Marland's tears were drying now, his trousers were still wet. He sniffed. They didn't offer him a tissue. The confession was over. It had been easy to break him.

Then a dark-green telephone on the desk rang. Mr Bride picked it up. The receiver looked very large against his small head.

'Show her in,' he said.

There was another moment of silence before Marland heard the door behind him quickly swing open. He turned and saw the big Bursar smiling and leaning against the doorknob as he opened it, making space for some person perceptible behind him to pass into the room.

It was Mummy!

Marland's heart leapt and he instinctively turned to run into her. She embraced him and immediately Marland was in the warmth of her soft dress and the smell of her perfume took him home and he was Michael again.

There was a muffled shrill from Mrs Gibson: 'Mrs Marland! It's such a pleasure to meet you at last. An absolute pleasure. So sorry that it's not in happier times.'

Michael looked up, across his mother's chest. She was looking down at him, smiling, ignoring Mrs Gibson and Mr Bride, who were shuffling against each other to reach his mother first. Slowly she looked up to address them, still holding her son.

'It's Mrs Taggart, not Marland. And the next time you question my son in my absence I can assure you there will be hell to pay. I would have thought you'd be more careful considering everything that's going on. I'm in a good mind to tell the police that you are questioning the boys this way. I wouldn't be surprised if it was against the law. In any case, I have no doubt that next week's inquiry will find this school guilty of neglect. You'll have more than enough problems on your plate then. Good day.'

Then she turned and walked with Michael in her grasp out of the door. When they were finally outside in the cold and the dark of the early winter night, Michael – who didn't understand any of the things that were going on around him – told his mother that he was sorry, and the tears started to rush. She grabbed him and held him in her breasts and they rocked together for what seemed like a very meaningful time.

'Come on,' she said eventually. 'I'm taking you home.'

# Chapter Sixty-One

They were back together – Michael and Sean, Marland and Clarke – back in that innocent cocoon they had first created for themselves under the *Star Wars* duvet when they were at St Luke's, that intimate space where they could comfort each other in the dark.

It was dark in the hotel room. No one was watching.

It felt strange at first, the chest and belly of another man. But then their bodies yielded and gave way to the boys within them. Sean's skin was suddenly smooth against Michael, Michael's chest hair was soft across Sean. In the end, it was the familiarity that felt strange – the knowing what to do. They remembered.

They pressed themselves into one another, the smell of cigarettes and alcohol breathing between them, the years meeting. They moved elegantly with a clumsy confidence, like drunken dancers.

Sean put one hand in Michael's hair and said: 'I've missed you.'

'I know,' Michael replied.

The drone of the air-conditioning unit fell into a faraway distance. They couldn't feel an outside, there wasn't an outside. There was only this room, this space between them. They saw each other in incredible detail.

Sean took Michael in his hand and let out a moan that came from somewhere deep within his throat that was terrifying. Their bodies jacked. They didn't have to wonder if they were doing it right. It was hard to remember to keep breathing.

When it was over they didn't break. Michael put his head in Sean's shoulder. They held each other, not saying anything. There wasn't anything to say. Everything made sense. They were safe.

Slowly, the sound of the air-conditioning swelled. The light crept back in from under the door. It had always been there. They looked up, their faces no longer burning, into the void of the ceiling, their legs entwined, letting themselves be lulled, curling into sleep.

# Chapter Sixty-Two

When Michael woke up the next day, Sean wasn't there. He heard the shower tinkling. Silver light cut through a small gap in the curtains. Michael could tell that it was raining. He got out of bed and went to look. Grey, drizzling clouds smudged the sea view, and the dreariness of day outside was somehow quickly within him, casting a long grey shadow over everything.

Michael felt his inner workings, his metabolism, lurch. He told himself it was just the comedown. His head still hurt and his nostrils were caked with dead cocaine. But then he remembered the prospect of having to return to Hong Kong and realized that it was more than just the drugs.

The bathroom door slammed open.

'Come on, mate, the ferry leaves at eleven,' Sean half shouted.

Michael turned to face him. Sean was pulling a shirt over his wet torso, quickly sweeping his wet hair back after adjusting his collar.

'Can't we catch a later one?' Michael said. He didn't want to go back to Hong Kong. He wanted to stay here, in Macao, with Sean.

'No. I'm meeting Candy for lunch, remember?'

Michael didn't remember, but he should have known, he supposed.

'You go on ahead,' Michael said. 'I'll catch a later one.'

Sean stopped putting Brylcreem in his hair, rubbing talc on his chest, coating his armpits with roll-on deodorant – some instant of vanity in a series – and looked at Michael.

Michael looked back at him.

'Suit yourself,' Sean said quickly and carried on rubbing, rolling, creaming.

Michael sighed and reached for the packet of cigarettes next to the TV. It was empty. He watched Sean squeezing on his shoes.

'If you don't catch the eleven o'clock you'll have to buy another ticket,' Sean said, not looking at him. 'And you'll need to get a taxi because I'm taking the Mini Moke back.' There was a pause in his out-loud thinking. 'Do you have any cash?' he asked quickly.

'No.'

'Well, I'm all out as well. I've only got my company credit card.'

Sean looked up at Michael and then got up and moved towards him. He swept his hand through his hair again. He looked so together, so sorted, so ready for the day. Michael found himself envying Sean's ability to rebound, to actually get out of bed.

'Everything's going to be OK, Mikey,' Sean said, looking at him gently. 'Tell you what, I'll buy you breakfast, yeah? They're showing football highlights on the catamaran. It's better if we stay together, don't you think?'

# Chapter Sixty-Three

The streets of Central were filled with a shrill squawking sound. It echoed off the skyscrapers and reverberated. Sean heard it from a district away but remembered too late and with dread that it was Sunday so Hong Kong's very significant Filipino *amah* population would be packed tightly in large friendly groups on the streets – eating, practising pop song dance routines and gossiping about their employers.

It was their day off and they had nowhere else to go. They certainly couldn't entertain friends in their wardrobe-sized rooms – their employers would never have allowed that. After all, they were just the help, and the far-inferior Filipino help at that. At least the Hong Kong government was considerate enough to close off downtown so that the poor ladies could congregate on the pavement. And the streets were clean . . . weren't they?

Anyone would have thought that in a place as wealthy as Hong Kong there'd be somewhere better than the pavement for the underclass to relax on their one day off a week.

Sean wished he'd come another route. He was suddenly back in the heart of it – the din of inequity – and the contrast with Macao was hard to stomach. It was also slow going through the intense crowds. He was going to be late for lunch with

Candy. The sun was beaming down and many of the women were huddling under awnings for shade. Sean knocked down two umbrellas as he tiptoed his way between the picnic rugs. Some of the younger *amahs* checked him out.

By the time he reached the edges of Lan Kwai Fong Sean was half jogging, running in little steps up the sudden steep incline. When he reached Shangrila his shirt was soaked in sweat. The waitress greeted him calmly as air-conditioning blasted from an outlet just above the bar. Sean hoped it wasn't messing up his hair.

'Hi,' he panted. 'I've got a reservation. Clarke. For two.'

'Yes, sir,' the girl replied in a Scottish accent. 'You're the first of your party to arrive.'

At first Sean felt relief. But then, as he sat down and realized that he was half an hour late, he instinctively knew that he'd been stood up. For a while he didn't listen to himself, instead ordering a drink, flapping his shirt so that it would dry in the cool and examining his hairstyle in the reflection of a spoon. Four buff homosexuals talked too loudly at one another in obnoxiously camp voices and occasionally glanced across at Sean. He was starting to get angry.

*She* was the one that had suggested this.

*She* was the one that had said *we have to talk*.

*She* was the one that had told him she was confused.

And now, as was becoming usual, *she* wasn't here.

When it got to her being forty-five minutes late Sean paged her. At the hour mark he paged her again – three times in succession. He left, furious. He'd felt like getting into a fight with the mincers at the restaurant but there were four of them and they were all huge. He stamped out into the street and thought about what to do.

He decided that he wanted to have it out with Candy, once

and for all. He wanted to tell her that she was the fucking bitch that she was. He wanted to hit her. No, better than that, he wanted to catch her in bed with someone else and then he wanted to kill her . . . no, both of them. First *him*, and then her. He thought about going round to her house in Pokfulam and he remembered that Candy's parents were on holiday. That wasn't unusual. What about the *amah*? It was Sunday. She'd be sitting in the shit on the streets of Central. He knew where they hid the key to the house. That sealed it.

He ran up to the top of Lan Kwai Fong and a cab immediately approached with its light on – Sean's chariot. Destiny was clearly in his favour. He flagged it down.

It didn't stop.

'Motherfucking cunting fuck,' Sean said with semi-psychotic calm before deciding to give chase. Sean sprinted after the cab, which accelerated away. Sean carried on running, telling himself he was going to catch the driver and kick the living shit out of him – serve the racist cunt right for not picking him up, for every cabbie that hadn't picked him up just because he was white. He was sick of being a second-class citizen in this city. It was time someone paid.

Two hundred yards later the cab stopped at a set of lights. Sean caught up with it, heaving, pink faced and dripping with sweat. He slammed a fist on the boot. He saw the driver's head snapping round the wrong way as Sean ran up to his window.

'YOU FUCKING CHINESE CUNT!' he screamed through the glass. 'OPEN THE FUCKING DOOR.' He shook on the handle but the door was locked.

The taxi driver sneered back at him with a dismissive twitch of his lip. Sean held a fist up. He was ready to smash his hand through the glass. The sun was hot. The taxi revved.

Sean had an idea. He pulled out his house keys, hid them

in a fist and presented one to the paint. They both watched for the light to turn green and then, as it hit orange, the taxi took off.

There was a satisfying screech as the key twisted its way against the metal.

Sean was slightly surprised to see the brake lights on the taxi flash and the car lurch forward on its own weight. He even felt his bladder as he watched the driver pile his way out of the vehicle and stare at the dull gash that screamed against its shiny red finish. The driver's face twisted horribly as he sprinted towards Sean yelling: 'I KILL YOUUUU!'

Sean stood his ground ready to fight. He was more than ready for violence. This was what it all came down to. In the few seconds it took for the driver to reach him, Sean had already decided to head-butt him. There was a moment of astonishment on the driver's face before a fleshy crack appeared on the bridge of his nose and he bounced down, sitting almost naturally on his arse in the street.

Sean towered over him menacingly for a second before he noticed people staring. There were one or two white faces but on the whole it was a pond of squinting yellow. As one or two men stepped out into the street towards him, Sean knew that he had to run. He spun on his heels.

Twenty minutes later, heart pounding, clothes drenched in sweat and hair everywhere, Sean decided that he was safe. He hailed a gypsy bus going to Pokfulam, but it was only as he arrived – *Lido m'goi* – that Sean realized he didn't have any money to pay for the fare.

He'd dropped his wallet.

# Chapter Sixty-Four

It had taken Candy a few hours after Stephen dropped her off at the pier without taking her to dinner to consider that she'd been raped. She hadn't known what to think at first. It had all seemed to be her fault. And in many ways that thought was the red flag that convinced her that she *had* been raped. She'd seen enough documentaries on the subject to know that rape victims usually blamed themselves.

The first thing she did was call Sean. It was purely instinctive, a natural reaction. For years, almost as long as she could remember, he had been the person she'd called when she needed somebody. She hadn't been sure what she was going to say exactly. She probably wouldn't have told him, even. She just needed someone to talk to, hold her.

But when Sean didn't answer her calls – she was too freaked out to leave a message – Candy went back to the gallery and sat in the dark. Evening was falling and she could hear activity in Lan Kwai Fong starting to build slowly, like a generator rumbling life into a party marquee. She sat there, alone, for at least an hour. She needed to talk to somebody, anybody. Who? She thought about calling one of her girlfriends but that thought seamlessly segued into: which girlfriend? Sasha? Ali? Emma? Hadn't Candy shunned them?

Could she still rely on the Group? Did she even want to?

Candy realized then that she'd thrown something away, burnt a bridge, and she regretted it. She felt alone and, for the first time, she understood a little better what Sean must have felt like when he was depressed. It might just have been the gallery gloom but everything felt very dark.

Rob found her. Quite literally. She was walking down to the corner of Wyndham Street after locking up the gallery and was about to hail a cab back to Pokfulam when he called out her name from the street above. He grinned and waved and then he was suddenly next to her. He looked extremely elegant in a plain white shirt (French cuffs) and designer jeans. She started crying instantly and hated herself for it. Of course, he wanted to know what was wrong and the next thing she knew they were travelling together back to her house. There had been some vague protests on her part – *no, don't worry, I'll be fine, you must be meeting people* – and the appropriate rebuttals on his – *don't be silly, I won't leave you this way, let's talk, I'm only meeting Tommy, he'll understand.*

But it was only when they reached the last part that it felt easy.

'Let me take you home,' he said.

And all Candy had to say was: 'OK.'

# Chapter Sixty-Five

Sean did call out when he got to Candy's house but not loud enough to disturb anyone having sex. Just loud enough to be able to say without lying that he *had* called out if he was asked.

His attempts at sneaking in surreptitiously were useless, though. As soon as he slid the key in the door and twisted the lock the dog went mental. Sean thought about legging it but he was worried that it might attack him if he ran. And, besides, he knew he wouldn't make it up to the top of the hill before being seen.

He stepped into the hallway and ruffled the Alsatian, which rather stupidly welcomed him. Sean headed straight towards Candy's room. He swung the door open and prepared himself for . . . what?

It was only when he saw that her bed hadn't been slept in that it occurred to Sean that Candy might be in some sort of physical trouble. Fear and guilt and everything else associated with real issues like death and paralysis flooded his brain. Sean instantly hated himself for not considering her well-being, but that only lasted a second because he realized that the *amah* would have raised the alarm by now if there had been a serious problem. Jealousy quickly took over again.

He scanned the room one last time before finally deciding to rifle through her drawers.

He didn't know what he was looking for. It was probably the stupidest thing Sean could have done in that moment. What better way to end things once and for all with Candy than to go through her stuff, invade her privacy, rape her soul? It was hardly going to get her back, if that was what he still wanted. Maybe he was simply looking for an answer, any answer – she'd left him with so many questions: *do you still love me?* Maybe he just wanted to make her as unhappy as she was making him. Or maybe he just wanted to sniff her knickers one last time.

Whatever the reason, it wasn't long before Sean found himself regretting it.

Mainly because all the things he did find – photo albums, letters, even a yellow Post-it note with a gushy message he'd written to her during a university lecture – made him realize that she did love him, very much, maybe even enough to never be able to stop loving him. She hadn't thrown anything away. He knew then that he was wrong to be doing what he was doing. He even realized that this act, this single event, could eventually end up overshadowing all of the amazing memories and moments he was steadily uncovering as he went through her stuff.

But he just couldn't help himself. Once he'd started asking the question, he kept finding the same bitter-sweet answer.

*Do you still love me, Candy?*

*Yes, Sean, I still love you . . . but it's over now.*

Sean wept and laughed his way through the rest of the day, methodically turning everything upside down and only making half an attempt to return it to where it came from. He didn't even try to hide the fact that he was searching through her stuff. There may have been some maliciousness in that but it was really that Sean wasn't there, in the room, as he rifled through it. He was bouncing around the last five years of his life with the girl that he loved. One minute he was grabbing Candy in a mountain of clothing, a huge blue sky and the Himalayas erupting around them, the next he was cringing over a love letter he'd written to her while she was in Spain. And once he'd taken all these memories out of their box or drawer, Sean found that he couldn't remember where they'd come from. There didn't seem to be a rightful place in the room for any of them. They all belonged to him.

# Chapter Sixty-Six

'**F**uck.'

Candy's pager was beeping again, a three-hour reminder call, and now she was squatting in her black knickers, her breasts small enough to stand against her chest, her hair falling forward before she pinned one side back behind an ear, reading the messages.

*I'm at Post where are u?*

*Still here*

*It's 2.30, I'm leaving in 10 mins*

*Thanks for nothing, Candy*

*Bitch*

'What's wrong?' Rob asked, propping himself up in bed. A late-afternoon sun was angling its way against the white-carpeted floor, the sound of the pool vaguely discernible even though no one was swimming in it. Maybe it was just the sound of the filter running.

It had been Candy that had suggested they go to D'Aguilar Peak instead of Pokfulam. She'd said that she couldn't deal with seeing her parents, even though she knew they weren't there. Secretly she feared the *amah* might say something – the Chinese loved spies.

'I've got to go.'

Rob didn't say anything. He didn't protest or claim her or beg her to stay. She started getting dressed in front of him, first pinning on her black bra, then sliding back into her tight office skirt with the grey pin stripe. It felt even sexier wearing it again the Morning After. She smiled at him as she picked up her shoes and walked over to the edge of the bed.

'Say hi to Tommy for me,' she said, standing by him.

'Will you be OK?' Rob said, taking her hand.

He'd been the perfect counsel. Not asking too many questions, nodding at the appropriate moments and actually listening to what she had to say. Candy hadn't told him that she'd been raped, or that she believed she had or whatever. She'd just talked, got a lot of what was going on in her life off her chest. Sean, her parents, the blind dates (she didn't say who with), the difficulty of being a Eurasian in Hong Kong. They'd smoked a couple of spliffs and she'd asked if she could stay the night. Making love that following morning (afternoon really, it was the best sleep she'd had in ages) had felt as natural as the day outside.

'Sure,' she said, nodding and smiling. 'I've just got to go and take care of something.'

'Can I see you again?'

'I'll call you.'

'OK,' he said, very relaxed.

She bent down to kiss him and as she did so found herself falling back into him, collapsing against the pillows as he wrapped his arms around her. He rolled her over and moved onto her. After a few minutes, she broke the kiss.

'I really do have to go,' she said, not wanting to leave.

'OK,' Rob said, releasing her.

Candy took a deep breath and jumped off the bed, brushing down the creases in her skirt before collecting her shoes and

bag and skipping out of the room and down the stairs bare-
foot. It was only when she reached the front door that she
realized she'd have to call a taxi.

will rhode

# Chapter Sixty-Seven

No one was home when Michael got back to the flat on Hollywood Road. That was one consolation at least. He didn't think he could handle Jamie and Roo in this condition. He was coming down hard off the coke, off Macao, off Sean.

Even though it was bright outside, the flat was gloomy and he had to turn the lights on to see. There was something exceptionally depressing about electric light in the daytime. Michael threw his keys on to the table and collapsed on the purple futon in the 'living room'. He rubbed his eyes and pinched the bridge of his nose.

On the wall there was a photo collage. Most of the gang had them on their walls. Picture upon picture of beaming friends, cut out in the shape of dismembered limbs and pieced together to create a big picture, a Cubist impression of happiness. Michael could see one of Sean being kissed by all the girls at the same time. There was another of someone picking up Sasha as she screamed. There were two close-ups of Emma and Ali beaming broadly, their faces pressed together. There wasn't a picture of Michael.

Michael reached for the remote control and turned on the TV but he couldn't see properly because the sun, which was unable to illuminate the apartment, somehow managed to reflect brilliantly off the screen. He drew the curtains. That made him feel a little better. A politics programme was on. Michael let the sound drone through him, the images anaesthetizing his eyes. This was the best thing: vegetation. Wait for the day to end. And then the next one, and then the next and the next, until somehow Michael would one day find himself somewhere that he wanted to be. That was all he could do. Fall from one day to the next, fall from one life into another, propelled by the hours. He wasn't in control of the situation. His life wasn't his. Never had been, probably never would be. He wished Sean were with him. They'd only parted a few hours before and already Michael missed him.

# Chapter Sixty-Eight

Michael woke up with a start. It was difficult to tell how much time had passed. A few hours at least, because it wasn't bright outside any more. With the curtains drawn it almost felt like night. He tried to figure out if he felt any better. It was hard to say. For the most part, he felt disorientated. Something had happened.

There was the sound of a siren out on the street.

Michael sat up on the futon. There was a wet patch from where he'd been dribbling. He thought about taking a shower. He couldn't face it. Maybe he should just go straight to bed, he thought to himself before knowing that he was too awake to do so now. There was a strange reverberation in the room. He couldn't tell what it was. Maybe it was the TV.

Another siren, maybe two.

Michael stood up and stretched. The word AIDS appeared in his mind but he forced himself not to think about it. It wasn't going to change anything. Best to adopt Sean's attitude towards life in this instance: straightforward denial. He tried to think about what might have happened between Sean and Candy at lunch. Would they be back together now? Michael hoped not.

There must have been a traffic jam outside – the sirens only seemed to be getting louder.

Michael walked to the window.

The phone rang.

He glanced between the window and the phone.

Somehow they were connected. He knew it. Something had happened.

He reached for the receiver.

'Hello.'

'Mikey?'

Blue light streamed in the street below.

'Who is this?'

'Can you hear me?'

Michael could hear sirens travelling through the receiver as well. The noise was everywhere – on the street, in the flat, screaming in Michael's head.

'Yes. Who is this?'

'Have you seen Sean?'

'Not since lunch time. Why? What's going on?'

'You'd better come quickly. There's been an accident.'

# Chapter Sixty-Nine

The street kept slipping away from him. The harder he tried to run, the more it seemed to pull him back, like travelling up the Escalators the wrong way, exhausting him, defeating him, taking him down, relentless. His shoes didn't grip. His thighs burnt. His lungs and throat were raw. He felt so weak, so helpless, too late.

He forced himself to look up, to see how close he was getting now. He was making progress, but the incline bore down on top of him, saying 'Go back, go back.' It would have been so much easier to go back.

Angry green smoke churned across the hill. Sirens screamed. There were people. So many people.

Michael drove himself upwards, knowing instinctively that Sean was dead. He was dead – dead, dead, dead. Michael wanted so badly to be there with him. It was safe in the dark.

He managed to puke as he ran. There were tears on a child's face. They don't deserve to cry. A woman's dress was torn. The hard bump of a shoulder in his. He was getting closer. Harder to breathe. He had to keep going. Had to keep going, had to keep going – up. Would he know when to stop?

Someone suddenly – a face. Michael recognized it.

Little Ali.

The mouth moved and there were words but they didn't go together. Everything was disjointed. Michael could only now smell the stink of his hangover through the acrid taste of upholstery burning.

*An explosion . . . gas . . . Can't find . . . Did you? . . . There's been no one . . . Ben heard it . . .*

Michael felt the swimming in his brain and knew he was going to be sick again. He was intoxicated by the flatness of the world around him now. He'd made it up the hill to Sean's apartment complex and it was flat here. He could feel it in his legs. They were breathing with relief. There was only one place to go – there was no point in resisting it. He made for the centre of everything that was happening.

He felt a big hand and shook it off. People blocked the way but they themselves were useless. He could take the whole lot with him if he wanted. Everything was being drawn towards the centre. They just didn't know it yet.

Smoke was around him now, curling across his vision like devastation on a battlefield. There was the occasional sight of flames.

Shouting. The very loud sound of machinery. People still running. Didn't they know?

Something collapsed. Michael could feel the heat. The pump of water. The clanking of tanks. He was close. There were still people. Blankets. The noise didn't hurt inside his head any more. He knew he was nearly there now. The cars were in the car park. Moments to the entrance way. One person fell.

And then he was down, suddenly horizontal, on his back. They'd come in charging, body blocking, shouting obscenely. The hard grit of the concrete against his head. He bucked against their heroic hold but they pinned him, the weight of muscle driving. Three firemen carried him away. He tore himself in their grip. There was pain again now. The further they took him away from the fire the more he felt it. All the things he knew.

Sean's flat was on fire.

Sean was dead.

Michael was on his own again.

He'd have to cope alone.

## Chapter Seventy

By the time Candy arrived at the Mansion, the fire had been put out. Candy remembered feeling surprised at how few firemen there seemed to be compared to the police, and shocked to see Sean's apartment gutted and gaping like a black cancer in the side of his apartment block. Almost all of the gang were there – it hadn't taken long for the news to spread. A lot of them lived nearby and had gone to see what was going on after they'd heard the explosion.

The worst thing was watching all of their faces – as they collected around her and celebrated her sudden appearance (Mikey had told everyone, after the firemen had dragged him out, that he feared she was inside with Sean) – when she told them that she didn't know where Sean was. It was even worse than the rising fear in her own heart that Sean might be dead. Their faces said the very thing she knew she'd always have to live with if he was dead: *So why weren't you with Sean?*

Candy didn't know if she'd be able to secretly bear the answer to that question.

The enormity of it all – that Sean was dead, that it was her fault and that she'd betrayed him all in one go – sent Candy into a kind of shock. At least, she went very quiet and everyone, particularly the girls from the Group who were fluttering protectively around her, interpreted this as shock. Maybe it was simply that she didn't dare say anything lest the truth leapt out.

Eventually someone took her home. She didn't remember who. Candy remembered insisting that she would be all right and she remembered walking into the house alone, and then Sean had simply been there, in the corridor, waiting, like a ghost, a strange expression on his face.

Candy almost knocked him over as she jumped on him, crying: 'I thought you were dead, I thought you were dead, oh Christ thank you thank you thank you . . .'

She wasn't completely sure what she felt most grateful for, the fact that he was still alive or that she wouldn't have to bear the guilt of his being dead. But none of that mattered as she kissed him all over his face – not then. In that instant Candy decided to right her wrongs. No one got second chances like this, she told herself. The dog had got jealous and had started barking and then tried to mount them as they'd held each other, Sean asking: 'What's wrong, Candy? Where have you been?'

She told him about the fire.

When Sean didn't say anything Candy took the opportunity to drag him to her bedroom, begging him to make love to her, desperate for him to be inside of her, needing him now, and swearing to be with him again, that she'd never leave him. But she stopped when she saw the mess that Sean had made.

Questions exploded in her ears.

Before she had a chance to ask them, Sean said: 'I . . . I thought there was someone else.'

Candy didn't say anything at first. Then she managed to say that she didn't care. The words felt forced, but she knew she had to say them. It was Sean that went on.

'Where were you?' he kept asking.

Candy told him that that didn't matter now. Christ! Hadn't he been listening? Didn't he understand? There'd been a fire – at his place, he could have died, but he didn't, everything was all right! They *had* to make love.

He wouldn't make love to her.

Did he know? Could he know? Candy refused to admit it, most of all to herself. She assigned the past, her betrayals, to a former self, a disillusioned, confused being that hadn't understood its true feelings. She knew her feelings now, though. With this second chance, she realized, she didn't want to lose Sean, let go of him. She'd do anything, forgive everything, she had to stay with him.

'Please . . .' she begged.

But it wasn't any use. Sean seemed to sense her guilt, as if her new enthusiasm for him was a sign. The more she pleaded, the more convinced he seemed to become that she'd actually done something wrong.

Did he know?

Eventually, reluctantly, she agreed that it might be better not to make love. They made one or two telephone calls to spread the news that Sean was safe. Then they tidied up her room, together. It felt very, very strange.

'How did the fire start?' Sean asked, practically as an afterthought.

'I don't know,' she said.

'Was anyone hurt?'

'I don't know,' Candy said. 'There were ambulances. I didn't see anyone.'

'What about Charlie and Alex?'

'I didn't see them.'

By the time they finished clearing up it was two o'clock in

the morning. In many ways, Candy told herself later, clearing up *was* the more appropriate thing to do. Sharing photos, going over old times, reciting their memories to one another. It was almost a celebration of themselves.

Eventually, when it was finally done, and their lives were stitched back together, they fell asleep in each other's arms fully clothed.

# Chapter Seventy-One

Seeing as they all had jobs, the Group collectively decided that they couldn't fly back to the UK for Charlie's funeral, so they held a makeshift memorial of their own on one of the dragon-back peaks. They'd congregated around a broken fortress, many of them still sweating from the one-hour climb. Candles and pictures of Charlie were propped up in divots of earth. The air was thick with humidity and the evening was already turning quickly to night on the mist. Streetlights winked along the shoreline far below.

The previous two weeks had been a nightmare. Charlie's parents had understandably wanted his body – or what little there was left of it – returned home but it had been difficult co-ordinating his dental records with the coroner in Hong Kong, so an official death certificate wasn't issued for a long time. Not that there was any doubt that it was Charlie – he, along with the woman in the flat above, was the only person unaccounted for after the fire. But still, the delay in paper-work only seemed to extend the hell.

And then, of course, there was the fact that the police were treating the fire as suspicious. The *Hong Kong Herald* had filed a front-page report the day after the fire with the headline ARSON! and that hadn't helped the general mindset. Now everyone in Hong Kong, particularly the Mid-level *gweilos*, seemed to take it for granted that there was a psycho pyromaniac on the loose. It was probably only a question of time before he struck again.

The Group found this upsetting. They had barely had time to digest the notion of Charlie's death before they had to come to grips with the concept of his being murdered as well. Who? What? Why? None of it made any sense. The police had questioned all of them: Michael, Sean, Alex, Candy, Sasha, Ali, even fat Nick, but they seemed to have very few leads. Principally, everyone in the Group agreed, because there could be no apparent motive for the fire. Who'd want to murder Charlie or even burn down Sean's flat, for that matter?

Indeed, there were a lot of question and exclamation marks in their discussions in the days following the blaze, and Michael received a grilling from the gang whenever the *Herald* ran a follow-up piece on the tragedy – maybe because the *Herald* so often quoted Michael as a source. After all, he did know Charlie. They'd run his first-hand account of the blaze on the third page to go with the ARSON! lead. Third page! It was Michael's first big break.

But he also faced quite a lot of moral grandstanding because of it. The gang told him things like how outrageous it was for the paper to suggest that Charlie had been murdered or that foul play was even suspected with so little evidence to back it up. OK, so there had been the traces of lighter fuel in the curtains and then there was the broken gas pipe, but the gang still found it very inconsiderate for the media to sensationalize their personal loss.

One or two people insisted Michael put a stop to it. He tried to explain that he was just the TV reviewer but they wouldn't listen. They were used to a Hong Kong where someone knew someone somewhere, and who could be relied on to sort out the situation accordingly.

Michael, still a relative new boy in town, obviously didn't have this kind of pull, and he wasn't used to this expectation of him. He got the vaguest sense – even though he knew it was ridiculous – that the Group felt that he owed them in some way. As if a Mafia organization had got him the job that he wanted (or something close to it) and it was now his turn to return the favour, use his position to serve the collective. No one ever said anything like that, of course, it was just a feeling he got.

No one ever mentioned the fact that he'd freaked out. Somehow they all seemed to think he was trying to be a hero.

Michael looked up and watched a cloud passing over his head, seemingly close enough to touch. He reached up and realized that the white wetness was actually much higher than he had imagined.

'Maybe that's Charlie with us right now,' Michael said, pointing to the ghost and turning to the rest of the gang, who were sitting on picnic rugs, smoking spliffs and drinking all around him.

'It looks just like him,' Emma shouted out drunkenly before starting to giggle half hysterically. The gang glanced briefly at one other as she started, already feeling nervous about what she might say, what she might do. Eventually, Ben took Emma by the shoulders and held her until the laughter turned into sobs. It seemed that they were back together again now, despite the public knowledge that Emma had betrayed Ben with Charlie. Ben was simply too nice to dump her, Michael supposed.

Eventually, Jimmy and Jules started strumming on their guitars and Jules started singing 'Redemption Song', overlaying

Emma's muffled moans.

One by one, they all joined in and Michael looked at them, genuinely feeling that they had all come together now in Charlie's death, now that he was gone, a bad element purged. Michael found his eyes meeting Sean's. Candy was sitting between Sean's legs, leaning back against him, singing.

Yes. Emma was back together with Ben. Candy was even with Sean now. And Charlie was gone. Everything was back to normal. The gang were all together. One great big happy family.

# Chapter Seventy-Two

It arrived with the rest of the Gallery post but it was clear that it had been delivered by hand. It stood on top of the pile – big and brown and blank, with the exception of a black felt-tip hand-written note that said: Attention: CANDY NEWMAN.

Somehow Candy immediately knew what was inside the package – the shape was pretty distinctive – but she had no idea why someone would send her such a thing so her mind blanked out the insight just as instantly and she found herself opening the envelope, genuinely bemused. She was alone, as usual. It was just before lunch and it was a Wednesday. It was raining. The other letters lay on the floor beside the door. The envelope tore haphazardly along the horizontal seam, pieces of fluffy cardboard bits falling to the floor. She glanced briefly outside. She didn't know why. Then she reached in and pulled out the contents, being sure not to miss anything, the way a child does with a present – *after all, there might be something else.*

But there wasn't anything else. There was just the CD-ROM. No box. Just the CD.

The label read:

*Amateur Allstars*
*Starring the Dirty Duo: Ben Melody and Jerry Langer*
*Special guest appearance: Jennifer Ames*

# Chapter Seventy-Three

They were in a trendy new bar that had just opened in Soho, right underneath the Escalators. It had sofas covered in purple velvet, and dark-red walls with mock Picasso paintings and big mirrors in gaudy gold frames. Somehow – it may have been the blood lighting or the faggot waiters in tight leather – the place suggested a sado-masochistic gay theme that was trying to be funny in a Jean-Paul Gaultier sort of way.

Needless to say, Sean hated it. The place, he couldn't remember the name – Let's be Gay or something – only had one waitress, who was pretty but she had all the attitude to match, and there were two male bartenders who were so camp they deserved to be shot. Sean didn't see why they couldn't have just met in Lan Kwai Fong. It was so much more *normal*.

Eventually, after he'd managed to order their drinks without telling the fudge packer to fuck off – *what a mincer* – Sean lit himself a Marlboro Light and squeezed into a standing booth that had a tall round table and a burning candle.

He managed to smile sweetly at Candy.

'Sorry, darling, what were you saying?' he asked.

Candy looked back at him. She'd just had her hair highlighted, with Cruella de Vil blond streaks coursing through her black, almost blue, hair. It was the fashionable thing to do, especially among the Eurasians, and Sean remembered that he might have mentioned to Candy that he liked it once. Why had she changed it now? Was it for him? He wasn't sure that he could appreciate the effort she was making. His suspicions still stood in the way of the heaven of having her back.

She was wearing the smallest amount of make-up (or at least, the kind of make-up that was meant to look minimal). She was wearing a skirt and a blouse, it was difficult to see what colour exactly in the darkness, but Sean could see that the blouse had pretty, doily-like cotton-work sewn into it.

How could any one person be so beautiful?

He could feel himself starting to hate her.

'I think this bar's great, don't you?'

'Yeah,' Sean replied flatly. 'It's t'riffic.'

Candy tutted at him but Sean ignored her.

'I think it shows that Hong Kong's changing,' she continued. 'For the better. It's becoming more liberal here, more open-minded.'

Sean just raised his eyebrows. More liberal? Yeah, right. In four weeks this city would be in the hands of a Communist, totalitarian regime. Who was Candy kidding? Herself? Why was she still trying to sell Hong Kong? Why couldn't she just face up to the truth? The place was a shit-hole. Always was, always would be.

There was an uncomfortable pause. Indeed, ever since the fire things between Sean and Candy had been on one long uncomfortable pause. He still couldn't bring himself to make love to her, even though he wanted to. Christ! How he wanted her.

But the question – the enormous question: where had she been that day when she was meant to meet him for lunch?

– still remained. It would not go away. None of their friends had known. And Candy still hadn't given him a straight answer.

For a while, Sean had managed to ignore the thought – after all, he'd other things on his mind. Charlie's death, for one. Poor Charlie. Sean missed him a lot. Charlie had been a sound bloke. What a way to go.

And then there was the thought that maybe it was his fault – the fire, Charlie's death. Sean felt both guilty and very scared over the police reports that the fire was started on purpose. He just couldn't get the fight that he'd had with the taxi driver that day out of his mind – and the fact that he'd dropped his wallet. All the taxi drivers had links with Triads, everyone knew that. What if they'd discovered where he lived? Had they come after him? Were they going to keep coming?

Finally, there was the fact that Sean had nothing now. All his possessions, all his memories gone, nowhere to live. The logistics of dealing with that – that had taken up a lot of his time, a lot of his mental and emotional energy.

Sean was staying with Jules now. Even though he lived near the Mansion he knew the Triads would never find him there. Thousands of people lived near the Mansion. He couldn't remember if there was a record of where he worked – a business card or something – in his wallet.

More than two weeks had passed without event. Which was probably why Sean had the energy now, the space of mind, to reconsider Candy.

Where had she been?

'The weirdest thing happened to me today,' Candy eventually said, taking a different tack.

Sean didn't say anything.

'Somebody dropped this thing – a CD-ROM – off for me at the gallery.'

He still didn't bite.

'It was called *Amateur Allstars*,' Candy said. 'Sounds a bit like a porno, doesn't it?'

Sean looked at her.

'What?' he asked, his mind suddenly racing.

'Yeah. This morning. Somebody. . .'

'Who?'

'I don't know.'

'How do you know it was for you?'

'It had my name on it.'

'Have you watched it?' Sean asked, his heart pounding. How on earth . . . ?

'No.'

'Then how do you know it's a porno?' Sean cut her off.

'I don't, it's just . . .'

'Well, it could be anything,' Sean said very fast. 'How can you assume it's a porno just because . . .'

He stopped himself. He could see Candy's face querying. He musn't let her see his panic. The fire . . . was it his? It had to be, didn't it? The coincidence was too much. Christ! Who'd sent it? Was this some sort of sick Triad warning? How could they possibly have known about Candy, where she worked . . . would they get to her too?

'I don't,' Candy said, shrugging her shoulders. 'I just,' she suddenly started beaming. 'I thought maybe we could watch it together. It might be fun.'

If Candy watched it she'd know. Jennifer Ames. Atlantis fire. The things he'd made her do. He felt sick.

'No thanks,' Sean said. He watched Candy's face fall.

'Come on Sean, what's the big deal?'

'Nothing. I'm just not into watching a porn film some sicko has anonymously sent to you. I think you should throw it away,' he added.

There was a very long pause. He could feel her looking at him.

'What's wrong, Sean?' Candy said eventually.

'Nothing,' he replied.

Candy looked like she might cry for a moment. Then she said, 'Do . . . do you still love me?' She was looking down when she said it. Funny how tables turn, Sean thought to himself, trying to tell himself that the CD-ROM wasn't important. The most important thing was for Candy not to see his fear.

'You know I do,' Sean replied.

'Then . . . why . . . why won't . . .' The sentence died. 'I want us to make love.'

Sean looked at her. Suddenly, he had to know, he had to know. He knew he should leave it but he just had to. Maybe it was his panic lingering.

'Where were you that day, Candy – the day of the fire?'

Candy's response was instant. 'Oh, for God's sakes do we have to go over this again? I've told you, I went to the gym, then I was in Stanley . . . Jesus, Sean, don't you trust me?'

Sean paused before saying: 'Not really, no.'

A tear did swell in Candy's eye then, but it was only for an instant before her face hardened.

'Well, there's not much point in us seeing each other any more if you don't trust me,' Candy said.

'Just tell me the truth,' Sean replied.

Candy looked back at him, straight into his eyes. She breathed. Sean made himself look back at her.

'I love you, Sean,' she said.

He didn't say anything. He just waited.

And waited.

Until . . . finally.

'I . . .' Candy sighed and her whole look fell away, unable to keep Sean's gaze.

He knew it. Christ! He'd always known.

'I was with Rob,' she said.

Gutted. That was the only way to describe it – literally, gutted. There and then and in an instant. Sean's innards, his very intestines, the body parts and nerves, they felt as if they were being ripped out and pulled down. Going nowhere, just internally destroyed. He'd been aware of the twinges. The fear and the anticipation. He'd known that this would be the way that he'd feel if she ever betrayed him. But now that it was happening it was so much worse than anything he could have ever imagined. The pain, the agony, the jealousy – he could feel his soul eating itself.

Candy was crying now, the words rushing: 'I'm so sorry, Sean, but it was only once and we'd split up and something terrible had happened and you weren't there when I called and he just found me I was drunk my parents had left for the weekend it didn't mean anything because I love you I've only ever loved you I know that now after the fire I was so scared because I thought you were gone but you weren't and we have a chance now and I swear Christ I swear it'll never happen again please Sean I couldn't bear it if you left me now because it was only once and it will never happen again and I need you it meant nothing.'

There was a quiet pause as the CD, playing some trip-hop trendy bent shit, selected another song. In the gap there was the sound of other people's conversations making a collage, individual words and spliced-up phrases meeting at different points and, somehow, making sense. Maybe because all bar talk was generic, there were only so many combinations.

Eventually Sean said: 'Was it good?'

Candy looked back up at him. 'What?'

Sean wanted to shout and scream at her then. But he didn't. That simply wasn't his style.

'Was it good?'

Candy managed to keep looking at him. He should have admired her for that, he supposed. But he didn't.

'Yes,' she said.

More guts ripped.

'Better than me?' Sean said.

'Don't, Sean.'

Very close to hitting her now.

'Just tell me.'

'He was . . .' Candy started. 'He was different.'

Sean breathed. Candy was talking about how she was only saying all this so that they could make a new start, so they could get on with their lives and not look back. They could be true to each other now, she said, but the words meant nothing because for the first time in his life Sean finally understood completely that he hated her.

Sean hated Candy.

A part of him always had, he realized. It was like a dormant emotion suddenly awakened. Maybe it was just the resentment bubbling to the surface. After all, she'd put him through enough grief. And now this!

But it was worse than that.

After all, Candy was a woman, wasn't she? And Sean hated women. Mother, Candy, Mrs Newman, Jennifer Ames – all of them: WHORES!

The Blackness was back.

Sean watched Candy picking at a piece of cream-coloured

candle wax that had melted onto the table and was now hardening into the shape of a dialogue balloon, the kind you see in comic strips.

A very, very large part of him wanted to hit her.

'Come home with me,' Candy said eventually.

Sean managed not to spit.

'No,' he replied.

Candy didn't cry. She simply looked at him, biting her back teeth together before saying, very quietly, 'I understand.' Then, in a series of smooth movements, she picked up her purse and turned to leave. 'I'll speak to you soon.'

'Yup,' Sean said, not moving, wanting to see her leave, the bitter-sweet taste of spite in his mouth, knowing that she'd be sobbing outside.

# Chapter Seventy-Four

'**W**eeeeyyyyyy!'

'Errm, yes, hello.'

'*Weeeeyyyyyyyyyyyyy!!*'

'Can I speak to Mr Quok, please?'

Michael could hear the receiver being put down against something hard, something that knocked into his ear, probably a table. He could hear a television in the background and then a woman screaming in Cantonese. A man replied in rumbles. Eventually, he could feel the phone on the other end travelling.

'*Wey.*'

'Hello, Mr Quok? Is that you?'

'Yes, Quok. Who is this?'

'It's Michael Marland.'

Silence.

'From the airport, you picked me up . . . couple of months ago. You gave me your number and said that you were looking for a writer, you know, for your company brochure.'

'I give my number to lot of people.'

'You dropped me at Tai-ping Shan, Mansion Flats, remember?'

There was a pause.

'Sorry, job taken, you too late.'

Michael could sense the phone moving through the air again.

'Wait, wait, Mr Quok. I don't need a job. I work at the *Hong Kong Herald* now. I need . . .'

Michael paused, waiting to see if he was still there.

'What? What you need?'

'Information,' Michael replied.

'What kind of information?'

'It's very sensitive. Can we meet in person?'

'No. You tell me now. What information you need?'

'I need,' Michael paused, relishing the investigative nature of it all – he was almost being a journalist. 'I need to know about a fire, a fire at Tai-ping Shan.'

'Sorry, don't know about fire. I drive taxi, run company, export-import. Goodbye.'

'We'll pay,' Michael said.

'Who pay?'

'The *Herald*,' Michael lied. Sean had agreed to front the money. He'd eventually confided in Michael about his fight with the taxi driver, losing his wallet, fearing that the fire was his fault in some way. Michael had tried to reassure him that it had just been an accident, but Sean had been very anxious, almost panicky. He'd said he was scared that Triads were after him. Michael had tried to tell him that he was being paranoid but when Sean explained how all taxi drivers were members of Triad rings because they protected their working rights, rather like a union, Michael realized that maybe Sean wasn't being irrational. Then Michael had remembered his taxi 'contact' and threw out the idea of making some calls. He hadn't known why he had said it – perhaps he was just trying to be helpful, or maybe he was simply excited to be able to help

Sean. He'd never told him how he'd freaked out at the scene of the blaze.

'How much?'

'It depends what you get us.'

'What do you need?'

'We just need to know anything you can tell us about the fire at Tai-ping Shan last month. We believe it could be Triad related. One of the residents in the apartments that burnt down was involved in an incident with a taxi driver near Lan Kwai Fong the day before. He . . . I mean, *The Herald* would be very interested to know if the fire was some sort of revenge attack.'

'One hundred thousand Hong Kong.'

'One hundred thousand!!' Michael exclaimed, noticing one or two faces in the *Herald* office turning. 'One hundred thousand,' he said more quietly. 'You must be joking.'

Silence.

'OK, listen,' Michael said eventually. 'We'll give you twenty thousand, ten up front and ten for the information you find. If it's good information we'll give you another five.'

'Ten.'

'OK, ten,' Michael conceded. 'That's thirty thousand Hong Kong for two phone calls. The easiest money you've ever made.'

'If so easy, why don't you make phone call?'

Michael tried not to get irritated. The Chinese always got the better of you. Just like Sean had said. Thirty thousand was three times the amount Sean and he had agreed.

'Just tell me where to meet you.'

# Chapter Seventy-Five

Candy couldn't figure out if was the sound of the foundation machine outside her house – essentially a giant hammer that was smashing a twenty-foot iron girder into solid rock with a deafening BANG! that made everyone blink – or her father's voice that was giving her a headache.

'I want to know why you don't want to see Stephen again,' her father repeated.

Candy didn't reply. She was still vaguely hoping that her parents would drop it.

'Everything seemed fine before we went away,' her mother stepped in. 'What's changed?'

'I bet she's seeing that boy, whatshisname, again,' her father said.

'You know damn well what his name is, Daddy,' Candy said – there was only so much stoicism within her.

'I knew it,' her father said, looking as if he were about to vomit. 'I knew she was seeing him again.'

BANG!

Blink.

'CHRIST!' Candy's father shouted. 'As if the goddamned *Taipan* doesn't have enough buildings already. Why does he have to build another skyscraper here, right in our view?'

'We don't have a view, Daddy,' Candy said, more to get back at him than anything else.

His eyes narrowed at her.

'Is it true then?' Candy's mum asked. 'You're seeing Sean again?'

Candy looked back at her mother defiantly, wanting to say yes, but already knowing within herself that she'd say no. She'd never been able to admit Sean to them – not his status nor her true feelings for him. They'd drummed the shame into her. She tried to time her denial with the next crash of the hammer, vaguely hoping that the lie would get lost deep in the foundations of the island, along with all of Hong Kong's other deceptions.

But it didn't work.

'No.'

BANG!

Blink.

'Then why?' her father picked up instantly. He never missed a beat, her dad. 'Why aren't you seeing Stephen?'

'Because he's a fucking bastard, that's why,' Candy said matter-of-factly.

'Why bastard? Why?' her mother said, giving away the fact that it made her angry to hear Candy swear. Her English always got worse when she was angry.

'He just is, that's why,' Candy stamped like a teenager. There was nothing to gain from telling them she'd been raped. A big part of her knew that they'd take Stephen's side anyway.

'I don't understand my own daughter,' Candy's father said, looking at his wife. 'I don't even know her. We try everything, we do everything we can to make her happy and look how she repays us.' There was the smallest of pauses as he turned back to face Candy, targeting her before dropping his bombshell. 'I don't want you in this house any more. Let's see how you survive on your own!'

'You're kicking me out?' Candy exclaimed. 'You're kicking me out because I don't want to see Stephen?!'

Candy's dad didn't say anything, but there was a small, 'Please, Sam,' from her mother before the sentence withered under his stare and then finally died as the hammer came down.

BANG!

Blink. Two tears crept out from Candy's eyes. She managed to say, 'I can't believe you, Daddy,' before sniffing stiffly and finally adding: 'I don't care. I hate this house anyway. There's plenty of other places I can go and stay. Who needs it?'

She went to her room to pack.

# Chapter Seventy-Six

Michael took the MTR to get to the docks, but only because Quok had told him to. If he'd been using his brain, he would have taken a taxi. After all, he was carrying thirty thousand Hong Kong in cash in his pocket so it wasn't as if he couldn't afford it. Plus it was the middle of the night, so public transport wasn't exactly the safest option.

But all of this only occurred to Michael as the hydraulic doors to the train hissed closed behind him and by then it was too late. He told himself it didn't matter. It would be cool. Only a few people had got on the train from Central and his train carriage was empty. Besides, Hong Kong wasn't exactly famous for its subway muggings. It was sterile that way. Even though things happened here, they tended to happen in dramatic isolation. At least, this was his new philosophy: gas explosions and Hong Kong went together, subway attacks were more suited to a 1970s New York.

He took a seat and rapped his feet. The train's overhead lights flickered – they must be passing through the harbour, Michael thought to himself. Adverts for a skin-lightening cream lined the carriage. He started to sing 'Ghost Town' by The Specials to the soft rhythm of the train tracks, seeing how low his voice could go each time he sang the *'This Town'* line. He knew he sounded terrible but he didn't care. After all, who was listening?

The train pulled into a station but no one got on.

Michael didn't know why he had agreed to meet Quok so late. Quok had muttered something about the end of his taxi shift, but they surely could have come to some other arrangement. Even though the city felt safe, Michael found himself becoming less and less comfortable with the idea of carrying so much money to a place he didn't know. Where was everyone? And could he trust Quok? After all, he'd only met the guy once before.

'Oh, Quok's OK,' he said out loud to himself, and instantly felt reassured by the sound of his own voice.

The train slowed down for another station. Still no one. How could a city become so completely dead? He thought to himself. After a couple of stops the train excreted itself from the bowels of the city and travelled in the open air. Three more stops after that and one more human sighting (no contact), Michael arrived at his stop. He sensed two other people alight from the train, but they were a long way down the platform and they seemed to leave the station via another exit.

As soon as Michael had climbed the stairs and stepped out into the open he was instantly lost. Nothing was recognizable to him. There seemed to be a lot of industrialization: factories and parked trucks. Michael was surprised. For some reason he had thought Hong Kong was all residential. He'd also imagined that the island would have been easily visible from any vantage point on the mainland – it stood so erect. But he couldn't see any of the skyscrapers that might have helped him get his bearings. The warehouse buildings that surrounded the station were crammed together, preventing a clear line of sight.

Michael scratched himself through one trouser pocket and held onto the money in the other. It was another muggy night.

A Chinese girl holding a handkerchief to her mouth walked quickly towards him on her own way into the MTR station. Michael approached her to ask directions but she trotted even faster as soon as she saw him coming. He called out to her but she dipped her head and scurried like a rat into the safety of the sewer. She was practically sprinting by the time she reached the top of the stairs leading down into the brightly lit underground. He watched her jiggling her way down without turning around to look at him.

Typical, he thought to himself.

He waited a little longer to see if a taxi might pull up before he decided to just start walking. Standing around aimlessly seemed to be asking for trouble somehow. He told himself he'd figure it out. He was almost late for the rendezvous already – the train journey had taken longer than Quok had said – so he figured he had to do something. There wasn't anyone around and even if there had been he knew that they wouldn't have helped him. He saw a small sign with a ship on it and decided to go in that direction.

A truck with green tarpaulin flapping drove quickly past, its headlights momentarily blinding him. When it was gone Michael thought he heard a voice, so he turned but he couldn't see anyone. He carried on walking. His trainers squeaked against the pavement. Then he heard the voice again. He started to walk a little faster, the squeak from his shoes picking up a pitch.

After passing three long factory-type buildings, Michael saw another sign with a ship on it, pointing to an incline leading darkly down to the right. He could see the sea from here, blacker than an oil slick, and rows of cargo containers. Quok had told him to look out for the taxi rank – couldn't miss it, he'd said.

'Yeah, right,' Michael said out loud to himself.

Then someone laughed. Michael spun round and was about to ask who was there but the words caught in his throat and didn't go away. He swallowed and started in earnest down the incline. Now he was nervous. The night shadows seemed to claw at him. He tried to walk in the sparse light, small yellow puddles left by single bulbs lighting intermittent doorways. Between the warehouses Michael could see long tracts of darkness but he didn't dare look too closely. He half-expected an army of Triads, karate chops and meat cleavers flashing, to surround him at any minute. That was when the thought occurred to him that he was walking straight into a trap. Maybe Sean had been right all along. Maybe he *had* incited the wrath of a Triad ring, and now they were on to them, ready to rob and then kill just for fun. What was Michael doing here? Was he mad? What had he been thinking? Was he doing it for Sean? Or had it been his wannabe an investigative journalist thing? Was any story worth this kind of terror? When did a journalist know the difference between bravery and stupidity?

Michael knew the difference.

He was being fucking stupid.

His feet had picked up speed along with the rhythm of his thoughts and by now he was jogging, his Nike's singing: *squeak, squeak, squeak, squeak, squeak . . .*

And then he tripped.

Everything went suddenly very quiet. The movement of air was vaguely discernible around him but time seemed to stop. No, it was more than that. Time shattered. And then the pieces rearranged themselves. Michael saw the moment ahead of him: he was going to fall on his wrist, and then the moment that had just occurred: the toe of his shoe catching on an upturned paving stone. He saw all the elements of the event from different vantage points. The paving stone itself and how it had long stood alone and proud in the street. Michael hurtling towards it, the stride of his legs perfectly measured to meet its edge. And then himself, suddenly in the present: flying.

Michael was flying.

And now he was falling.

And now, just as he had foreseen, he was crumbling onto his wrist.

There was pain.

And then a laugh.

And then the voice, as clear as the day he'd first heard it.

'JOEEEYYYY DEAAACONNN!'

Michael sat upright, ignoring the burning in his arm.

'WHO'S THERE?' he called out, finding the words that had remained in his throat.

Nothing.

'WHO ARE YOU? WHAT DO YOU WANT?'

Michael was close to crying now, terrified, the pain in his arm (the same one Baxter had broken) making everything worse. There was a shuffle of feet and then a horrific feeling. Michael didn't dare say it, lest the admission made it real.

But he had to. He had to know.

'S . . . sh . . . Sean?'

Silence. Shadows. The wind. Michael stared down the empty street, squinting.

'I know you're there, Sean.'

Still nothing. Michael could feel him very close now, he was certain of it. He just had to talk to him. What did Sean want? Why was he following him?

'Don't,' Michael said gently. 'Don't do this.'

'Do what?' a voice suddenly called out from behind him.

Michael spun around and looked up.

It was Quok.

# Chapter Seventy-Seven

'Jesus, you scared the fucking shit out of me,' Michael said. 'You have money?' Quok said.

Michael felt his eyes narrow, his heart still racing, all his senses alert. 'What information do you have?'

Quok paused and stared down at him. 'Why are you lying in the street like a dog? Who are you talking to?'

Michael rubbed his wrist and got up, inspecting the raw graze jumping across his palm and wrist.

'I fell over.'

Quok looked at him. 'You are alone?'

Michael half turned. 'Yeah,' he said. 'I'm alone.'

Quok's eyes narrowed.

'I'm alone,' Michael said again, feeling the tension in his voice. 'Now come on, let's get this over with. What information do you have for me?'

'Money,' Quok said.

Michael gave him an envelope. Quok peered inside. 'There's no point counting it,' Michael said. 'It's only half. You'll get the second half after I hear what you have for me.' He'd learnt his lesson from the Witches.

Quok sneered but Michael's expression must have been stony because he started, 'No Triad.'

'What do you mean?'

'Fire no Triad. No Triad,' he repeated.

'Are you sure?'

'Yes, sure. I even know taxi man your friend hit. He angry. Very angry. Want to kill your friend. But . . .'

'But what?'

'He don't know who he is. Don't know where to find him. Can't kill him. But now . . .' An ugly grin broke across Quok's face mid-sentence.

'*The Herald* won't pay you more than this,' Michael gulped.

Quok looked at him and didn't say anything.

'Do you know who started the fire then?' Michael asked, more to change the subject than anything else.

'No,' Quok replied. 'But people . . . they say . . .' Quok paused as if for effect.

'What?' Michael pressed.

'They say *gweilo* – he start fire at Tai-ping Shan.'

'A *gweilo*?'

Quok nodded.

'How?' Michael started. 'How do you know?'

'*Gweilo* evil. Everyone in Hong Kong know. *Gweilo* are ghosts, *gweilo* are reason for all things bad here.'

Michael snorted at him. 'Yeah, right, OK, whatever. Listen to me. Did anyone actually see a *gweilo* start the fire?'

'No,' Quok said.

'Typical,' Michael huffed, shaking his head. 'You brought me all the way out here to tell me that. For Christ sake. You could have told me this on the telephone,' Michael admonished, being sure to tower over Quok.

'Maybe,' Quok replied calmly.

'Well, I don't think your information is worth thirty grand. You haven't exactly told me much, except that the Chinese reckon the British are to blame for everything, and that's hardly news. I suggest you and I simply go our separate ways, Mr Quok.'

Michael started to turn to walk back to the MTR station when he heard Quok snap, 'No! You pay me. Pay me now.'

Michael didn't dare show his back to him. 'Why should I?' he said, remaining.

'Because otherwise I tell taxi man where to find your friend.'

Michael snorted cynically. 'I knew you never needed a writer.'

Quok's face queried. 'What?'

'Your English seems pretty good to me.'

Quok smiled – sort of. 'Only for business. Business English OK.'

Michael handed him the second envelope with the other fifteen thousand inside and turned to walk.

'You pay me every month now,' Quok called out to him as Michael stepped away. 'Thirty thousand each month.'

Michael carried on walking, hoping that moving away would make Quok go away.

'I call youuu,' Quok called out after him. 'I call you. You bring money. Every month.' Quok was half shouting now but Michael ignored him. He'd had enough of this misadventure for one night. He'd have to consult Sean from here. He'd know what to do. He'd know how to get rid of Quok. A shadow within a shadow moved in the corner of Michael's eye and he turned to look but he didn't want to stop walking because of Quok and, in any case, the movement wasn't there when he focused on it. Michael found himself smiling. Yeah. Sean would know what to do. Sean would know how to clear up this mess Michael had made.

He always did.

# Chapter Seventy-Eight

The sun was blazing and the outdoor pool was a delicious cold that made the English summer feel fresh, like it should feel: late and eventual but definitely there. There was the sound of cricket bats thwacking cricket balls and the distant buzz of lawnmowers and the smell of grass. Pigeons lilted from horse chestnut trees. The boys all splashed each other and plunged and ran around. Wasps darted near their feet.

Yes, it was definitely summer in England at last and everything was different, so very different, from the cold, dark winter months of before. Exams were over, term was ending, Baxter was dead and Fishface was leaving – sabbatical, the school said.

Marland was leaving, too. At the end of the year, his mother had finally decided. After the inquiry failed to reveal anything, she thought it best. She didn't want to create a *stir* by taking him out in the middle of the term as he had originally hoped she might. *He could hang on for a bit longer, couldn't he?*

Clarke's mum was the same. He had his Common Entrance to finish and a place at Millfield already secured. His dad had gone there. They didn't want to mess up the boy's chances by removing him at the same time as the scandal.

In some ways, it worked out best that way for everyone.

With Baxter gone, Marland was one of the most popular

boys at St Luke's now. It hadn't taken long for him to assume the position – half a term at most – after the 'accident'. Maybe it was because everyone was scared of him – him and Clarke. Somehow, even though there'd been a big cover-up, Michael's interpretation of the events leading to Baxter's death had got out and subsequently been accepted as truth. Maybe his version simply made as much sense to everyone else at St Luke's as it did to him. After all, Clarke had only just come back from his suspension before it happened. It seemed far too coincidental for it to have been an accident, even if Clarke did deny it.

In any case, the story was folklore now, another school legend, like the Bummer Man and the boy that had gone missing five years ago in the Elms. It was one of those tales that would get handed down through the generations of boarders, late in the night when the lights were turned out. There'd probably even be a story about a ghost – the vicious bully named Baxter, who had been murdered and now roamed the halls of Holland House ready to terrorize and mutilate the new boys, the young ones, looking for revenge on the weaklings. Those sorts of stories lasted for ever and somehow always ended up becoming true.

'TIME!' Mrs Webster shouted before whistling the end of swimming break, and all the boys who weren't in the pool made one last dive bomb, their skin feeling sharp in the breeze and goose-pimples standing on their thighs.

Marland was in the pool squirting water out of his mouth at Jeffreys and Miller, who were both laughing and making sure they only squirted water at each other and not back at him. Everyone was climbing out now and shivering themselves into towels that were too small. Boys from another class, two years below, were lining up along the hedgerow that bordered the swimming area, their teacher, Mrs Gibson no less, in front of them waiting by the dark-green wooden gate.

'Come on now, Mrs Webster,' Marland heard her wobbling. 'Your boys have been in the pool for long enough. It's Year Three's turn now.'

Marland found it hard not to stare at her, hating her still for the way she had interrogated him that time in the Headmaster's study, the way she had turned the situation to her own advantage. Mr Gibson was going to be Holland's new House Master. He was taking over after Fishface left.

'Yes, boys, come on,' Mrs Webster clapped. 'It's time for your biology class now.' Everyone groaned. 'Come on, Marland,' she said, looking down at him as he continued to dawdle deliberately in the water. 'Let's go. Chop chop.'

Marland just stared at Mrs Gibson, willing her to try and exert her authority over him but knowing she wouldn't because he was leaving so she knew that he didn't care what she said any more. Marland even believed that maybe she was a little scared of him now as well.

Then Marland heard Jeffreys whisper to Miller, 'Look, that's Baxter's brother,' and Marland turned his head quickly to see a young head, a flash of brown hair just showing over the hedgerow. Marland felt a brief surge of fear as he recognized the squinting, sneering look in the boy's eyes, even though he looked quite different from his brother. He reminded himself that he was the most popular boy now and that Baxter's brother was two whole years below him – so much smaller. 'He's a day boy, same year as Mrs Gibson's son.'

'What? The Bender?' Marland said.

'Yeah,' Miller and Jeffreys said together.

Marland's class filed their way out of the swimming pool area and only Jeffreys, Miller, Marland and a tutting Mrs

Webster remained now. Mrs Gibson was holding open the gate for her class as they rolled in, squealing as they quickly leapt into the pool, water splashing up around them. Marland moved to leave the swimming area and then, just as he was walking through the gate, little Baxter crashed into him.

'OI! WATCHIT!' Marland shouted as he body blocked him, the boy's skinny pre-pubescent frame bouncing off his chest and crumbling easily to the ground.

Marland felt Mrs Gibson staring at him, Mrs Webster too afraid to look, Marland's black shadow towering over and consuming the small body lying on the grass before him. Marland ignored the teachers, feeling Jeffreys' and Miller's presence not far behind – his back-up boys. He felt powerful, big, strong. Still, little Baxter sneered up at Marland and, for an instant, Marland felt genuinely threatened.

'Bloody Joey,' was all he could think to say, stepping over him.

A few seconds passed before he heard the words.

'I'm going to get you for what you did.'

Marland pretended not to hear.

# Chapter Seventy-Nine

The Russian was a trading magnate – or at least the heir of one. He didn't seem to do very much of anything, except throw parties. But his parties were unlike any other in Hong Kong. For starters, not everyone was invited. In fact, the guest list was very strict – only the Beautiful People could attend. Wannabe models pined for an invitation: it was the kind of endorsement that could make or break a career. And all of Hong Kong's colonial male population lusted for one – for obvious reasons.

Maybe that was why images of perfect breasts and six-pack-powered whoops of fun sprung instantly to Candy's mind when she received her invitation, even though she didn't know why she had been invited. OK, so she knew that she was beautiful – but what had been the catalyst? How had the Russian come to hear of her?

Of course, she had wanted to go. This was one of Hong Kong's few remaining secrets. The only things that Candy knew about the Russian's parties were that they were usually held in his private suite at the Canton Hotel or on his wooden junk-cum-yacht. A cordon bleu chef cooked dinner and apparently the finest drugs were always served for dessert. He also had a Gauguin.

Sean still didn't seem to want her, so what did she have to lose?

But as the tender that had picked Candy up from the dock growled its way alongside the Russian's yacht – Repulse Bay's streetlights rippling in the night sea – Candy understood why she had been invited.

Beautiful People were drinking champagne and laughing on the floodlit deck. The men were dressed in tuxedoes, the women in designer dresses. Candy was wearing her black number again, the same semi-transparent one she'd worn for Stephen Ching.

She saw Rob, looking as dashing as ever, smoking a cigarette, in a white dinner jacket, peering down as the tender landed, clearly waiting for her. Before she had a chance to ask the driver to take her back to the dock – she owed Sean that much – Rob had waved and was stepping towards the back of the boat to greet her. She felt herself moving, drawn towards him like innocence is to danger: aware that there might be consequences, but still vaguely and naïvely believing that she could outwit them.

Rob took her hand as she reached the final rung of the ladder leading up to the back of the boat. The brightness of the deck seemed to fill her as he smiled and moved to kiss her cheek.

'I thought you might not come,' he said in her ear.

She smiled back at him without saying anything as he pulled away, still holding her hand. She glanced at the other guests, immediately noticing how many more women there were than men. She saw that the dinner table had already been elaborately laid.

'Come here,' Rob said. 'I want to introduce you to Jordan.'

Candy let Rob lead her through the knots of people towards

a tall man who was talking intensely with a fat man in a chef's hat. As they approached, Candy feeling Rob's broad smile shining, the chef whispered something before leaving through a gangway door. The man was still nodding seriously by the time Rob began his introductions.

'Jordan, this is Candy,' Rob said, moving to stand alongside him so that they could both admire Candy together. 'Candy, this is Jordan.'

The Russian smiled warmly at her, black eyes twinkling. 'I'm so pleased you could come.'

'You have a beautiful yacht,' Candy replied, thinking to herself how benign he looked.

'Thank you,' Jordan replied. There was a brief pause before he added, 'Would you excuse me?'

Candy nodded as he moved away. 'He's much taller than I had imagined,' she said to Rob.

'Jordan's a lovely guy,' Rob said simply.

'How do you know him?' Candy asked as a waitress delivered a tray of champagne. Candy took a glass and Rob replaced his. Candy watched Rob thank the waitress, looking into her eyes earnestly, before turning back to her. 'Tommy introduced us.'

'Where *is* Tommy?' Candy asked. 'I haven't seen him in ages.'

'He's around, but you know how he is – he likes to be alone.'

'Is he recording?'

'Yeah,' Rob replied, his voice lilting hopefully. 'He seems to be doing some really good stuff.'

'I'd like to hear it,' Candy said, sipping on her champagne as Rob pulled out his cigarettes and offered her one.

'You should come over,' he said, reaching into his jacket pocket for a lighter. Candy watched herself lean towards the flame as it kicked in the breeze. 'You owe us another visit.'

Candy smiled. 'So where's this Gauguin I've heard so much about?'

'It's in the living room at the front of the boat,' Rob replied. 'I'll show it to you if you like.'

'Ooh yes,' Candy replied enthusiastically. 'I'd love to see it.'

Rob smiled and moved to lead her but then there was the chime of a teaspoon against a champagne glass as Jordan said: 'Please, Beautiful People . . .' a pause and some twitters of ironic amusement. 'Take your seats. Dinner is now served!'

Rob looked at Candy and shrugged his shoulders. 'It can wait till after dinner,' he said, looking into her with the same intensity with which he'd thanked the waitress. 'It'll look better then anyway.'

# Chapter Eighty

The MDMA had a way of illuminating everything. Candy was finding herself being mesmerized by Rob's blue eyes. They seemed to sparkle, flash out towards her. He looked like an angel. He was smiling at her, as if to say he could hear it too – their vibration. They were dancing, close. So close. She could feel his breath, the brush of his stubble. She wanted him. It was there again! The dazzle in those deep azure pools. His eyelashes sparkled. Candy was falling, she could feel herself going. The rest of the room was becoming darker, the other couples and the Gauguin (oh, the Gauguin! She'd come up hard when she'd seen it) slipping into a tunnel-vision void. Rob's face dominated everything now. He was smiling. She was falling, falling. Was it love?

The beat in the music changed and she felt Rob place his hands on her hips. Their groins moved together. He moved to meet her. She could see his tongue. She wanted to feel its warmth. She opened her lips. She was ready, waiting, she wanted it, she wanted it, she was going to do it, yes, she . . .

Something seized her. What was it? The drugs were making it hard to think. What had just happened? Nothing. Where was time? Rob was still moving into her. Wait! Stop. Candy felt quickly disorientated. No. She realized. This was wrong.

What was she doing? What was he doing? Stop, go back, let go. She tried to breathe and then somewhere she found the words.

'Wait,' she snapped, the panic quickly in her throat.

Rob ignored her and pressed their groins harder together, keeping the beat in their hips.

'Rob.' She pulled away. The rest of the room emerged from out of the borders of the dark tunnel and she could see where she was again. In the middle of the room, in a very tight space with Rob. Other people were dancing, kissing, two girls next to them.

'Rob.' She managed to smile this time.

She felt the warmth from the mudma flood through her again, lulling her into that big feathery heaven, but she resisted. She didn't let herself melt. She tried not to look into the Angel's eyes. They were dangerous, magical. She couldn't look.

'What?' he said, still staying close.

'I . . . I need some fresh air,' she managed, her voice shaking.

'No you don't.'

'I do, please.'

She managed to break and turn quickly, pushing her way quickly between two couples and towards a door. She didn't know where it led to. She felt wonderfully warm. Her face was glowing. The outside air lifted the hem of her skirt and then she felt the sea on her face. The smell of wood from the boat. Every nerve in her body was alive and tickling with strange information. Rob's hand was on her back. It felt so good.

She stepped away from it.

'What's wrong? Are you OK?' he said, behind her.

She leant against the gangway barrier and sighed heavily, trying to catch her breath, trying to make sense of the wonderful way her body felt, wanting to control it. She mustn't fall. 'I was hot,' she said, feeling her voice still shaking. Come on, Candy! Get a grip. 'That stuff is really strong.'

'I know,' Rob said.

They didn't say anything, Candy just focusing on her breathing, trying not to let the fishing boat lights on the horizon become too blurred, a small part of her wishing she would come down, the biggest part of her wanting to turn around and kiss Rob and feel this heavenly way for ever. Did she love him?

Could she trust that?

She was scared. She couldn't bear to look at him. If she looked, she'd never turn away. She had to get off this boat. She could not do this. She would not do this. He was close to her again now. She wanted him. She tried to move away but her body wouldn't react. He was moving in. Was this real? It felt real.

She turned. He was beside her. His strong chest reaching. She felt her hands clenching. Another shivery sigh. She was shaking.

'Are you cold?'

He took her shoulders in his hands. She felt them slide down her upper arms. He held her by the elbows. His fingers gripped. The smallest of pulls. She was being drawn in again. She looked up at his face. She could kiss him now. It would all be over. Sean. She could. He was coming closer. The air. Somewhere a moon. She was slipping again. That fog of ecstasy coming in at the edges. Her lips moved. His hands travelled firmly round and across the small of her back. Sean. The word appeared.

Rob was going to kiss her now. The word started flashing. It started flashing in her brain like a big neon alarm. Don't say it, don't say it. Don't say *that* word. Please. But she had to. She couldn't do this. Sean. Rob's lips were touching hers. She was falling. Stop!

'NO!'

It hit both of them violently – something very beautiful had been smashed.

Rob tried to ignore it but it didn't work. Once she'd said it the word poured out of her just as it always had – hatefully, destructively, defensively. Why was he making her do it? Why did they all make her say it?

'No, no, no, no – get OFF ME!'

She snapped herself out of his grip and felt herself falling backwards. Some part of the boat caught her and she managed to stay upright. Rob kept coming.

'Leave me alone,' she said, still backing away.

'What's wrong, Candy?' he said, still coming towards her, his features darkening.

'I can't do this.'

'Do what?'

'I said no.'

'I know you want me.'

He was still coming. She hated him now – for everything. For coming between her and Sean, for nearly destroying her, for making her responsible, for making her hate herself, for being just like all the others, for making her say that word.

'Stop it, Rob, or I'll scream.'

'You've said that to me once before.'

'I mean it this time,' she managed to sigh. Another wave of the drug was overcoming her.

'I don't believe you.'

'You have to understand,' she managed more softly now. The ecstasy was calming her, the sea soothing too. 'I can't do this. I love Sean. I can't leave him. He's a part of me. I could never leave him. If I left, it would kill him. He can't live without me. And I can't live without him.'

'He doesn't want you any more, Candy.'

'I'll wait.'

'What if it's too late?'

She shook her head.

'How do you know?'

'I just know,' she said. 'We were meant for each other. We'll always be together. I want to be with him.'

Darkness came into the angel eyes.

'Are you sure?'

She nodded.

He looked at her terribly.

'Please, Rob, I want to get off this boat.'

'Don't worry,' he said. 'I'll make sure you and Sean are back together soon. I promise. You deserve each other.'

'I just want you to leave us alone. Please.'

'No, really. I owe you that much.'

'You don't owe me anything.'

'You don't understand.'

'What don't I understand?'

'You and Sean are made for each other. He loves to fuck whores.'

Candy felt her bottom lip starting to quiver involuntarily and she twisted her features and bit back the hot flush of hate she could feel quickly coursing through her, killing the mudma and making her feel sober. Her senses returned to her and she felt a moment of relief before scrambling though her brain, desperate to find the words, the right insults to fight back with. He'd caught her so off guard – she was still in shock – she literally couldn't find a single word to say.

So she hit him.

He was quite a lot taller than her, even while she was in stilettos, and he was turning away when she did it so she only clipped him on the back of his head. But then, once she'd started, she found she was unable to stop and she was suddenly unleashing a flurry of half-clenched fists on his shoulders, against his neck, on the back of his head. She didn't yell, or scream, or say 'Bastard'. She just felt the rap of her knuckles whenever they struck hard bone.

And then, quite suddenly, she was paralysed. Somehow, in the midst of her fury – she must have had her eyes closed – Rob had turned and caught both her wrists and was squeezing them, very hard.

'Oww,' she moaned, real tears flooding her eyes now from the pain and the fear and the outrage she could still feel burning. 'Stop it. You're hurting me.'

Rob was staring darkly into her, all his features hateful now, looking so ugly, so violent. He wasn't an angel now. He looked like the Devil – at the very least, she could feel evil. She suddenly feared for herself – a fundamental fear, an animal fear, the kind of fear that could kill. She was completely powerless. Whatever was to happen next she had absolutely no control over. She felt so fragile. Everything, her whole life, indeed all life, seemed in that instant to hang precariously on a string. And it was being stretched – stretched to its very breaking point. Life hummed around her, ready to snap at any moment and then it would be over, gone for ever. Candy felt herself squeezing her eyes and her ears, wincing and shrivelling, bracing for the blow. Any moment now . . .

And then he let go.

Quite suddenly. And he was standing tall, not bearing down into her any more. All his features were normal, all his composure resumed. Cool as ice, just as she had always perceived him. The evil was simply gone, and Candy couldn't help feeling she'd imagined it. He even appeared to look at her quite compassionately. He didn't brag in his domination, he didn't remind her or humiliate her or say anything to her, even make her do anything.

And in that moment, he must have known, he could have done anything to her. He could have raped her, beaten her, killed her even. She was infinitely fearful of him. She didn't know whether to laugh or cry. She didn't know whether to start hitting him again or hugging him. Somehow she felt grateful. She tried to say something, she wanted to, but she was still paralysed, mesmerized maybe.

Rob didn't say anything. He stood there for a moment, the breeze stroking him, looking as handsome as ever, his white dinner jacket cutting a dashing silhouette against the darkness. He looked like an advert for chocolates. And then, he turned. Silently and slowly, he walked back through the gangway door and into the room where they'd been dancing.

Candy refused to let herself sob and she moved quickly towards the back of the boat, desperate to get as far away from Rob as she could. As her shoes clipped across the gangway she felt the ache in her wrists and she looked down to see black bruises breaking against the milk of her skin and she couldn't hold down the feelings of wretchedness and self-hatred and humiliation and fear. The tears erupted.

A couple emerged at the top of the yacht's ladder, naked and dripping and laughing, and she had to quickly compose herself. She could feel their looks. For a dreadful moment, she thought the woman was about to ask if she was OK, but then they were gone and she was finally alone. She looked up in the sky for stars but the brightness of the island drowned them. The world seemed darker out to sea. She wanted a cigarette but she knew that she'd left them inside somewhere. She thought of Sean and she knew that she'd leave Hong Kong with him now. She promised herself that as soon as she got back she'd tell him – beg him if she had to. The next day if possible, whatever flight – she didn't care.

But then she remembered what Rob had said.

# Chapter Eighty-One

After it happened it suddenly seemed so avoidable.

Michael had noticed the guy beforehand. Like everyone else, he had been drinking and smoking and laughing. It was the weekend. It was hot. White people had laid themselves out on the upper decks of the Lamma ferry, arming themselves for the journey with shiny sickly looking buns filled with tuna fish, mini cans of Heineken and copies of the *Hong Kong Herald*. The Chinese sat below, in the shaded but stuffier cool. They sat on the moulded plastic seats that were bolted to the floor in rows.

Michael saw one girl reading his column. She had plaits mimicking dreadlocks and bright ribbons woven into her hair. He might have introduced himself if he hadn't found her so unattractive. She didn't look like she was enjoying it much, anyway. She was grimacing but that might just have been her squinting in the brightness.

They'd already passed the harbour, consciously breathing deeper as they slowly moved towards the open ocean. Michael needed the break from Hong Kong Island and the stuffy, dark, humid heat. He stared at Kennedy Town as they passed; the way the millions were piled on top of one another in sky-scrapers. Row upon row upon row. All of them the same. The odd pastel colouring in the concrete, only ever reinforcing the point: everyone was the same, everyone was trapped. Lost and boxed in, no life. Inside those apartment blocks they were just another number: 33F, 55A, 29D – everyone looking out onto each other from their windows, hearing every conversation through their walls, living in each other's shadows. Enormous skyscraper shadows that bore down on the streets in a terrible maze with no end, no solution. Just a world that weaved and hemmed the players in. No one could see beyond. They couldn't jump or give someone a leg up to take a peek over the hedgerow borders, catch a glimpse of the broader perspective. Ha! The skyscrapers practically laughed in their domination, their huge-ness. Everyone was *inside*.

Unless you lived on the Peak, of course.

But there was a way out, a way to see. And this was it, this boat journey. It was impossible not to marvel at the cityscape. The magnificence of it. It was so beautiful from the outside. Or was that just the relief of the escape? Probably both.

Lamma took a tantalizingly long time to reach. It was a haven to so many. There were no vehicles allowed on the island and the restaurants sat on the water and there were plants that blossomed and there was space to walk. Even the Chinese were nicer. Well, not exactly nicer, just less in-your-face nasty.

Michael didn't know what he'd do on Lamma once he arrived. He didn't know anyone there. Christ, he didn't know a single person from beyond the Group – that was how weak the dynamic had made him. Maybe the smallness of the set was another side-effect of living in the city maze, he thought to himself. Urban life was so disorientating and overwhelming that it was impossible not to congregate into teams, pool together into small puddles. It was the only way to forget the fact that they were lost in Hong Kong or, at least, not be scared of it. And having found that security, it was hard to venture out alone to other puddles, make new friends. After all, you might not find your way back to the one you came from.

Even so, it felt good to be on his own now.

It was hot and he was sweating but he was in the open. He was wearing shorts. He'd be swimming later. They said the water was safe around Lamma, despite the enormous power station. Michael didn't think too deeply about it. The beaches looked clean even if the water was too warm in places and the algae made your skin feel slimy after you got out.

Time to relax, that's what he told himself. It was the weekend. The boat was chugging. There was more laughing. And then some shouting. One of the engines died as the island loomed suddenly large and the captain began the negotiation for the sweeping, reversing, looping park onto the pier. Michael liked that bit, picturing himself handling the controls like some Starsky and Hutch driver, drifting the boat in like it was actually a high-speed car stunt shot in slow motion.

It all happened so quickly.

He couldn't have been much older than Michael – a man-child: fun and young. A little drunk, a little boisterous, definitely not very intelligent.

'I'm swimming in,' he announced.

Those must have been the words, though Michael never heard them. He was looking at the guy but only glancing as he scanned the crowd for what must have been the tenth time. All Michael knew was that he'd seen him saying something before suddenly standing, stripping his shirt off and then leaping up onto the wooden railing.

That was the moment that would remain. That lull in the act, that pause, that eternal instant. It would replay over and over and over in everyone's minds long after it had passed. The moment when the catastrophe could have been averted. No one made a move to stop him. Not because it happened too quickly but because no one had properly thought through the consequences. Michael certainly hadn't. For a moment he'd even thought it was a decent piece of showboating.

But when he finally jumped there was a scream and then there was a sudden rush of people to the railing before an alarm of some sort sounded and then there was lots of shouting. Michael quickly ran to the back of the boat and into the throng to see what had happened. Maybe the guy had banged himself against the boat on the way down. Hit his head or something. Michael expected to see him in the water. He still hadn't figured it out yet.

A girl was shouting: 'DAN, DAN, DAN!'

Michael finally found the fear. He soon understood. The engines were still chugging. The water washing and tumbling and turning and sucking in. Michael could see underwater channels churning. But no 'Dan'.

It was like a magician's trick – a vanishing act. Dan had gone. The moment he hit the water he had been sucked down, into the pull of the propellers. Then he was chopped into pieces, which sank. Of course he was. Anyone who'd been thinking could have foreseen that.

It was only two hours later, when the police fished out the parts of his body from the sea and onto their boats, lights flashing in the bright day, that anyone saw Dan again. The sight of a torso and an impossible arm and half a head hanging.

People collected on the pier.

Death.

It was freaky. The way it hung in the air. Dan's death felt physical. Like a part of the scene, a member of the crowd, weaving its way round, a shadow in the sun, black and true and among them. Death looked on from that pier, along with everyone else, as the police fished Dan's mauled remains from out of the water. It was difficult not to feel it.

And then there was the way people cried and hashed their way through the previous minutes, analysing, dissecting, rethinking, racking their brains – Christ! Should-have, could-have, would-have. Eventually in the grieving process Michael assumed – just as with Charlie – people would let go, they'd learn to accept that they couldn't have controlled this situation, that they can't control everything, in fact – they might even come to understand – they don't actually control anything.

But in those first minutes after the catastrophe, that feeling of failure, limited foresight, should-have, could-have, would-have . . . it went round and round and round relentlessly. And always at the end of each thinking, in the pauses between the circles, there was the immutable. The fact and the event. There'd been an accident. A boating accident.

And now Dan was dead.

Just like Charlie.

Just like Baxter.

# Chapter Eighty-Two

'I love you.'

There. Done. At last. Whatever happened now, it didn't matter. Michael had decided, somehow, somewhere, that he just had to say it. He didn't care any more what she might say. In many ways, this wasn't even about her. It was about feeling trapped by the secret. And Michael had to break free. The two scenarios: she'd either reject him, and then he'd move on, or she'd say that she loved him too (could she? might she? he wished!), and then they'd have to deal with things from there. All Michael knew was he couldn't bear not saying anything any more. He'd done that for five years. It was time to get things off his chest.

Candy was sitting opposite him, very close, across a tiny table in a five star hotel bar, their knees almost touching. She was wearing a leather mini-skirt and fishnet stockings, which Michael might have thought was a good sign if he didn't already know that she'd dressed for a cocktail party earlier in the evening. They were both drinking flavoured vodka. There were cashew nuts.

There wasn't even a pause before Candy replied: 'I know.'

Now Michael had considered that Candy might say this so, initially, he wasn't surprised. But when she left the statement hanging without any sort of elaboration, simply reaching for her drink and another cigarette as Michael looked at her, he realized that this was the one scenario he hadn't counted on.

What did she mean by simply saying, 'I know'? Did it mean she knew but didn't care? That seemed harsh, considering. Things had been tense between them at times, but, still, if you knew that someone had been in love with you all that time wouldn't you sympathize a little? Seemingly not, Michael thought, as he watched Candy drop her smoking black match into the ashtray.

Or maybe Candy really did have nothing going on in her head. Michael had always found her opaque. Indeed, that was partly what had made her so beguiling. Who knew, or more to the point, who'd get to know, the passions and intelligent insights burning beneath that veneer? Then again perhaps Candy didn't have any passions. Maybe it wasn't a veneer, maybe she was just dull. It certainly didn't seem to register with her, Michael's lust, his longing for her, and the sheer will it had taken him not to say anything, for a noble cause, no less! Her and Sean. He'd never interfered. That was what he had promised himself. Couldn't she see that? Didn't she *admire* him for it?

Maybe the message wasn't getting across.

'I've always loved you,' Michael said, looking at her intently now, deliberately furrowing his brow so she could see all his suffering.

'I know,' Candy replied.

'Don't you . . .' Michael started. What was he going to say? Don't you love me? He knew the answer. It was obvious. His wildest dream – that they might be embracing now in a tumult of repressed desire – definitely wasn't happening. In fact, Candy seemed more interested in beckoning the waitress for another drink.

OK, that's cool, Michael told to himself. It didn't matter what she'd said, or even how she'd said it. He'd done what he'd come here to do. He'd come to tell her that he loved her and now she'd told him in not so many words: *I don't love you*. Fair enough. At least there wasn't a secret now, at least there wasn't any misunderstanding. Michael was free from Candy at last. From here, he could move on, safe in the knowledge that she didn't love him, never wondering any more 'what if', never fantasizing. She didn't love him. In many ways, that was the best thing, right?

'I just . . .' Michael said, changing direction. 'I just wanted to get it out. Do you know what I mean? You know, so we could move on, yeah?'

Candy nodded and sucked on a cashew nut.

'Right,' Michael half laughed, wondering if Candy was going to help him at all or if she'd make him squirm all night. 'Good.'

'Can I ask you a question?' Candy said suddenly.

'Yeah, of course, anything.'

'Has Sean ever slept with a prostitute?'

'No,' Michael replied, genuinely enough. 'Not that I know of.'

'He hasn't slept with anyone then?' Candy pressed.

'I think you should ask him that, Candy. I don't want to get involved.'

'So he has.'

'I didn't say that.'

'But he has.'

'Candy, I don't want to talk about this,' Michael started. He felt a soapbox coming on. 'You know, you didn't exactly want me telling Sean about Bob, did you? So I don't see how you can expect me to tell you who Sean may or may not be sleeping with.'

There was a pause.

'Fair enough,' Candy eventually said.

'How is Bob anyway?' Michael said, more out of spite than anything else. There he'd been proclaiming undying love and all Candy had seemed to be thinking about was asking Michael about Sean, using him as a spy. What a cow!

'I wouldn't know,' Candy replied tersely.

'What? So you're not still seeing each other then?'

'No. That guy's a fucking arsehole.'

'Really,' Michael said, genuinely interested. 'Why?'

Candy sucked air in between her teeth. 'I don't want to talk about it.'

Michael didn't say anything. Candy picked up her drink and finished it, gobbling some crushed ice at the bottom of the glass.

'Do you want another one?' Michael said.

'No,' Candy said, shaking her head. 'I think I should go.'

He wasn't disappointed when she said it.

'I'll take you home.'

When the taxi pulled up, Michael got out with Candy. Jamie and Roo's flat was walkable from Emma's apartment anyway, which was where Candy was staying now, ever since the argument with her parents. He followed Candy to her front door. Maybe because he thought it was the gentlemanly thing to do.

Candy was about to put the key in the lock when she suddenly turned to Michael and said: 'Do you want to come up?'

Michael looked blankly at her.

'Emma's staying with Nick tonight,' she added.

It still wasn't registering with Michael.

'You can stay,' Candy said finally.

Michael felt his palms immediately turn sweaty. Was this a

platonic invitation? It wasn't rare for members of the gang to crash at each other's. But this didn't seem like one of those moments. After all, he had just told her that he loved her. It suddenly occurred to Michael: Candy was offering to sleep with him. Finally, after all these years of waiting, Michael was going to shag Candy!

His heart raced.

Did he really want to go up? Did he want to fuck his best mate's girlfriend, ex-girlfriend, whatever she was now?

He looked at her. Yes. The answer was definitely yes . . .

In fact, no.

No?

Why no?

Because Candy was Sean's girlfriend! Of course Michael couldn't sleep with Candy. It was out of the question.

Michael felt his heart slip as he realized – only now, as the opportunity finally presented itself – that he was too scared to sleep with Candy, that he could never sleep with Candy. His long-held fantasy – the one where she wept as he penetrated her, confessed her passion and swore her forbidden love to him for ever – was suddenly shattered. Michael suddenly had flashes of impotence. There was too much pressure, too many years of waiting, too much desperation for it to be perfect – he knew that he'd fail. Michael would never have been able to handle that kind of humiliation. That was even worse than rejection. Sexual inadequacy, a total fucking soul destroyer. Sean had marked his territory with Candy and Michael, the Omega Male, didn't dare go near it. He simply didn't have the balls. And he certainly didn't have a nine inch dick.

'I don't think that's a good idea, do you?' he said eventually, looking into Candy's eyes.

Candy turned the key in the lock and smiled gently at him, as if she was quietly pleased (even proud?) that Michael finally understood, or at least that he was making this decision for them.

'Yeah,' she said softly. 'You're probably right.'

She kissed him on the cheek and walked into the building.

'Night,' Michael said to himself after she'd gone, and he was just about to walk away without looking back, feeling pleased with himself, when, suddenly, out of the corner of his eye, he saw Candy's arse – her tight, gorgeous arse – moving up the stairs, her leather miniskirt riding against her long fishnet thighs. An immediate ache stirred in the pit of his groin. Michael groaned.

How had he just said no to *that*?

# Chapter Eighty-Three

Appleton Smythe was a dated skyscraper in Central. It had become dwarfed over the decades by the Bank of China building, the Landmark complex and numerous other architectural monsters. Even so, it still commanded perhaps the best view for watching the fireworks, which was part of the reason Michael wanted so badly to attend the company's Handover party. The other reason was because practically all of Hong Kong's VIPs were going to be there.

Michael reached inside his hired dinner jacket pocket one more time to feel the mini tape recorder whirring. He knew it wouldn't be long now before someone called his card at the *Herald* and then the show would be over – he'd be out of a job for sure. Which made it all the more important that he break out of the review pages and get himself onto the news desk. The Witches piece hadn't done it, his feature on the fire at the Mansion hadn't done it, not even his breaking-news piece about the Lamma ferry accident. Hopefully a little inside information from the Handover party at Appleton Smythe would crack it.

Michael took the lift to the top floor and then got out, as the invitation instructed, to take the private lift to the Directors' Suite in the penthouse. Michael had to admit that that was a classy touch and he couldn't help hearing the faint whisper of *I Have Arrived* once again in his head. It had been ages since he'd last heard himself thinking that, even though he'd only been on the island for four months now.

An elderly Chinese man turned a key that shut the doors and operated the lift as Michael stepped inside. It was the only indication that he knew Michael even existed. Michael said, 'Good evening, sir,' in a very posh, colonial accent, more as a wind-up than anything else, but then he found himself getting irritated when the man didn't respond. Michael was in half a mind to have a word with Tommy's father about him – rude bastard – when the lift doors quickly opened and he instinctively knew that it wouldn't be a good idea.

The open-air terrace dazzled with diamonds, champagne-glass crystal and the general exuberance of excessive wealth. A six foot ice statue of a swan with a spotlight shining through it added to the sparkle and there was the overwhelmingly distinct pitch of private education in the air. Michael's hired DJ felt suddenly very tatty. He was going to have a hard time not looking like the inferior with the chip on his shoulder as it was.

He stepped carefully through the buzzing crowd, a little disappointed that it wasn't a more private affair (the invitation had seemed extremely exclusive) and more than a little desperate now to find a face that he recognized. Everyone, particularly the women, seemed to turn and glance with dismissive disdain as he *excuse-me*'d his way between them.

Eventually, gratefully, he spotted Bob, who was smoking a cigarette with Tommy in one corner. Michael stepped immediately towards them and was very pleased when Bob waved him over encouragingly.

'Mikeeeey,' Bob exclaimed as Michael approached, making him cringe.

'Bob!' Michael said, moving to embrace him. 'Hi, Tommy,' Michael said, turning. He noticed that Tommy's bow tie was skewed and the front of his dress shirt wasn't tucked in. He still managed to look much better turned out than Michael, though. Maybe because his DJ was designer.

'Hi, Michael,' Tommy said, quietly dopey, his French cuff flapping because he hadn't threaded the cufflink all the way through. At least he had his name right, Michael thought to himself. He liked Tommy a lot for that.

'Pretty fancy party,' Michael said with approval as Bob offered him a cigarette. 'Thanks,' he said, taking one. 'Where's your Dad?' he said to Tommy.

'Over there, talking to the Governor,' Bob said for him.

Michael glanced over and saw the two men, looking so normal in reality and yet so indistinguishable from the media images that had flashed repeatedly in the previous months. They were talking next to a large flowerpot with a palm tree inside it and Michael thought to himself that that might be a good place to stash his tape recorder.

'Are you going to introduce me?' Michael asked Tommy.

'Probably not a good time,' Bob said stiffly. The social sensitivity sounded funny coming from him. Michael had thought Bob and Tommy were all about being anti-establishment, doing drugs in Daddy's pool, shunning the privilege. There was no such thing as public school cool, it seemed. Even Bob and Tommy weren't the anti-class. They only rebelled because they could afford it.

'That was a good piece you wrote on the Lamma ferry accident,' Bob said, changing the subject.

'Thanks,' Michael said, drawing on his cigarette.

'I wish I could write like you,' he added.

'Honestly, Bob, journalism has got nothing to do with writing. It's all about information,' Michael replied.

'But I love the way you have the power to make something real.'

'How do you mean?'

'Well, you're the media.'

'I don't understand.'

'Well, let's say you were never on that ferry. Let's assume you never saw that boy, what was his name?'

'Dan,' Michael said. 'Dan Wood.'

'Yeah, Dan Wood. Let's say you never saw it like you did. His death would probably have just been a tiny little announcement on page five or something. No one would have read it.' Bob was beaming. 'But the fact that you saw it, the fact that you were there and then wrote about it, and that it was printed on the front page, that made his death real for everyone. Otherwise it might have been as if he'd never even died, or lived, for that matter. Do you see what I mean? As far as the rest of the world could have cared, Dan Wood might have come and gone and no one would have been any the wiser. Except for your story.'

'I don't think so somehow,' Michael said, feeling a little embarrassed by Bob's morbid fascination. After all, weren't they at *the* party of the year? Weren't there less important things to talk about? 'A ferry accident was always going to be big news. They would have got the right pictures somehow and then there would have been witness interviews for the piece. It had nothing to do with me being there.'

'It's not the same,' Bob retorted quickly. He paused and Michael waited for him to elaborate but then Bob simply added, 'It's not the same at all.'

Michael shrugged his shoulders and let his cigarette fall to the ground, crushing it under his shoe. He half turned and looked over his shoulder, just as a buzz quickly zig-zagged its way through the crowd.

Stephen Ching was arriving.

# Chapter Eighty-Four

Everyone – Stephen Ching, Rob, her parents, Sean, Michael and the rest of the gang from Leeds – they were all there by the time the fireworks started, and Candy was having a hard time negotiating her way safely through the evening. She'd decided that the best way to stay out of trouble was to simply avoid other people's eyes.

Candy was standing next to Fat Nick, her arm threaded through his. She could feel him sweating in his DJ, like all the other men. It didn't make much sense wearing formal wear on a night as humid as this. It felt even more sticky than usual and the clouds were very low in the sky, ruining the firework display. Still, the rest of the view was impressive. Hong Kong's multi-coloured lights throbbed like an enormous power station that sprawled into the dark distance. Boats filled the shallow harbour – they'd gathered there for a clear view of the firework display – their blue and red navigation lights adding to the urban rainbow. There was a sightless explosion.

Nick leant towards Candy's ear and whispered: 'Do you want a line?'

Candy shook her head. She could feel everyone's eyes as it was. Leaving with Nick to the loos would have been too much.

After all, her parents were here. Nick started moving away. She pinched his forearm.

'Where are you going?' she hissed.

There was an *ahhhh* from the crowd as a big red firework suddenly exploded clearly between two continental clouds.

'Well, I want one,' he said.

'You can't leave me like this,' she said flirtatiously, hoping he wouldn't be able to tell how much she meant it.

Another impressive flash of green and yellow in the clouds: *Wooooo!*

'I'll be back in a minute,' he said, before pulling away completely.

Candy suddenly felt herself standing alone and exposed. She shifted closer towards the wall of the building, her back to the party.

Nearby she saw Mikey smile at her genuinely and move towards her.

'Good fireworks,' he said.

Candy could see two thick streams of sweat trickling from each side of his hairline, his face looking very pale.

'Tomorrow night will be better,' she said. 'The Chinese will want to outdo the British display.'

'Where'd Nick go?' Mikey asked.

Candy touched her nostril.

'Oh, right,  see you in a bit then,' Mikey said, before quickly walking away.

Typical, she thought to herself. Candy was about to find someone harmless to reattach herself to when she suddenly heard a voice from behind her say: 'Hello, Candy, I'm surprised you're not wearing the necklace I gave you.'

Candy didn't reply but continued to look out towards the fireworks, as if she was interested in them.

'I haven't seen you lately,' Stephen said. 'Are you well?'

Candy stepped forward again, away from Stephen and as close to the edge of the building as she could get now. There was a large flowerpot with a palm tree in it beside her.

'I'd very much like to see you again,' Stephen said flatly as another firework boomed without light. In the distance a cloud turned momentarily blue.

'Go away, Stephen,' Candy said.

Stephen laughed sharply. 'Ahh, Candy Newman – always a tease. I wonder what your father would say if he knew.'

'You wouldn't.'

'Wouldn't I?'

'Leave me alone,' Candy said, despairing.

'I want to fuck you again.'

'Please, just go,' Candy said.

'No,' Stephen said.

Candy didn't say anything. She just stood there, willing Stephen to go away, knowing that she couldn't risk moving – what if he created a scene? After all, he *was* a total psycho. She prayed for someone to save her.

'You're nothing but a whore, Candy Newman,' Stephen said eventually. 'I always knew that you were. All I had to do was give you some junk jewellery to make you mine. You let me come inside you for a piece of glass.'

Candy was having to summon all of her strength not to scream, and she was glad that she'd gone to the edge of the building. She was frozen to the wall, unable to move. She stood staring at the fireworks, telling herself over and over that he'd be gone soon, he'd be gone. Then she felt a hand move inside her dress, which had a plunging back. It edged its way across the tops of her buttocks. She couldn't bear it any more. She swivelled round, feeling the grip quickly fall, and she was about to press herself past blindly and move as far away as possible when she suddenly noticed that Stephen wasn't standing beside her now.

It was Sean.

# Chapter Eighty-Five

The rave was being held in the basement of a shopping arcade Kowloon-side. They'd all queued for an hour to get in. It had been over two hours since the end of the Appleton Smythe party. Sean had already done a pill, which explained why he was being so soft with Candy now. He'd said that they needed to talk. She'd put her finger to his lips and shaken her head. There was nothing to say. Let them just enjoy this one night – together. They deserved that, didn't they?

Overweight *gweilo* bouncers manned the door and body searched people randomly. There were separate queues for those who already had tickets and for those who still needed them. Everyone ended up with an invisible stamp on the back of their hand that only showed up under the UV lights that lined the final entranceway to the dance floor.

Three Chinese girls dressed in canary yellow mini-skirts and yellow T-shirts advertising a brand of vodka, one of three corporate sponsors for the event, checked that everyone had their stamps. The UV lights made the glitter on their glossy tights twinkle, their black hair blue and the whites in their eyes and teeth turn yellow. Combined with the sense of moving through a number of stages to get into the party, Candy felt that the vodka girls were like some strange arcade-game interpretation of alien sirens attracting contenders to the gates of a final championship level. One of them smiled at Candy as she went in, a cap on her front tooth staring blackly out as if it was missing. Candy told herself to remember to keep her own mouth closed during the party. At the end of the day, UV was not a flattering light to be cast in.

Inside, with the exception of a brightly lit and very crowded bar that seemed to only sell flavoured spirits and small bottles of mineral water from ice-filled oil drums, it was very dark. No one from the gang wanted a drink (like everyone else they'd stocked up on water and gum in the Seven Eleven outside and were anxious now just to get straight onto the dance floor) so they joined the main stream of people attempting to surge its way into the flash of strobe-struck blackness beyond.

Candy could feel the air as they shuffled: a dense cloud of hot bodies, sweat and the sound of bass. The sense of anticipation she'd started to feel as soon as she'd popped her ecstasy in the taxi started to swell and she reached out now for Sean's hand in front of her. They held on to each other tightly as their stream of people linked with another line of bodies that was circling the dance floor like an eddy trapped in its own current. Then, quite suddenly, they were a river, and the jostling became more intense, bodies banging and pushing to make way for feet that had no space to stand.

Candy banged her shin against the corner of a box-like, carpet-covered podium that was acting as a makeshift stage for two *gweilos* who were wearing white gloves and had fluorescent day-glow sticks plaited between their fingers. She watched them jutting their outstretched palms into the air, making shapes out of the red laser light that beamed in smoke-swimming razor-sharp shafts directly at them. They looked like mime artists piling up imaginary building blocks.

When they got past the podium Candy could smell euca-lyptus mixing with the sharp chemistry of amyl nitrate and she smiled. It was just like the old days. One big love-in – just what Hong Kong needed, she thought to herself as the first rush of ecstasy started to glow through her spine.

Several years after the rest of the world, mainstream rave culture was finally arriving in Hong Kong. It felt good, it felt right, it felt like a future. Maybe this was the space where she and Sean, the Eurasian outcast and the wide *gweilo,* could find a space that was comfortable, a space without judgement and prejudice. Perhaps raving would change Hong Kong – brew a new, more open-minded post-Tiananmen Square generation of Chinese that wouldn't begrudge couples like her and Sean.

And as she started to come up, Candy found herself hoping that this moment might be the beginning of a new start. Here she was, holding hands with her Sean, her pill kicking in strong now as she shuffled and bumped against old friends, people all around them dancing and grinning and bouncing and whistling. She found herself beaming as another shock of hap-piness fired through her, her fingers moving in Sean's hand, wanting to feel the touch of his skin. She hadn't felt this good since, since . . .

# Chapter Eighty-Six

It was four in the morning and Candy was feeling like shit. She'd just popped her third pill but not in time to negate the comedown from the first two and she was finding it hard to ignore the looks she was getting from the Chinese – particularly the men. She'd noticed them eventually, some time after the initial excitement of arriving had worn off and the initial eye-fluttering moments of her first pill had subsided enough for her to see clearly.

She knew what they were all thinking – there was nothing new in their naked hostility. But it stunned her slightly that it should be so obvious even on E. Hong Kong was the only place she'd ever gone out clubbing where the ravers seemed capable of hate. Even in Leeds everyone had got loved up – the locals and the public school, the ex-cons and the Southern pooftas: they'd all hugged and kissed and rubbed Vicks on each other's shoulders. A big part of Candy used to believe in the revolution that raving offered the world. Ecstasy could end war.

Now she wasn't so sure. Even pilled off their faces – and they were definitely mashed, their moon faces creasing and screaming with rapture – the Chinese were still cognizant enough to know that they should dance noticeably away from the *gweilos*. The attractive Chinese girls caught in the strobe lights on the stage seemed to sneer at no one in particular and there wasn't a single hug exchanged between a Chinese person and a *gweilo* as far as Candy could see.

For the first time in her life it was the Chinese that Candy hated and most of all her Chinese half. She felt embarrassed by them, as if she should apologize to the Group on behalf of a race one billion strong.

Maybe it was just that they weren't used to the love-in culture yet. Maybe it was just that she was still angry because of Stephen Ching.

Whatever the reason, Candy immersed herself unashamedly in her *gweilo* gang, proudly and rebelliously snogging Sean every second she got with him on the dance floor, making sure that the Chinese boys saw her and desired her and hated her all at the same time. Fuck you, she found herself thinking in the brief moments of clarity, realizing sadly and gladly in the mix of a strange hallucinatory happiness that she and Sean were back together, they were finally back together. Did they have to have put themselves through all of their heartbreak?

Sean was shuffling his little dance and beaming at her. He was sweating and red faced and he looked awful but Candy fancied him madly. She grinned at him (she'd long since forgotten to hide her teeth) and moved in to kiss him again.

'I love you,' she said, for what must have been the tenth time that night.

'I love you too, baby,' Sean replied into her neck.

Candy started to bounce on the balls of her feet as a melodic break in the music cracked into a dark rhythm that thumped. She put her head down and decided that the only thing to do was dance. She could feel her third pill kicking in and she was starting to rush, the sense of universal love coming back to her now. She told herself to forget the Chinese, just have a good time. It didn't matter. It was probably just the pills talking anyway. They were quite up and down, not very steady, not like the mudma. It didn't matter. After all, this was the Handover! Blow-out time. This was the party they'd all been waiting for. It was time to go mental!

The next day, everyone slept.

# Chapter Eighty-Seven

Sean had it all prepared. He'd decided. He wasn't exactly sure of when or how or even why he'd decided, but he'd decided. Maybe it had been the ecstasy. He'd felt all his anger and hatred for Candy simply slip away as soon as he'd seen her at the Appleton Smythe party. He found he didn't even care about her sleeping with Rob any more. Truth was he hadn't exactly been a hundred per cent faithful himself.

His sky was no longer a sea of darkness, there was now a sun to light the way. A rising sun no less. Sean was going to take Nobucorp's job offer in Japan. He was finally going to leave Hong Kong, and he was going to take Candy with him.

They were going to leave – for a fresh start and so much more.

The boys from work had come good on the Bank of China. He had an entire office just for them, looking directly out onto the harbour, several hundred floors higher than they had been on top of Appleton Smythe the previous night. At least it seemed that way. There was a clear view this time – no clouds. Two bottles of champagne chilled in a bucket. There was air-conditioning.

Sean waited.

He wished Candy would arrive. The fireworks were going

to start any minute. And his nerves – he couldn't stop fidgeting. He found himself peering out into the corridor every time he heard the lift chime. He worried that maybe she'd got lost. After all, the lifts here were complicated. He'd had to take three different ones to reach the ninety-third floor because of the building's design. Quite stupid, when one thought about it. But Sean knew he was deceiving himself. He could hear the thump of other people in the adjacent offices – the whole building seemed filled for the night. If Candy was having any trouble she could always ask somebody the way, right?

He checked his messages. Zero. He thought about paging. But then he held himself. She was only an hour late. She'd been later. She wouldn't stand him up. Not this time. Not for the Chinese celebration. Would she? Could she?

No, no way, not after last night. It simply wasn't possible. The way they had come together: first at Appleton Smythe and then at the rave. Somehow they'd lost each other before the dawn party on the beach at Deep Water Bay. He'd expected to see her there but when she didn't show he figured she must have stayed in town. He'd half expected to see her back at Jules's place but she hadn't been there either. He wasn't worried. The whole gang had splintered after the Kowloon rave. He'd ended up passing out on Jules's sofa.

As the fireworks began, a glow warmed from within him. She'd be here soon, he said to himself.

# Chapter Eighty-Eight

Sean watched the boats leaving the harbour, their lights turning and then moving collectively like an enormous Greek flotilla in a modern-day epic. He watched them through the glass, putting silently out into the dark, open ocean. One by one they blinked and then were gone. The show was over. Everyone was leaving. No one would be coming back. This was Hong Kong's last day – the Fall of Hong Kong. It had had its time. Shanghai was to be the new gateway to China. Hong Kong was destined to sink into the past, into the sea. This was history in the witnessing. This was the Takeover. The End.

Sean felt himself lurch. The desk he was lying on felt like it was bobbing on the harbour below. He could feel the height of the building beneath him. Here he was, floating on the ninety-third floor, impossibly suspended. Everything was swimming. He could taste an acidic nausea in his gills. He was alone. All alone.

Why hadn't she shown?

The question kept turning in his mind. It made no sense.

He'd paged her – a hundred times it felt like. But she never replied. Why? Was she angry with him? Maybe she'd found out – about his whoring, all his infidelities. What had happened?

There were moments when he cried.

Sean gathered himself and took out the ring – the one she had liked and that he'd bought for her, nearly two years ago now, waiting for the right opportunity . . . just in case.

Tonight was meant to be the night.

Where was she?

Maybe the Others knew.

One by one, nervous but not knowing it, he paged the gang. Steadily the replies came in:

*No, I thought she was with you . . .*

*Are we still meeting later for the Grace Jones concert?*

*What? She stood you up again?*

*She'll be there, don't worry.*

Mikey's message was the last one to get through.

*We have to talk . . .*

# Chapter Eighty-Nine

They met in the Pirates Bar at the Canton Hotel. It was dimly lit. A Filipino band played off-key cover versions of Chris de Burgh and Sting songs. Well-dressed prostitutes managed to move through the bar without looking bored or lonely. Apart from a Chinese couple in the corner, Sean and Michael were the only punters there – everyone else was out on the streets, having a 'wild' time. The whores never approached them. Maybe they didn't look rich enough, or maybe it was simply hotel policy. No soliciting – everything had to be arranged through the concierge-slash-pimp.

Sean was smoking his eighth cigarette in as many minutes. Michael was trying to calm him down, not let him drink too much more – he'd never seen Sean so destroyed, not in person anyway. Michael couldn't help but despise him a little bit for it. Sean seemed to be blaming himself for everything. He kept saying it was all his fault, shit like that. Couldn't he see that he wasn't to blame? It had been her all along – the fucking slut. Michael couldn't believe it when he'd found out the whole truth. It seemed incredible. But there was no denying it.

Candy Newman – what a bitch.

'I've fucked it this time, Mikey,' Sean was saying, his eyebrows branching across his forehead. 'Really fucking fuckered it.'

'No you haven't,' Michael said, staring into him. Secretly he was still torn. He wasn't quite sure what to do. Why had he agreed to meet Sean here?

'Well, why else wouldn't she show? She must have found out about our trip to Macao.'

'How could she know about that?' Michael said coolly.

'Dunno,' Sean shrugged, sniffing, squinting into a whip of smoke that was lashing into his eyes. 'I dunno,' he said again, more quietly.

There was a pause.

'I just hope she's OK,' Sean said suddenly, looking up into Michael's face with a crushed expression. Michael could tell he didn't mean it, though. Michael could see there was a big part of Sean that hoped Candy wasn't OK, that she had been hurt in an accident or something, prevented by forces beyond her control from meeting him. That way, at least, the dream – that she wanted him – could stay alive.

But they both knew that that was a lie.

'I'm sure she's fine,' Michael said, again a little cold and clinical in the face of Sean's distress. After all, Michael had all the facts at his disposal. He'd found out that evening, before the Chinese firework display, quite by chance. He'd almost never even bothered to check. Christ, a big part of him wished he'd never checked. But he had. And now he was distant from it all. He was objective, scientific. He could see Candy for who she was. He knew the Truth, he wasn't blinded by her. And he had to show Sean the truth, he had to enlighten him.

Didn't he?

Sean placed a small box that he'd been handling on the circular table between them, next to a cheap candle that was floating on water in a piece of porcelain shaped like a petal.

'I was going to ask her to marry me,' Sean said.

Michael thought he was going to be sick.

'I don't know what I'm going to do without her,' he said, his lower lip quivering.

Oh, for crying out loud, Michael said to himself, exasperated.

'If she's left me, I going to . . .'

'What, Sean?'

'Nothing.'

Michael felt his anger surging. Not the suicide thing again. Michael started to shake his head. But Sean wasn't looking. He was staring into the peanuts.

'It's all my fault,' Sean said again, suddenly sobbing. 'I've ruined everything.'

And that was it. Michael couldn't take it any more. He reached into his pocket and pulled out the tape recorder. He thought about preceding it in some way, giving it an explanation of some kind, give it some context, stress the fact that Candy was nothing more than a slut, a whore. But he could see Sean was too far gone to listen. He was lost in a swamp of self-pity. And Michael had to save him. This was it. It all ended here. Michael had had enough. He was finally going to do what he'd come to Hong Kong to do. He was going to break the spell that Candy held over Sean. He wasn't going to let her destroy him.

The Filipinos were singing 'Killing Me Softly' – the Roberta Flack version.

He placed the tape recorder on the table and pressed play. There was a long hiss, which shook Sean momentarily into the present and the place, and then the sound of voices and laughter and the crack of a firework that quickly transported both of them back to the previous night. Then, over all of it, there was the sound of a loud male voice saying:

*Hello, Candy. I'm surprised you're not wearing the necklace I gave you . . .*

## Chapter Ninety

When he saw the headline in the *Herald* Michael instantly realized that he hadn't checked his messages. So stupid! Three whole days of hell had passed and he hadn't once thought about the office. After all, he figured Sean would have contacted him at home – if he was going to call at all.

Rain was screaming against a slice of corrugated iron serving as a roof for the news stand, the tips of umbrella ribs stabbing and jabbing at Michael's face as ten thousand Chinese people pushed and shoved their way along the street. Their umbrellas were at just the right height to poke Michael in the eyes every time it rained, which, incidentally, was every fucking day now. Maybe they did it on purpose. He wouldn't be surprised. Michael turned his back so he could stare properly at the headline again, the paper wrinkling in the wet.

TAXI DRIVER FOUND DEAD AT DOCKS – FOUL PLAY SUS-PECTED.

Quok had been dead for two days, so the coroner was quoted as saying. Hung with a piece of telephone cord in a warehouse – on the very same street where he and Michael had met. It made sense, Michael supposed. After all, Sean did follow him there.

*Was it Sean?*

Underneath Quok's story, there was another piece about Candy – the third in as many days. It said that the police were looking for Sean in Japan now. Apparently he'd taken a flight the day after Michael had met him that night in the Canton.

That night.

Michael remembered it like yesterday. The strange look that had come into Sean's eyes, the almost-smiling look, nearly bewildered. He'd asked Michael to play the tape again. When Michael had refused, worried then that he was making a mistake, Sean had told him it would be OK, everything would be OK. So Michael had played the tape again. And again. And again. They'd listened to it four times before Sean eventually stood up. Michael had stood up, too, to meet him, and somehow their bodies had come together quite naturally and then Sean had embraced him, deep and warm. And then he'd left.

And now Sean was Hong Kong's Most Wanted: the prime suspect in the most high profile missing persons (read: murder) case of the year. The gang were in state of shock – fuck, the whole island was reeling. Everyone, not just the Leeds crew, seemed to know who Candy Newman was – she had all the makings of a truly glamorous *Tai-tai*, the papers claimed.

And then there was all the loose talk of a serial killer, what with the fire at Tai-ping Shan and everything. Maybe it was just that so many things had happened in such a small space of time and more especially place (Hong Kong had never felt so tiny) that it seemed impossible they weren't in some way connected.

But, in many ways, the connections only made things more confusing. Why would Sean have wanted to burn down his own flat? Or kill his friend Charlie, for that matter? And what about the link between Quok's murder and Candy's disappearance? Was there one? The newspaper couldn't explain it. But then again, why would it?

Michael was the only person who could truly understand.

And what he understood now, for the first time, standing in the rain, looking at the newspaper, was that this had all been his fault. All of it. It all came down to him. The man that had driven him from the airport was dead now. His two friends were both mysteriously missing. And he was the connecting point between it all. He understood now what he'd suspected the moment he'd pressed Play on the tape recorder that night in the Canton Hotel: he should never have told Sean the truth about Candy. He shouldn't even have come to Hong Kong. He'd thought he was helping but he was only making things worse. Much worse. Just like before, when he told Sean about the Elms and the Bummer Man.

Michael should have learnt by now: telling Sean only ever made things worse.

He noticed a payphone at the end of the street. He couldn't use his phone at home, the police were tapping it. Maybe that was why he hadn't thought about checking his messages until now. The police had been so determined that Sean would eventually contact him there, Michael had never even thought about his office. Why had he listened to them? Yet another mistake.

He reached into his pocket and checked for change, then he folded the newspaper into his armpit and snapped his umbrella open, angling it to charge. After all, that was what umbrellas were for – to fend off everyone else. Forget the rain. Far better to be wet than blind. A waterfall cascading from a channel in the corrugated roof momentarily crashed against the black nylon on his umbrella and then splashed down his neck as Michael stepped out into the sea of spines. The water felt warm against his skin. Michael kept his head down, just in case of any errant spokes, and looked at the ground as he walked. His visual memory guided him to the telephone booth. A puddle rippled as a tram vibrated its way along the street.

He stood by the open-air box, balancing the umbrella between his shoulder and neck and using his hands, which were trembling now, to pick up the receiver and deposit the coins. Once he'd dialled the number, he held the umbrella again in his hand and cradled the phone so he could push his way through the touchtone instructions.

*Hello, you have reached extension 358 at the* Hong Kong Herald.

Three second pause.

*If you want to leave a message, please press one . . .*

Michael waited patiently for the next instruction.

*If you have come through to the wrong extension and wish to speak to an operator, please press zero . . .*

Jesus, who came up with the order of these prompts?

*For subscriptions, press eight . . .*

*For . . .*

At this point, Michael's mind trailed off. Where were all the humans?

*To return to the main menu, please press the star key. . .*

Fuck! He'd missed his option. 'I JUST WANT TO GET MY MESSAGES FOR CHRISTSAKES!' Michael shouted into the phone. No one seemed to take any notice.

He pressed the star key and waited.

*If you wish to collect your messages, dial nine followed by your six-digit pass code . . .*

'At last!' Michael said, trying to remember what his code was. He tried his birth date.

*Hello, extension 358. You have one new message and three old messages.*

There was a bleep as he pressed the 1 key.

*Message received on July 2, 1997. . .*

Three days ago now. The dawn of the Chinese takeover, the day after he'd met Sean in the Canton, the day Sean had run away, the day Sean had . . .

*At 2.05 p.m.*

Come on, Michael thought to himself. His sense of fear burnt. A car drove past and splashed a puddle up into him. He didn't think to swear. There was another pause and then the sound of someone breathing.

'Hello, Michael.' More breathing. 'This Quok.'

Michael's heart stamped in his chest. It was disturbing to hear a dead person talk.

'I have message for you from . . . old friend.'

He said 'old friend' like it was an ancient Chinese proverb or something, the kind of catchphrase you'd expect to find in a fortune cookie. Maybe that was Sean's idea of a joke. Michael didn't find it very funny.

'Take ferry to Lamma for another scoop. She's under the pier.'

Everything was quiet for a moment after the message ended. The line, Michael's mind. Then the screaming rain started to fill the void, slowly at first and then quickly getting louder, as if someone was turning up the volume.

Another scoop? Under the pier?

The rain screamed.

It could only mean one thing.

Screaming. Michael's head started spinning.

What had he done? What had he done?

Images started to melt. The telephone booth started moving away from him.

It had happened again. He had happened again. *They* were happening again.

There was another sound now – a rhythm, within the screaming – like the distant thump of helicopter blades. Michael couldn't breathe.

What had he done?

Michael held his face. It was burning. He pinched his temples with one hand, stemming the urge to puke. He wanted to sob – but he was dry inside. A puddle glared his reflection back at him accusingly. He felt himself lurch. Breathe. . . he told himself. Just breathe. . . .Slowly his thoughts started to realign themselves. Air flushed his system. The wave of panic started to fade into a remorseful wake.

'If only,' he semi sobbed.

*If only, if only, if only . . .*

It kept going round in his mind, as if Michael's desire to turn back the clock kept catching on the same phrase, unable to travel the time and fulfil the final words.

*If only I hadn't come to Hong Kong.*

*If only I hadn't told Sean.*

*If only I hadn't gone to St Luke's.*

*If only I hadn't told Sean.*

*If only, if only, if only . . .*

Eventually he noticed that his umbrella had fallen to the ground beside him and was collecting water in its belly. His shirt was soaked through. There seemed to be a strange light in the sky. Was it the storm passing?

Breathe . . .

Michael started to understand what he had to do. He'd take the last ferry, the midnight boat.

Breathe . . .

When it was dark. When no one else would be around.

Breathe . . .

He wouldn't let Sean down this time. Not like last time.

Breathe . . .

He took the newspaper out from under his arm and looked at it again. Candy looked out at him. Stunning as always.

Breathe . . .

That was when he knew.

Breathe . . .

He wanted the first picture to be of her face.

## Chapter Ninety-One

No one saw Candy leaving the rave with Tommy because they got separated from the Group and then Tommy offered to give her a lift to the Deep Water Bay party in his father's Rolls Royce, rather than leave her waiting in the street for a taxi. It never occurred to her that it was a trap . . . but then again why would it? Candy didn't think Tommy even understood what he was doing, not truly. Maybe it wasn't a trap at all. Maybe everything that happened afterwards was simply accidental.

But when the chauffeur took a turn for D'Aguilar Peak, Candy did get nervous.

'I thought the party was that way, Tommy,' she said, looking down the road that led to the beach.

Tommy didn't say anything.

'I thought the part—' Candy started again.

'I need to get my drugs,' Tommy interrupted, almost snapped at her.

Maybe it just sounded that way because Candy had mis-timed Tommy's communication delay – her timing was off cue because she was nervous, scared even, to bump into Rob again. She definitely didn't want to be on her own with him – not after the last time, on the Russian's boat. She told herself that he probably wouldn't be at Tommy's house. Why would he be? This was Handover night – party time. No, no one was at home now.

Ten minutes later, the Rolls ramped up the estate drive and then circled past the tennis court and the swimming pool before pulling up in front of the house. Candy watched Tommy climb out of the car and felt herself not moving until she saw that the chauffeur had walked round and was opening her door for her. She got out more out of politeness than anything else. Following Tommy to and then through the front door seemed like the only thing to do after that. There didn't seem much point standing out in the final moments of the night.

She noticed dew collecting on the lights that lined the path leading into the house. Then there was the sound of central air-conditioning at they stepped inside. It was very dark inside. It felt empty. Tommy switched on the lights and moved purposefully through the hallway, then into the living room. Candy watched him skip up the stairs, three at a time. She waited in the living room for him, hovering. She was anxious to get to the party, anxious to not squander the pill she'd just taken, anxious to be with Sean again, anxious to leave . . . just anxious. She found herself scanning the room, desperate for distraction.

Minutes passed. There was the sound of a grandfather clock ticking.

Candy waited, not knowing if time was passing or if it was just her being impatient. She thought about calling out for Tommy, but she didn't dare. The night felt so still. It would have felt like shattering glass. She didn't dare go upstairs and look for him.

On the other side of the living room Candy noticed that

there was a set of dark double doors with brass handles. She remembered that they led to the dining room. She'd eaten there several times before when she was a teenager. She saw that one of the doors was open. A lamp inside the room was on, its yellow light pressing itself against the floor.

Candy stepped inside.

There was a long table with candlesticks, stiff straight-backed Chinese-style chairs surrounding it. To one side there was a large cabinet that touched the ceiling. There were wine glasses and crystal decanters inside. At the end of the room there was a table with drawers, presumably for the silverware. There were paintings on the wall. Above the table there were photos. She walked up to look.

Some of them were very old. A Victorian woman from the nineteenth century. One said *Preschute House 1938*. Another one said: *1st XI 1941*. Candy noticed the *Taipan*'s name on that one. He looked very handsome in whites, and the way that he sat you could almost see that he was destined for big success. He seemed very large within himself. Further to the right the photos melted from black and white into sepia and finally into colour. There was one, a very long one, for a whole school: *St Luke's 1983*.

The name rang a bell in Candy's mind but she didn't know why. She looked at all the faces – all of them just little boys. Very individual, very young, some just changing, but really all of them just little boys. There was a row for the teachers. They sat very stiffly in chairs and stood out because they weren't in the uniform – the green and black striped blazers – that dominated the picture, practically glaring. At their feet sat some very small boys – small, six, seven years old, no more.

A row of names.

*Geoffrey Hewitt, Daniel Jones, Benjamin Sirota, Thomas Gravelle.*

Tommy! She corresponded the face with the name and almost let out an ahhh! He looked so sweet! The sight of his cherubic lips and fat cheeks and only the faintest sign of the Orient in his eyes – it gave her a slight lift on her pill. She carried on scanning the blur of names and she was only looking aimlessly now, not trying any more because she'd found the one name that was relevant – the very reason for the picture to be on this wall in the first place. That was how she recognized the school. There wasn't anyone else that she expected to see. And then, suddenly, there they were, all three of them – just the names, standing in a strangely shaped triangle, supposedly corresponding with their places in the rows that lined the long photo.

*Michael Marland*

*Sean Clarke*

*Robert Baxter*

Candy lined up Sean's name first, feeling the anxiety she'd first felt when she walked into the house. There was no mistaking him. He was very handsome, even back then, his refined features very pronounced already. Then Mikey. God, *he* had changed. He was standing shoulders pinned too far back, chest puffed out, chin too high. The guy looked like he was about to explode. Next to everyone else he looked very strange, obviously tall for his age but still looking too young, like he should have been on the bottom row, cross-legged and in shorts at the teachers' feet.

And then Rob. Candy practically gasped when she saw him. Jesus. They were within feet of each other. All of them, in the same frame, the same school. They all knew each other.

'What?' Candy said out loud to herself as the coincidence sank in.

'It's not a good one of me, I know,' Rob's voice suddenly said behind her.

Candy yelled out instinctively then and spun round, immediately falling back against the wall.

Rob was at the other end of the dining room, the long table dividing them. Candy felt suddenly exposed, naked. The ecstasy quickly drained out of her system and was immediately replaced with a new drug, adrenaline, like fresh water flowing into a flushing toilet. Her heart was suddenly bumping, she could feel her hands shaking.

'Jesus!' Candy panted. 'You scared me.'

Rob stepped towards her. 'Well, well, well – Candy Newman,' Rob said.

Candy tried to smile, fake a blush, anything to hide her fear. Somehow she sensed that she was in danger – real, physical danger.

'How are you, Rob?' she said, cringing inside because she could hear that her voice was shaking.

'Candy, Candy, Candy, Candy Newman,' Rob sang, brushing one hand over the tops of the Chinese chairs as he paced slowly towards her. 'What are we going to do with you?'

Then a very strange look came into his face as he said: 'Mr Crewe goes to the loo with Benny Lemanu the big fat poo!'

He laughed sharply.

Candy tried to control her breathing.

There was a pause before Rob said, 'Oh, Candy. I don't ever want you to think I didn't like you. I *was* using you, I know. I'm sorry for that. But I always liked you. Please don't forget that.'

'What's ... what's going on, Rob?' Candy said, not sure what she was actually asking as she said it but finding that she was still trying to smile for some reason.

'I think you know,' he said simply.

'No, I don't,' Candy said, finding her feet and shuffling against the wall now, trying to keep the table between Rob and herself. She brushed against a photo and it immediately fell to the floor, smashing.

Candy jumped and glanced behind her and then got very scared because Rob ignored it completely, simply saying: 'I wish you hadn't come in here.'

Candy started to panic. 'Why?'

'I can't have you telling them.'

'I don't know what you're talking about,' she said quickly. She gulped to hold down the tears and felt the wall behind her with the tips of her fingers, needing to know that it was there, petrified that something might grab her from behind.

'You should never have seen that picture. I'm going to kill them – you know that now,' Rob said, standing near the wall of photos where Candy had been when he'd first walked into the room. Candy was approaching the end of the drinks cabinet by now.

'Wh . . . what? Why? What are you talking about? Please, Rob, you're scaring me,' Candy panted. 'I don't know why I'm here, please. Just . . .' The words died as she saw him opening one of the drawers in the desk under the photos and pull out a long carving knife.

Candy started to weep then.

'Clarke and Marland killed my brother,' Rob said, looking at the knife as he turned it in his hand. 'And I am going to kill them. I've been waiting, years – all my memorable life, in fact . . . they say seven is the age of consciousness.'

'Please, Rob,' Candy sobbed. 'Don't.'

'Everyone at school knew. There was this fat bitch called Gibson. She had a big mouth. And her son. I got rid of them years ago. It's taken me longer to get to Marland and Clarke. I don't know why – I think they were just very big in my mind. You know, almost like gods. Ha!' he snorted. 'It's hard to believe that now. They're pathetic, don't you think?'

Candy didn't say anything. Rob's words had given her time to gather herself slightly, control the panic and the tears. She found herself noticing for the first time that Rob was still dressed in his tuxedo from the party on top of Appleton Smythe. He looked very elegant, very dashing, everything done-up and neat and tight. She was nearing the double doors now, she could feel the hinges. She was close. She knew what she had to do.

'So, so it was you that started the fire at Sean's.' Candy found her voice, knowing she had to stall. Just a few inches more now.

Rob nodded and stepped casually closer. 'I'm sorry about Charlie,' he said. 'I suppose I've only got myself to blame. If we hadn't spent the night together, well . . . I think they would have been there, don't you? Clarke and Marland, I mean. But then again . . . you might have been at the Mansion as well. I know how much you all liked to hang out together on Sunday nights. The gang.'

Candy blindly found the handle for the doors.

'Then again, that might have been the best thing. I think in some ways, Candy – and this is the real tragedy for me, because I always liked you – you had to die with them. You were so bound up together.' Rob winced. 'If only you'd broken free. You should have broken free, like you told me that time, how you wanted to. I gave you a chance. But, well . . . it's too late for all that now.'

Candy didn't think after that. She swivelled round and caught the brass handles in her hands, yanking them with all her strength so both doors flew towards her and opened completely, the space beyond expanding in enormous relief. Candy felt herself beginning to run just as the sound of Rob's footsteps started to fill her ears. She immediately screamed for help. Her shoes slipped on a piece of carpet. She managed not to fall. She felt her thigh crash against a large, soft chair. Then, suddenly, out of nowhere, Tommy was blooming into view from the stairs, coming at her. Candy quickly recoiled away from him, just as he reached out to her. Then she felt her foot catch on something very unyielding and she knew it was bad because everything went instantly quiet.

She felt herself hanging in the air.

Then she saw the corner of the table approaching.

It accelerated very, very fast and all in a final instant.

She didn't have time to put her hand out or break her fall.

She might have said 'No', but she couldn't be sure.

Because after that, everything went black.

# Chapter Ninety-Two

Sean only found out when he finally turned up for work at the office in Tokyo. He'd taken the previous week for himself, travelling, thinking, crying. He'd done a lot of that. Maybe that was why there weren't any tears when his new boss, a *gweilo*, called him immediately into his office and told him that Candy was dead, explained how the police had been looking for him, that he'd missed the funeral. Maybe it was simply that he'd already killed Candy in his own mind, after Mikey had played him the tape and he'd found out the truth about her. It didn't seem to make that much difference, now, that she was dead. Or maybe he was just in a state of shock.

'You know Thomas Gravelle?' the *gweilo* boss said gently, rhetorically. The day was bright behind him, flooding through a large window and giving the man – Sean didn't get the name – a slight glow in his white shirt and tie. Or maybe that was just Sean's imagination. The man seemed to have so much information, all seeing, all knowing, he appeared as a kind of angel.

Candy. Dead. Murdered. Body discovered. Police suspicions. Thomas Gravelle . . .

The sound of the trading floor coming to life was discernible through the wall.

'I think so,' Sean said.

'Apparently he made a full confession to the police,' the angel said. 'He cleared your name. Said that he witnessed the murder. Told the police about a certain Baxter, Robert Baxter. Have you heard of him?'

Baxter?

It couldn't . . .

It wasn't possible . . .

Sean just looked at the man, as if in a dream, the long nightmare that had started a week ago.

Life without Candy. She was gone now. For ever.

'Thomas Gravelle says that Robert Baxter knew you,' the angel said. 'That he had tried to frame you, you and a, err . . .' The angel had to refer to a piece of paper now. 'A Michael Marland.'

'Mikey,' Sean said simply, confirming the names in his mind.

'Yes,' the angel said. 'Michael Marland. He's been trying to reach you. Says he has to talk to you.'

Sean didn't say anything. The world didn't feel like it was moving any more.

'Are you all right, son?' the angel said.

Sean couldn't see the man's face, the brightness beyond him seemed to be all engulfing. Sean nodded.

'What . . . what about Baxter?' Sean asked eventually.

The angel breathed in heavily. 'I'm afraid . . . well, no one knows where he is. Everyone is trying to find him, I can assure you of that. The police here . . . they want to interview you. They want to know everything, anything, you might know about him. Apparently he's very dangerous – a sociopath. He'd been planning some sort of revenge, for his brother's death, and somehow your girlfriend . . . Miss Newman . . . she found out about it and that was when . . . well, Thomas Gravelle says that was how it happened. He . . . they think he's in Thailand now. He's extremely dangerous.'

'Thailand?'

'Yes. Robert Baxter fled Hong Kong after he discovered that you'd left the country – so Thomas Gravelle says. Presumably to make sure that he wasn't in some way linked to the case. Possibly arrested.'

Sean didn't say anything.

'They . . . I don't want to worry you, son,' the angel breathed. 'But they say he might come for you – that you should be careful. Where are you staying? Are you living alone?'

'It's OK, I'll be careful,' Sean heard himself say, finding that he was half praying that Baxter *would* come after him.

*Clarke wanted to kill Baxter.*

'We understand if you need to take time off,' the angel continued.

'No,' Sean replied, looking ahead now, into the light.

'Sure, sure,' the angel said, nodding. 'I understand. You want to stay busy. Maybe that's the best thing. But . . . well, if you ever need to . . .' he paused, 'talk – you know where to come.'

'Thanks,' Sean said, standing up, noticing that he was in a daze now.

'I've asked Moshe, my secretary, to show you to your desk,' the angel said. 'I've put you on swaps, OK? I know you'll do well there. You've come highly recommended.'

At that very moment the door to the angel's office swung open and a tall Japanese girl stepped into the light. For the first time in as long as he could remember, Sean found himself looking at a woman without thinking what she might be like in bed.

Candy . . . poor Candy . . . she was dead . . . she'd died trying to save him . . . them . . .

There was a moment when he thought he was going to break down then. But he caught himself as the roar of the trading floor filtered through his thoughts, his emotions. It was simple. Sean had to work. Not think. Like before. He'd learnt that much in his life. It was the only way to handle it. He could not think. Must not think. He could feel himself collapsing.

He walked to his desk.

# Chapter Ninety-Three

'Michael?'

'Yes?'

'There's someone here to see you.'

Michael looked up. He saw Mr Newman immediately, even though he was waiting at the other end of the long and chaotic newsroom, across the rows of desks with telephones and computers, beyond the glass doors with the words *HONG KONG HERALD* etched in frosted italic font. Maybe Michael managed to spot him so quickly because he'd been expecting him. Even so, his anticipation of this meeting did nothing to stop the immediate racing of his heart, the sudden sweat on his back. Had he really expected to get away with it, without questions being asked, without some sort of accountability? Was an explanation even possible?

Michael felt like he'd been caught. Doing something terrible, very terrible.

'Can I use the conference room?'

'Yes,' the middle-aged Chinese receptionist said. 'It's free until three.'

'Thanks a lot,' Michael said, still trying to gather himself. 'Show him in, will you?'

It suddenly struck Michael how unprepared he was for this,

even after the police questioning, even after Candy's funeral (only family could attend) and his letter of condolence, even after all his explanations to the gang.

*How did you find Candy?*

*Why did you take pictures of her?*

*Did you really think it was a boat accident – why did you write that?*

*Who is Robert Baxter?*

*Why did he kill Candy?*

*Didn't you know? Didn't you know who he was, that Candy was in danger?*

*Why couldn't you see?*

*Why didn't you warn her?*

*Why did you take pictures of her?*

*Why is she dead?*

Somewhere along the line, usually in the terror of a quiet night, Michael had started to see. The illusion had slowly lifted and Michael had seen the Truth. It had all been him – Baxter's murder had been his delusion. His best friend Sean wasn't a killer, never had been. And now – Candy, Quok, Charlie – they were all dead because of his madness. Clarke had never killed Baxter. It *had* just been an accident. Marland had got it all wrong. And for all those years, Michael had got it wrong too.

It *was* all his fault. He *was* to blame everything. All the dark things in his heart. Whatever anyone said, Candy was dead because of him. His friend's lover. Would Sean ever forgive him?

After all, how could he? Not after what he'd done. Taken all those pictures of Candy and then sealed the scoop for the *Herald*. Would Sean understand how Michael had been terrified that it had been Sean? Would Sean understand why Michael had believed this? Because of what happened at school, because of what happened to Baxter? What would Sean think when he understood that Michael believed his best friend removed people that got between the two of them? Baxter, Charlie, Candy. What would Sean think of that? Would Sean forgive Michael for all of this madness if he knew that Michael only took the pictures because he was trying to cover up Candy's death for his benefit, as 'repayment' for Baxter's murder, to make amends for Marland's confession to Mrs Gibson and Mr Bride? Would Sean see any of that? Would he thank him for it?

And it had almost worked, the attempted cover-up. Even the police seized on the boating accident hypothesis at first. Sean was quickly in the clear. The police no longer needed him to return to the island. Anything was better than a missing persons case, Michael had supposed, anything was better than a murder investigation.

And the editors – they had seemed happy with the BOAT TRAGEDY! angle too. They quickly gave Michael a permanent position on the newsdesk. Everything had seemed sweet, so very sweet. Michael had saved his best friend from prison and got himself the job he'd wanted for so long – all in one fell swoop.

And then Tommy had confessed. Just like that. At least, that was how it had seemed. The police had been conducting a routine inquiry to confirm that Candy had gone to the beach party at Deep Water Bay (they assumed she'd simply swum off the coast from there). Someone had come forward to say they'd seen Candy leaving the Kowloon rave with Tommy and so the police had gone over to the estate to ask him a few questions and then he'd simply caved. A full confession. Who knew why? Maybe because Robert Baxter had left him stranded, vanishing into the Asian ether like that, leaving Tommy to cope on his own. Tommy couldn't cope on his own. He was just like Marland. He told on his best friend.

Suddenly it was a murder. Suddenly it was Baxter. Suddenly it wasn't sweet any more. Suddenly everything was messy again.

Sean still hadn't returned his calls.

And now, Mr Newman was here, in the office, wanting to see him, wanting answers.

Michael watched himself move through the moment. His feet stepping across the brush-carpeted floor, the way one or two other journalists looked at him, his editor glancing, the chrome door handle slipping slightly against the sweat in his palm as he gripped it, the way he was having to control his breathing, the way the light turned as he walked into the room, the sound of his voice as the words came out.

'Mr Newman.'

Candy's father was standing by the long windows on the other side, looking out over the bay, the brutal scars of a land reclamation programme dominating the peninsula opposite. He was dressed tightly in a dark suit, the creases seemingly supporting him. He didn't turn round.

'You wanted to see me,' Michael said, inviting the onslaught.

*MY DAUGHTER IS DEAD BECAUSE OF YOU!*

*YOU TOOK THOSE PICTURES!*

*IT'S ALL YOUR FAULT!*

'She wasn't mine, you know,' Mr Newman said quietly but steadily, still not turning round, still not facing Michael.

Michael saw that it was a beautiful day outside.

'I'm sorry?' Michael said, even though he'd heard.

There was a long pause before Mr Newman spoke again. Michael saw that one of his hands was trembling slightly.

'Candy,' Mr Newman said eventually, turning now. Michael

could see a thick rub of greying stubble across his face. His eyes were crowded with dark lines. He looked dishevelled in an immaculate way. 'She wasn't my daughter.'

Michael didn't say anything. What was he meant to say? This wasn't what he'd been expecting.

'I married her mother to save her from the shame, the loss of face,' Mr Newman continued impassively, looking across the room, away from Michael, at nothing. 'Some no-good *gweilo*. . .'

Somehow Michael understood that Sean was a 'no-good *gweilo*' in Mr Newman's eyes.

'Bastard just pissed off, never to be heard from again.' Mr Newman paused and then added as if reading Michael's thoughts: 'It was difficult to have abortions back then.' He paused again. 'She loved him too much to get rid of the child.'

Mr Newman moved slowly towards one of the high-backed leather chairs surrounding the table. Michael sat down across from him.

'Why you?' Michael asked, feeling his journalism take over. *Keep questions to a minimum. Let the source do all the talking. Everyone wants to tell their story.*

'We were friends, Candy's mother and I,' Mr Newman said, looking up at Michael now, his pale-green eyes looking hollow, without light. He suddenly sighed. 'No. I loved her. I was prepared to do anything.' There was another pause. 'Back then.'

Michael didn't say anything.

'So you see,' Mr Newman said, still looking at Michael now, 'I'm not really here for me. I feel . . .'

Words suddenly failed the man and Michael watched as the grief tumbled over his face. Michael found that he desperately wanted to say how sorry he was. For everything. For trying to cover up Candy's murder because he thought Sean had killed her. For using her death to get his promotion to the news desk at the *Herald*. For knowing Robert Baxter. For being a part of the reason Candy was dead. For Candy being dead.

But he held himself.

'I feel that we owe you our thanks,' Mr Newman continued.

Michael felt his face twist with confusion.

'For trying to help her, when you found her,' Mr Newman said. 'The police explained how you touched her, how you must have panicked. It must have been awful for you, simply awful to find her like that.'

'Mr Newman . . .' Michael started.

'Please,' Mr Newman interrupted him. 'I know what you're going to say. I've been trying to explain it all to Muriel. You had to take those wretched pictures. You probably thought the police would need them for their inquiry. And I heard how the editors seized them from you, forced you to hand them over so they could print them. See? I understand everything.'

Only now did Michael start to see that Mr Newman couldn't cope. He couldn't handle the truth. So he was making one up, one that he could cope with. Just like Marland had done.

'It's just, well . . .' Mr Newman broke, a sudden flurry of tears cascading without sound down his cheeks. He stared ahead at Michael as he spoke, the drops rushing and then streaming. 'I blame myself, you see. I should have been more careful, I shouldn't have pushed her away like I did, I shouldn't have let her leave the house. It's all my fault.'

'Mr Newman. . .' Michael tried again.

'No,' he said, suddenly standing, the chair making a strange sound as it scraped across the carpet. 'I don't want you to say anything. I just wanted . . .' He paused for a very long time.

'To see you. I had to tell someone, you see. I had to tell someone. . .'

'Yes, Mr Newman. I understand.'

Mr Newman got up and walked round the desk towards the door. Michael thought he was going to leave but then he stopped and stood opposite him. The two men looked at each other. Michael thought he saw a corner of Mr Newman's mouth move.

'It's Muriel who will really suffer. . .' he started before trailing off.

Michael didn't say anything. He couldn't. The silence seemed to hang for a long time. There was the sound of their breathing.

Finally, after an expectant pause, Mr Newman said coldly: 'Don't try to call.'

He turned and left the room.

# Chapter Ninety-Four

'Why haven't you returned my calls?'

Michael – always too heavy, always too serious.

'Sorry, mate,' Sean said. 'I've been busy. You know how it is . . . I've called you now, haven't I?'

Michael sighed. He could hear the *Hong Kong Herald* news desk buzzing in one ear, the scream of the Tokyo trading desk in the other, coming through the phone. The sounds crashed together somewhere in the middle of his head.

'How's Tokyo?' Michael asked.

'It's OK,' Sean sniffed in a seemingly positive way. 'It's all right.'

'Job's OK?'

'Yup.'

'Well, you were right about the stock market,' Michael said, as a conversation starter more than anything else. Three months after the Handover it had collapsed more than fifty per cent. Ironically it had had nothing to do with Chinese rule, though – the whole of Asia had simply gone to shit. Even so, that hadn't stopped Michael from writing a couple of articles on it as part of a series he was doing on the terminal decline of Hong Kong. 'You must be loaded.'

'Yeah, well, I did try to tell you,' Sean said.

Michael could feel his smile through the receiver. 'It doesn't matter,' Michael said. 'It's not like I had the money to invest.'

'Anyway, you're not doing too badly yourself from what I hear,' Sean said. 'Apparently you're some hotshot reporter for the *Herald* now.'

Michael winced when Sean said it, worried that Sean would have put the pieces together, understood that Michael only got the promotion to the news desk after his scoop on Candy.

'I always knew you'd make it,' Sean said.

There was a pause.

'So how's Hong Kong otherwise?' Sean continued. 'How're the Leeds crew doing?'

'Place is a fucking ghost town. Pretty much everyone has left. Now that the Handover's been and gone.'

'Yeah, I heard about Emma and Ben leaving.'

'Fat Nick, too.'

'Yeah?'

'You always said this place would sink into the ocean, Sean.'

'Just make sure you get off before it does.'

Another pause, a long one.

Eventually Michael said, 'How are you, Sean? Aren't you . . . well, aren't you lonely out there all by yourself?'

He was surprised when Sean gave him a straight answer.

'I miss her,' Sean's voice said simply.

'Yeah,' Michael said quietly. 'I miss her too, Sean.'

Sean didn't say anything. Michael wondered if he should say something more. But what was there to say that hadn't already been said, hadn't already been understood? They both loved Candy and now she was gone.

'So what else is new, Mikey? Are you going to stay in Hong Kong?'

It felt like they were circling the conversation, the one they were both on the phone for, like timid air pilots trying to land.

'Dunno,' Michael said. 'Job's good. I'm living on Lamma now.'

'Yeah?'

'Yeah, it's much nicer there.'

Michael didn't mention the fact that he could see the beach where he'd placed Candy's body from his terrace.

'Good,' Sean said. 'That's good.'

'Oh and I, err. . . I've got a girlfriend.'

'Yeah?'

'You might remember her.'

'Not Karen,' Sean said.

'How did you guess?'

'Christ! What's she like?'

'She's a very sweet girl,' Michael said. 'In a Jennifer Ames sort of way.'

They both laughed very hard at that. It brought the relief they needed.

There was a long pause. Eventually, as he listened to Sean breathing into the receiver, the background noises underlying everything, Michael finally managed, 'I miss you, Sean.'

There was another long pause. It felt as long as the three months that had passed since the Handover, since they'd last spoken, that time in the Canton.

Slowly, gently, into the receiver, privately, Michael said: 'Do you think . . . well.'

'What?' Sean replied.

'Do you think we'll see each other again soon?'

'Maybe,' Sean said.

'It's all my fault, isn't it?' Michael heard himself saying then, stunned that he was cracking up now, that there were tears in his eyes. Or maybe he was crying because he understood that he'd never see Sean again – they were finally over.

Sean sighed. 'It's not your fault, Mikey.'

Michael sobbed for a while, shielding his eyes with his hand, looking down between his legs, away from the office, at the carpet between his feet. He failed to notice what colour it was.

Sean listened to him.

'I should never have told on you, Sean,' Michael said eventually, sniffing, gathering himself.

'I already told you, Mikey,' Sean replied gently, 'it doesn't matter.'

'Of course it matters!' Michael snapped, exasperated now. 'Candy's dead, Sean!'

Michael smarted as he said the words because he knew that they were violent and that a big part of him wanted to thrust Candy's death into Sean's face, wanted to hear his reaction, find out if Sean hated him now. He suspected, even hoped, that Sean hadn't returned his calls because he blamed Michael. He deserved that.

'It wasn't your fault, Mikey. Everything that happened to you at school – none of that was your fault. You mustn't blame yourself.'

. . . *for wanting Baxter to be dead*. . . Michael could almost hear the unsaid words.

What about Candy?

Had Michael wished her dead?

And Quok?

Why did Bob Baxter have to kill him? Was it just for the frame?

Charlie?

Wasn't Michael ultimately to blame for all of them? Even if he didn't do it? Even if Sean didn't do it? Wasn't Michael still the link?

'But if I hadn't told on you . . .' Michael whined.

'You were just a kid, Mikey. You didn't know what you were saying. There was no way you could have known what would eventually happen. You can't blame yourself for Candy.'

'You're not angry with me then?'

'Of course not.'

'I thought it was you, Sean.'

'I know.'

'Why don't you hate me?'

Sean sighed. 'I can't hate you, Mikey. You're the only person I've got.'